The Luck of

By

John Poulton

"This is a fictional work based upon actual historical events. The characters and incidents described herein are solely the concepts and products of the author's imagination. They are used to create a fictitious story, and should not be construed as real."

ISBN 978-0-9956763-1-2

CONTENTS

ACKNOWLEDGE-MENTS

Thanks to my wife/editor Anne for her support, patience, inspiration and suggestions. Thanks also to all those who read the feedback edition and gave me helpful advice and much needed encouragement especially; James Boylan, Allison Cowley, Andrea Murphy, Michelle Whittle, and Sue Williams. A massive thanks also to Janet Riley for the cover artwork.

A big thanks to everyone in the Rwanda Group Trust and to all our RGT partners in Rwanda. Your stories have moved, inspired and changed me forever.

I first went to Rwanda in 2011. With the help of Odette Kayirere, and the Rwandan widow's charity Avega East, I met a woman called Feza Mediatrice, in the village of Musha in Rawamanga province. She summarised all that has captivated me about Rwanda and its people. Feza is woman who has suffered much and yet lives her life with generosity and courage. I hope people put this book down thinking that hideous cruelty need not overcome virtue, indeed with people like Feza on this earth, virtue cannot be overcome.

This book is dedicated to

Feza Mediatrice

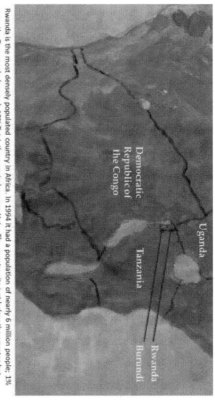

Rwanda is the most densely populated country in Africa. In 1994 it had a population of nearly 6 million people; 1% were the Twa people (pygmy), 10% Tutsi, the remainder were Hutu. The country sits just below the equator but most of it is 1500m above sea level, so it has plenty of sunshine and rain.

Rwanda has few natural resources unlike its neighbour the Congo (called Zaire in 1994), but it is a very fertile country and exports tea and coffee. Due to the fertility of the land it is understandable that farming is the main source of employment but most of it is subsistence farming. You can grow enough to feed a family (just), and even sell your surplus at local markets, but it's an economic trap. Though things have improved enormously since the genocide this is still how many Rwandans live.

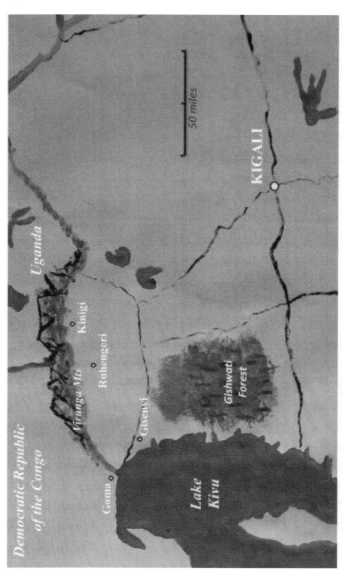

Rwanda is often called the land of 1000 hills with good reason, much of the terrain resembles an egg box. Traveling times are a lot longer than one would expect, as the roads have to wind through valleys and traverse so many hills. In the north of the country these hills rise to become a range mountains covered with a vast rain forest shared with the Democratic Republic of the Congo and Uganda. At its widest point Rwanda is about 200 miles wide, it is about the size of the American state of Maryland or the country of Wales in the UK.

ABEL KEPT FLOCKS, AND CAIN WORKED THE SOIL

1

A lone grey crowned crane circled in the sky. In the silence below it, a vast forest draped over the mountains of northern Rwanda. It spread north into Uganda, and westwards where the same green canopy conquered the vastness of the Congo, a country as large as Western Europe. The crane could see the long shard of Lake Kivu that marked the border between the Congo and Rwanda. The lake glittered in the sunshine, pointing southwards to its bigger sister, Lake Tanganyika. Apart from the blue waters of Kivu, the only colour the bird could see was green. All the shades of green were there, from the lime green of spring pastures to the dark avocado green of mountain slopes. Infinite shades of it ruled the rippled landscape of steep hills and deep valleys.

Occasional wisps of smoke from cooking fires drifted into the air, as they had unchanged for thousands of years and, as the author of Genesis wrote "it was good". The inhabitants believed that God roamed the wide earth by day but chose to sleep every night in Rwanda.

Rwandans believed the crowned crane brought luck. Alas, the good version of it had been in short supply for many years. Most lived lives that their Iron Age relatives would have recognised. They farmed with ancient tools, fetched water from ancient wells, and died of ancient diseases. The jets that flew overhead marked the progress that passed these people by. The colonialists had come and gone. Their cartographers had drawn neat borders on their maps, without consulting the tribal societies they arbitrarily divided. The Europeans left behind broken countries. The modern world sucked the natural resources out of the old, precious minerals were mined by enslaved peoples, who were ground under the heel of gangster tyrants. Perhaps the crane bestowed its luck on them.

After hundreds of years of peace, the Belgian colonisation, which began in 1916 had, by 1959, left tiny, pastoral, crowded Rwanda, in a state of murderous tension. After favouring the minority Tutsi tribe for around forty years, the Belgians had left the Hutu tribe in charge. The 90% Hutu majority persecuted the remaining Tutsi population for everything that went wrong, and this in a country where not much went right. The passing years since the Belgians scuttled away in 1959 were marked by pogroms, massacres, and Tutsi refugees fleeing for their lives. Prices for Rwanda's crops plummeted on the global markets, and poverty got even worse. For three decades old jealousy mixed with new prejudice to produce a lethal cocktail of racist hatred that was, ultimately, Belgium's parting gift.

But one cannot blame the grey crane which swooped down to the Virunga mountain range seeking seeds and insects for food. The breeze rippled its spiky crown as its wide wings flicked and worked the currents of air rising from the forested slopes. It will have seen the roofs of the humble village laid out below, their gardens, fields and plantations. It might have seen three children playing in the sunshine, children who sorely needed the blessings the crane no longer brought.

*   *   *

Grégoire was a Hutu, a farmer, Joseph was a Tutsi, a herder. In childhood neither the race nor the job descriptions mattered to these two boys. It did not affect the regular rhythm of sunshine and rain that the sky shared equally amongst all Rwandans. The 'poverty line', as defined by the United Nations and World Bank, was up above their heads, and out of reach. These people aspired to that level of so-called poverty. But the children had family and friends, a blanket to sleep under, just enough food to eat, cast-off clothes to wear, a school to learn in, a Catholic Church to pray in and, on the open ground in front of Grégoire's house, a place to play in; which is where they were on this hot, dry afternoon as the shadow of a crane's wings passed over them.

A thousand metres beneath Mount Sabyinyo, near the northern border of Rwanda, thirteen-year-old Grégoire swung his machete with wild energy. His targets were the weeds in the clay yard of his home in the village of Kinigi. His younger friends Joseph, twelve, and Denyse, nine, watched warily. Baked and brittle, the weeds shattered and snapped, tumbling into the brown dust. As he held the blade aloft, he watched the sunlight sparkle on its edge and it glittered in his eye. He was a dancer and the '*panga*' (machete) was his partner. Quickly he whirled;

'Fall under my sword! Die! See, I show no mercy,' shouted Grégoire as he thrashed around.

'Kill them all, Grégoire,' Joseph laughed, 'they are Belgian weeds!'

'No. They are Tutsi weeds like you, Joe!'

'That's nice,' said Denyse.

'Well, Joe is skinny... like a weed,' panted Grégoire.

'That's true. And I am a Tutsi,' said Joe, seeing the logic in Grégoire's remark.

Joe was elegant and tall for his age, with a long face, a sharp nose, and girlish almond eyes set above angular cheek bones. He had light skin for an African, even for a Tutsi. When placed next to Grégoire, his physical opposite, people would comment on the contrast. Joe's balletic grace was in marked distinction to his friend's muscularity. Grégoire respected strength and was proud of his physical potency, whereas Joe admired intelligence and enjoyed school. Denyse was a tender, female version of Joe; readier to laugh and less prone to sulking. She was some years off being a beautiful woman, but clearly; it was already her destiny. If they stood in a line, then Grégoire was the thorn between two roses.

The weeding job was soon done, much to the others' relief because neither Denyse nor Joe felt safe when Grégoire pirouetted with his father's machete. Finally, he sat sweating on the doorstep, the blade still trembling in the hard dirt in front of him. He leant back against the wall of dried mud that was plastered onto the wooden frame of his home. The corrugated tin roof heated the house up, so it was cooler to sit outside in the sunshine and enjoy the faint breeze.

'Get your breath back, Grégoire,' said Joe, 'or today I shall beat you to the top of the hill.'

'Joseph, I do not need all my breath to beat you,' laughed Grégoire. 'Just say when you want to try. I'll be ready for the race.'

Joseph was ready, or so it seemed. As the boys prepared to run, Denyse looked around and spotted the old, red, transistor radio on the window ledge. On her tiptoes, she could stretch just high enough to turn it on. After some crackly adjustment of the plastic wheel, the tinny speaker blared out the big hit of that year, 1988; Michael Jackson's 'Bad'. She sang along and, thanks to her English lessons at school, even understood some of the words. The scenic grandeur of the mountains deserved a better soundtrack than Jackson's brittle pop kitsch, but that was what they played. Like many African children, Denyse idolised artistes like Michael Jackson. Successful Afro-Americans were icons for them. They enjoyed wealthy, western lifestyles and 'lived the dream'. Even an inaccessible dream held out some hope. The radio piped that fantasy across the continents, and it fed the aspirations of children like Denyse, Grégoire and Joe.

As the music played, the sun etched out the boys' shadows across the line that was scratched into the red clay. They stooped in their starting positions, like Olympic sprinters, twisting their feet for better grip. The beat pumped through them both. However, the lyrics to 'Bad' distracted Joe. He thought Michael Jackson was good, very good, and so when he sang along to the chorus he changed it; 'Because I'm good, I'm good, I'm really, really good…' he did not know why the wonderful Michael Jackson, of all people, should call himself 'bad'. It did not seem right. As he awaited starter's orders, he twitched to the rhythm of the music and hummed the tune.

'On your marks…

… get set…

… GO!' shouted Denyse.

Instantly Grégoire shot up the slope, his strong and powerful legs thumping at the hard earth. As he predicted he led from the start but, alas, Joseph did not rise to the challenge. For Joe the music won out, and he preferred to sing and dance along with Michael Jackson and Denyse in the dusty yard. On the shout of 'Go!' he merely jumped up to join his hero on an imaginary concert stage. His 'moves' consisted of bouncing, stamping and flicking an imaginary long-haired wig around. This was far removed from the 'moonwalk', but Joe had never seen Michael Jackson dance. He assumed Jackson performed the traditional Rwandan dance steps. When he wasn't singing, he grinned manically, with his eyes widened as far as they would go, just as the Intore dancers did. Denyse and Joe merrily kicked up the dust outside Grégoire's house. For them the race was forgotten as soon as it began.

A hundred thigh-burning yards later, Grégoire celebrated his triumph up the slope with leaps of joy, pumping his fists into the air. He knew he would win, he always did, and today he could not even hear Joseph panting behind him. However, when he looked down on the scene below, he saw it was a hollow victory. Joseph and Denyse cavorted madly in the yard with only the faint background of Michael Jackson as evidence that they weren't insane; merely dancing. He sat down to catch his breath, laugh, and rest for a moment.

Behind him, soaking up the sunlight, small rectangular terraces of fertile earth stretched up the hillside planted with potatoes and sorghum. Each individual plot of land was the proud mini farm of a Hutu from the village of Kinigi. These little holdings perched on the mountainside like rough tiles on a steep roof. Each was a different shade of green depending on the crop, the quality of the soil, and the skill of the farmer. This organised procession up the slope halted where the farm land stopped at the edge of the forest. Nature's anarchy began at the boundary of the Parc National des Volcans.

Towering above Kinigi and Grégoire, Mount Sabyinyo sat in the middle of the Virunga Range, a row of eight volcanoes, fifty miles long and rising over 3500 meters above sea level. Yet beneath this incredible richness of animal and bird species, with its wealth of plants and trees stretching into the misty distance, there lived some of the poorest humans on earth. Indeed, if they dared seek food in this bountiful larder on their doorstep, the world condemned them as poachers; as if they could be thieves in their own garden. The rain forest was being conserved, but not for the people who lived next to it.

Grégoire did not dwell on this injustice. With his back to the mountains and facing the land to the south, he could make out the busy market town of Ruhengeri seven miles away. It was now famous across Rwanda because one of its sons, Juvénal Habyarimana, was the President. Grégoire knew this and, though he was vague on the details of how it had come about, he was pleased to feel associated with the town. Others would call the northern province of Rwanda, especially Ruhengeri, the muscle of the president's strength. It was the power-base of Habyarimana and the stronghold of his ruling 'Hutu Power' party. His Hutu government believed in power and wealth only for the Hutu tribe, much as the Nazis favoured Aryans during the Third Reich and, as it had been for non-Aryans, if you weren't a Hutu you were effectively sub-human.

The President was currently in Arusha in Tanzania half-heartedly negotiating a peace deal. Across the table from him were his enemy, the leaders of the Tutsi rebel army, The Rwandan Patriotic Front (RPF). A civil war had simmered on for several years. The RPF was made up of Tutsi refugees, and their descendants, who had left Rwanda in fear of Hutu persecution. The United Nations wanted President Habyarimana to share power with the rebels and end the fighting.

There was no chance he would abide by this agreement and nor did his party wish him to. But wherever the United Nations shone its beam of sweet reason, it was always nice to bask in the limelight. Habyarimana enjoyed the frisson of global attention in Tanzania because it made him feel important. To placate the United Nations, he would say anything and sign anything, but back home he would only do what he wanted. Meanwhile, Rwanda and his hometown of Ruhengeri appreciated his dimly reflected glory. Though the town did not have a building over two stories high, Grégoire shared the local, civic pride that said 'our Leader, our President, he is one of us'. There was a feeling of being blessed here and that life would get better. It seemed to the young boy that everyone in the country was patriotic and loyal to the president. But Grégoire knew little of history and less of present reality.

As he looked down the hillside, he saw his father, Jean Damascène, walking up the path to their home on the edge of the village. With a big grin, he jumped up to his feet, waved frantically, and ran down the slope to greet him.

2

Jean Damascène trudged slowly up the hill to his home. He

was not in a good mood, but seeing his son brought a smile even to his tired face. He felt the heat as a burden to be carried, he was already weary, and it was only midday. He shaded his eyes from the sun's glare and saw his son sprinting down the hill to greet him. As Grégoire neared, Jean called out;

'Get yourself ready Grégoire, we have work to do. Say good bye to your friends now.'

At his voice, Denyse peeped shyly round the open gate and smiled. When he waved at her, she gave a timid flutter of her hand in response, then she was quickly gone, round the back of the house, and away to her mother. As Jean arrived at the house, Grégoire had already snatched up a hoe, ready for work. Farming was hard, sweaty labour but, like his father, Grégoire took great pride in it. Owning land, even if it was only a small patch, meant that you had status. It gave you a lifetime's income, it fed your family, and any food left over could be sold at the market. Farming connected Grégoire to his father and all his ancestors; they tilled the meagre parcel of soil that had been passed down to them. Even the tools had changed little in hundreds of years. The bond to the past was as deep in their souls as their genes were in their flesh and bones. They were born farmers, and they died farmers.

Joseph tugged at Jean's tattered jacket sleeve.

'Can I help you today?'

'No, Joseph, I'm sure your mother needs help with her cattle. You must go to her now.'

'But she hasn't got many, and they smell horrible.'

'Joseph, this is our job and you have yours. Go to your mother now. She cannot milk the cows on her own.'

As Joe left, Jean took off his jacket and adjusted the angle of his cap. Within seconds Joe had forgotten his disappointment and was skipping through the grass singing his 'good' version of Michael Jackson's 'Bad'. As he scampered off, Jean and Grégoire strode up the hillside to the family plot. Grégoire was keen to impress his father and made a point of keeping up with him without looking like he was struggling to do so. His father knew this and deliberately walked fast to give Grégoire his chance to prove himself a man. He chuckled when Grégoire's panting gave the game away. He was breathless by the time they reached their field near the top of the hill.

'Do you need to rest, boy? You seem tired already. Clearing those weeds must have done for you.'

'No, I'm fine. I had a race with Joseph just now. That's all. You should have seen me. I won easily.'

'Well done, but he is a year younger than you. Perhaps your skinny little Tutsi friend will catch you up one day?'

'He'll never beat me.'

'Good lad,' his father laughed and clapped his son on the shoulder. 'Yes, you are strong. Now take your hoe and show this field how strong you are.'

They set to the task that was the rhythm of their lives. The blade of the hoe swung into the sky, then it thumped into the clay, it flicked in the sunlight, then punched the earth once more. They worked hard as the sun rose high, bleeding sweat from their pores. The soil was hoed so finely that it looked like sand. Mechanical farm tools were unheard of but with a wealth of cheap labour, and little else to fill a farmer's time, the soil received better treatment than any machine could hand out. Their sorghum grew in the neatest rows as if directed by a surveyor's theodolite. Pointless perfection, but a neighbour would comment disapprovingly if the line of plants looked sloppy. Each row was raised a nearly a foot above the drainage gulley's in the field so the rain would flow away quickly and not wash away the soil from the roots. The sorghum was used for porridge and it provided fodder for animals. It fed the family goat, if you had one, which gave you regular milk and, one fine day, goat stew.

After a few hours, they stopped for a drink of water from Jean's plastic bottle. They sat under the shade of a tree at the edge of the field and tuned in to the familiar soundtrack of crickets and birdsong. In the distance near the edge of the forest, a group of men and women were preparing a new patch of ground for planting. They swung their long hoes over the shoulders into the scrub, like a horde of angry golfers looking for a lost ball. The soil and climate were perfect for growing things but not everything that grew was wanted, weeds, wild celery, bamboo, any number of unwanted seeds could be blown down from the forest on a breeze. A farmer had to make order out of the chaos of nature and once planted, the crops had to be looked after night and day. Life was hard, and Jean Damascène had to prepare his young son for it. As he mused on this problem, he spotted an opportunity to give Grégoire a little more of a man's responsibility.

'Grégoire, it is our turn to look after the hillside tomorrow night. We have to protect our crops and keep a watch for wild animals that might eat or trample them. You are ready to be a guard, I think. What do you say, boy?'

'Yes,' replied Grégoire, both thrilled and scared by the thought. He realised this showed his Father's confidence and trust in him. It was a small step towards becoming a man. At the top of the slope, under the eaves of the rainforest, was a small hut for the night watchman. There was just enough room for one person, or two small people, to sit inside and spy on the fields. If an animal came out of the forest, the watchman had to scare it away by throwing sticks or stones at it. The trespassing animal was usually some kind of deer, and they were easy enough to frighten off. However, buffalo could sometimes come out of the Parc; he would have to run and get his father if that happened, they were dangerous. 'Can Joseph come with me?' He asked.

'Ah...' Jean paused and weighed his thoughts. 'Yes, but only this once, if his mother will let him.'

'Good. He is my best friend. One day we will farm together,' said Grégoire enthusiastically, but at this comment Jean's expression clouded.

'Now Grégoire, I hear what you say, and I am concerned. There is something you must remember; yes, Joseph seems harmless, but you can never trust him. Always be careful. Joseph is a Tutsi. His ancestors did terrible things to Hutus. They made us their slaves, forced us to work for nothing. Your grandfather fought to get rid of the Tutsi kings and free the Hutu people many years ago. You must watch Joe carefully because you do not know what he is planning. This wickedness is deep inside all Tutsi, it is in his bones. He cannot change what he is, so you must be on your guard.'

'We must be careful the Tutsi cattle do not trample our crops.'

'Yes, Grégoire,' he replied. 'We must be careful. You must be careful. They are not like us, Hutu have always been farmers in this land. The Tutsi came from the north with their cattle many, many years ago. Sometimes we live in peace and sometimes we must fight to protect ourselves. We are different, that is the way it is. Notice how thin and tall Joseph is while you are broad shouldered and strong.' Jean pulled his son closer to him and looked into his eyes. 'Do not tell him your secrets. When he grows up Joe will be dangerous!'

Grégoire's eyes were downcast and he spoke quietly. 'But Joe is my friend!'

'No Grégoire, he is your friend now and, tomorrow, he can help you watch the cattle. But not for much longer. I'm only saying this for your own good.'

Jean knelt down so that he was directly face to face with his son. 'You may need to end your friendship with Joe soon.

3

Joe skipped back from Grégoire's house on auto pilot; he knew his way through the maze of informal paths that connected all the houses in Kinigi together. There was a bare main road through the village, a red dust track that a car could drive down. It was a bumpy ride even if you had good suspension, and if it was the rainy season, the journey would best be postponed. Joseph could see the road below him, one day he dreamed he would drive along it. He would wave at his friends and they would see how well he had done to be sat in a motor car. One day.

Many homes had hedges to border their land and provide privacy, but the wily traveller knew where the gaps were. Joe even knew who was likely to be in or out, and whether or not a shortcut through someone's yard was safe. He skipped along his zig zag route barefoot, his feet long since hardened to any small stones he could step on. He was soon out on the common scrub land where the Tutsi's cattle wandered sleepily in the sunshine. He spotted his cousin moving between the cows in the small herd. His wiry frame towered above the dozen or so younger boys who scampered around him trying to be helpful.

'Pascale!' he called. Pascale turned and waved.

'Joseph. Good to see you. But you are late; your mother's two cows have missed you.'

'Sorry. I was with Grégoire and Denyse,' said Joe as he ran over and stood resting his arm across the back of his favourite cow called Umuseengo. He gently stroked the back of the animal's head and listened as Pascale gently chastised him.

'Well, I have been watching for you, you owe me Joe.'

'Have Clement and Claude not been helping you?' asked Joe with a smile.

'What? The twins are only four years old. Today they have been putting flowers in their hair, not looking after cattle. We should have one boy for every cow. What if somebody came to steal them? We have to look out for one another.'

He was right, but Joe knew he wasn't really mad, Pascale never got angry. He was an intelligent young man who had been allowed to stay on at school, and Joe looked up to him for that. Pascale had been accepted into university in Kigali and would be leaving the village later that year. He was a father figure to Joe and advised him as such.

'Clement and Claude know how to milk the cows.' Joe said.

'The milk should end up in the bucket, not your mouth. These two feed like hungry calves,' replied Pascale.

Clement and Claude lived on the same hill as Joe. Their father was called Charles, and his two Ankole cows looked grand with their big, rippled horns splaying three feet from their heads. Their milk was the family's main source of income. Looking after the cattle was not arduous, and all Joe needed was a stick to make sure they stayed on the pasture land and away from any crops. All the boys took pride in their task, and they made it look more complex than it was for the benefit of passers-by. Being the eldest, Pascale carried a spear, supposedly to protect the herd from any big cats that might threaten a straggling young calf. This was a position of responsibility, Joe liked to be the boss, and he was also keen to play with the spear. Even though he was late, Joe felt Pascale would still give him the chance.

'Pascale, can I carry the spear today?'

'Hmm...' Pascale ran his eyes up and down the eager Joe. 'I guess I could do with a nap.'

'I know what to do,' replied Joe.

'OK. But stay near. Keep your eyes open and watch the long grass carefully. If you see any big cats, you must wake me. Is that clear?' Joe nodded. 'A leopard or a lion would kill you.'

'I'll be very watchful.'

'Remember what I told you,' said Pascale and headed to some long grass where the twins were sat playing with dried grass and pebbles. Joe called after him.

'Can I practise throwing the spear at that tree?'

'Yes, but not near the cattle, and..,' said Pascale over his shoulder and wagging a raised finger as he walked away. '...definitely not near me!'

Pascale lay down to snooze while Joe strutted manfully with the spear a safe distance away. At first, he wore the responsibility heavily like the spear across his shoulders, but he soon tired of his swaggering pose and settled down to some throwing practise. He threw it at a tree but did not have the strength to make it stick in the trunk, so it bounced off. After a few more unsuccessful tries, he settled for patrolling the edge of the herd, shading his eyes in the sunlight and kept a wary eye on the long grass. The cows followed Pascale's lead and lay panting in the sunshine, occasionally swishing their tails. Pascale rested contentedly, safe in the knowledge that the nearest lions were two hundred miles away in the Akagera National Park; but today was not the day to share that information with Joe.

Herding cattle took lots of their time, but it was pretty much a leisure activity as long as they didn't annoy the farmers by letting any animals stray onto their precious crops. The work was not much more than a gentle stroll in the sunshine, and Joe quite enjoyed it. He liked to talk to Pascale though and was pleased when Pascale awoke after an hour or so.

'Do we have a game this weekend, Joe?' He asked with a yawn.

'Yes, we play Kampagna from the other side of the village. Do you remember? Jean de Dieu is their captain.'

'Ah...' Pascale paused for thought. 'I don't like them, or him, actually. There are no Tutsi on that team Joe, they are all Hutu. Tutsi boys live round there, they just don't get a game.'

'That is a shame, Pascale. They will not get spotted by the scouts from Europe. I think Manchester United are watching this one.'

'Really? Have you packed your bags, Joe? You are sure to be flying to England very soon when they see your skills. Make sure you score some great goals.'

'I will, and they will know it's me. I've written 'Sharp' on my shirt, that is their sponsor, and my name is on the back,' said Joe.

'Well, I hope it is not Real Madrid's turn to watch football in Kinigi this week. They won't like that.'

'No. It is Manchester United.' said Joe with a confident nod of his head. He liked to indulge his dreams and Pascale let him.

'Do they have many Rwandan players in Manchester?'

'I do not know. I may be their first.'

'And, when you are rich, what will you do with all the

money you will earn?'

'Hmm, I will send ten Rwandan francs a week home to my mother.' Joe replied before thinking a little more. 'No. I'll take her with me, and I will send tickets for you to watch my first game.'

'Well, you are generous. I guess I'll pay for the flights myself.'

'Do they cost a lot of money?' asked Joe.

'More than ten dollars, Joe. Anyway, I hope to be playing for Musanze by then.'

Musanze Ruhengeri football club was the nearest 'professional' league team, and thousands of people flocked to the home games. They streamed down from the hills and wound through the valleys to watch. A five mile journey was not considered too far, it was a social occasion and bottles of beer passed among the football pilgrims along the way. Attendances matched those of the Catholic Church, indeed most people attended both. The priests and the football league made sure there were no clashes sporting or ecclesiastical. Win or lose, soccer was an excuse for everyone to party, drink beer, and feast on goat kebabs; clerics included.

All the boys played football if they could, and there were teams at school and Church for all ages. Joe was a midfield player, and he had an eye for the pass that could split a defence wide apart. Pascale was an excellent centre forward where his height gave him first pick of any ball crossed from the wings, and therefore plenty of headed goals. Football provided another pipe dream of escaping the backwater of poverty; they fantasised they could be the next Roger Milla who played for Cameroon and in the French league. The boys passed the afternoon talking football while the cattle got up and slowly drifted around from one clump of grass to another. The afternoon sun soaked and drizzled over the thousand hills of Rwanda. The dust rose, the birds and cicadas sang a lullaby by babbling streams in their sleepy Eden.

Four hours later Joe sped back home. His mother,

Angelique, sat outside their tiny one-room shack listening to angry voices on the radio. As she saw him skipping up the path, she quickly turned it off. Then she stood up to greet him, with her arms held wide open for a hug. Joe's wrapped his arms around her waist and clasped his hands behind her back as he pulled her close. When he pulled back, his eyes darted around, and he sniffed the air for a hint of cooking food.

Joe's home was even more humble than Grégoire's, lacking the corrugated tin roof. The best you could say of the cracked mud walls was that there was no need for air conditioning. The air came in through the many gaps and 'conditioned' for free. There were two rickety homemade chairs and a battered table. Their beds were pallets of straw covered with blankets. A cast-iron pot suspended over an open fire outside the front door bubbled with vegetable and bean stew; it smelled fine to hungry Joe.

'Did you keep my cows safe today, young warrior?' She asked.

'Yes, mother. Pascale let me carry the spear and keep watch.'

'Did you see any lions?'

'I think I saw one crouching in the distance, ready to attack. But it saw me and went away. It was probably afraid.'

'Well, that was a very sensible lion! You have earned your evening meal but wash yourself first.'

Joe helped himself from a yellow plastic jerry can and splashed the cool water on his face and hands. Angelique washed the dust off his back and legs with a wet cloth, patting him dry with an old tea towel. It was a warm evening and Joe was dry in seconds. She ladled some stew into a battered tin bowl, and he ate quickly. Before long he was sat in her lap outside their home watching the world go by.

Not that much of the world went by their house, but a beautiful small bird hopped around in the puddle near where Joe had washed, pausing to drink from the few remaining splashes of water. It had a golden orange breast, brown wings and white stripes on its head. Mother and son drank in its beauty while Joe's eyelids grew heavy. His yawns grew larger and more frequent.

'Sing a song for me, like when I was little,' mumbled Joe.

'Ah, which one?'

'Sing "My Little Rock". That was my favourite.'

'Yes, 'my little rock is very pretty'. He still is,' laughed Angelique as she began to sing.

'Kabuye Kanjye
Kabuye Kaniye ni keza pe
Kabuye Kaniye ni keza pe
Enda nawe ukarore
Nawe ukarore
Ni keza pe...'

He was asleep before the end and she carried him in to his bed. As she did every night, she picked up the faded picture of Joe's father, Daniel, and touched it to the boy's lips. 'Say goodnight to Daddy, little Joe,' she whispered. Then she put the photograph back on the window sill.

With Joe tucked in, she went back outside and turned the radio back on at a low volume. She listened while the fire spat sparks into the cool evening and kept the darkness at bay. She missed her husband and longed to feel his arms around her on nights such as this, with the stars overhead and the fire warming her legs and outstretched hands. The flames comforted her, but the announcer on the radio did not.

4

Radio Télévision Libre des Mille Collines

'Brothers and sisters. Bad news, very bad news comes to us from our neighbour Burundi. More of our Hutu family were massacred there by the Tutsi cockroaches; remember at Ntega and Marangara only five years ago. Many refugees are crossing over the border into Rwanda. You may know some of these people. They come to us seeking help. Seeking shelter. Seeking food. We will welcome them with an open hand. Our land is so full. Our people so poor. Yet we will welcome them with an open hand.'

'But do not forget. Do not forget who has slaughtered your cousins in Burundi. Keep a watchful eye on your Tutsi neighbour. Our fathers were their slaves. They forced us to work for nothing, so we rose up against our arrogant masters. Those tall Tutsis, those tall trees. Keep a watchful eye brothers and sisters.'

5

Denyse's mother, Grace, woke her at six o'clock on the Sunday morning as there was much to do. She had to fetch water for cooking and washing and all of this had to be done before Church at eleven. Denyse picked up a small plastic jerry can while her mother balanced a much larger one on her head. They were fortunate that Kinigi had a water tap that was only a twenty-minute walk away from their home. Grace greeted friends and neighbours with a 'good morning' as they passed;

'Mwaramutse Grace. Amakuru.' 'Good morning, how are you?' came the replies.

Even the grumpiest elder would smile back to acknowledge the winsome Denyse's greeting. Part of Grace enjoyed the attention her daughter attracted, and part of her was worried that it would go to the little girl's head. She had a speech prepared for the day when she had to warn her about men. Traditionally girls were brought up to be good wives and mothers, but Grace wanted that and more for Denyse. Education would give her more choices later on in life. She wanted her to have that and a husband who could give her a future better than merely bearing children and cooking. As she juggled these thoughts, her daughter looked up at her smiling and Grace put her concerns aside. It was the Sabbath, a day of Church, football and beer. Everyone would be scrubbed clean and wear the best clothes they had.

For most people, Sunday was a day of less work, if not none. Cows needed to be milked and farmers cast an eye over their crops, but attendance at Church marked the start of a day of recreation. Mothers socialised, daughters and sons played, fathers drank in their favourite local bars called 'cabarets'. These things happened most days, but on Sunday nobody needed an excuse, and so all were done to excess.

At the Holy Family church, like everywhere else in Kinigi, the two Catholic priests, Father Patrice and Father Ishimwe, prepared themselves. As the senior Parish Priest, Patrice would lead the eleven o'clock mass and consecrate the bread and wine. His physique was muscular and strong, as were his traditional religious views; both were developed in his now distant youth. He had a loyal and unbending faith. Ishimwe assisted as his curate. The younger priest was a product of spiritual renewal in the Catholic Church; he was flexible and moved lightly with the times. When they were ready in their best, least grubby, vestments they went to the vestry where the altar boys awaited. Quickly they formed a procession with the smallest and youngest at the front and the older and taller to the back. Behind the line of servers Ishimwe, languid and graceful, was matched by the tall, slim cross he carried. Patrice brought up the rear carrying the covered communion chalice. With his robes gently flowing he looked majestic, like a galleon in full sail.

The first hymn began, and the congregation rose to its feet and sang with gutsy enthusiasm as the altar boys led the way into the packed church. Paradoxically, for the poor, the offer of a blissful afterlife was made more tangible by the reality of suffering in this one, not less. Surely God would not dump on them twice! The Catholic Church also made them feel connected to the power and privilege of the first world; the vestments, the gestures, the prayers, even the shape of the well-fed priests, was universal. The Sunday rituals of Christianity were a global connection, a sign they were not a forgotten people after all.

The sun poured through the high windows behind the altar onto the upturned faces of the people gathered in their brightest clothes. The boys and men were scoured clean. The girls had bows in their pigtails. Women wore mascara, lipstick and figure hugging dresses of peach, green, and red. The pews looked like a garden of flowers, chaotic in bloom. Heady perfumes and scents mixed in with the smell of sweat. The sorghum farmers and the Ankole herders sang as one before their God.

As he walked down the aisle, despite the joyous occasion,

the elder Patrice stared at the back of Ishimwe's head in a melancholy frame of mind. Absentmindedly he noted the trim line of neatly cut hair on the nape of his neck, there were no creases in the younger man's skin as yet. Disconnected from the religious pageantry that unfolded around him he returned to the dark thoughts that often plagued him. The fog of incense which preceded them to the altar was like the fog of self-doubt in his mind. Now in his mid-fifties he questioned his vocation to the priesthood knowing it was too late to undo his choices. Each night he crossed off another day on the calendar of life. One day less to live, one day nearer death. He rarely slept through the night and usually awoke at four am. Lying in the dark he did not light a candle to see his confidant; the silent Christ on the cross who had no words of comfort for him. There was no wife to reach out to and hold, to soothe the panic in his pounding heart. All he had was prayer, a monologue offered to a mute God.

He knew that Ishimwe, only thirty years old, did not feel this way. He had once been a young priest like him, eager to serve, enjoying the prestige of the position. Patrice was cynical of his curate's certitude and was sure it would fail him as he got older. At the beginning of his priesthood the choice of obedience and celibacy could be undone, a life and a wife could still be found. Part of him wanted to tell Ishimwe get out now while he could and part of him wanted him to stay to drink the same bitter cup. If the futile burden could be shared, maybe its weight could be halved. As he climbed into the sanctuary of the altar, he realised he hated Ishimwe; the smug, jolly Tutsi with the possibility of a future ahead of him.

It was too late now for Patrice; the only security lay in faithful service. The only pleasures to be had were what the Church allowed, and the parishioners would accept. He was a Holy Man in the eyes of his congregation, almost a saint, and within the limits of the faith he still had power. He felt that potency surge around him in the voices booming in song, gradually it cheered him knowing that he was the focus of their fervour; not Ishimwe. When he spoke, his sermon would have the seal of authority of Christ and the Pope. His words were validated by the spiritual power of the white man's religion, their truth demonstrated by the white man's omnipotent strength, technology and wealth.

The bare, whitewashed, walls reflected sunlight into the congregation's faces who were oblivious to Patrice's musings. Mass was an opportunity to promenade, to be beautiful and enjoy the beauty of others. Though empty of statues and icons few churches in Rome were graced by such singing as everyone here gave it their best shot. The finer points of the melodies were sacrificed for power and enthusiasm, but all were uplifted by a communal roar worthy of a football match.

The mass was lengthy, but no one begrudged the two hours of liturgical theatre in Church. The big wooden front doors and the windows, their metal frames with rust crisping the paint off them, were wide open to let in cooler air. Hymn books served to fan faces when they weren't being used for singing. The Bible readings were taken to heart, and the sermon was greeted with heads nodded in agreement. After the Lord's Prayer, at the sign of peace, everyone smiled and shook hands with the people around them. The room buzzed with communal affection and harmony. When the bread and wine were consecrated at communion, the congregation broke into applause to acknowledge the miracle of Christ coming amongst them. On the surface it seemed that this branch of Christianity had been successfully grafted onto its deeper African root.

Later, after the mass, the two priests hung their faded costumes in the vestry. Patrice smelled the familiar odour of extinguished candles and heard the echoing footsteps as the last stragglers of the congregation left. In his mouth a remnant of the flavour of altar wine had given him a taste for more. The urge to drink was a gentle yet insistent tap on his shoulder, he made a mental stock take of how much beer and wine they had in that day. 'Was there enough?' he wondered as he looked in the mirror and arranged his thinning hair to cover his round head; he reckoned there was. Meanwhile Father Ishimwe was eager to leave, as he made his way to the door he called out.

'Patrice, are you still coming to the football this afternoon?'

'Of course, but have a Primus,' said Patrice, holding a bottle out. 'We have done our work for the day.'

'Give me five minutes, I have an appointment. Keep it cold for me.' And with that Ishimwe stepped out into the sunshine ignoring Patrice's frown of disapproval. Outside the presbytery several men from the village were waiting, among them was Jean Damascène.

'Good morning gentlemen. I have something for you'. Ishimwe produced a cardboard box from inside his shirt and began to distribute condoms to the men. They were supplied free by the UN and the priest had the connections to get lots of them. He wholeheartedly believed that condoms were not just essential contraceptives in a poor country where people had children they could not feed, but they were the first and last line of defence against AIDS. The Catholic Church was at the forefront of their distribution because it had far more Churches than the UN had clinics.

'Thank you Father. It is good of you.' One of the men said. 'Perhaps I can get you a beer later at the game.' Ishimwe smiled.

'Have you brewed some urwagwa Jean?' he asked.

'Of course, Father, only the finest banana beer for you.'

'Ah well, if it is truly the finest then I would be crazy to say no!' The men laughed, more than was merited, showing their relief. It was not a secret that Father Ishimwe gave them free condoms, but it was not something to broadcast for fear he would get into trouble and the supply dry up. The men got their contraceptives and Ishimwe got strong, free beer that would make even Musanze Town look like a good team.

Back in the vestry Patrice had nearly finished his first Primus when his colleague returned.

'Ishimwe,' he said without looking at him. 'Back so soon?'

'Yes, I was just chatting to some men from the village.'

'Just chatting? Nothing else?'

Ishimwe took a deep breath. He knew what was coming next from past experience. 'No. Not just chatting and you know what else.'

Patrice turned to face him. 'Then we both know that I do not approve of what you have done.'

'I understand your views on this Patrice, but I must follow my conscience, many of our fellow priests agree with me...'

'Then they are wrong,' snapped Patrice. 'There's no safety in numbers with regard to sin Ishimwe.'

Ishimwe paused and said with a sigh. 'It is but a little sin, and a little forgiveness is all that is needed.'

'The size of the sin is not the issue Father. It is the frequency that concerns me. It is your defiance of the Church's teaching every week and your defiance of my authority...'

'For which I apologise,' cut in Ishimwe. 'I try to be a good priest; alas I am not a perfect one.'

'You do not try to obey this particular teaching however imperfectly. Do you think it is wrong? Old fashioned maybe? Which teaching will you reject next in your arrogance? The sin of Adam was not eating the fruit of the tree, his undoing was his decision to make his own laws. He defied God.'

'I am not defying God, only Pope Paul the 6th.' Ishimwe replied. He needed to end this debate, Patrice would get over his anger, but he was his superior, and he could report him to the bishop. He picked up his bottle of Primus and made to leave the room. 'I'm not disagreeing with you and I respect your opinion in all things. I ask that you indulge me in this one weakness if that's what it is,' he needed to leave the room before the argument heated up. 'Excuse me Father. I need to change and freshen up.'

As he left the room Patrice finished his beer and opened another bottle. For the second time that day he found himself resenting Ishimwe. He took his defiance personally it was an affront to his authority as parish priest and, he fancied, a snub to Rome. He believed that a good priest understood the value of loyalty and it was about time Ishimwe paid the price for his arrogance. In his mind he began to put together a letter to the Bishop.

6

Joe, Grégoire and Denyse had arrived at Church with their families but did not sit with them. They made their excuses and huddled together at the back. As the congregation awaited the priestly procession, the adults chatted with their neighbours and the children did the same.

'Are you looking forward to tonight Joe?' asked Grégoire.

'Yes!' He nodded excitedly.

'Are you watching Jean Damascène's crops?' asked Denyse, leaning into the two boys and determined to be a part the adventure.

'Yes,' replied Grégoire.

'Can I come with you?'

'No!' snapped Joe, his eyes wide with indignation. 'This is man's work.'

'But I could be a good look out.'

'It would not be safe for you,' advised Grégoire.

'There are wild animals,' explained Joe. 'You could be eaten.'

'Yes, eaten.' agreed Grégoire. Denyse sat back and stuck her bottom lip out to make her feelings clear. Grégoire tuned to Joe and winked at him.

'But you can help us Denyse.'

'How?' She replied, leaning back on the pew with her arms folded.

'It will be a long night and we will need something to eat.' Grégoire explained. 'As soon as mass starts, we are going into the forest to find something.'

'I don't want to go with you. I like Church.'

'It's boring,' hissed Joe and Grégoire in unison.

'I like the singing.' She replied.

'So do I.' Added Joe.

'Shut up Joe, you idiot. Whose side are you..,' he stopped in exasperation as the priests and altar servers entered. The congregation rose to its feet.

'Let's see who is saying the mass today.'

When Denyse saw the order of procession her shoulders slumped in despair. 'Oh no. It's Father Patrice again. He never tells any jokes.'

'Come on. We're going,' said Grégoire.

Covered by the singing and the shuffling of feet the children sneaked out of the back doors and into the sunshine. They crept round the side of the Church and stood close by the outside wall to share their secret plan.

'Promise you will say nothing to anyone about this Denyse,' said Grégoire. 'And you Joe,' he added as an afterthought.

'Promise!'

'What are you going into the forest for?' asked Denyse.

'Honey,' replied Joe with a grin.

'Honey?' said Denyse, shaking her head. 'How are you going to get that?'

'My father found a bee hive yesterday. It's near the edge of the forest, I've seen it,' said Grégoire.

'Are you insane?' said Denyse.

'No,' said Joe, puzzled at the question. 'Honey is very nice.'

'So how do you get it?'

'It's easy,' said Grégoire. 'Someone climbs the tree and knocks the honeycomb down with a stick. We wrap it in big leaves and put it in the night-watchman's shelter for later tonight.'

'And who is going to climb the tree?' asked Denyse suspiciously. The boys were quiet for a moment.

'Well...' began Joe.

'The branches, they are not strong, it would need to be someone smaller and lighter than us,' said Grégoire.

'And the bees?' asked Denyse.

'They will be OK,' replied Joe confidently.

'They make the honey for us. They are used to this,' said Grégoire. 'They will be pleased to see you.'

'If you think I am going to risk my life falling from a tree while being stung by a thousand bees...' At that moment Placide, late for Church, skipped innocently around the corner. Denyse turned to him. 'Placide...' She asked with a sweet smile, beckoning him over with her little finger.

After a swift twenty minute sprint they were at the wall that separated the farmers' fields from the forest and following Grégoire to the tree his father had shown him. It did not take long to find it and soon the four children stood looking up at the cloud of bees enveloping the big honeycomb that hung from a branch thirty feet above them.

The day was warming up, and the bees were already active. The main body of the pendulous swarm swayed slightly as it hung from the branch. It was surrounded by a cloud of insects flying back and forth from the surrounding forest, each delivering its cargo of nectar.

'The queen is in the middle,' said Denyse.

'You can smell the sweetness of the honey,' said Joe gazing hungrily up at the prize.

'Are you ready Placide?' Said Grégoire handing him a large stick he had found on the forest floor. Denyse and Joe quickly gathered some big leaves and placed them under the swarm above.

'Should we not make some smoke to calm the bees down?' Asked Placide.

'No, you don't need that. You will be fine,' said Grégoire.

'What if I fall?'

'I will be underneath to catch you. You are not heavy. See!' said Grégoire lifting him up to a foothold on the trunk. Placide quickly leapt down.

'What if the bees sting me?'

'They won't,' said Denyse.

"I don't like heights.'

'It's not that high,' said Joe.

'I don't need to climb up anyway,' said Placide.

'Why not?' said Grégoire.

'I'm a good shot with a stick. Watch.'

'No, wait...' cried Denyse, but it was too late. And Placide was indeed a good shot. The stick whirled through the air and caught the swarm bang in the centre, knocking a big chunk down to the ground.

'Honey!' shouted Joe.

'Bees!' shouted Grégoire.

'Run!' shouted Denyse over her shoulder, sprinting from the scene.

The bees were dazed by the assault upon their home, but it did not take them long to identify their assailants. They gave chase.

As they ran screaming down the forest path it crossed Grégoire's mind that the bees would attack the rearmost member of their party. 'Thank God I am the fastest' he thought to himself; only took look up and see the other three ahead of him. Finding renewed energy in his fear he powered on to catch up to them. The children ran faster than they had ever before. As they got to the border of the Parc National each of them cleared the wall in a single leap, aided by the downward slope. As they crashed on heedless through the farmer's crops, they eventually began to feel safe and finally collapsed laughing on a path.

'Did anyone get stung?' gasped Denyse.

'Not me.' 'Nor me.' came the replies.

'Did anyone pick up the honey?' said Joe.

'The honey?' asked Grégoire. 'No. I forgot. That was careless of me. Tell you what, Joe. Why don't you go back and get it?'

'Hmm,' replied Joe rubbing his chin thoughtfully. 'Do we

really need honey tonight?'

'Let's go back to Church.' Suggested Denyse as she stood up and dusted herself down. 'Before we are missed.'

'Who is saying mass today?' asked Placide.

'Father very boring Patrice,' said Grégoire.

'Let's take our time then,' replied Placide.

By the time they got to Holy Family Church the congregation was filing down the central aisle to communion. The four children tagged onto the back of the queue as if they had been there all the time.

7

On the front steps of the Holy Family church Jean Damascène met Grégoire, Joe and some of the boys from the village who collectively formed Colline Kinigi United. Joe wore his red shirt with 'SHARP' written in felt-tip pen across the front and a smaller hand drawn badge to make it clear this was a Manchester United top. He was proud of his kit even though a line of white buttons went down through the centre of the 'A'. Everybody had heard of George Best and Bobby Charlton; they hadn't realised it was twenty years since they had retired from the game. To wear their colours was to access their powers, or so they hoped.

Narrowing his eyes, he surveyed the group of excited boys who surrounded him. With a bare, discrete nod Jean Damascène provided the essential equipment, handing over a single sachet to Grégoire. He kept the rest for himself.

'There you go boys,' he said.

'Thank you Jean,' came a chorus of appreciation.

Quickly the boys pooled their resources to make the ball.

Though it was a flimsy and thin the condom was the perfect template and it was quickly stuffed with banana leaves, dried grass and litter. Once it was the required shape and size, it was carefully bound with string to make it strong enough to survive the game. Within twenty minutes the footballers of Colline Kinigi United were ready for kick off.

On the edge of the village was an uneven patch of land void of shrubs and trees. Cattle often grazed here, and a pile of dung could deflect an otherwise accurate pass, or worse - the ball could get stuck in the shit. Most of the 'pitch' was patches of bare earth, there were some green areas of short grass, and occasional sections of 'rough'. The variations in terrain could make even a skilful player look a fool. The goal posts were the simplest wooden frames of approximately equal size. The crossbars sagged in the middle and a bored goalkeeper could easily leap up to swing from the middle section in a moment of boredom. This Sunday about thirty boys from the local area had gathered. Joe and Grégoire's team only added up to nine regular players from their village but they happily added occasional extras, or just played against opponents that outnumbered them. The team they played against was made up of older boys, at least two of whom were fifteen. A few adults watched, swigging from bottles of beer, ready to encourage, cheer, or laugh at a mistake.

Today however Joe was aware of a different atmosphere. There was no laughter, as though the game was serious. He felt the grown men were surveying the preparations with an odd intensity, like they were waiting for something to happen other than the football. Maybe they had heard a scout was coming from England, maybe he was one of this tiny crowd, dressed like a local to blend in. He scanned the people hanging around the perimeter of the pitch, but there was no one in the thirty or so people there who fit the bill. A voice in his head told him his dream of footballing fame was a foolish child's fantasy; he chose to ignore it.

Presently some boys from Kampagna arrived on homemade 'bicycles'. Cobbled together from scrap wood and utilising a couple of mismatched wheels it was probably quicker to walk. On a downhill section you could get a free ride, uphill they had to be pushed. These prized bikes were owned by the larger boys in the team and, after they dropped them by the side of the field, one of the watching men called the Kampagna players over. A secretive team talk began with glances being thrown at Joe's side as they waited for the game to start. Joe tried to listen to Fabrice's team talk, but he kept looking nervously towards the Kampagna group.

'Grégoire, Jean de Dieu does not look happy today, he is giving me bad looks,' said Joe.

'He never looks very happy Joe,' replied Grégoire.

'He probably has splinters in his arse after riding his bike.' offered Cyprien in a bass voice that welled up from deep in his chunky frame. His remark was intended to get a laugh and when it did, he chuckled, and a smile broke on his big round face.

'He's not looking at you Joe, trust me,' said Fabrice. 'Jean de Dieu always looks like that. He's trying to frighten you, it's his job. He's OK, I know him from school.'

'No, I know what you mean Joe,' said Pascale. 'I swear him and his friends have been giving me evil stares since I arrived.'

'Fabrice is right,' said Patrick, faithful as usual to Fabrice's every word. 'But they are sick of you scoring goals.'

'Good, and I'll be scoring some more today,' said Pascale with a wink at Joe.

'Yes, that will teach Jean de Dieu,' Joe replied.

'I'll kick him in the bollocks.' said Cyprien the enforcer, getting a laugh once more.

'Good idea, but don't do it in our penalty area,' advised Pascale.

The conversation stopped when Jean de Dieu came over to check out the ball and say 'hello' to them yet, somehow, Joe felt the greeting was not aimed at himself or Pascale. When Jean de Dieu shook hands with Fabrice, their handshake seemed to go on for too long.

As the sides took the field, the men watching them fell silent. One put two fingers to his mouth and gave out a piercing whistle to start the game. As ever Pascale took up a forward position ready for a long ball booted up field. With Pascale being a good six inches taller than the defenders the tactic often worked. In past games Jean de Dieu had shadowed him closely and tried to knock him off the ball, today however he held back. Ten minutes into the game Joe spotted Grégoire with the ball while a big gap on the left wing opened up in front of him. He recognised the opportunity to set up an attack.

'Grégoire, here,' he shouted, waving a hand in the air. Grégoire saw Joe's plan and flicked the ball out wide to him. Quickly controlling the pass, Joe sprinted down the wing ready to knock a cross into the penalty area. He noticed again how Jean de Dieu had given Pascale too much space. Joe clipped the ball in, and Pascale had plenty of time to receive the ball and turn.

As the ball winged over to Pascale Joe saw Jean de Dieu sprint forward and dive feet first into the small of Pascale's back. He hit him well before the ball arrived and did not attempt to hide the assault; the vicious look on his face told Joe he had enjoyed it. Pascale collapsed with a roar of pain clutching his back. Jean de Dieu stood threateningly and over him.

'You fouled me you dirty Tutsi bastard!' Jean screamed and Pascale's head jerked backwards as Jean kicked him in the face. 'Did you see what he did?' he shouted as all the players ran over to the scene.

'The cheating fucking cockroach,' yelled Alexis, Jean de Dieu's friend, and he too kicked out at Pascale's head.

Within seconds, like it was planned, the Kampagna players gathered round to kick at Pascale's prone body. Joe's team ran in to break up the 'fight'. Grégoire was first there and launched a blow at Jean de Dieu which, to his surprise, never landed as Fabrice grabbed his arm and pulled Grégoire a few paces away from the fight.

'Stay out of it.' shouted Fabrice pushing at the confused and angry Grégoire.

'But...' began Grégoire. Jean de Dieu came over quickly and squared up to Grégoire but, though both had their fists clenched, neither threw a punch preferring to stare and dare the other to make the first move. Fabrice moved in between the two.

'Stay out of it Grégoire,' repeated Jean de Dieu.

Separated from the fray the two stood face to face in silence, each still daring the other to hit out. In the background the watching men jeered and laughed at the writhing Pascale. Albert broke up the assault, grabbing Alexis by the front of his shirt and shaking him about like a rag doll.

Joe ran over to the melee but only slowly, as though his feet dragged through mud in a nightmare. He was trembling with fear and felt a sickness in the pit of his stomach. He wanted to protect Pascale, but he could not fight, he could take a punch but he could not hand one out. He did not like to see people hurt, and he did not like to be hurt himself. It was the most he could do to run among the boys and plead for peace.

'Stop, stop, we are all friends,' shouted Joe, pushing into the crowd of kicking boys. 'Stop!' Jean de Dieu stepped away from Grégoire, gripped Joe by his throat and squeezed it so that he choked and could not speak.

'Never, ever call me that again, Tutsi,' shouted Jean de Dieu an inch away from Joe's face. 'Do you understand? I am not your friend.' At this Grégoire stepped in and grabbed Jean's arm tightly.

'Let him go Jean,' said Grégoire as he stepped in to square up to Jean de Dieu. 'He is my friend.'

'He is your friend? So am I, and I am more than your friend Grégoire,' said Jean de Dieu, matching Grégoire with his controlled anger and even voice. 'Me and you, we are on the same side. We are Hutu, he is a cockroach.'

'On another day Jean. Today he is a footballer on my team,' said Grégoire.

With that Jean released his grip on Joe's neck, who fell sobbing into the dirt by his cousin Pascale. This seemed to amuse the other team and the men looking on who laughed hard, swaying with mirth.

'Look at the little coward cry!' they jeered. 'Pick up your friend, the little cry baby, and go home. This is a man's game.'

By this time the violence had simmered down. With Joe's help Pascale stood up slowly and unsteadily, leaning on the smaller boy. Grégoire went round the other side and led Pascale away. Joe expected his friends to go with them, but they stood uncertainly, as though awaiting a call. Albert, Cyprien and Patrick deliberately looked away; Placide swayed back and forth looking into the middle distance, as if something else had caught his attention. Fabrice stood side by side with Jean de Dieu as though he played for their team.

'Come on we're going,' said Grégoire. 'Albert, Cyprien, are you coming with us? Placide, Patrick, are you coming?'

'We are playing a game of football,' said Fabrice. 'We are not cowards. It was a fair tackle; people get hurt in contact sports.' Grégoire turned his back and began to lead the stumbling Pascale away. Fabrice continued. 'Hey! Where are you going? Stay with us and play. Yes?'

'I must take Pascale home Fabrice. He is hurt,' said Grégoire looking back, as Fabrice and Jean de Dieu walked over to him.

'Come on,' said Fabrice. 'He's OK. But you might be making trouble for yourself farmer boy. Face it. The Tutsi got what he deserved. He fouled Jean de Dieu.' This remark set the Kampagna players smirking with barely suppressed giggles.

Grégoire let go of Pascale and stood face to face with Fabrice.

'Fabrice, don't talk to me like that just because your father has money. I have a great idea. Let me tell you about it. If you want to make trouble with me, you know where I live. Come and see me. Then I will see your trouble. How does that sound?'

Fabrice backed away and said nothing. After a moment Grégoire turned and led the two boys away; Pascale barely able to walk, Joe gasping for breath and in tears.

'Grégoire. I am not picking a fight with you,' shouted Fabrice. 'You know I am your friend. Come on man. We are on the same team.' Grégoire ignored him and carried on walking. 'Grégoire!' shouted Fabrice once more, this time Grégoire turned and gave him a cynical half smile.

'Don't call me a farmer again Fabrice. Just because your father has an office and a desk in town.' With that they left.

'Young Grégoire seems not to know who his friends are Fabrice,' said Jean de Dieu when Grégoire was out of earshot.

'Not yet. But he will. He is a good Hutu. His father is a good man.'

'I hope so. My father has told me of Jean Damascène. He will come round.' Some of the men who had been watching came over to the remaining players. They held bottles of beer and offered them to the older boys.

'Here, have a drink, you deserve to celebrate. You taught that cockroach a lesson. He was a cheat, he spoiled the game,' they said. 'Yes, drink some beer with us. You have become men today. You can walk with us to Ruhengeri to watch the game this afternoon.'

All the Colline Kinigi United players, except for Fabrice, felt pulled in two by the invitation. They knew they were selling out, but they wanted to taste beer and be accepted by the men.

'Well. Who wants to go with Grégoire and the cry baby Tutsis and who wants to stay here?' asked Fabrice with a smile. 'They've got cold beer boys!' The question was met with silence while they made up their minds. 'Don't worry about Grégoire and Pascale. It'll all blow over. It always does.' Finally, keen as ever to appear Fabrice's friend, Patrick spoke.

'Yes, we have seen fights before. It happens. It doesn't frighten us.'

'One thing first,' grumbled Cyprien. 'Jean de Dieu.'

'What?' he answered.

'Try that trick with me, and I'll kick you in the bollocks.'

'Cyprien,' laughed Jean de Dieu. 'Trust me. I will never do anything that would cause someone of your size to kick me in the balls! Come on. Have a drink,' he held a bottle of beer out to Cyprien who took it from him. 'Guys. There's more. Albert, a beer for you?' Feeling part of the gang Albert accepted the drink. 'You. What's your name? Would you like a taste of beer?'

'That's Placide,' said Fabrice. 'He doesn't say much.'

'Ah, the strong silent type?' said Jean de Dieu.

'No. Just silent,' said Fabrice pushing Placide's outstretched hand away. 'And he's too young to taste beer, so I'll have his.'

As the first beers were drunk only Placide seemed to have doubts.

'Do you think Pascale and Joe are OK?' he asked Fabrice.

'Oh, they'll be fine. It's just one of those things. There's trouble between Hutu and Tutsi from time to time. It happens,' he ruffled the younger boy's hair. 'A week or two passes and then it is forgotten. We can check on the guys later. Grégoire will come round. He lost his temper, that's all.'

As the boys shared the beer between them more of the men came over to join them. The mood calmed, and it was almost a party. Most sat on the grass enjoying the beer while some of the players showed off tricks they had learned with the football. Sure, the players in the Kinigi team held Joe and Pascale as their friends; but there were forces stronger than the friendship of boys. Those forces tugged at them.

8

Later in the afternoon Jean Damascène sat and snoozed outside his home enjoying the late afternoon sun. It had been a good Sunday so far. He had been to church in the morning and enjoyed a good sing song. After this he had gone into the Parc National des Volcans to check on his traps. Several men from the village set traps in there though, now it was illegal, not as many as in the past.

Game, such as wild deer, was a valuable source of protein in a place where meat was rarely affordable. For most people illegal game was the only source of meat they could put on the table; even Tutsis who had several cows rarely killed one for the steak. The trapping was not illegal because it killed small bushbuck or monkeys; the problem was that the traps sometimes caught gorillas. A young gorilla could be killed or maimed as the trappers could not discriminate between their victims. The mountain gorillas brought in the foreign tourists and their dollars.

Jean was careful and so far he, and most of his traps, had escaped detection by the park rangers. When he got to the spot, he saw that his prayers at Church had been answered; a young deer, an okapi, close to death, struggled to pull free from the wire that had its foreleg in a bitter grip. The more it struggled the deeper the wire cut, and blood leeched onto its fur. Jean ended its struggles with a single blow from his machete and, after re-setting the trap, sneaked out of the parc with the carcass over his shoulder.

With the meat safely delivered to his wife, Gloria, Jean was nicely set up for the day; he had a few beers watching the football, and a couple more swigged on the walk home. He had a look at his crops and admired the straight lines and the finely hoed soil. He had no intention of doing any work and, thankfully, there was none to do. He chatted to a few neighbours as they compared their craft in the fields. When his eyes grew heavy, he headed back down the slope for some bean stew and a quick nap. His wife, Gloria, indulged his beery demeanour, gave him his meal and let him sleep it off. Later he would head off to his favourite bar. She would chat to her neighbours and enjoy a few drinks herself without Jean getting under her feet.

A couple of hours later she had finished washing the pots and dishes. The sun was just above the horizon. She flicked a tattered, wet kitchen towel over her thick forearm as she picked up the bowl of tepid, dirty water and emptied it in the corner of the yard. She surveyed her snoozing husband and noted the position of the sun. It was time for Jean to rouse himself and be off, so she filled the bowl with clean water and placed it at his feet. Then she gave him a shake to wake him.

'Come along Jean. It is nearly sunset. Your friends will be waiting for you. Mine are waiting for me. Let's be going.'

Jean rubbed his eyes and took a deep breath which he exhaled as a yawn and elaborated with a stretch of his arms.

'Yes, yes. I am ready,' he replied and removed his hat to swill his face in the cool water. There was a stale taste of beer in his mouth and he was keen to replace it with a fresh one very soon. Feeling more awake he popped his faded leather cap back on his head.

In the daytime it kept the sun off, in the evening it kept his head warm, but all the time it was his trademark 'look'. He was quite vain about his hat. As a young man he had seen a movie poster for 'The Wild One'. It showed Marlon Brando looking cool, slouched over a motorcycle. Jean wanted to be cool like that. He could not afford the bike, but he found a similar hat, and that was good enough. His hat was part of his character and he was rarely seen without it. When he removed it to mop his brow in the fields people did a double take as the top of his head was a rare sight. He had some tight grey curls remaining beneath a bald patch on top. Jean believed his cap took a few years off him, nobody else thought that, but he did not know.

'Is the meat prepared?' he asked.

'Yes, there are two full legs for us, one for Laurette and the rest you can sell at the cabaret.'

'Is Laurette going to pay?'

'She and Oscar gave us meat last time.'

'It was a while ago. Oscar does not set good traps.'

'The day will come when he has meat and we don't, then you'll be grateful he owes us a favour. And don't forget that Grégoire is watching the crops tonight.' Gloria reminded him.

'I haven't. He was very excited. Joe will be with him.'

'Tutsi Joe?'

'Is there another?' Jean thought for a moment, he needed to do something about Grégoire's friendship with Joe. 'With any luck one of them will manage to stay awake.'

'If there is a problem, he will come running for you. Will he be able to wake you up?'

'I doubt it, but he'll wake you up trying.'

At that he laughed, tweaked the peak of this cap, gave her a wink, and set off for the cabaret. Gloria watched, him toying with the idea of throwing the dish cloth at his departing back.

'Don't. You'll miss.' Was Jean's final remark, delivered over his shoulder. Gloria decided he was right in that. She'd end up fishing the dish cloth out of the dust and have to wash it. Instead she went in to prepare herself for the evening, yet no sooner had she walked through the door than her neighbour Laurette was right behind her.

'Are you not ready yet Gloria?'

'Soon, soon, Laurette. Jean has only just left.'

'Yes, I saw him go. Oscar is already there. Here, have a taste of this. It will help you get ready quicker.' She held out her bottle of home-made urwagwa to her friend. Gloria took the straw and drew in a good mouthful.

'Ah, thank you. I'll just wash my face and I'll be ready. There is some meat for you on the table. Jean has been lucky again.' In five minutes both women were walking arm in arm down the dusty path to call on friends and neighbours. They carried drinks and shared them on the way. By the time they reached the cabaret there were half a dozen more women primed for the evening.

9

Jean made his way up the rough path to meet his friends with the remainder of the okapi wrapped in a cloth over his shoulder.

Evariste's cabaret was much like any other in the country. Essentially it was a shed that served alcohol. Flimsy walls of bamboo surrounded a courtyard, in the centre of which was a fire in a stone hearth where goat kebabs cooked over the flames and were served up on flat breads. Some benches were placed around the perimeter of this area and there was a covered section near the bar in case it was raining. The 'bar' consisted of a plank shelf behind which stood Evariste and from there he served his customers. There were bottles of urwagwa with straws in; depending on how much money you had you could buy it by the glass or the sip. If someone's wallet was full, there were a couple of cases of Primus beer though, inevitably in Kinigi, this was gathering dust. The secretive could sit in dark corners and talk in low voices while the more gregarious could join the general banter as the beer flowed... or trickled.

As Jean walked into the courtyard of the cabaret, he saw his friends Thierry, Daniel, Oscar and Vincent were already there, drinking, talking and laughing around the bar plank with Evariste. He tilted his old cap back on his head to reveal more of his face and stood amongst the old gang. Ordering a drink from Evariste he shook hands with the bartender and discreetly placed the okapi out of sight by Evariste's side. The men nodded to each other, and the deal was done. The meat would be cooking on the fire before tomorrow was over. With business concluded Jean turned to nod at his drinking buddies making brief eye contact with each.

Evariste's confident smile and professional manner demonstrated the standards of civility he demanded from his clients. He did not serve anyone considered too young and he did not tolerate rowdy behaviour from customers if they had run out of money. He was the boss and, as such, exercised the right to guide conversation in his bar.

'Have you heard the news today Jean?' He said handing him a bottle of out-of-date Primus beer.

'Burundi? Yes. Of course. It is a long way south of here, but near enough to affect us I think.'

'You are right Jean,' said Oscar. 'There are thousands of refugees. Rwanda is small, but they are our brothers, we must help them. Fifty thousand were slaughtered; terrible, terrible.'

'It is bad news for Burundi but it is also a warning for us,' replied Jean. 'We have our own Tutsi cockroaches here to keep an eye on. If a few heads look like they are too far from the ground, they can be cut down to size. We have done it before.'

'It's not just the Tutsis around here,' came Vincent's agitated voice. 'In Uganda there are many more waiting. The rebels are a threat and their spies may be any Tutsi we know, even in our village.' This comment drew murmurs of agreement.

'This army is not so far away as Burundi, it is waiting on our doorstep,' added Oscar. 'And their friends are in our village.'

'Then we would be wise not to trust them,' said Evariste. 'They made our ancestors slaves, and that's why we gave them a beating thirty years ago. They should stay in Uganda for me. There is no room for them here.'

'Maybe we should make some room for the Hutu refugees?' mused Oscar. 'Clear some Tutsi weeds from their land? Perhaps we should sharpen our pangas for the harvest? Our President needs to be strong on this problem.'

'Habyarimana is strong, his wife is even stronger,' said Jean.

'Well he is wasting his time in Arusha..,' said Vincent, but he stopped as he looked over to the bar's entrance.

He fell silent because he noticed that a new customer had walked into the bar. It was Charles, a friend, but also a Tutsi and he had heard some of their talk.

'Good evening neighbours,' he said then, after a pause.

'Shall I buy a drink or am I not welcome here?' The group was quiet at first; Jean took a long, slow, swig as an excuse not to speak. It was Evariste who broke the uncomfortable silence.

'Charles. Do not let our talk worry you. Beer and bad news are a not a good mix. We meant nothing. All my friends are respected in here, you as much as anyone.'

'Of course, Charles,' said Jean, who had now decided to be conciliatory. 'If there is any trouble, we will look after you. You are a good man. People worry about bad news but, all the bad things that happened, that was years ago. You are OK with us.'

'Yes, naturally,' said Charles. 'Well, here is your chance to prove it. Who is going to buy me a drink? After a pause it was Evariste again who dictated the mood.

'Charles. Have some urwagwa on me. Let's drink to my wedding next week.'

'Ah good man Evariste!' exclaimed Charles, hoping to change the vibe with some forced jollity. 'Yes, to your wedding. And we will drink more on that great day.' Evariste took a sip of the drink, as tradition demanded, to prove it had not been poisoned, and passed it to Charles who held the glass aloft for a toast.

'To Evariste and his wife to be.' The toast provided a way out of the previous conversation as all the men joined in.

'To the couple.' 'To Evariste,' came the replies.

The men became more light hearted when reminded of next week's wedding celebrations, it was a long awaited party. The beer passed back and forth and everyone grew more and more relaxed. Vincent became so relaxed he fell off his chair. Around midnight, customers began to drift away, either full of drink or because their money was spent.

Charles made his way home from the cabaret deep in thought. He had heard this kind of talk before and it was something he had come to accept. From time to time there was trouble; that was life. Sometimes it made sense to keep a low profile. He had once hidden in the forest for a week till things calmed down in the village. At the time his wife Uwase had been pregnant with Clement and Claude. He did not like the mood of the country right now, but politicians often spoke like bullies to keep themselves in favour with the radicals. Nor did he believe his friends would do him harm. But this night he was aware of the shadows between houses and in banana plantations behind his back. The calls of night birds seemed too loud, as if they could hide footsteps. He was glad of the moon and the starlight in the alleyways, revealing what the dark could have hidden. Yet he was more glad to get home and shut the door behind him.

10

The same moon and stars whirled slowly in the dark sky above Grégoire and Joe as they sat outside the watchman's hut. Between them was the tiniest fire made of small twigs sending sparks and smoke up into the night. It kept them a little warmer and served as a warning to wild animals. They had a plastic bottle with some water in it and an old drum to bang if they needed to scare any beasts away. The noises of the night, insects and a skylark, surrounded them. At first they were conscientious guards, peering into the shadows ready to spring into action, but when nothing happened they relaxed and forgot why they were there. Joe wanted to talk about the trouble at the football, he sensed Grégoire did not, but he could not stop himself bringing the subject up.

'I don't understand what happened today. Do you think Jean de Dieu and Fabrice are friends? Why did Jean de Dieu do that to Pascale? His team joined in like it was planned.'

'It was planned and you know why. Pascale is a Tutsi. There has been trouble in Burundi and people get angry, don't be such a child.'

'I'm only twelve, I am child.'

'Yes, but you are not stupid.'

'You were very brave standing up for Pascale.'

'I did not do it for Pascale, I stood up for my team. I'm not scared of Jean anyway, but Pascale needs to be careful and so do you Joe.'

'Me? Why? I have done nothing wrong.'

'Yes you have. You are a Tutsi.'

'That's not something I have done. I wish I wasn't a Tutsi.'

'I wish you weren't too but you are and... look Joe,' he paused '... it is too much of a risk being your friend.'

'What do you mean?'

'No Hutu trusts a Tutsi. We have to be careful, your cattle trample our crops, your ancestors made us slaves and forced us to work for them. You know this so don't make me explain it to you.'

'But I did not do those things. Do you not trust me?'

Grégoire paused and looked out into the field. Of course he trusted his friend but his father had been clear. He could not betray his father. He could choose his friends but not his family or his ancestry. For the second time that day he felt confused. He tried to compromise with his answer.

'I trust you now Joe, but you will change when you get older. My father has told me,' he faltered as he realised his logic was weak. 'Look, you are a target for people like Jean de Dieu. If I am your friend, then I am a target too. Do you want me to get hurt? Is that what you want? That's what will happen. It is dangerous for me.'

'Are you not my friend anymore?' said Joe. 'We have always been friends.'

'Do you want me to get in trouble? Why? I am not a Tutsi! We must spend less time together.' Grégoire cringed at his own words. 'Look Joe, I face a choice. I have one friend, or many. You, or the rest of the guys on the team. What would you do in this situation? Do you want them to beat me like they did Pascale?'

As he spoke, Joe sat in silence, his eyes filling with tears.

'Well? What would you do?' he demanded. Joe said nothing and Grégoire felt sick as he knew he had done the wrong thing. Finally he saw a way out of the conversation. 'Anyway. That's enough. We should be listening carefully,' he threw a pebble over his shoulder into the field and leapt to his feet. 'What was that?'

Grégoire walked a few paces away from the fire and scanned the slopes below them; Joe stood by him and peered into the darkness. For the next fifteen minutes they crept along the paths and ditches between the crops. Grégoire's ploy worked as both of them wanted to change the subject. A few minutes later they sat down again, and they did not broach the topic again. As the fire died down, they grew more tired and it was not long before Grégoire was asleep. Joe watched him for a while trying to understand the change that had taken place. Though he did not fully understand it he sensed the conversation was a kind of goodbye. He lay down and, exhausted by confusion and the day's events, fell asleep himself.

Just before dawn they were unaware of two brown eyes under a thick carpet of black hair, peering at them in the brief half-light. They did not see the almost human hand reaching out to tweak their toes and enquire what strange bald creature slept in a grass hut instead of a tree. Nor did the boys see the silverback call its child away as the group of gorillas headed back into the forest. The boys missed the show that tourists paid $500 an hour to see. They did not know that if the eyes of the world ever fell on Rwanda it was to gape at the mountain gorillas, they barely glanced at the human beings who carried their bags.

11

A week later, Jean and Gloria arrived at Evariste's house at ten in the morning to help them set up for the wedding that afternoon. Most of Jean's friends had volunteered; given Evariste ran the cabaret they guessed the beers would flow early, and they were right. The drinking had already begun and Jean looked a little surly until Vincent, one of his cronies from the cabaret, thrust a cold Primus into his hand.

'Ah, now I see why you wanted to get here so soon Jean,' said Gloria.

'I wanted to be here to support my friend. It is a great day for him,' replied Jean, winking at Vincent.

'Yes. Any day with free beer is a great day,' said Gloria, snatching the bottle off Jean and helping herself to a good swig. 'Now finish that and let's help set the place up.'

The wedding took place on the village football pitch. There was a central stage area where the bride and groom would sit and their families faced each other formally in rows. The groom's guests lined up behind his family and the bride's guests behind hers. Gloria, Jean, Vincent, Laurette and Oscar help decorate the trees with bunting. Sheets were stretched out over the branches to provide some cover from the sun. Everyone helped out and brought chairs from home to seat the guests. The work of some men was hampered by the fact that they only had one hand free as the other was clutching a bottle of beer. Within a couple of hours the area was prepared, and the guests were warned of the bride and groom's imminent arrival. They took their places in serried ranks, like armies awaiting a battle.

Evariste and his bride Sonia arrived wearing traditional clothes in cream, beige and gold. The opening ceremony consisted of speeches by the two families. Men from both parties stood up and gave their opinions on the proposed marriage. The younger ones tended to support the match, but the older and more experienced speakers played it for laughs. The bride's fidelity was questioned to a chorus of 'oohs' and 'aahs', in response Evariste's ability to give her a child was challenged. In the past these had been real negotiations but by 1988 it was pageantry and a nod to tradition. Evariste gratefully accepted the dowry price of two cows, however.

'Two cows!' shouted Jean. 'Evariste will think he is a Tutsi.' Jean's joke got a mixed response some laughs, some boos, and a sharp poke in the ribs off Gloria. The bride, Sonia, was Tutsi, a fact which was a concern for Evariste. Identity came with the father however, and though Sonia would always be Tutsi their children would be considered Hutu.

The cows were blessed by a singer representing the bride's family and, following this, another singer representing the groom's family performed. This was the cue for the couple to come together to be married. With the afternoon sun hot in the sky they went to the stage in the middle and Sonia fastened the beaded crown, the *ikamba* on Evariste's head. This concluded the formalities and now the partying could begin in earnest.

Joseph and Denyse watched the ceremony, side by side, from their places at the back of the crowd on the bride's side of the family.

'Will you get married one day Joe,' she asked.

'Yes. I guess I will have to. Everybody does.'

'Do you not want to get married Joe?'

'Yes. No. I don't know. What's the point?'

'We can have children.'

'But I don't... What? Oh! I see! It's 'we' now is it?' replied Joe. Denyse laughed and slapped his leg.

'No. I will not marry you Joe. Your family only has two cows.'

'Well. I will not be interested in you Denyse. You have none. What would be your dowry, an old goat and a chicken?'

'My dowry will be my beauty Joe. You will change your mind. I will be a beautiful, graceful wife.' With that she leaned her head on his shoulder looking up at him and though he wanted to shrug her off he did not. For some reason it was nice.

The little scene did not go unnoticed on the other side of the green where Grégoire sat with Albert, Cyprien, Patrick, Placide and Fabrice. Joe smiled and waved when he noticed them looking over but the only response he got was a shrug of the shoulders off Grégoire. Joe knew a change had come over all his friends since the fight at the football match last week. What he did not know was that Jean Damascène had had another long chat with Grégoire when he heard of the events. He frowned on his son's friendship with Joe and ordered him to end it. It was not safe for Grégoire to be close to a boy who may grow up to be a marked man. Such a friendship could cost Grégoire dear if the Tutsi's day of reckoning came. It was time to grow up.

Meanwhile the wedding turned into a party worthy of a cabaret owner. Grégoire and his friends decided on some tactics to get their hands on the alcohol their parents wanted to deny them. They found the best approach was to circulate among the guests waiting for one to put a half empty bottle or a glass down. This could be discreetly removed and shared by the boys out of sight behind the trees. If they got caught, they claimed to be tidying up for Evariste. The more people drank, the more willing they were to believe they had merely misplaced their drink. However, the more success the boys had the less skilful they became, and their fumbles were rewarded with a friendly slap on a couple of occasions. Joe longed to be a part of the fun and with Denyse off dancing he decided to try to join the game.

He walked over to where they stood in a circle passing round a bottle of beer. The boys saw him coming and whispered to one another. As he tried to join the circle the gaps between the boy's shoulders closed and he was left on the outside. When he moved to where a gap appeared, they moved, and it quickly disappeared. He was left circling the group looking at their backs. Finally, he spoke.

'Hey guys, can I join in?' He asked. 'I'd be good at this. It's really funny. Grégoire, I saw you take that beer right from under your father's nose.' Joe laughed nervously but nobody laughed with him. Fabrice turned around.

'Stealing isn't funny. Did you here that Grégoire?' said Fabrice. 'This boy thinks it's funny that your father lost his drink.' Grégoire said nothing.

'You're right Fabrice, that's sick,' said Albert.

'Yes, go away Joe. You're sick,' said Cyprien. 'Don't bother us anymore. You're not our friend. Go and be sick somewhere.' At this the boys laughed and turned away once again. Joe backed away and stared at the backs of the closed ranks. He knew if he left he could not come back, but nor could he stay. After a few moments he turned and ran, tears brimming in his eyes. Grégoire turned to Fabrice.

'I don't like this. It makes me feel like a coward.'

'Hey, come on. You're better off without him Grégoire,' replied Fabrice. 'Who needs a friend who runs off crying just because of a little joke? He's the coward. Would you have done that if we had played a joke on you?'

Grégoire felt the hint of challenge in Fabrice's tone. He didn't like the idea that Fabrice might get one over on him front of the others.

'Would you try a joke on me Fabrice?'

'What do you mean?' asked Fabrice, the smile freezing on his face as he saw Grégoire's expressionless face.

'Any jokes planned for me Fabrice? Anything you'd like to try?'

'Hey, we're friends, what would I do to my friend?'

'Nothing,' replied Grégoire as took the bottle from Fabrice's hand and took a long swig of beer whilst staring Fabrice down. 'Nothing at all.'

Joe intended to run out of the wedding party and go home but he did not see clearly through his tears. He stumbled into another person. Strong hands held him firm to stop him falling, when he looked up it was into the face of Pascale.

'Pascale, it's you. Are you well? Are you better now? I thought they really hurt you.'

'I'm OK skinny Joe. I am not made of glass and it will take more than those bullies to hurt me.' Pascale replied. 'But you look upset, what's the matter?'

Joe told him what had just happened.

'Well, it doesn't like we're on the football team any more Joe.'

'But I want to play for Kinigi, with my friends. Grégoire is my best friend.'

'No Joe he is not and the others are not either. They are not good enough to be your friends. You deserve better than them. Come over here and sit with me,' he led Joe over to a shady, discreet spot where there were some empty chairs. Joe slumped down with his elbows on his knees and his head in his hands. For a while neither spoke, but Pascale rested a comforting hand on the young boy's back.

'It's OK Joe.'

'Why is life like this?'

'You know the answers Joe. It is because we are Tutsi. We have no rights in this country. I know you are young but one day you have to face the truth. I'm sorry, but today might be that day.'

'You played for the team. You are a Tutsi.'

'Oh, of course, yes, they let me play. They know I'm a good player. They act as if they like me most of the time.' Pascale shrugged. 'But they don't mean it. At the end of the day I'm still a cockroach.'

'I have heard them call me that sometimes.'

'Don't let it get you down.'

'Why do they call us that?'

'Because their parents call us that, their teachers call us that. Even the government calls us cockroaches.'

'It's not right.'

'No, it isn't,' replied Joe, and the two boys were silent for a few moments.

'I wanted to try some beer,' he sniffled.

'Never mind them. Wait! These chairs are not very comfortable.' Pascale stood up. 'Something cold and hard is sticking in my arse. What can it be?' Joe looked up to see Pascale smiling and holding out a bottle of beer. 'Here Joe, try this. It has your name on it.'

'It does not say 'Joe' anywhere on this bottle. It says 'Primus'.'

'Yes. That is your new name. Joe Primus; Joe the first, the

number one. Cheers!' Pascale chinked the younger boy's bottle. Joe looked up and smiled gratefully, he was not alone after all. Joe looked over in the direction of Grégoire and the other boys. He would never call them friends again.

AN AMERICAN
IN RWANDA

1

Six years later and 7000 miles away, Positano Ristorante did everything it could to appear an unpretentious trattoria nestling on the Amalfi coast. The restaurant's Italianate facade looked the part, and the aroma of freshly cooked garlic tempted passers-by. But instead of Positano's narrow streets winding up the cliffs above the Tyrrhenian Sea, Positano Ristorante squatted beneath a three-storey block on Mulberry Street, in Manhattan's 'Little Italy'. Street-side al fresco diners had to contend with four lanes of slow traffic sloughing past their tables.

Inside the illusion was more successful but unnoticed by Melanie Hickman as she shuffled the final piece of tiramisu onto her spoon. In khaki trousers and a brown checked shirt Melanie was dressed for trekking not socialising. However, the colours complimented her shoulder-length, straight brown hair, with blonde highlights, one strand of which made a solo journey down her face. Her boyfriend Tom watched as she brushed it back into place, knowing that he would never see her do that again. His gaze dropped from her face and admired, for the last time, the way her broad shoulders sloped into her slender waist. Melanie's physique was firm yet graceful, and he realised with a pang that he still found her sexy. He knew he would miss her, but not enough to change anything now. Melanie caught him in the act of observation and felt an urge to speak, but there was little that hadn't been said. It was nearly time for goodbyes and he would not be her boyfriend in an hour's time. She selected a noncommittal smile and served it his way; he returned the same with a little nod of his head and fidgeted uncomfortably.

'My lasagne was delicious!' He offered.

The blandness of the comment nearly made her laugh, but she stopped the chuckle and decided to stick with the pleasantries. 'Mm, mine too,' she replied, then popped the spoonful of tiramisu into her mouth to prevent a cutting response escaping out. She raised her eyebrows and gave him a friendly grin. Members of her family also sat around the table, facing empty plates, and everyone was aware that the time was 'goodbye o'clock'. Their glasses of wine had become half empty rather than half full. It was time to go.

Melanie had prepared herself for this moment and had played the scene through in her mind to help her deal with it. She reminded herself why she was going to Africa to teach English. Her reasons were mixed. On the negative side her relationship with Tom had grown stale because he would not commit to anything permanent, after a four year wait this amounted to a rejection. She wanted and needed to end it. It was typical of Tom that he hadn't faced the truth. More positively her recent thirtieth birthday had been a wakeup call; if she didn't take a chance in life soon, she was afraid she would lose her nerve. Travel, making a difference in the world and helping others, risked becoming an unfulfilled childhood dream. She didn't want to be telling her grandchildren she had missed her chances in life. Ahead of her lay a take-off, a flight, and a landing far from everything she knew and loved; and she needed to set off on the journey.

'OK everybody,' said Martin, her father. 'A toast everyone; to my beautiful daughter and her exciting year of adventure. To Mel.'

'To Mel,' came a chorus of voices.

As the glasses chinked Mel felt butterflies in her stomach

but managed to keep her emotions under control. Her father gave her a wink, but she noticed his upper lip tremble and she had heard the catch in his voice. Her mother wore a mask of composure. Two taxis arrived and the party set off. Her father insisted Mel and Tom share a taxi.

'You'll want some time together,' he suggested. Melanie raised an eyebrow.

'Thanks dad.'

Throughout the journey they sat side by side but not so close as to be sat together. As they drove to JFK airport for her evening flight Melanie made a mental note that, in a tiny way, her adventure had begun. At least this part of the journey was familiar, once they were out of Manhattan and over East River the buildings were just as dense, but not as high. Although Mel and Tom had nothing more to say except goodbye, the silence was uncomfortable.

'What time's your flight again?'

'Six o'clock.'

'Nearly fourteen hours. That's a long time.'

'It's a long way. When I get to Nairobi, I have a short wait, then it's just another hour or so to Rwanda.'

'Kigali, the capital. Right. Well I never met anybody who's been there.'

Their conversation was a stilted and embarrassing but it was better than riding along mute. At the risk of seeming rude Melanie made a mental note to get the goodbyes over quickly and escape into the departure lounge. It was going to be a difficult farewell, there would be tears, some of them would be hers, but there was no backing out now. The taxi pulled up outside the terminal and sure enough, her mother had a tissue at the ready.

The mildly stressful business of; spotting her flight on the departures board, digging out tickets, rooting for her passport, finding the right desk, checking in, and moving luggage around provided a distraction for a while, but the moment had come.

'OK everybody. Thanks for a lovely meal and thanks for giving me such a lovely send off. Give me a hug.'

She went around the small group and hugged everyone, even Tom who whispered 'take care' as he held her. Mom and Dad were the hardest to let go and her voice was choked with tears as she tried to hold it together.

'Well, it's only a year, I'll write, I'll phone and if I don't like it, I'll come straight home.' The impromptu poem brought some relief and a smile. She could see her Mom was struggling the most, so she took her hand and squeezed it.

'I'll be fine. I'm a big girl, I'm 21!'

'You wish,' said her father.

'Ah well. This will be great and I'll see you all in years' time. I'll bring everyone a present from sunny Rwanda.'

'Super, just what I needed, a grass skirt,' said her Dad at which everyone laughed gratefully if a little too much.

'If they do your size, I'll get you one. OK gotta go. I'll phone when I get there, soon as I can. Bye.' With that she turned and headed towards the security check area. When she got there, she gave one last smile and a wave. This made her eyes fill up again, so she took a deep breath and began fishing for electrical items and metal bits to pop in the tray for the scanner.

Being alone put things into perspective and she focused on the trivial realities of making sure she was ready at the right gate at the right time. The airport security staff reassured her with their professional indifference and faux authority. She passed through their lives without touching them, as if she was just more luggage gliding along a conveyor belt. Next, she stepped into the materialistic limbo of the departure lounge, where nervous fliers gorged on retail therapy. Lit up like Las Vegas it was both alluring and repellent. 'So many pay so much for so little' she thought, blinking in the lurid, bright lights.

At a Starbucks she ordered a coffee, to put off the moment when she would order a glass of wine, and stood in the lounge looking out at the runway. Although she had flown plenty of times, the raw power of a jet taking off and landing still gave her a thrill. Hypnotherapy had cured her fear of flying and she could smile at the unreal images her phobia had fed her; the runway was not filled with smoke, burning wreckage, wailing sirens, and the screams of the dying after all.

Just recently she had realised where her fear had come from. It wasn't a fear of flying; it was a fear of heights. It started when she was eight years old, stood on the staircase of a fairground helter-skelter ride. The flimsy wooden tower was shaking as the other children ran gleefully past her to the top. She had climbed back down the stairs sobbing and ashamed; then embarrassed when the ride owner refused to give her Father his 50 cents back. Strange, that memory still had the power to hurt her. 'Fuck that helter-skelter' she thought and then stopped in horror. That was not a thought; she had spoken it out loud. Nearby an elderly lady got up and moved away. Mel laughed and gave up on the coffee she was not enjoying. 'I can enjoy flying and I can enjoy it even more with a glass of wine' she thought to herself. She headed off to the bar.

Ordering a large glass of chardonnay, she pulled out her purse to pay the bartender. Inside was a small envelope, instantly she knew what it was, and who it was from. Mom. Several times when she had gone on holiday her mother had sneaked a little card into her purse, wash bag, or camera case. It was always a little note to remind her that, though she may be miles from home, she was always close to her mother's heart. In various ways the messages said 'have a great time and come back safely'. Melanie filled up as she flipped the miniature envelope open and removed the card. The cover was a picture of herself as a child asleep in her cot. On the back was a message; 'Dearest Melanie, you know you are always in my thoughts and prayers. If it gets hard out there in Africa always remember you can only change the world one person at a time. Love you, Mom.' She had to take a deep breath to avoid a sob of tenderness. The bartender caught her mood.

'Here's your wine miss. Are you OK?' He was sympathetic but his gaze also took in her figure.

'Oh God. Yes. Thank you,' she replied, 'just having a moment!' Melanie was just about able to hold it together and not slump on the bar in tears. 'Err, thanks, yes, how much for the wine?' The bartender's response brought her back to reality.

'That will be ten dollars, thank you,' he said with a smile that hinted at a tip. Given she could have bought a bottle in a supermarket for the same price Melanie withheld on the gratuity, but gave him a tilt of the head and a raised eyebrow.

'Ten dollars, OK.' She withdrew from the bar to a table near a panoramic window where she could watch planes take off and land.

Two hours later she was sat belted in her seat, and after offering a glimpse down the stretch of runway, the plane turned through ninety degrees and enjoyed its momentary rest before take-off. Everybody waited as the captain looked to the control tower for clearance. Mel felt air traffic control's response as a punch of acceleration in her chest that pushed her back into her seat. The engines kicked in with a roar and, with grace and power that cast aside gravity, the jet took off into the evening sky.

Back at JFK her family and Tom watched the plane's ascent. Her mother prayed as she felt the weight of her love for the plane's precious cargo. Carol and her Father looked to each other, then to Mom, realising her need of them both. Tom felt confusion knowing the love that had just flown away had really left him some months before. When she decided to go, it meant she did not want to stay with him. He wanted it to be different, but he knew she had made the choice he had ducked. There was also a thrill of freedom, he could move on if he wanted to; and he did want to.

Melanie craned her neck to see what she could of the disappearing eastern coastline of New York State. It was stunning, it was home, and it would still be there when she got back. Still climbing over the featureless grey blue of the Atlantic she settled down and tried to anticipate what lay ahead. All she could envisage was the dark night that covered the continent she was heading to.

2

Melanie slept for six hours until, at six thirty in the morning, the cabin crew sprang into action triggered by the daylight outside. A cup of coffee was a welcome alternative to the taste of stale wine in her mouth. She felt grubby and knew her hair was a mess, but she woke up feeling energised and excited. She visited the tiny bathroom to tuck her untidy hair under her blue New York Yankees baseball cap, leaving a pony tail hanging out the back. In her seat she looked out of the window and peered between the clouds at the land beneath. Africa! Even the word gave her a thrill.

With an hour till landing the dawn sun washed over the Kenyan countryside and the view commanded the attention of every passenger who could see it. Grassland with occasional clumps of trees as far as the eye could see. In any other country this would be protected, sanitised, and called a national park, but here it was just... Kenya. The passengers looked down on millions of acres where the only 'development' was where humans made tracks besides grazing cattle.

Eventually civilisation encroached onto the landscape as the plane descended to Nairobi's Jomo Kenyatta airport. The city loomed as an island of concrete and glass set in a sea of shanty town poverty. Melanie smiled when, as usual, the landing approach stilled conversation on the plane, and the relief was palpable when, after a couple of bumps, it slowed down with a roar. People found their voices as they taxied to the airport building, and they got up to root through the overhead compartments for their hand luggage ten minutes before it was needed.

The terminal building was jaded and run down. In contrast to JFK there was not enough electric light and the dawn brightness did not penetrate the dirty windows. The airport shops were seedy and crowded with junk. People sat sullenly waiting and half asleep, she saw no smiles. Melanie searched uneasily for a screen showing flight information, fighting down her rising panic. Already she wanted to be out of this place.

Yet, like a Church anywhere in the world, there was a common floor plan. There was a group of people staring upwards and, yes, there was the dimly lit departure board. Her flight to Kigali was on time and left in an hour. Melanie felt relieved, but not confident enough to sit on her own at a cafe table and get a drink. She was worried in case a stranger spoke to her and she wouldn't know what to say. Trying to act like an experienced traveller she strode to the departure gate for Rwanda and prayed her luggage was making a parallel journey to the same flight.

As she got her bearings, she realised that the seeming darkness of the airport was merely in contrast to the sheer brightness of the sunshine outside. People weren't staring menacingly at her; she was merely receiving the admiring glances she got at home. At a counter near her exit gate she relaxed enough to buy a coffee and a croissant. The young man who served her spoke rather too gently, like a lover, and his smile was too... she stopped and was aware of prejudices she would have to drop quickly. 'He's not making a pass', she told herself, 'he's just a nice guy, lots of Africans speak gently'.

Throughout the flight to Kigali with Sabena Airlines the announcements, starting with the apologies for the two hour delay, were given first in French, then Kinyarwanda, and then English; the pecking order reminded her of the political reality of the country she was going to. Rwanda was Francophile; when the country looked out to the developed world, it looked first to France. Everyone in Rwanda spoke Kinyarwandan, and everyone with an education spoke some French. Not many schools even taught English but there was a view that it was a useful language to know, which was why the Peace Corps had found Melanie a placement at a secondary school.

On the flight to Kigali Melanie got a look at the landscape

of Rwanda. It was like an egg box of hills and valleys, with every spare inch cultivated. Tiny fields of greens, greys and browns left little space for the wilderness so prominent in Kenya. She remembered her Peace Corp training, per square mile Rwanda was the most densely populated and intensely farmed country in Africa. It made for a striking patchwork panorama from her window on the plane.

Stepping down off the plane the temperature was warm but not too hot. She got her two suitcases off the only baggage carousel at the small airport and made her way to customs. As she handed her passport over the female official gave her a smile and spoke in the by now familiar gentle manner.

'Good morning. What is the purpose of your visit?'

'I am going to be teaching here. I have a visa permit for one year.'

'Have a lovely time and welcome to Rwanda,' came the reply along with her passport.

'Thank you, oh... I mean, murakoze! Did I get that right?' The immigration officer laughed,

'Excellent. Murakoze cane. Thank you very much. Welcome to Rwanda.'

Melanie stepped through the barrier under the indifferent gaze of a nonchalant, armed, soldier. She made her way into the arrivals lounge to meet her contact and driver; a Catholic priest by the name of Father Ishimwe. Melanie had hoped he would be stood clutching a sign with her name on it, but there was nobody there. The only thing in her favour was that it should be obvious to Father Ishimwe who his passenger was; she was the only white person in the airport. She sat down with her bags and waited. Five minutes dragged by, her flimsy self-assurance dissipated, and she began to feel vulnerable and isolated.

After sitting alone, and nervously, for twenty minutes she remembered she had a number to call in case of emergencies. However, when she found that she then realised she had no currency to use in the pay phone. She picked up her suitcases and made her way over to a cafe counter where the prices for items were clearly displayed; inevitably in Rwandan Francs. The assistant read her nervous looks.

'It's OK we accept American dollars.'

'Oh good. I need change… for the phone.' She held out a ten dollar bill feeling a little stupid that she had no idea of its worth out there. In fact, it was more than a month's salary to the girl. There was an embarrassing pause.

'No please, err… for the phone.' She held her thumb and little finger to the side of her head. The sign proved to be universal. The assistant smiled, fished two Rwandan coins out of her purse and gave them to her, waving the dollar ten bill away.

'Thank you very much, murakoze.'

'Do not worry. The phone is over there.'

Again, she picked up her bags, fearing they would be stolen, and lumbered slowly across the arrivals lounge with them. The instructions for the phone were in French and Kinyarwandan and she could read little of either. She picked the phone up and dialled the number she had on a piece of paper tucked in the back of her passport. All she got was silence so she pushed one of the coins in, as she did so a high pitched continuous tone came through suggesting failure. She looked at the number. Damn! The first few digits were for overseas callers, they would be irrelevant in country. She wondered which ones to omit and she had only one coin left. She missed off the first three and made another attempt. A ringing tone informed her she had got through. 'Please pick up and please speak English' she thought. Someone picked up.

'Muraho,' said a male voice.

'Err… hello? Could I speak to… oh God!'

'Muraho?' the voice repeated in some confusion.

In desperation and embarrassment, she put the phone down.

'Shit, shit, shit,' she said, louder than she intended. She turned around and was a little startled to see a man standing directly behind her. He was in his early thirties, tall and elegant, wearing grey trousers and a black shirt open at the collar. He tilted his head sideways and looked her with a wry smile on his face.

'Good morning, I am Father Ishimwe, but you can call me 'shit' if you like.'

Melanie's shoulders slumped in tired relief and her hands came up to her face. 'Oh, thank God. I mean, sorry.' She laughed.

'I assume you are Miss Melanie Hickman?' He held out his hand. 'Please accept my apologies for being late. I knew you were delayed, but I forgot we are one hour behind Nairobi. Are you OK?'

Melanie was so pleased to have met her contact she barely took in what Ishimwe said so, grinning and embarrassed she replied,

'Sorry. I was panicking there. I didn't know what to do,' she replied to the tall, gangly priest.

'Yes, you are a long way from home. But do not worry; can I get you something to drink? A bottle of water maybe?'

*   *   *

An hour later Ishimwe was behind the wheel of a white Citroen 2CV with Melanie sat beside him, watching the sun bathed countryside pass by. It was a fine day, with a clear blue sky. In Kigali the road was asphalt, just like home, but it soon turned into a rutted track when they got out of the city centre. The car bounced around and Mel had to tense her body and hold on to avoid banging her head. Being a passenger was physically tiring.

It was a Sunday and along the sides of the road thousands of people walked to Church, the women wore bright dresses in the boldest colours with matching headscarves and most carried a large handbag. Mel guessed the clothes needed to be bright to stand out against the colours of the land; the green of the banana trees and crops, the stunning flowers. You couldn't have got away with those choices back home but here they worked just fine. There was almost no other traffic except for bicycles, and minibuses crammed with people that stopped to drop off and pick up wherever they were needed. She saw no one working, and the streets had the relaxed ambience of a seaside promenade.

A lot of people checked her out through the car window and she quickly realised it was because she was a white Westerner. Children's faces lit up as they waved and smiled at her. It was an hour before she tired of waving back but it became a distraction as she wanted to talk to Ishimwe. Occasionally she picked up a word 'mzungu' that was often aimed at her.

'Ishimwe, I keep hearing people shouting something at me, what does 'mzungu' mean? It doesn't sound friendly. Are they insulting me somehow?'

'Ah, mzungu, it is hard to explain. It means several things like 'boss' or 'you who are above us'. It isn't a compliment, but nor is it really an insult, it is a statement of fact. It is not reserved for whites but it is often used for people who are travelling around, and they are usually white tourists. People have shouted it to me just for driving this car. They assume the car is mine I think. They assume the car is mine I think. If I have car maybe I'm a rich man and above them, so I am mzungu.'

'OK. Wow. I guess there's so much I don't know, so much that's so different from back home.'

'Yes and no. I've never been to America and I'm sure it's different but, well, people are people, and there will be many similarities too.'

'But I could make so many, like, terrible mistakes just by not knowing a custom or something like that.'

'Not really, people know you are from another country. They will expect you to be different, and will make allowances for that.'

'That's good to hear. I have a million questions to ask.'

'Well, we have a seven-hour journey, ask anything you want.'

'OK. Wow. I don't know where to start.' There was a lengthy pause while Melanie tried to prioritise what she didn't know.

'Oh my God... I can't think of anything!'

Ishimwe laughed. 'Well we can start with the American habit of saying 'oh my God'.'

'Oh, I apologise, I meant no offence.'

'I am not offended, but some people would be, certainly my fellow priest Father Patrice. Rwandans respect authority, and that includes the Bible. We are an obedient people.'

'Hmm. OK, I get that, but as a teacher, I want the children to think for themselves. You know, like, weigh the evidence.'

'What if the only evidence they have is the rubbish they have been told?' Ishimwe smiled. 'But do not worry. The teachers, the children and their families are all excited to meet you. They will treat you with respect. You will be made, like, very welcome.'

'Ishimwe, did you just, like, mock me then?'

'Yes, like, I did,' He laughed. 'Like.'

'Do I use that word a lot?'

Ah, I am only joking. Please don't stop, it is already part of your charm.'

Melanie and Ishimwe chatted through the journey which, although it was a long ride, was an introduction in itself to her new home. Everywhere was farmed with crops or tall banana plantations, except for fields where long horned cattle grazed. The homes were tatty and dilapidated, stained with the red brown mud. Most people looked too thin, and the children were barefoot. People of all ages trooped around with large containers balanced on their heads, running water was clearly a rarity. The condition of the road would not be tolerated outside a farmer's field back home and she could see it would be impassable in the rainy season. Yet, set against the obvious problems, the verdant lushness of the countryside and smiles of the children gave her a sense of hope for her stay. Around mid-afternoon they stopped for a drink by the roadside.

Ishimwe bumped the car over the dusty verge outside a shack as he explained; 'this is called a 'cabaret'. I have spoken to the owner many times. It has a toilet you can use, and it's clean. We can get a drink here.'

To Melanie It looked like a market stall selling drinks and snacks. 'I'll get them.' She volunteered and then remembered she had no Rwandan francs.

'No. I'll pay. I can get it cheaper. You would have to pay mzungu prices.'

'You mean I'd be ripped off?'

'Kind of. But they are poor and you are rich.'

Ishimwe bought two Fantas, and they looked for somewhere to sit. There was only one table and four chairs available, it was plastic garden furniture. The place was occupied by a man who, without being asked, stood up, smiled, and gestured to his now vacated place.

'Please, good morning,' he said and moved away to stand near the counter. Melanie nodded her thank you as Ishimwe spoke briefly to the man.

'That's strange. I mean, I'm not royalty.' Melanie said to Ishimwe as she sat down. 'I'm not poor; I'm just average back home. I know its relative but... I feel so weird, it's like they look up to me.'

'Of course, but in Rwanda a person earns about, maybe five US dollars a month.' Ishimwe shrugged. 'There is a lot to understand, but you'll be fine. It will take some time to adjust. Soon you will have servants to look after you.'

'I don't think I like the sound of that. Servants!'

'Yes, a cleaner, someone to carry fetch your water, someone to wash your clothes, and a gardener. They will not cost you much.'

'But I can do all those things myself without exploiting some poor person.'

'It's not exploiting them. They need the income. It will be

expected of you and they will be hurt if you refuse their offer of service.'

'But a cleaner, it makes me look like a lazy colonial.'

'A cleaner is useful. It's the gardener that's the worst.'

'Why?'

'You don't have a garden.'

'But I will have a gardener?'

'Yes. You will have a clay yard in front of your apartment, with bits of grass. He will sweep that, make sure there are no weeds and bring you fresh flowers for the window sill.'

Melanie leaned back to look around and soak in the scene. Talking was stopping her observing. A large truck lumbered slowly up the steep road in front of them. Behind it a man on a bicycle leaned over his handle bars and held onto the back of the lorry getting a dangerous free ride. He smiled and waved, Melanie waved back.

'Why does everyone smile at me?'

'We are a friendly people, I think. Most people like to see foreigners, especially white people in the countryside because you don't see many outside Kigali. Having visitors says we are part of the modern world and that people want to be here. Rwandans are proud of their country. Anyway, we have a few hours journey ahead of us and we need to get going.'

When they finally arrived in Kinigi, it was dark. Father Ishimwe left the engine running as he stepped out of the car to unlock the gates to the school grounds. A weather worn sign showed the school badge, and the name painted above it; 'Holy Family Catholic School'. Once inside he shut the gate behind them and drove a short way to her small apartment in the school compound. After Ishimwe had lit the two kerosene lamps, she could see the place was small, only two rooms, but it was clean, and it would be fine.

Ishimwe stood by the door ready to leave. 'Are you sure you will be OK? You have everything you need?'

'Yes, I can see it has been made ready for me, someone has been very thoughtful.'

'You will be well looked after. But you must be tired after the journey, it was a long drive.'

'Yes, I am ready to sleep. Maybe I'll read a little.'

I did ask Angelique, she's your maid, to leave you a little welcome gift. Ah there we are,' he found a bucket of water by the sink; it contained four bottles of Primus beer. 'Rwanda's finest and it's chilled too. I'll call tomorrow at seven o'clock and take you to meet the Headteacher.'

'Thanks, I'll set my alarm.'

'Angelique's son, Joseph, will bring you fresh water at half-past six. Goodnight Melanie.'

After Ishimwe left a silence descended on the darkened school grounds, it was punctuated only by the calls of night birds and cicadas. Melanie sat on a small chair by her bed and pretended to gaze casually around her room, when in truth she was looking for scary insects. To her relief she saw none. Suddenly it hit her that she was a long way from home, from the people she loved and a pang of loneliness ached in her stomach. She realised she needed to occupy herself. A quick search located a bottle opener in a draw and she helped herself to a Primus. The first mouthful settled her nerves, 'some things are universal' she thought as the beer fizzed, delicious and cool on her tongue.

Bottle in hand she plucked up the courage to open her door and peer out into the night. She had never seen darkness like this in New York, then she looked up and exclaimed out loud;

'Oh my God!'

Melanie walked away from the building and gazed up-wards. Stars, more numerous and bright than she had ever seen before blazed overhead. On the clay floor she could see that she cast a star shadow. She stood open mouthed and stared in wonder. As she looked out into the darkness, a smile grew on her face as a simple truth dawned upon her; she had done it, she was really here!

3

When her alarm clock rang, she stared upwards in confusion and wondered why she had slept in a tent. Thoughts quickly bubbled up in her waking consciousness; 'I'm in Rwanda', 'that thing... it's a mosquito net!' Shards of light found gaps in the curtains and lit up her room. 'No spiders, thank God'. She flicked back the cotton mesh and sat on the edge of her bed.

A quick glance at her watch reminded her that the water boy was due. Quickly she slipped on some jeans and a t-shirt and opened the curtains and the front door. It was a bright day, with a clear sky, and a rangy, athletic looking teenager approached her door carrying a large plastic canister of water. Even with his weighty burden he managed to look graceful. She opened the door and went out.

'Good morning Miss Hickman!' He said with a bright smile. 'Where can I put this water for you?'

'Oh, you speak English? That's great. Thank you for the water. Here is fine.' She said, pointing at the path. 'I'll take it in. Its Joseph isn't it?'

'Yes, but please, call me Joe,' he replied. As he put the water down, he looked up at her uncertainly. 'Are you sure you can manage this?'

'Yes.' She grunted as she tried to lift it with both hands. All she could do was drag a little nearer the house leaving a wet trail in the brown dust.

'Wow, you are stronger than you look!' Said Melanie with a laugh.

'Shall I take it inside for you? I can put it on the table next to the sink, there is a tap on the bottom for you to use. See it's just like being in a hotel.'

Joe carried the water inside and Melanie followed him. She knew that things she took for granted may not be available here, but actually seeing it opened her eyes. Every drop of water she used would be carried in by this young man. She would be frugal with the precious water from now on.

'There, this should last you all day.' Joe smiled and leant against the sink.

'Thank you, I really appreciate this. Hey! Your English is very good. Did you learn to speak it at school?'

'Not really, though I did have some lessons there. I don't go to school anymore. All my family speak English. I learned it as a child in Uganda.'

'So, you're not Rwandan then?'

'Ha, of course I am, but I suppose it's a long story. We lived in a refugee camp in Uganda.'

'Oh! I see. Well, no, I don't, actually. You'll have to tell me the story some time.'

'Sure, some time I will. But I had better be going now. I have cattle to watch over.'

'Oh. OK. So, I won't see you in school later?'

'No. Like I said, I don't go to school. I left when I was 12 years old. I look after my mother's cattle most of the time, with my friends.'

'Oh. I see. That's sad.'

'It's OK. We have some good cows,' he looked up at her cap. 'Is that a real baseball cap?'

'Yes,' said Melanie, a little surprised. 'New York Yankees. They're my team. Do you like it?' She took it off and handed it to him.

'Ah, this is the real thing, not a cheap copy. You can tell by the weight. It's very nice,' he said, then as he handed it back he added. 'New York Yankees,' quietly and reverently. 'New York, yes.'

'It will keep the sun off my head.'

'And the rain. I have to go now. It was very nice to meet you. I will come again this evening to bring you fresh water,' he looked at her cap. 'Nice hat, but best not wear it for school!' He grinned and skipped off through the doorway with a wave of his hand. He was right about the cap, Melanie thought, she flicked it off and threw it onto her bed.

*   *   *

At seven a cheery Father Ishimwe arrived. Melanie was sat outside her rooms sipping a cup of water gingerly; she had not mastered the stove so making a hot coffee had proved problematic. It crossed her mind that she did not know if the water was safe to drink but she resigned herself to the process of adjusting to it.

'Good morning Melanie. Did you sleep well?'

'Yes. A beer or two helped!' She replied, as she looked up and shielded her eyes from the sun to look Ishimwe.

Ishimwe smiled. 'Good! Are you ready to meet the teachers and the boys?'

'No girls then.'

'You know girls do not go to secondary school, don't you?'

'Yes, I do know, but I don't agree with it.'

'That's a good point and neither do I, but we must take one step at a time. One day they will, I hope, one day,' he replied cheerfully but then added, gently and inquisitively, 'how are you feeling?'

Melanie paused. 'I'm a little nervous but also excited.'

'You'll be OK. It will be fine. They are going to like you I am sure. Classes start at seven, but you are on what you might call Africa time now. It will take some getting used to but don't let it frustrate you. Teachers get to class around half past seven and by eight they will have most of the students that are going to show on that day. All the children will have done chores at home before school and for some the farm work may keep them off for the day. Feeding the family comes first. Come. If you are ready, we can go.'

Ishimwe walked her to school, it was only ten minutes away and she could have found her own way but, being with Ishimwe, talking to him, helped her to cope with the stares of every passer-by.

*   *   *

By seven thirty Ishimwe had gone and she had been placed in the care of an experienced teacher to get a feel for the job. Clement was in his late forties, chunky and stocky with short grey hair. From Melanie's point of view, he seemed quite 'old school' and was quite cold and stern with the boys even though he was essentially welcoming them back to school. They had a kind of respect for him, but it was based on fear not admiration.

Boys were arriving in small groups and being directed to their classrooms by staff. The boys wore brown denim shorts and white shirts; nearly all were barefoot. Each boy was checked to make sure that they had the correct uniform and a pencil or pen to write with. It was clear that not all had the correct equipment and various items were being passed around amongst friends just in time for teacher's inspection. If the staff spotted this, and Melanie suspected they did, they turned a blind eye to it. Eventually, by eight o'clock, most of the bare wooden benches in Clement's class were full of boys aged between eleven and thirteen. He had finally been given a list to check, and he called the group to order.

'Good morning. I will take the register now please answer 'Yes Sir' clearly after I call your name.'

As he began Melanie noticed something odd.

'Charles, Hutu.'

'Yes Sir.'

'Dominique, Hutu.'

'Yes Sir.'

'Yves, Hutu.'

'Yes Sir.'

'Charles, Hutu.'

'Yes Sir.'

'Patient, Tutsi. Stand up.'

'Yes Sir.'

'Michel, Hutu.'

'Yes Sir.'

And so it continued until thirty-six names had been read out leaving four children standing in their places. These four; Patient, Christian, Thierry, and Faustin were all Tutsi children, they stood patiently awaiting their fate.

'Now then, you were all warned about this last term. The school has its quota of Tutsi children this year and we cannot fit you in. You must leave now.'

Clement spoke without a note of sympathy. Silently the children filed out of the room. As Faustin made his way to the door, one of the seated children reached out and snatched his pencil from his hand.

'You don't need this, cockroach.' The boy said.

Faustin did not attempt to reclaim the stolen pencil and Clement did nothing to help him. Melanie watched in silence, not understanding what was said and not knowing what to do.

Clement had asked her to watch his first lesson so that she would grasp the etiquette of a Rwandan classroom. It was not like back home. Obedience was demanded and given without question. Education was a privilege, not a right. The children were compliant and seemingly cherished the chance to learn. Clement told Melanie he was giving a revision lesson about basic Rwandan history.

The lesson sounded like a sermon and, even without knowing the language, it was evident Clement was a firebrand preacher. The word 'Hutu' was received approvingly and the word 'Tutsi' evoked contempt. Melanie could tell from his tone that the message was an angry one. She was reminded of Adolf Hitler shouting and banging the rostrum at Nuremberg rallies. When break time arrived, she confronted Clement.

'Clement, thank you, you are a very energetic teacher, so full of life.'

'Ah yes Miss Hickman. It was just a history lesson. I am passionate about our history, enthusiasm is caught not taught. A young nation has little history so what we have is precious to us.

'Why were those children sent away?' she asked.

Sadly, we do not have enough funds and we cannot afford to educate all our children. I know this might seem a little strange to an outsider but we have to make some difficult choices in Rwanda. Traditionally it has been the Tutsi who got everything, so the government is addressing that balance to make it fairer. It is the children of the poor Hutu farmers who need education, so we target our resources on them. Tutsi make up ten percent of the population, so they get ten percent of the school places.' Melanie was already deflated before she made her lame response;

'But... it seems so unfair.'

'It is unfair. Of course. Poverty is unfair and, you are a good person, you are right to feel sympathy for the poor who lose out in life. But, really, Hutus must cease having pity for the Tutsi. For so many years we have been kept down. That has been our history. It is surely right that we have our day in the sunshine, is it not?'

'Well, I guess so, but wait, you said 'we'.'

'Yes. I am a Hutu.'

'Well if the Hutu have been so oppressed how come you qualified as a teacher?'

'Excellent,' replied Clement and laughed a little too hard. 'You are an intelligent woman. Yes, I am a Hutu and I am a teacher. Maybe I am the exception that proves the rule? Do not be concerned about this Miss Hickman. Come. We will meet our senior students in the next class. They mostly aged about 18. I think you will be impressed with the standard of their English. I find they are good at learning the words but not good at structuring the sentences. They need to converse with a native speaker. Did you know that not many Rwandan schools even teach English? They prefer to teach French. Of course, our country has strong links with France, but we recognise English is the language of business these days. That is what these children will need in the future.'

Melanie felt uneasy; something was wrong, but she could not put her finger on it. Somehow, something had not been said. There was a Tutsi elephant in the room.

After break, Clement introduced Melanie to the older pupils, and she was relieved, at last, to be doing some teaching. Clement gave the class an hour to write a short essay in English explaining what they had done over the holidays.

'I think you will find these boys have been very busy this summer Miss Hickman. Why don't you tell her about it Grégoire?'

'Ah yes Miss, please take a look at my writing.' Melanie went and sat next to Grégoire and asked him to read out what had written so far. Some boys near him stopped work to listen and join in the debate. His written English was reasonable, and he gave a nice picture of a summer camp with games and fitness training. It sounded like the Boy scouts.

'What did you like best about the camp Grégoire?'

'It felt as though I was being treated as a man instead of a boy. I liked the physical training. The soldiers helped us to become fit and strong.'

'Yes,' chipped in another young man. 'We will have men's work to do soon, maybe.'

'I see, it sounds very exciting. And what is your name?'

'Fabrice. It was great being with the soldiers, one day I too shall be a soldier.'

'Well every country must be ready to defend itself Fabrice, that is a noble calling.'

'Yes. We are being ready to fight the Inkotanyi if they attack,' said Grégoire.

'Sorry. The Inky... what?'

'The Inkotanyi, the Tutsi cockroach army. They want to kill us all.' At this the agreement of the surrounding boys grew louder and Melanie sensed a level of anger in the young men. She tried to turn the topic back to the English language.

'Well, you've expressed yourself well in English. Did you learn some on the summer camp?'

'No, there we speak to each other Kinyarwandan or French,' said a big, powerful, young man called Albert. 'We should learn French not English. French is good language for Rwanda.'

'Yes. The French is on our side,' said Cyprien excitedly, raising a clenched fist. 'French is our friends.'

'You mean France is our friends.' Suggested big Albert cautiously, but Clement had come over and he cut across the conversation.

'Close Albert, but not quite right. Now I suggest that you listen to Miss Hickman, let her speak, because her English is better than all of ours.'

The day passed quickly enough, and Melanie was tired by the time the final bell rang at three o'clock. Clement congratulated her.

'Well done Miss Hickman, the first day is tough but it will get easier.'

'Thank you for saying that, and for letting me in your class today. I have learned a lot. The children were very nice.'

'Yes, they are always well behaved. My only advice to you is not to get too close or too friendly to them. I think Rwanda is more traditional than what you are used to. Try to be the teacher your mother and father had.'

As Melanie left the classroom, she found Father Ishimwe waiting for her with a young woman, who she recognised as being one of the teachers. She was in her mid-twenties, had big eyes, short straight hair, and an elfin lightness to her frame. Melanie was reminded of a painting of a ballerina that she had cherished as a child; Rosine had the dancer's delicate poise.

'Hello Melanie,' he said. 'You have survived the first day. Who knows you might even come back tomorrow! I have brought along a friend of mine who wants to meet you. Melanie, this is Rosine Isaro.'

The two shook hands. Rosine introduced herself.

'Hello Melanie. Ishimwe and I were worried you might be a little lonely. If you don't mind, I would like to show you around. But, please, only if you want to. I'm sure you must be very tired.'

'Rosine that would be wonderful, thank you.' Melanie replied, thinking she might have someone who could at least show her how her ancient stove worked. She could not even switch the gas bottle on.

'Rosine speaks great English as you can see but is determined to learn even more. She is using you for private lessons I fear.'

'Well that's OK by me,' replied Melanie.

'Ladies, if you would not mind, please don't think me rude but I need to be back at Church now, I must dash. Melanie, I leave you in capable hands.' After saying that he left the two women on the path and walked away. Melanie decided to open with practical matters.

'Would you mind coming to have a look at the stove in my kitchen? I am dreading having to cook on it tonight. I can't get it to do anything.'

'Yes. I know the type you have, they are very old. There is a kernack to it.'

'A kernack?'

'Yes. A kernack... a skill!'

'Oh, in English you don't pronounce the 'k' in that word; you can ignore it when you speak.'

'Ah, my first lesson! Thank you!'

Melanie walked with Rosine over to her rooms. It turned out she had a similar place just 50 yards down the path, so they were neighbours. The two women instantly felt comfortable in each other's company. Melanie loved Rosine's dreamy, soft African voice, although she had to listen carefully to catch every word as she told her story. She was from a town a hundred miles away called Ntarama. She had trained to be a teacher in Kigali and took the job here because she had a fiancé, Pascale, whose family lived in the area. He was doing his final year of study at University, but she saw him some weekends and in the holidays. For a moment Tom's face flashed into her mind and Melanie was pleased to discover there was no sadness or regret attached to his memory.

*   *   *

At five o'clock Joe arrived with the water.

'Good evening Miss Hickman, good evening Miss Isaro. Shall I put your water in the kitchen?'

'Yes please Joe, but, another bucket of water? We have plenty surely.'

'Ah, it's not the water Miss Hickman; it is what is in the water. It is a present from Father Ishimwe,' he grinned as he pulled out a bottle of beer and the clinking inside the bucket suggested there was more. 'Well, I have to go. Goodbye Miss Isaro, Miss Hickman, sleep well, I'll see you in the morning.'

As Joseph left Melanie turned to Rosine.

'Will Father Ishimwe be sending me beer every night? I'll leave here an alcoholic. Or fat. Probably both.' She said.

'No,' laughed Rosine. 'He just wants to make you feel welcome and Rwandans like their beer. I see you have Joseph fetching your water. He is a good boy, he is very bright too, and he is my Pascale's cousin.'

'Did you teach him English? He is very articulate.'

'Yes, when he was at school, but he did not need much teaching his mother is fluent. They spoke English in Uganda.'

'Why did he leave school? I saw children leave today. Clement explained about quotas and Hutus and Tutsi and, well I'm not sure, but it cannot be right to throw a child out of school just because of their race or tribe or whatever. I don't know what to make of it. I don't want to say the wrong thing, but, well I don't know. Sorry if I offend, I don't mean to.' Melanie decided to change the subject. 'Would you like a beer?'

'Yes, I'd like a beer, I am Rwandan! But I understand, it is difficult looking in from the outside. This is only your first day; as you get to know us better, you will understand more. For today let's just say that this is a divided country, there has been trouble between Hutu and Tutsi for many years.

'Why?'

'It is just our history, really. People are angry and people are scared. The Hutu are always being told the Tutsi will enslave them once more. They see bad things happening in Burundi, the country next to ours, and they think that the same might happen here. So, the Tutsi are being pushed out of society, boys like young Joe are pushed out of schools, and we all fear violence.

'Are you really afraid?'

'Yes, sometimes. I am a Tutsi. But trouble may not come, and, anyway, I doubt it will come soon; certainly not before we have finished this beer.' Rosine laughed, tilted her head back, and had a mouthful of it. 'Do not worry! Come over to my rooms. I will cook you something to eat and you can tell me about your home. Where are you from in America?'

'New York.'

'Ah,' said Rosine. 'That's where 'Friends' is set!'

'Yes! Where did you watch that?'

'In Kigali, in bars at university, I always loved the opening scenes, the big buildings in Manhattan. All those lights twinkling at night. I must be amazing to see.'

'That was my view driving into work every morning. Yes, I suppose it is amazing.'

'New York stands for freedom in my world Melanie. Who could not dream of going there? You have everything.'

'Yes, but there's me, in my apartment in New York, dreaming of going to Rwanda. Where I don't even have running water.'

'Ah, but what about goat stew? They won't have that in Manhattan.'

'No, you are right there.'

Melanie and Rosine spent a pleasant evening cooking,

eating, chatting, and drinking, while the night sky slowly chased the sun to the horizon. At sunset, the green slopes of the mountain changed colour as they were flushed with the golden orange rays of the sun. A heat haze rose sleepily from the ground as the air filled with the chirping of birds and insects. The combination of the view, the sounds, and the alcohol had a hypnotic effect on Melanie; she felt as if she were in a trance.

4

As the days turned to weeks Melanie got into a rhythm in the classroom and found her style as a teacher. Clement popped in occasionally and seemed satisfied with her progress. She learned as many names as she could, but it was hard with so many children in front of her. The children's first names were French, but the surnames strung together letters that you wouldn't usually connect in English.

She tried different ways of teaching, but the children learned best with rote learning, and copying off the board. The children wrote fast, they had to, as a pencil that finished a sentence in one hand was passed to a neighbour to write the same thing again. One pencil, three children, was their economy of writing. While she taught in the classroom, there were always children looking in at the window. She did not know what to make of this and asked Clement.

'Should those children be in other classes? Should I send them away?'

'No. They are not in school for different reasons. Some may be unable to pay their school fees, or to buy the uniform, or the correct equipment to study. They are trying to learn what they can.'

'Correct equipment? A pencil?'

'Yes, or paper. Some will be Tutsi children who have been told to leave school.'

'That does not seem right.'

'Maybe not but we have few choices. Not all Tutsis have to leave school, if one is very bright and doing very well, they are allowed to stay. It happens.'

'Like Pascale?'

'Yes, Pascale was a good student. He is at university, of course, you are friendly with Rosine.'

'Yes, but the boy Joseph, who brings my water, he seems a bright young man. Did he have to leave?'

'Joseph. Joseph Shema? Yes, I remember him. He was OK, but no brighter than the other in your class,' replied Clement edgily.

'Yes, but...' began Melanie

'Yes, but, listen. Life is hard for everybody. The families our children come from have a little patch of land to farm. They have barely enough food to live on, if their tiny crop fails, then they are in trouble. There are not enough places in school. I wish there were.'

'I understand but Joseph...'

'How do you understand? How long have you been here? Six weeks?' Clement's enquiry was half question and half challenge. Melanie did not reply.

'Joe's mother has cows I expect. They are not so poor. These Tutsi complain too much,' he shook a finger in front of Melanie's as he finished speaking then, when he realised he had overstepped a mark, he turned and walked away.

*   *   *

Later that day Melanie was turning the dial on her radio searching for some music. The Rwandan radio station was filled with angry, strident voices that reminded her of Clement. As Rosine approached singing a Rwandan song, she turned it off. Melanie found the traditional Rwandan music strange but beautiful. They spent most evenings together and Rosine often sang.

She was singing outside Melanie's apartment this evening when Joe stopped by with his burden of water. He stood silently to listen, and it was a couple of minutes before they spotted him.

'Miriwe, Joseph.' Melanie said and on hearing this Rosine looked over and stopped.

'Ah, good evening to you both,' said Joseph. 'You sing well Miss Isaro; you are the best, after my mother.'

'Thank you,' said Rosine.

'Is your mother coming around later? I've yet to meet her; she always comes during the day when I'm in school. I need to pay her.' Said Melanie.

'She will be here soon,' replied Joe, 'I said I would wait for her, we will walk home together.'

'Good, don't let her walk alone after dark..,' said Rosine but stopped and looked over to Melanie.

Melanie felt as if a secret had been let out. 'Why? Why can't Angelique walk home alone after sunset?'

Joe and Rosine looked at one another as an unspoken conversation flashed between them. Rosine pursed her lips then gave him a short nod of permission.

'Yes, I'm sorry', Joe began, choosing his words carefully, 'you deserve an explanation.'

'And you don't need to worry about our problems.' Rosine chipped in. 'First, I must reassure you that you are perfectly safe. You are not in any danger.'

'Well, who is, and why? said Melanie, shrugging her shoulders. 'I know there's a lot of tension around here but, surely, the United Nations are negotiating the peace, everybody is in agreement.'

'The leaders might sign, Miss Hickman,' said Joe. 'But the president's signature means nothing if his party doesn't agree. It's just a piece of paper and it will blow away in the wind. The Hutus will not share power if they think they can keep it all for themselves, nor would the RPF rebels. There will be more fighting.'

'Well, Joe,' said Rosine. 'You don't know this.'

'I do and you should Miss Isaro. Talk to your students. Ask them what they did over the summer holidays, where they go at weekends, camping and training. You know what they call themselves? Interahamwe; it means 'those who work together'. Ask them what their work will be. Talk to bastards like Fabrice and Grégoire...'

'Joseph!' He was cut short by the arrival of his mother Angelique. Tall and athletic she strode towards them wearing a traditional red pange decorated with yellow flowers. Her hair was piled up majestically, and with her large eyes and dramatic cheekbones she looked like the wife of an ancient Pharaoh. The impression of haughty royalty was thankfully undone by her generous smile and the mock horror of her raised eyebrows. 'Such bad language from my beautiful boy. He has turned into an angry young man! Oh dear!'

'Hi Angelique,' said Melanie, and, a little relieved to change the subject, she gave her an envelope and resisted the urge to kneel like a faithful subject. 'Here you are. Thanks for all you have done. It's always so clean when I come home.'

'It is my pleasure, I'm glad you are satisfied. Hello Rosine.' Rosine smiled back at her friend.

'Would you stay for a cup of tea Angelique?' asked Rosine.

'Yes, but we cannot stay long, it is getting late.' Clearly, she did not want to be out after dark either, but with the tea made the three women sat down on chairs in the sunshine while Joe sat, frowning, against the wall. Angelique also wished to change the subject.

'So, I imagine Rwanda must be very different from America Miss Hickman.'

'Yes it is, in many ways.' She paused. 'It's only been a few weeks. It's hard to form an opinion. The children are lovely in school.'

'That is children the world over I suppose.' Angelique replied. 'Do you have children?'

'No. Not yet. I had a boyfriend back home but, well, no children yet. I'm only 27.' This caused Angelique and Rosine to laugh.

'In Rwanda you would not be far off being a grandmother,' said Angelique, 'I am 36, someday soon a girl will see how beautiful my young Joe is and he will make me a grandmother.'

'Joe has an eye on Denyse, he has known her a long time,' said Rosine.

'Yes. She is sixteen now. She likes Joe and always smiles when she sees him,' said Angelique.

'Good job Joe isn't here to be embarrassed by all this talk,' said Joe.

'Does Joe smile when he sees her?' asked Rosine.

'Oh always. He can't take his eyes off Denyse,' said Angelique.

'They would have beautiful children.'

'Really? Please!' groaned Joe.

'Oh, Denyse Kirezi?' said Melanie. 'I've seen her. She's a very beautiful girl.'

'She is, and she's not a girl anymore, she is a woman,' said Rosine.

'I wonder where Joe could be?' said Joe. 'Oh, look there he is leaning against the wall. Listening to the women talk, good thing they aren't talking about him, he would be so embarrassed.'

'Oh, she is beautiful. Perhaps one day I shall drop a subtle hint to Joe that he should ask her out,' said Angelique.

'Only a subtle hint?' said Joe. 'Please spell it out, he might miss it.'

'Was that you Joe?' said Rosine. 'What did you say?'

'It will be about Denyse. He never shuts up about her,' said Angelique.

'I'll leave you to it. I'm going for a walk.' And with that Joe retreated from the glare of the women's attention, they laughed as he waved over his shoulder to them.

'Poor Joe. He is such a lovely boy Angelique, he does you credit,' said Rosine. 'He's so intelligent and speaks so well.'

'Thank you. He has always been a good boy and he will be a good man,' replied Angelique, 'just like his father.'

'If you don't mind me asking, where is his father?' Said Melanie, 'sorry, I hope you don't think I'm being intrusive.'

'No, not at all, replied Angelique, 'Joe's father, Daniel, is a soldier with the Rwandan Patriotic Front. The RPF, as they are called, are usually in Uganda to the north, or they are sometimes in the Congo. I don't know exactly where he is at the moment.'

'Are you in contact?

'Yes. He writes to me when he can, but the fighting has got worse since 1990. The mail is not reliable.'

'Do you ever see each other?'

'We used to meet in the forest at night. We had a secret little cave on the mountain! It sounds silly, but it was exciting and romantic!' She laughed at the memory. 'I used to take Joe with me but I have not seen Daniel for two years now. People round here know who he is and what he is. I know they suspect me as a spy. We are a family split up by war but that is not a rare thing here.'

'Oh, I'm so sorry. That's such a sad story.'

'Yes, but it is also a romantic one,' replied Angelique with a smile. 'It has certainly been an adventure. We left Rwanda when we were teenagers, we ran after one of the massacres, fearing for our lives. For a few years we lived in a refugee camp in Uganda, eventually we got married and Joe came along. But it was a hard life, and I had a home here, some family to welcome me back, so I chose to return.

'Could Daniel not return with you?' asked Melanie.

'Yes, he could have done. I wanted him to, but he wanted to return to Rwanda with dignity; not come sneaking back to live in fear. He believed we should stand up and fight. Like many Tutsis in exile, he became a soldier and fought in the Ugandan civil war that made Yoweri Museveni President.

When that finished the Tutsi soldiers formed the RPF and began to attack the Habyarimana's Hutu regime. Daniel felt it was his duty to be part of this.'

'That must have been so difficult.'

'It was, but he was right, I agreed with him then and I still do now. However, a refugee camp in Uganda was no place for Joe to grow up. We said goodbye, and I brought Joe here, he was only a little boy at the time.'

'Oh my God, that's such a sad story Angelique. Do you miss him?'

'Yes, I love him. But I understand why he has to do this.' Angelique smiled faintly and looked into the distance. 'I get on with life and his picture sits by the window. One day we will live together again. My hero will come and find me. He will pick me up in his strong arms and carry me into the house, like we are newlyweds, and then he will make love to me.'

'Oh!' chorused Rosine and Melanie.

'For many hours!' shouted Angelique.

The women laughed, but the sun had not been still in the sky. Joe appeared walking towards them.

'Angelique it is getting late,' said Rosine. 'Will you be safe walking home on your own? We were talking about that when you arrived.'

'We are safe today Melanie, we are probably safe tomorrow and the day after. But the day after that? We watch, we listen, we read the signs.'

With that she stood up and wrapped her pagne round her shoulders. They walked her and Joe to the compound gate and then said their goodbyes. The pair walked off in the fading light, down the dusty clay road to their home. As they closed the school gates and locked them Melanie realised they were doing this to be safe, but how safe could a gate keep them?

Angelique's story had filled in some of the blanks in her understanding. It was as though the nation was holding its breath, waiting for something to happen. The surrounding tension was making her emotionally tired. She looked forward to the coming weekend in Kigali. School broke up for October holiday and she had a ride to the capital. It would be a chance to get a hot shower, wash her hair, and wear something nice away from the dust of Kinigi. All the Peace Corp volunteers would be there. They go to a bar and have a good drink. She needed a blow-out. A good night out and some fun. 'Yes!' She said with a smile as she got into bed that night. She was open to all possibilities...

5

Kigali city centre floated like a floodlit cruise ship on the dark tide of Rwandan poverty. The Kifalme Park Hotel was one of the few establishments capable of offering the comforts international tourists expected. Most of the guests and visitors sat around the pool drinking ice cold beers, cocktails, and quality South African wines oblivious to the destitution surrounding them. The dozen Peace Corps teachers had pulled two tables together and formed an increasingly noisy party. Social drinking was not the purpose of the gathering; they were getting hammered. Melanie had drunk plenty and was ready to down some more. She had quickly made friends with a fellow American teacher, Sarah, and it was she who stared at the empty wine bottle and struggled to read its label.

'Meerlust Chardonnay. There's a joke in that somewhere.'

'No. There's only a crap pun. Don't pursue it,' said Melanie.

'You're right, but we'll have another bottle of 'lust' anyway,' replied Sarah, and motioned for the nearby waiter to come over. 'One more please garcon. Do we say garcon here? Oh well. One more... no. Better make that two. We're drinking this piss like it's Budweiser.' The waiter smiled indulgently, inclined his head, and left to get the drinks.

'But this is a great Chardonnay.' A smooth French voice intoned. 'It has hints of lemon and tangerine, there are citrus notes within a piercing seam of lime zest and...' the owner of the voice sniffed brought a wine glass to his nose, 'a detailed finish of vanilla; perfect with grilled fish.'

'Whoa, amazing!' Said Sarah.

'Bullshit,' said Melanie.

'Yes, you are correct, it is bullshit. I haven't even tried the wine. Please allow me to introduce myself, my name is Michel. It is a pleasure to meet you.'

He raised himself off his seat and held out his hand for Melanie and Sarah to shake. He had silky brown hair that was parted off centre and swept back, and it reached the collar of his button-down Oxford shirt. He wore khaki chinos, scuffed brown moccasins, and a chunky gold watch dangled loosely on his wrist. With his air of languid insouciance Michelle could tell he was not one of the gorilla tourists, they were more excited to be here. Michel took was the kind of man who took everything in his stride. He gave Sarah a civil smile, he reserved his charming one for Melanie.

Michel had joined their party with a friend earlier in the evening and though no one could remember inviting them over, it did not seem intrusive. The Europeans and the Americans happily formed an ex-pat community in the alien African surroundings.

'So, you are teachers? Is this your first night in Kigali?

'Yes to both,' said Sarah. But Michel directed his response back to Melanie.

'You made a good choice; this is the best hotel in town. I know the manager personally. He has the best wines, the best restaurant, and so the best people come here. We French are particular about our food, the Kifalme Park Hotel is the only place that comes near our high standards.'

'There's a lot of French guys round the hotel, I keep hearing the accent,' said Melanie. 'They're all military people.'

'Yes, France and Rwanda have close links,' said Michel.

'So, you are here doing some linking?' asked Sarah.

'I have a meeting with the big guy over there, he is General Bizimungu.'

'He is one big guy,' said Melanie.

'Yes, he has an overactive... err... what is the word in English?' said Michel. 'He has an overactive...'

'...Thyroid?' said Melanie.

'...Knife and fork?' offered Sarah.

'Aha, yes, both perhaps. The General likes the fine things in life,' said Michel. 'He is high up in the government.'

At this moment Bizimungu looked over at them as though he knew they were talking about him. Michel was quick to wave and smile, earning a grin and a nod of approval from the General, albeit, after a pause. His face was honest and open, the smile was genuine and yet somehow calculated. Melanie figured he hadn't smiled spontaneously, he had made a rational decision to smile on this occasion. He may not on the next. She turned to Michel.

'What is your meeting about? She asked.

'I don't want to bore you with the details but, essentially, I work in the armaments industry. My company has contracts with the Rwandan government, and I am here to oversee them.'

'Do you work for the French government?' asked Sarah.

'Not directly, but everything I do is with their knowledge and their approval. My company has connections at the highest levels of our government. We are a part of French foreign policy.'

'Sounds mysterious,' said Melanie.

'Sounds illegal,' said Sarah.

'We are just doing our bit, helping this country. For progress in this world you need peace and that means protection. There is a rebel army on the northern border and innocent civilians need protection from them,' he smiled and leaned towards them. 'Even American teachers may need that protection.'

'Oh... My hero!' swooned Sarah at which Michel leaned back and laughed. 'Waiter! Do we have any wine fit for a hero?' shouted Sarah. The waiter smiled and strode off to get another bottle of Meerlust.

The evening continued under a banquet of stars. By midnight most people had drifted off to their rooms and finally, as they had both hoped, Melanie and Michel found themselves alone. Some twist or turn of their conversation caused Michel to rest his hand on hers, he did remove it and she did not wish him to. Half an hour later, in a pause, they looked into each other's eyes for a moment, that look turned to a smile and both knew they could risk leaning forward to kiss. So they did. Conversation was no longer required. They went upstairs and joined the secret silence of the night.

Five hours later Melanie awoke, in Michel's bed, to an African sunrise. Half drunk, half asleep, she sat up and tried to remember how she'd got there. She looked at the slumbering man beside her and recalled his name with relief. She laughed at herself and took a mouthful of tepid water from the tooth mug on the bedside table.

The noise from the city caught her attention, so she slipped into Michel's bathrobe and went to the veranda for some fresh air. The sky was clear and there was a slight breeze; with few cars there was no pollution in the city. The pedestrian traffic flowed chaotically around the streets. Some people rode their bicycles, while others pushed them supporting sacks of vegetables on the cross bar as if they were handcarts.

Kigali aspired to be a modern city, but the high-rise buildings had sprung up in an unkempt garden of shanty town improvisation that littered their feet. The streets buzzed with rude colour and commerce as hundreds of farmers hawked their produce from makeshift stalls. This was where they turned their hard work into money. As she soaked up the scene Michel came up behind, wrapped his arms around her and gently kissed her neck. Melanie was sure she had seen someone do that in a movie; but what the heck. It was another hour before they went down to breakfast.

Melanie spent the next couple of days with her friends, but Michel was often around, or leaving messages at the reception desk for her. She needn't have paid for her stay at all; Michel's suite was superior to her tourist class room, so she slept there every night after meeting him. She rationalised that her fling with Michel was a way of shrugging Tom off; back in New York in a closed chapter of her life.

On Wednesday, her last day in Kigali, Michel made her an offer.

'How many more days till you are needed back in school? He asked.

'I need to be back on Saturday at the latest. I am pretty much free. I have promised to help my gardener with his English.'

'You have a garden?'

'No.' Michel looked puzzled as she continued. 'It's a long story, but I do have a gardener and he's a kind of pupil.'

'OK, but we have a couple of days. Would you like to come with me to Gisenyi on Lake Kivu for a night or two? I have some business that takes me out that way and it's very beautiful up by the lake. It's the nearest Rwanda has to a holiday resort. There is a beach there and I know a nice hotel and some restaurants. I have some business in Ruhengeri, it's near your school, I can drop you off.'

Melanie's teaching allowance covered a trip to Kigali, but this was a treat beyond her budget. She would be mad to say 'no', so she did not. After breakfast they set off in Michel's 4X4.

6

It wasn't long before Kigali's tarmac roads gave way to the dried mud and gravel tracks that served the majority of the country. As they travelled along the route a pattern emerged; hamlets and villages coalesced into small towns, then the buildings drew back as little farming communes took over the scenery once more. Every scrap of land was cultivated, small holdings and plots dotted every hillside. Their car was the only evidence of the 20th century in what was otherwise a medieval landscape.

Melanie, drowsy from several days of partying, slipped in and out of sleep. In a dream she heard Michel say he was stopping for a while just outside a town he called Kayove. He closed and locked the car door behind him. After he had been gone for five minutes, the silence roused her and she became aware of her surroundings.

They seemed to be in some kind of woodland scout camp. Though she could not have named it, Gishwati Forest rose up on the hills behind the area. There were wooden huts, big tents, smoke rose from cooking fires, and she heard the voices of men singing in the distance. She could see Michel talking to some military looking guys outside the only brick building. Everything looked fine, they were laughing and shaking hands, she felt safe as she watched Michel go inside with them.

What she could see of the scenery was gorgeous, and she wanted to see more. As she looked a beautiful bird strutted out of the forest undergrowth. It had long legs that supported a plump body of slim, black, white and silvery grey feathers. Behind the long beak its face was patched black, white and read beneath a spiky crown of golden grey quills.

Melanie longed to get a closer look. The door was locked, but she found the release catch, swung it open and stepped out carefully towards the bird. She crept to within ten feet of it then crouched in silence. The crane strolled nonchalantly about, unfolding its long neck to peck at food on the ground. Occasionally it glanced her way, blinking a jet-black eye. When she put a hand on the ground to steady herself, the bird noticed the move and stood to its full height with its wings at full spread. Aware that she was intruding on its space Melanie backed off to leave the bird in peace.

The fresh air had woken her up, and she decided to explore further. She walked over to the hut Michel had entered but chose not to go in as she did not want to interfere. Instead she walked further into the camp.

After a minute's wandering she came across a parade

ground, and at one end of it something caught her eye. A row of dummies made of cloth and rags, stuck on poles. She'd seen this in many war movies; 'bayonet practise'. The dummies were a mess, ripped apart by regular assaults. Some of them had heads missing. 'But, of course', she smiled and thought to herself. Michel dealt in arms; he wouldn't be arming the scouts, this was a military base.

She took a closer look. The last dummy in the row had a weapon sticking out of it, the blade had penetrated the rags and stuck in the wooden pole. It was a machete, hardly state of the military art, more of a farming tool. She looked at it closely; it was cheap, with a basic wooden handle stamped 'made in China', but it had a sharp blade. As she examined it, she was aware that the singing was getting closer, accompanied by the stamp of running feet and, bizarrely, the sound of referee's whistles.

Melanie felt an urge to run away but, as she had nowhere obvious to run to, she decided to stand her ground. She had done nothing wrong, so she was waiting as the crowd of chanting, running, Rwandan men came into view. Whistles blew and machetes waved above the heads of the brightly coloured mob. The clothing was peculiar, too vivid and garish to be scouts or soldiers. Some wore 'cool' shades and bandanas more suited to a beach party than a parade ground. There was an air of carnival. It was like someone had invited a hundred young men to a frat party where the theme was bad taste and violence; for all the bright colours and party atmosphere the men oozed naked aggression. For a second it seemed that evil turned towards her; and she was suddenly afraid. She froze, hoping to God someone would step in, as if someone could be in charge of this seeming chaos.

At that moment three men in khaki uniform stepped out of a nearby hut and quickly stood between Melanie and the staring mob, the Capitaine barked commands in French.

'ATTENTION!'

As he gave the command, he did not look at the group, instead he gazed at the distant trees with the confident assumption that his order would be followed. Slowly the rabble took on a recognisable shape, ranked in orderly lines. A measure of calm descended he re-enforced this with;

'REPOS!'

The men began to relax to 'at ease' on his word. The Capitaine slightly inclined his head and acknowledged the change in atmosphere.

Next he strolled nonchalantly along the front of the line. His swagger showed he was in charge, his lack of fear at their aggressive demeanour showed that he was not threatened by them. He assumed natural authority; so they gave him automatic deference. It was a system that had worked in armies for millennia and it did not fail Capitaine Moreau on this occasion. He oozed discipline and power, his eyes glittered with controlled menace. The militia responded like a Rottweiler called to heel. They stood panting and sweating; their whistles silenced, and their machetes hung by their sides. In their gaudy clothes they never became an army, but they looked less like a mob.

Pausing to enjoy their subservient silence he finally released them from his thrall;

'ROMPEZ VOS RANGS.'

Quickly the crowd dissolved into smaller gatherings of friends and comrades, chatting and heading off to their tents. The threat had receded, though Melanie noticed an occasional glance come her way.

'Madame...' The Capitaine started...

'I'm sorry I don't speak French.' Melanie replied, frustrated that her voice trembled. 'Thank you.'

'I understand English. Thank you? What for?'

'Err... nothing, just... thank you. I was frightened.'

'What are you doing here? This is a military camp. You should have been stopped by security. C'est des conneries!'

Melanie guessed the last bit was profane, and she was right, the Capitaine thought the situation was bullshit. He looked around for someone to blame, clearly he was unhappy that a civilian had witnessed anything.

Still shaken because she had felt threatened Melanie took control of her feelings by breathing deeply. As she did so her heartbeat slowed down and her head cleared. Her attitude of gratitude towards the French officer shifted; if he was in charge, then he was in some way responsible. He wasn't angry with his wolf pack, he was angry with her. In fact, she realised, he was angry because he had been exposed, as if he had been caught doing something wrong. It was almost as if she was a witness to something; but what? Melanie was relieved to see Michel approaching with another officer, in a uniform visibly better tailored than that of the Capitaine.

'Melanie! Here you are, I was worried about you. It is not safe to go wandering off in an army training camp,' he exclaimed, in too jolly a fashion for Melanie's mood. 'I thought you were asleep in the car. Instead you came to watch the soldiers training,' he turned to the well-dressed officer. 'See General? It's not a problem. There're just men running around here and a woman watching them.'

Capitaine Moreau and the General were not really listening to Michel being deep in a conversation of their own. The Capitaine had been complaining, but it was evident the General had calmed him already. Michel took Melanie by the upper arm steering her back towards the car.

'Come I'll walk you back. I don't think the soldiers like to have civilians watch them at work. Especially not women.'

'Why? What have they got to hide?'

'Nothing. But, come now, I'll walk you back, please stay in the car, I'll only be a couple of minutes, I just need to finish things off here and say my goodbyes. We'll be on our way soon I promise.'

With Melanie in a safer place Michel returned to the hut. He walked up to a wooden packing case that lay on the table and patted it like it was a friend's dog. He smiled and winked at the General.

'Ah... I'm sure you will enjoy the cognac, it's Remy Martin.'

'Yes, it's my favourite, thank you, the case should keep me going for a few days at least!'

'Only a few days?' Michel laughed.

'I cannot drink the shit beer they serve out here.'

'I know what you mean General. But that's Rwanda for you.'

'God Michel, this job, these fucking Rwandans; trust me,' he pulled a bottle out of the case and tuned it over in his hands. 'I need more than a glass of brandy at the end of the day in this place,' he tapped his finger on the label and pursed his lips as he replaced the bottle. 'Speaking of home comforts, you seem to need something more at the end of your day too. Who is the girl in the car? She's not a journalist I hope.'

'No, just some American teacher I met in Kigali.'

'A teacher, that is all?'

'Yes. I'm taking her up to Lake Kivu for a couple of nights,' he added with a wink.

'Oh, very nice. It must be a nice change to fuck something white eh?' The general nodded his head as Michel smiled and replied.

'Yes. More expensive than a Rwandan whore but, like you say, a nice change.'

'Ah, Michel you are always the same. Let me know when you've finished with her.'

'I'll keep you in mind general. But I need to get going now. I need to get over to Gisenyi.'

They shook hands and Michel turned to leave.

Back at the car Melanie mused over what she had seen and felt. She felt violated by the stares of the 'soldiers' who looked more like a gang than an army. 'Anyway, what army uses machetes' she wondered?

She could not see the parade ground from the vehicle as a copse of trees obscured the view, but when she looked at them the once pleasant greenery seemed to be merely cover for prying eyes. She locked the car doors and was starting to feel a little more secure till she made the mistake of looking in the rear-view mirror. A face stared back at her. She was about to scream but stopped when the face smiled, a charming smile, and she recognised him; Grégoire.

The young man walked round the side of the car and Melanie wound down the window to speak to him.

'Grégoire. What are you doing here?'

'Do you not remember Miss Hickman? I have told you before. I am training to be a soldier in the militia.'

'Oh yes, I forgot.' Melanie was shocked to find she had a connection with the place. 'But aren't you a bit young? I mean, to be a soldier.'

'Most of us are young; of course our leaders are older.'

'But the officers, they were French.'

'Yes, they are real soldiers, they are training us.'

'But what for?' Melanie furrowed her brow. 'I thought peace was... that's why the UN are here.'

'Yes, but we have to be ready to protect our people from the RPF rebels. Our communities may need us.'

'Who are you? What are you called?'

'We are Interahamwe.'

'Interahamwe? What does that mean?'

'Those who work together. My comrades and I, we work together.'

'Work... what work...?'

'I am not supposed to say, we are a secret but...' Grégoire stopped and looked up as he heard voices approaching.

'I have to go now. Don't tell anyone you saw me. I will see you at school next week.' With a wave of his hand he turned and ran off, out of sight under the trees.

Michel approached the car, and the general walked alongside him, his hand resting on Michel's shoulder. After brief goodbyes the two men shook hands, Michel got into the car, started it and pulled out of the camp onto the main road. Melanie sensed that he was angry about something but was choosing to say nothing. She tried to relieve the tension by dealing with it head on.

'Did I do something wrong by having a look around? You don't seem very happy about it.'

'No not wrong, you weren't to know, but it didn't go down too well with the officers. They are the military and they like to have their secrets,' he let out a deep breath. 'It was my fault, I should have told you, I thought you were fast asleep.' Michel managed a smile. 'No harm has been done.'

'I saw those Rwandan men Michel, they weren't proper soldiers, and some of them were very young.'

'Well, yes, some of them are young, and they aren't soldiers, really. They are a militia. We are training the general public to defend themselves.'

'We?'

'Well, the French army.'

'With machetes? I doubt the Rwandan Patriotic Front will come armed with swords.'

'Guns are expensive. Rwanda is poor. Machetes might be all they have to work with.'

'Only butchers work with machetes for God's sake.'

'Well, unfortunately, war is butchery.'

'Yes, well, that militia, butchery... yes, that's the right word. They were horrible... mean, evil even.'

'Well they are soldiers, in a way. You don't want soldiers that are good at improvisational drama.' Michel laughed. 'They have to be fighters. It's their job.'

'OK, point taken.' Melanie calmed down somewhat. 'So, what is it that you do? I don't see you running around with a machete.'

'With these shoes? No chance!' Do you know how much they cost? Michel smiled. 'I provide logistical support.'

'Really? What's that?'

'Today it was brandy for the general. I picked it up at the Kifalme Park yesterday, and I have good news,' he turned and winked at her. 'I've saved some for us. It will help you forget the bad men.'

'Well, at least I got some good photos,' she said casually.

'You what!' shouted Michel, as he turned and made the car swerve.

'I'm joking!' laughed Melanie, pleased to have scored a point.

As they drove along she spotted another of the exotic birds she had seen earlier.

'Michel. Do you know what kind of bird that is? It's so beautiful.'

'Yes. It is called the grey crowned crane. The locals believe it brings them luck.'

'Really?'

'Well, if that's true they could do with a lot more of them.'

7

The lakeside resort at Gisenyi was superb with sandy beaches fringed with trees and nice hotels all set against the majestic backdrop of a stunning volcano; Mount Nyiragongo. Melanie and Michel could have been on a mini break in the Caribbean.

Two days later Michel dropped her off at her small rooms on the school campus. It was Sunday morning and as they approached Kinigi, she saw all the local people going to Church in their bright clothes. She usually enjoyed mass at the Catholic Church, especially the exuberant singing, but she didn't feel right attending today, after a week of boozy sex with a man she had just met.

She had pretty much enjoyed their time together. He connected her with a different, more glamorous, world. Neither Kigali nor Gisenyi was New York but there were a few bright lights, enough bars, and some music to create a bit of nightlife, an echo of home. Michel gave her the phone numbers of his apartment and office in Kigali with the invitation to give him a call next time she was in the capital. His usual knowing smirk fell short of romance however, and she knew she was an accessory for a fun weekend, nothing else. That was OK as far as it went, but it didn't really go far enough. She was worth more and if more came along Michel would not be getting a call. Then again, she reflected, she wasn't going to be here for long and a woman has many needs; Michel ticked a lot of boxes. She grinned in the mirror above the sink and gave herself a wink. In her bedroom she threw her bag on the floor, flopped onto her bed and slumped into a deep sleep, snoring, flat on her back, without unpacking a thing.

In the warm mid-afternoon she was tugged from her drowsy slumber by someone knocking on her door. It took her a few moments to register where she was and what was the noise was. Joe's voice brought her back to reality.

'Miss Hickman? Are you home? I've got fresh water for you. I'll leave it in the shade out here.'

'One moment, I just need to put something on.' She answered although she was actually fully dressed. She just wanted to bring herself round. She poured out a saucepan of cool water, tipped it over her head and wrapped a towel round to dry it off. When she opened the door, Joe was walking slowly away.

'Hey Joe.' She called. 'Come back. We can practise some English'.

Joe stopped but did not turn round. 'Oh, not today Miss, I don't feel up to it.'

'OK then. Thanks for the water,' she replied. 'I'll see you soon.'

Joe carried on, gingerly walking away. Melanie sensed something was not right.

'Are you OK Joe?' She asked. Joe stopped with his head bowed. Melanie stepped over towards him.

'Joe? Look at me. Are you...' But she stopped as Joe turned towards her. His face was a mess of cuts and bruises, both eyelids were swollen and blackened. 'Oh my God Joe, what happened?'

'I had a fight.'

'Who did this to you?'

'It was just a fight Miss Hickman; it happens, really, I am fine.'

'Can I get you a painkiller?' Joe paused before he replied.

'Actually, thank you, that would help.'

'No problem. I'll get you one.'

She went into her room and quickly returned with a blister pack of tablets.

'Here, take one of these, every four hours with some food. It's a medicine called ibuprofen, it's really good for swellings.' She poured him a glass of water. In his gratitude Joe didn't bother to point out that he didn't eat every four hours.

'What happened to you?'

'It was a fight that is all. I'm OK. I will get over it,' he attempted a smile. 'You ought to see the other guy.'

'The other guy or guys?' It was obvious to Melanie that this was more than a brawl; Joe had been given a beating. She reached out to him to rest a hand on his shoulder and comfort him. The tender gesture undid his composure, and he crumpled into a sob, his head slumped low on his chest. Melanie put her arms around him and pulled him close. Welcoming the chance to hide his face Joe sobbed into her T-shirt. The emotion he had been bottling up spilled out of him. Rage and shame. Rage that he had to take a beating, shame that he could not hurt them, shame that he wanted to fight like a man but could only cry like a boy.

She let him stay like this for a while, he would not be able to talk or listen till he had calmed down. After five minutes Joe regained his composure and stepped back from Melanie. He struggled to speak without his voice cracking.

'I'm sorry. I'm OK now. There's no point in... well... there's just no point is there?' He stood with his hands on his hips facing the gate to the school compound. There was little to say but finally Melanie settled on a course of action and popped into her room. As she pulled the brandy out the suitcase her New York Yankees baseball cap hooked onto the neck of the bottle.

'Here, this will help,' he turned around to see her offering him a drink of some kind. 'What is this?' He asked as she popped the cap onto his head.

'It's called brandy; this one is a Remy Martin, a very good brandy actually.'

'Will it do me any good?'

'No. But that's no reason not to have a glass!'

'Dear me Miss Hickman, a double negative in a sentence. What shall we drink to?'

'Me being a good teacher; you spotted a double negative. Cheers. Drink it slow, it's not like beer or that urwag... waggy... banana, drink, thing.'

'Cheers,' said Joseph tweaking and adjusting the peak of the cap while Melanie poured them both a shot. He sipped carefully at the brandy and narrowly avoided a coughing fit. 'Wow!' He croaked.

'Have some water too.' Advised Melanie, she put two plastic cups on the table as they sat down.

'I like this hat. Do I look cool?' asked Joe.

'Very cool.'

'Do I look like Michael Jackson?'

'Ha! I guess so. Do you want it? It's yours.'

'No. I could not keep this,' he replied, spinning the hat around in his hand. 'It has your name in it, see?' He tapped his finger on a little label inside that said "Melanie". 'You need it.'

'I don't need it.'

'You do, it will keep the sun off your head. It is dangerous, we are high up and very near to the equator. I am used to the sun, you are not.'

'No. I want you to have it.'

'OK I'll make a deal with you. When you go home, you can give this to me as a leaving present.'

'OK. It's a deal.' She held out her hand and Joe shook it and smiled.

'Tell me about Michael Jackson. Was he bad or good?'

'What do you mean?'

'Well there was this song we used to hear, and he said he was bad. I do not understand that.' Melanie leant back and laughed out loud, Joe joined in.

'OK... Michael Jackson...' Melanie began.

The two of them sat sipping brandies, and before long Primus beer, watching the afternoon wear away and comparing their very different lives.

*   *   *

An hour before sunset the compound gate squeaked and scraped open on its rusty hinges. Rosine, Angelique and Denyse walked in and shut it behind them.

With a third of the bottle of brandy gone and four empty bottles of beer on the table Melanie and Joe were in better moods; their greetings were louder than they intended. Ominously Angelique lugged a heavy bag that clinked with bottles.

'Ah! You have started without us,' said Rosine. 'How was Kigali? Did you have a good time?'

'Yes, thank you, it was good, a nice change.' Melanie replied.

'I was expecting you back a few days ago,' said Rosine.

'Yes, but I met a man, an old friend, and we had a couple of days at Lake Kivu,' said Melanie, correctly guessing her story was transparently not true, but she didn't care. Rosine and Angelique laughed straight away.

'Ah! An old friend, you have so many of those in Rwanda! You must introduce us to him sometime,' said Angelique. 'Perhaps he'll take us all to Lake Kivu.' She turned to her son. 'And how is Joseph this fine afternoon?'

'Well. I am drunk mother. And very nice it is too,' he replied.

'Drinking beer? This early?' said Angelique.

'Beer? Beer? This isn't some scruffy cabaret in Kinigi. I am sharing a glass of brandy with my teacher. We are discussing...

err... What was the topic of conversation my fine teacher?'

'You were telling me how pretty Denyse was.' Melanie offered.

'Oh, not again,' he held his hands open to Denyse, 'Denyse do not believe them.'

'But, don't you think I'm pretty Joe?' inquired Denyse.

'Yes, but I keep that a secret,' he replied.

'Miss Hickman what are you doing to my son? He drinks brandy and shares secrets with you that he never tells me! Whatever next?' said Angelique while Rosine handed round the beers, though Denyse declined.

'Yes, I'll have a beer before I turn in. I can't drink anymore of this brandy,' said Melanie.

'You can't go to bed Melanie,' said Denyse. 'We have to talk about Rosine's wedding. We need your ideas.'

For the next half an hour the women talked through the plans, the wedding was only a week off. The couple had wanted to get married at the start of the half term, but Pascale was tutoring at the university in Kigali and they had different holidays. Sadly, Rosine would get married on the Saturday and be back teaching in school on the Monday morning; there was not much of a honeymoon for the couple. This however did not dampen Rosine's enthusiasm; it was the gateway to a lifetime of happiness for her and her husband to be.

As they chatted Joe had dozed off. Melanie joined in the wedding chat, but Joe's situation preyed on her mind more and she took Angelique to one side while other two talked dresses.

'What really happened to Joe?' She asked. 'He said it was just a fight, but I don't believe him.'

'Ah well, no, it wasn't quite that. He was very brave. He is not a fighter by nature. I will be quick; we have to go home before sunset. It was the Friday night you went away to Kigali, the start of the holiday. Joe and I were home, maybe about nine at night and we heard noise outside our house. I went out to see what was going on. It was a group of men, about ten of them. They were drunk, passing by and shouting things at me. Disgusting things, that they don't have the courage to say when they are sober.'

'These were the boys from school?'

'They were there, but they weren't doing the shouting and they weren't drunk. That was the men from the village, the loud mouth Jean Damascène, with Thierry, Daniel, Oscar and a few others, maybe. It was dark.'

'Jean Damascène? Grégoire's father?'

'Yes. Unfortunately, Grégoire will end up as stupid as his old man. I said nothing to the fool. I can shut him up with a look. His wife is more of a man than he is. But Joe could not stand there and watch me being insulted. He came out and stood before them.'

'Did the men beat him?'

'No. They got the boys to do it, Grégoire and his friends. Like setting a pack of dogs on him. He had no chance. As quick as I could I got a broom and chased them off. I cracked a few skulls! The men did nothing; they like to watch a fight.'

'What happened next?'

'When they saw Joe on the floor they left, laughing, and telling their boys how brave they were; to pick on someone who was outnumbered six to one. Jean Damascène said they would come back for me another day.'

'Oh my God! What does he mean by that?'

'I don't know. I'm not afraid of him, he's a coward, but he is dangerous because he leads the others.'

'What might they do?'

'I won't give them the chance to do anything. There are always signs before trouble. Joe and I will escape, don't worry about us, we have lived as exiles before. From time to time, in 1963, 1967, 1973 Tutsis were attacked. This is how we mark the passing of the years. Maybe 1994 will be a year to remember. I have noticed that the behaviour of some round here is getting worse. The boys are less respectful and it's these Interahamwe gangs that are training them. Even Jean

Damascène's mouth is getting bigger.'

'But these people are your neighbours. How can they do this?' asked Melanie.

'They have been taught to since they were children. Grégoire, Denyse and Joe were friends when they were young, but as they grew older, they grew apart. Jean Damascène would not allow his son to be friends with a Tutsi. From being children they are taught to blame us for everything. We have no rights, no vote, most of our children are denied education, the list goes on. It is very difficult for a Tutsi to get a paid job, and if you do you have no rights at work.' Angelique added.

'I will never be promoted at school,' said Rosine who had been listening in, 'and I can be sacked without being given any reason.'

'This is awful, it's like, it's like how the Jews were treated in Nazi Germany,' said Melanie.

'Exactly. That is an excellent comparison,' said Rosine.

'So, have you told the police about the attack on Joe?'

'It would do no good. The police would be on the side of the boys who beat him, they are all on the same side. That is the meaning of Hutu Power,' said Angelique. Habyarimana's government is behind this.'

'Oh God. Is there any way I can help you?'

'Would you?'

'Yes, of course.'

'Thank you, I'm glad you said that. We might need a place to hide if there's trouble. You will be safe. They will not touch a white woman and they would not dare search your house.'

'I'll do anything I can Angelique.'

'Thank you. Well, sunset is only half an hour away. We need to get home before it gets dark. I'll wake Joe up, your brandy has made him sleepy, but thank you, he needed to relax.'

Angelique roused Joe and before long Melanie found herself alone and yawning outside her front door as the stars began to come out in the night sky. She thought over the events of the last week and thought about where she stood in all this; an American, a teacher, a short-term guest in a land where violence against some people seemed to be expected and accepted. She wondered if she really could protect Angelique and Joe if trouble started. Life had never asked her to be a heroine before now, she feared she might be miscast in the role.

An image of her chance meeting with Grégoire popped into her mind. That was after this despicable attack. She made up her mind to question the boys in school. Perhaps she could get them to see things differently. She tried to think of a lesson that would give her the chance.

8

Denyse made sure that the route they took meant that they got to Angelique's home first. Once there, the conversation they had on their arrival went as she had planned it.

'Oh, what were we thinking?' exclaimed Angelique, 'Denyse, we should have gone by your house. We'll walk back with you; you don't want to be out at night alone.'

'It's alright. Joe can take me home.'

'Yes,' added Joe, stretching his arms above his head and yawning. 'The walk will clear my head. The drowsy has made me brandy,' he announced confidently. Angelique managed to suppress a chuckle and replied.

'Well it's a good idea then. Don't be too late, you have jobs to do tomorrow. Goodnight Denyse.'

As Angelique went inside her door the two of them set off. When they were round the corner Denyse slid her hand into Joe's giving it a squeeze.

'So, do you like brandy then Joe?'

'It's OK. It's stronger than urwagwa and has a lot cleaner taste.'

'Have you actually ever had urwagwa?'

'I've tried it.'

'Is it nice?'

'It's like warm, banana flavoured mud.'

'Sounds lovely.'

After a pause Denyse stopped walking and turned to look up into Joe's face holding both his hands. Joe raised an eyebrow and in response Denyse stepped onto her tiptoes offering her mouth to his. They had kissed before, but the alcohol made Joe bolder than in the past. He pulled her too him, hoping he had guessed her mood correctly. As their lips met Denyse pressed forward against him and pushing herself into his loins. Joe's stomach muscles tightened in a mix of pleasure and trepidation. Unsure of himself for a second he pulled back then, quickly, he realised he wanted to feel the excitement and tension again. He pushed himself against her once more. They wound their arms around each other and hugged each other close. Joe breathed in the fragrance of her hair and skin as she surrendered to his embrace. He could feel her heart beating against his chest where his own heart pounded giddily. They enjoyed a few minutes of this freely given tenderness until Denyse pulled back with a giggle.

'Joe!' She laughed with her eyes wide open. He quickly realised what had come between them.

'Well, what do expect?' he chuckled. 'I am a man you know.'

'That much is obvious,' laughed Denyse.

'Oh God, said Joe, looking down at his groin. 'You've let me down,' he said, addressing the bulge in his trousers. Denyse kissed him gently once more.

'Don't be embarrassed, come on, we don't want to be late.'

'I don't mind being late,' replied Joe, 'it's a beautiful evening.'

'It's a beautiful night now but we both have to be up early,' said Denyse leading him by the hand.

Outside her home they paused and faced each other, holding hands and looking into each other's eyes.

'It's not that late,' said Joe.

'It's late enough and you've had a tough few days.' Joe was silent as she hinted at the beating he had received. 'I want you to know I'm here for you Joe.'

Joe looked at her and tried to find the right words. 'I know you are Denyse. I'm here for you too.'

Denyse rested her hands on his chest and did up a button on his shirt. 'Good! Maybe you'll find an excuse to walk me home tomorrow as well then!'

Saying this she kissed her finger tips and brushed them across Joe's lips, 'goodnight my love,' she whispered gently and went into her house. Joe walked home with a smile on his face and a warm glow spreading throughout his body. He felt full of life and joy; his cuts and bruises hurt no more. Had he met his tormentors again he could have taken them all on and won. He looked forward to walking Denyse home again the next day; he'd find a way to make that happen. He did not realise that his 'tomorrow' would be very unlike his 'today'.

9

As Holy Family was a Catholic school the day's learning began with prayers or, if the teacher wished, a reading. As Melanie started the day with the class containing the boys who had beaten Joe, she decided to address their behaviour subtly. She chose a reading that had meant a lot to her as a child; The Good Samaritan. The class stood respectfully in their places as she led them in the sign of the cross.

'In the name of the Father, and of the Son, and of the Holy Spirit...'

'Amen.' The class responded.

'Could I have a volunteer to read please?' She asked, most of the boys put their hands up. Melanie chose Grégoire.

'A man was travelling was travelling from Jerusalem to

Jericho when he was set upon by robbers...,' he began.

As he read Melanie looked around the faces in the room to see if any of them made the connection between the story and what they had done a week or so previously. Albert, Cyprien, Placide, Patrick, and Fabrice all seemed to pay attention. When Grégoire had finished, he handed the Bible back to Melanie who closed prayers with the sign of the cross. She told the boys to sit down and addressed them.

'Thank you Grégoire, you read very well.'

Grégoire nodded thoughtfully.

'So, what was that story about do you think?' she asked. It was Albert, honest and straight as a die, who answered first.

'It is about a good man who help his neighbour,' he said. 'The priest and the other guy they are do nothing. They are looking other way. This Samaritan he is the good.'

As usual he played safe and stuck with the present tense she thought, but most of the boys did except for Fabrice and Grégoire. As she looked to these two to take the discussion further, she sensed they were suspicious of her motives; she had never discussed a morning reading before. They flashed glances at each other. Fabrice tilted his head back and looked down his nose at her. Grégoire leaned back on his chair.

'Grégoire.' Melanie continued. 'What do you think?'

'About what?' he asked, playing dumb.

'About The Good Samaritan'.

'What about it? It is a well-known story.'

'Who would you want to be in this story Grégoire?' she probed.

'Well. I would want to be the good man.'

'And who is that?' asked Melanie.

'Hmm, I'm not sure, I need more information.'

'More information!' said Melanie, taken aback.

'Yes,' said Fabrice. 'It looks like the man from Jerusalem who gets beaten up is the victim. But how can we know that? What if he was a thief and the so-called robbers are just getting their stolen things back?'

'Yes, this priest and this Levite. Maybe they know this, and that is why they do not help. They think he got what he deserved,' said Grégoire.

'Well, I see your point but... they could have killed him.' Melanie was thrown by their reasoning.

'Is a hangman a murderer if he hangs a killer Miss Hickman?' said Fabrice. 'Sometimes justice demands the death penalty does it not? It does in America for example.'

'Yes. But that is not the point of this story. The Good Samaritan is the good person because he helps the victim. He knows the commandments, you should love your neighbour, it is right that he had pity on the beaten man. Do you not want to follow this good example?' Melanie replied.

'Should I love my neighbour? Yes, I love my neighbour Miss Hickman,' said Fabrice. 'But who is my neighbour? I know of another commandment. It is one of the Hutu Commandments, the eighth one. It states; Hutus must cease having pity for the Tutsi. You see, I have Hutu neighbours, I have Tutsi neighbours. I must protect my Hutu neighbour from the Tutsi enemy. Pity is weakness, it is more important to fight for justice. That is a duty.'

Melanie needed an answer and paused too long thinking one up. The class sensed she had been outwitted by Fabrice.

'Fabrice, the story is not called the 'The Bad Samaritan' or the 'The Foolish Samaritan'. It is the 'The Good Samaritan' because he does what we all should do; help our neighbour. Like Jesus said; Love your neighbour.'

'Miss Hickman.' Offered Grégoire. 'I respect Jesus. But was his neighbour a Tutsi?'

'That's silly Grégoire,' said Placide, whose shy voice was never heard in the classroom. 'They didn't have Tutsis back then.'

'What do you know Placide?' said Fabrice stunned, like everyone, that the normally silent Placide had chosen this day to begin his public speaking career.

'Speech!' shouted Cyprien, looking round the class for

their approving laughter. The boys joined in calling; 'Speech! Speech!' Now all eyes were on Placide, who felt obliged to say more but was too embarrassed. Melanie tried to help him out hoping he would support her cause, even accidentally.

'That's true Placide. What do you think the story is trying to teach us?'

'Err, we should be nice to one another?' He mumbled.

'Brilliant Placide,' laughed Fabrice. 'You should become a priest! Father Placide. We should do prayers like this more often Miss Hickman. Placide can do the sermon, don't you think Grégoire?'

'Yes Fabrice,' replied Grégoire. 'Placide by name, no longer Placide by nature.' Placide was embarrassed and grinned sheepishly.

Melanie realised she was up against it, Grégoire and Fabrice were the leaders, Cyprien was their policeman. He only ever truly spoke with his eyes and she did not like what they said, as they followed her around the room. Placide was weak, physically and mentally, like the other smaller boys in the room he was a follower. She held out more hope for Patrick who had an inquisitive mind. In growing desperation she turned to him.

'Patrick, Fabrice and Grégoire can turn the Bible on its head it seems. What do you think?' She paced up and down the front of the class while Patrick thought of an answer. 'Does this story relate to the 10 commandments, perhaps?'

'Yes Miss. You are right. One of the commandments fits here. If the man who was beaten was a Tutsi, then the robbers and those who passed by did the right thing; 'The Hutu should stop having mercy on the Tutsi', that is the eighth of the Ten Hutu Commandments.' Melanie was mystified, but Patrick's recollection stirred Fabrice and Grégoire into a round of applause which the rest of the class quickly joined in with. Melanie knew she was beaten.

'The what commandments?' she said in exasperation.

'The Hutu Ten Commandments,' came a voice of authority from the rear of the classroom. Melanie looked up to see Clement had popped in to see what the noise was about. Melanie did not know how much he had heard. 'You will not have heard of them Miss Hickman.'

'No.' She replied. 'Please, tell me about them.'

'Certainly, let me summarise them for you. They are a line of defence for the Hutu people so that never again will we be slaves of the Tutsi. The Hutu Commandments are a shield against the rebel army that waits, ready to attack, from Uganda. These boys will be on the front line if that day comes. They need to be warned that the Tutsi are bloodthirsty and power-hungry and want to take Rwanda by force. Commandment number one; every Hutu male should know that every Tutsi woman is a traitor and a spy; therefore, they must not marry them or work with them. Number two; every Hutu male must know that our Hutu daughters are better women, wives and mothers. Three; every Hutu male must know that all Tutsi are dishonest in their business dealings. Any Hutu who does business with a Tutsi is a traitor. Four; Hutu women must teach these truths to their husbands and sons. Number five; Hutus must lead the country in government and, yes Miss Hickman, six; in education. Number seven; the Army must be 100% Hutu and no soldier must marry a Tutsi woman. Eight, as you have heard, the Hutu should stop having mercy on the Tutsi. Nine; Hutus must be united in solidarity; they must be firm and vigilant towards their common Tutsi enemy. And finally, number ten; the ideology of Hutu Power must be taught to Hutus at all levels. Any Hutu who disagrees shall be deemed a traitor.' Clement ended his speech holding his clenched fist in the air, the boys cheered and clapped. Clement nodded to them while gently encouraging them to be silent by waving his hands.

'I am sorry if this sounds harsh to you Miss Hickman, but Rwanda is not the USA. We have seen enormous suffering and freedom means everything to us now. Of course we are angry to see our liberty threatened. The Hutu was liberated from

Tutsi oppression in 1959, we will not return to that state. We are ready for war with the Tutsi.'

'I understand, to an extent, but shouldn't you be ready for peace? President Habyarimana signed the Arusha Accord agreement,' replied Melanie. Her comment was met with a stony silence from her colleague. Finally, he took a step towards her and spoke.

'Then the President needs to be careful. It may be that he has signed his own death warrant.'

Melanie and Clement faced each other in the silent room. Though he acted calm, Clement's expression and trembling tension gave away the bitterness and resentment that boiled within. She could see where Fabrice and Grégoire got their ideology from. They were primed, ready, and the Hutu Power ideology would justify anything. They could beat up Joe because they saw him as less than human. Melanie looked at the faces of Grégoire and Fabrice and saw that innocence had long since been drained from them.

There was nothing else to be said and, thankfully, it was the end of registration time and the first lesson of the day was due to begin. Melanie dismissed her class.

'Off you go boys. I'll see you later.'

The class filed out leaving Melanie and Clement facing each other alone in the room. Clement spoke first.

'Our job is not just to teach our subject Miss Hickman. Our job is to teach people. That is my job. I am a teacher.'

'Teacher? Indoctrinating children with hatred is not teaching Clement.'

'You do not understand the Rwandan context Miss Hickman...'

'Melanie. My name is Melanie. Why don't you use it?'

'It is a sign of respect to use your surname...'

'Not from you it isn't Clement, it's just a way of keeping me at arm's length, you don't respect me one bit.' She continued. 'I'd like you to leave my classroom.'

'It isn't your classroom, you're only borrowing it for a

year, then you'll be gone,' replied Clement with a bitter smile then turned and headed for the door.

'One more thing Clement.'

'What?' he replied, turning to face her.

'I have something to add.'

'Really? What is that?' said Clement with a raised eyebrow and a sneer. Melanie smiled sweetly back at him.

'Fuck off.'

Clement marched out of the door.

10

Melanie had no class to teach but a minute after she sat down to mark some work, she was up again, and pacing round the room. She had to move around to relieve the tense energy whirling round her body. She decided to go for a walk, anywhere, she did not need a destination, she just needed to move. Outside her door she was onto the clay playground with its reluctant covering of grass. That space felt too open, so she slipped between some classrooms, and headed for the scrub ground that separated the school from the Church buildings.

At the glassless windows at the back of the rooms she saw the usual line of raggedy children straining to hear what the teacher said to the lucky pupils. These children were desperate to get an education in the feeble hope it could save them from a lifetime of subsistence farming. It was not much of a life, thought Melanie sadly. For most pupils education ultimately meant they would still end up toiling in meagre fields; with the swing of the hoe punctuated by an odd remembered line of Shakespeare, or poem proclaimed to a cow's arse as its hooves sucked and slopped through the red mud.

She could smell the stale sweat on the children from a distance. But the expression on their faces, their desperation to learn, dissipated her cynical rage. It wasn't the children's fault.

They turned to her with nervous looks in case she should shoo them away, but with a smile and a wink she bade them stay. These kids were united by poverty. It might say Hutu or Tutsi on the identity cards, but for everyone it said 'zero' on their bank book. She knew that it was kids like these she wanted to reach out to.

She had been close to tears, but the children's state of need reminded her; the pain was theirs to feel, only hers to sympathise with. Blubbing wouldn't help them. Across the weedy waste ground she spotted Father Ishimwe in the Church garden. Even the priests were part-time farmers and he was tending to some plants. She picked her way over to him.

'Good morning Father,' she called. 'How's your cassava doing?' Ishimwe looked up and smiled.

'It's good, and it's ready,' he replied. Would you like to try some? The root is cold and juicy straight from the ground.'

'Sure. That would be nice.' Melanie replied, though a list of vegetables that tasted finer than cassava was already growing in her mind. With a knife Ishimwe quickly peeled the root and handed it to her. It looked like a white carrot and tasted starchy, like potato; but it was moist and surprisingly cold.

'Wow! It is juicy! And it's like it's straight out of the fridge.' She said.

'Yes, it is amazing how it is so cool, even one foot beneath the surface. But, how are you? Shouldn't you be teaching?'

'I don't have any lessons this morning.' She paused and changed her tone. 'Actually, there is something I want to talk to you about. Have you got a few minutes?'

'Of course. Is something troubling you.'

'How did you guess?'

'You were too polite about raw cassava and didn't spit it out.'

Melanie laughed. 'No... it's OK, it doesn't taste of much really,' replied Melanie.

'I don't eat the shit myself.' confessed Ishimwe with a grin. 'Father Patrice can't get enough of it. Come inside, I can offer you a glass of water.' Melanie followed him into the cool of the presbytery on the side of the big Church. As he gave her the water he asked, 'What's the problem.'

'Clement's the problem, but not just him. There's something, I don't know, evil going on round here.'

'That's putting it strongly. What is so bad?'

'Clement gave a speech in class today. In English for my benefit. Have you heard of the Hutu Ten Commandments?'

'Ah, those, yes.'

'Ishimwe, they are horrible.'

'Yes, but you must not take these things too seriously. It's just something these Hutu Power extremists have made up. It's all hot air. Things are not going too well, people are angry, they want someone to blame, so they blame the Tutsi. A peace deal has been signed and, of course some people do not like compromise, but it is only by working together that we can solve our problems. That is common sense and most people believe in common sense. It's just these mad few.'

'Working together? The Rwandan word for that is 'Interahamwe' isn't it? Does it ring a bell?

'Interahamwe? He replied thoughtfully, his eyes downcast. 'I have heard of them.'

'Most of my senior boys are in it and I reckon that every one of them would agree with what Clement said. It's like he is their leader. They've been training with this Interahamwe thing for months. I've seen one of their camps up near Gisenyi. I saw Grégoire there.'

'Really?'

'Yes, and I'll tell you this. Those boys are taught to hate the Tutsi. They know their Ten Commandments.'

'They are young men; young men are often angry. They will mellow as they...'

'You are a Tutsi. What does it feel like to know that the boys who sing in your church, sit in your school, make footballs from your condoms...'

'They're not strictly 'my' condoms Melanie! Please, I am a

priest.'

'Don't make this a joke Ishimwe. It's real. People have a right to equality.'

'We are all equal before God Melanie, they are only boys and they will grow out of this.'

'Do you really think so? You know Joe who helps me out? He was beaten up last week. Just for being a Tutsi. It's wrong.'

'Yes. Of course, it is wrong. If there is a danger of serious trouble Angelique will take herself and Joe to a safe place.'

'Hide in the forests? Like animals? We should do something about this Ishimwe.' As she spoke Father Patrice poked his head round the door, Melanie realised he had been listening outside.

'What is going on here? I heard angry voices on such a sunny day. Miss Hickman. Are you not teaching today?'

'Father Patrice, I'm glad you are here. I was just saying to Father Ishimwe about, well, about the politics going on around here.'

'Miss Hickman, I thought you were here to teach English, not politics.' Father Patrice replied with a smile.

'It's about right and wrong Father.'

'Ha ha!' He laughed. 'That sounds like the Church's job Miss Hickman.' Father Patrice responded. 'You must understand you have come here from... the outside, if you like. You should not judge us by the same standards you would use at home. Rwanda is different.'

'Different? 'The Hutu should stop having mercy on the Tutsi?' 'All Tutsi are blood thirsty', 'all Tutsi are dishonest'. That kind of stuff is the same the world over Father Patrice. We call it racism. That's what Hutu Power is; Racism.'

'I am a Hutu Miss Hickman,' replied Father Patrice. 'Am I a racist?'

'I am not saying that Father. I did not say...'

'I am very glad to hear that Miss Hickman. Your command of English is excellent, but it does not qualify you to teach us politics or morality, it qualifies you to teach English. And that is why you are here. The children need a teacher of English. They do not need political interference, nor does the school, and nor do I. However well intended that interference is.'

'I do not mean to interfere, and I did not call you racist...'

'No, you did not, but you seem to be critical of all Hutus. Maybe you should ask yourself some deeper questions. Are you always right because you are from the West? Because you are from a rich country? Because you are white? Find the answers to those questions before you lecture us on racism. Please. You have a dream Miss Hickman,' he chuckled. 'But it is a dream deeply only rooted in the American dream. That one day this nation will rise up and live out the true meaning...'

Father Patrice's voice tailed off into silence as he walked out of the room and into the body of the Church. Through the door Melanie watched him genuflect before he stepped onto the sacred space of the altar and disappear into the vestry on the right, still intoning the words of Martin Luther King. Melanie and Ishimwe stood in silence. Ishimwe wanted to speak but struggled to find the words. After a minute or so of silence Melanie at last heard her own feelings vented quietly, but sincerely, at the end of a long-exhaled breath of despair.

'I don't know what to say, I am so... so angry,' said Ishimwe in a low, resigned voice.

'I know what you mean,' said Melanie and nodded to nobody in particular. 'Well, I have to get back to school. I am paid to be a teacher. Father Patrice was right about that much. Sorry if I came over a little crazy just then. Clement upset me, but, I've gotta get back in there.'

'I understand. Maybe I'll see you later.'

'Yes, thanks Ishimwe, maybe later.' Melanie left the vestry and headed back to school.

*   *   *

The rest of the day passed uneventfully. Clement stayed

out of her way and she did not see her class of senior boys again. As she made her way back to her rooms in the early evening, she saw Ishimwe walking towards her.

'Hello, Melanie, I'm glad I caught you.'

'You are lucky Ishimwe, you timed your visit well. I was just about to go the cinema, after a visit to the bowling alley of course, and maybe dining at a Chinese restaurant later.'

'Yes, of course! I was going to see the Manet exhibition at Kinigi art gallery myself, his still lifes are exquisite. The evening entertainment is so abundant round here. You must have a busy social life. Shall I call by another time?'

'Well, since you're here. I suppose I could re-schedule my engagements.'

'That would be marvellous. Would you like to go for a walk with me? I can show you the sights of Kinigi.'

'Will there be Ankole cattle and banana plantations to look at?'

'The finest. I know where there is a field of sorghum too.'

'Sorghum! Really? Well, how could I say no to life in this fast lane?'

Melanie put on her baseball cap and the two set off down the road to the village centre.

'Have you always lived round here Ishimwe?'

'No. This is my home village, but I have travelled a little. I studied in Kigali and spent a year in Rome.'

'Rome! Wow! I'd love to go there. What was it like? I bet it was an amazing place.'

'Yes. I loved it. The mix of old and new is wonderful. You can sit at a street cafe having a coffee in this century, staring at a building from 2000 years ago.'

'What was your favourite building? The Vatican?'

'No, the Vatican is big and powerful, but it is not beautiful. It just stands there and says; 'Look at me! I am the Catholic Church. Big and Powerful'. It has no charm. Most of all I loved the Pantheon. The temple to all the gods, mine included.'

'I like that idea.'

'One day I will go back there.'

'Will you be allowed?'

'I am allowed a holiday once every few years. Or I could go and do further studies. The Church likes to pull you back into the centre once in a while. To remind you who is the boss.'

'Overseas travel must be seen as quite a perk in a country like Rwanda.'

'Oh yes, not many people get the chance to fly, it is a privilege. Priests have a high status in this country, and we are treated with a lot respect.'

'Don't you have to take a vow of poverty?'

'Only if you are in a religious order. Mind you, you could take a vow of poverty round here and still be richer than your neighbours. We take a vow of celibacy, so I am not allowed to have a wife or a girlfriend.'

'Or sex.'

'Or sex. And I cannot have a boyfriend before you ask.'

Melanie laughed, 'Ishimwe! I was not going to ask that.'

'Good. Actually, you will not hear homosexuality even mentioned in this country, nor in many African countries that I know of.'

'Why? There must be just as many people inclined to be gay.'

'Yes, but the cultural taboo against it is very strong. In a way it is seen as a white man's condition.'

'Do you regret not being able to have a wife and a family?'

'I am married to the Church. My exclusive relationship is with God. That gives me time to be a better priest,' he opened his arms and indicated the surrounding countryside. 'I have a family, it is massive, everyone in the parish of Holy Family are my children, my brothers and my sisters. Hutu or Tutsi, I don't care which.'

'You're a hero Ishimwe!'

'No, I'm not. I'm just trying to live out my faith. Trying to make a difference.'

'I wish I had your faith.'

'I sometimes wish I didn't.

*   *   *

The walk to the centre of Kinigi didn't take long. It had been market day, but the stalls were closed or closing down as they approached. A man walked past balancing a banana tree on his head, a little boy followed him pushing a wheel attached to a wooden stick. He was pretending it was a car. He made noises, revving the engine up, then skidding with imaginary brakes. The boy waved and smiled at them, and then he ran towards Melanie with his arms outstretched. His father called him back before he reached her.

Melanie had grown used to drawing interested stares from the locals, she felt she was fair game as they didn't see many white people around. They knew who she was by now however and she was rarely pestered. There were small stores and cabarets around the square and they were open for the few shoppers that remained. Ishimwe and Melanie went into a shop that sold groceries and basics, oil, flour, salt and the beer they had really come for. He bought a 12-bottle case. The shopkeeper was happy to arrange an instant delivery so they would not have to carry it back. A lanky teenager appeared, popped the box of beer on his head, and set off to Melanie's address.

They stepped out of the shop and walked through the bare frames of market stalls. The very emptiness of the square invited introspection. As they set off on the journey back to the school Ishimwe spoke.

'You've had a tough day. I worry about you. You came here to teach, and you have to deal with all these bad things. Are your still glad you came?'

'Yes, I am, even now I guess.' Then she laughed as she said; 'it's been an experience! I feel like I've got more than I bargained for. I like the teaching part, I suppose I am 'doing good', if you like. I can't bear all the tension I feel around me. They didn't tell us about that before we came.'

'But you are doing good! Trust me. The boys in your classes will be proud to a have a real American as their teacher. They will be showing off to their friends about that,' said Ishimwe. 'You will not realise but you are doing good just by here. Rwandans feel forgotten by the world, especially the young ones. They know enough about the lives of their age group in America and Europe to know they lag behind. Just by being here you connect them to the bigger, wider, world.'

'Thanks, that's a nice thing to say.'

'But it's true. People like you are the beginning of a new future. Deep down all the people know we need to change if our children are to have happy, long lives. We have to move forward. And we need peace to prosper, that's why I am not worried about all this Interahamwe nonsense. Most people are good; the only problem is they believe too easily that others are bad.'

'That's what makes them so angry.'

'Yes, but everyone knows we need peace and harmony, not violence and anger.'

*   *   *

Back at Melanie's rooms Ishimwe's shopping was waiting for them.

'Ah look! I see our delivery boy has left the beer outside your door. Twelve bottles, far too much for you Melanie, I'd be worried if you drank all that this evening.'

'Well perhaps you would be able to help me?'

'I'd consider it an unwelcome duty. The idea horrifies me, But, if you are twisting my arm...'

'You don't take a vow stay sober then?'

'Quite the opposite. You need a drink to live with Father Patrice. To be fair, he needs one to put up with me.'

'You seem very different types, of priests, of people, of Catholics even.'

'Yes, Patrice is of the older generation. Thank you,' said Ishimwe, opening a beer.

'What was I saying? Ah yes. Patrice. The second Vatican council in the 1960s changed the Church, but not the old guys like him. He's a good man, but he doesn't like change. But then, who does?'

'Patrice is a Hutu, isn't he? You are a Tutsi. Is that a problem for you? Or him?'

'No no. We are brothers in Christ first, fellow priests. We have our disagreements but, as Saint Paul wrote, neither Jew nor Gentile, slave or free, male or female, Hutu or Tutsi, it is being a Christian that counts. That is our bond.'

'Now I don't believe Saint Paul actually mentioned Hutu and Tutsi, did he?'

'Well, you have me there, now that you brought it up, I'd have to check the Bible.'

'Damn, you've just reminded me of those Hutu Ten Commandments,' said Melanie.

'Sorry.' Offered Ishimwe. 'Do you know, they were published in a stupid magazine about four years ago,' said Ishimwe, but then he fell silent and it seemed a shadow passed over his face. After a moment he continued.

'Today, walking into Kinigi, we passed my family home.'

'You did not say anything.'

'No, because, really, it is the just the site of my family home. There are some broken walls left, that's all. It was destroyed.'

'When? What happened?'

'Over the last fifty years, Tutsi history has been a series of periodic massacres, burnings, and beatings. My family got caught up in one in the 1960s. Fortunately some good neighbours warned us, and we escaped with our lives. We survived; several thousand were not so lucky.'

'Several thousand people were murdered? I never heard

about this.'

'The world is not interested in our tragedies.'

'Where are your family now?'

'We lived in a refugee camp in Uganda for a while. When I was eighteen, I decided to become a priest, largely as a result of my experience with the Church in the camp. The priests gave us so much; education, medicine and most importantly, hope. That is why I am sat here now with this collar on. I guess I want to give something back, to say thank you to those that helped me back then.'

'It's one hell of a thank you. You're a good man Father Ishimwe.'

'Well it is nice of you to say so. Do not forget that you are also doing very good things; especially teaching Joe. The kids at school will get an education, but he is so lucky to have you.' As Ishimwe finished speaking Rosine came running up the path towards them.

'Quickly turn on the radio,' she shouted. 'Bad news.'

'What's happened?' asked Melanie. She leaned through the window into her room and switched her transistor radio on. She asked Ishimwe and Rosine to translate.

'There is more trouble in Burundi. The army is rounding up peasants and massacring them.'

'Why?' asked Melanie.

'Last year Burundi's President Ndadaye was killed,' said Rosine. 'It was a military coup, and it led to a civil war. Many people have been murdered.'

'Is this a problem for you? Said Melanie.

'Yes, Hutu refugees will come here because Rwanda has a Hutu government. Hutu Power will use this as an excuse to create trouble for us.

'Angelique said something like 'there's always signs before trouble'. Is this a sign? Are you in danger?' asked Melanie.

'Maybe,' replied Rosine. 'It depends how people round here react. I need more information.'

'I am going into Ruhengeri this evening,' said Ishimwe.

'Can I come with you?' Asked Melanie.

'Yes, why not? We'll see what we can find out there.'

What they found at Ruhengeri was not what they expected.

11

Later that evening Jean Damascène and friends joined in a noisy debate at Evariste's cabaret.

'If the government will not stand up to the Tutsi cockroaches, we will show them how to.' Jean shouted at his friends.

'Our Hutu brothers should be avenged,' said Oscar. 'But what are we to do?'

'What has been done before. We must not show weakness, we must not show mercy,' said Vincent.

'The Rwandan Patriotic Front will not show any mercy to us,' said Jean.

'RPF spies are everywhere.' Added Oscar. 'Kill a few and show them who is boss.'

'Well said!' Said Jean, waving his drink at Vincent and Oscar, spilling some beer as he did so.

'Careful Jean, beer is more precious than blood to you.' Laughed Evariste, but Jean did not smile.

'No! You be careful Evariste.' Slurred Jean. 'You be careful your Tutsi wife is not a spy.'

'Who do you think you are talking to?' Shouted Evariste, stepping out from behind his bar. 'Are you making trouble for me?'

'Stop! We must not fight amongst ourselves,' said Oscar stepping between the two. 'There are enough enemies without making extra ones.' But Evariste was too angry and Jean would not back down.

'Jean, you are too old to fight,' snarled Evariste, face to face with Jean. 'You have to send your son to do it for you I hear.'

'Remember what I say Evariste.' Jean wagged a finger at

him. 'When the fighting begins, make sure you are in the thick of it, if you want to save your Tutsi bride. Then you can prove whose side you are on.'

This silenced Evariste and he paused. He controlled his anger because he knew Jean was right. He would have to be careful, but he was not going to let Jean get away with that threat in his own cabaret. 'Oh, don't worry about me Jean. I'll be there. I know whose side I am on. I am proud of who I am. And nobody talks to me like you just did in my own cabaret. So, you apologise, or you never drink in here again.'

'Listen, I don't need to...' began Jean.

'I said apologise,' said Evariste firmly. The two men stared at each other in silence for a few moments.

'Come on Jean,' said Oscar. 'Evariste is our friend, you should not have said what you did. Let's calm down.' Jean mumbled something into his drink.

'What was that Jean? I didn't hear it,' said Evariste as Jean backed away from him.

'I said I did not mean it. I am just angry like we all are. You are my friend of course. I am sorry, I did not mean to offend you. How could you think I meant that?' said Jean, fidgeting with his cap.

'Good. Now get out,' said Evariste and went back behind the bar.

The men stood silently, knowing that this exchange had put an end to their evening. Jean put an empty glass on the bar and walked out into the darkness. He guessed he could leave it a few days and hopefully things would be forgotten. He also knew that it was Evariste who had the problem, not himself. Thierry, Daniel, Oscar and Vincent finished their drinks slowly enough, but conversation was slim, and they were soon ready to make their ways home.

'Hey Evariste. It's late for me now. Thank you and good-night,' said Oscar as he placed a conciliatory hand on Evariste's shoulder, 'forget what Jean said. He says too much when he's had a drink.'

'Yes, sure Oscar. It's not a problem,' replied Evariste, as he cleaned a glass with a cloth.

'Good man Evariste, Oscar is right, we are all friends here,' said Vincent as stood beside Oscar. 'Shake my hand. See? We are good. I'll see you tomorrow.' Oscar and Vincent left together.

All the group left in a similar manner, each making his peace with the bar owner. Within twenty minutes Evariste was left alone to pour himself a beer and make plans.

By the time Jean arrived home his mood had improved. He found Grégoire sat outside in the yard. He sat down next to him.

'How was the cabaret?' asked Grégoire.

'It was... interesting.'

'Did you talk about the troubles in Burundi?'

'Yes, of course. Everybody is angry; we need to teach the Tutsis a lesson. We have done it before.'

'Tell me about that.'

'Like the weeds in this yard, when they get too big they need to be chopped down. It is work that has to be done. You have to protect your people. Remember! Mercy is weakness.'

'It would be easy to kill a cockroach, they are not like us.'

'This is what they tell you in Interahamwe,' replied Jean. 'It is true, but they bleed like us, they cry, and they beg to be spared like you or I would. That is when you need to be strong.'

'I am ready to protect my family whatever it takes.'

'It is harder if you know them, a neighbour perhaps,' Jean looked carefully at his son, 'or an old friend or acquaintance.'

'I could do it.'

'Are you sure? What if you had to kill Joseph, the boy you used to play with?'

'Easy. I hate him. You watched me beat him last week, didn't you?'

'Yes. You did well,' said Jean, nodding and patting his son on the shoulder. 'You did me proud. You cannot show mercy to the Tutsi. You cannot let your friends think you are not

100% with them. It is dangerous to do that. I have been there, I know what I am talking about.'

'When the time comes, I will be ready. I will do what I have to.' Grégoire stood up, 'I am not tired, I'm going for a walk for a while. Goodnight.' Grégoire left his father on his own.

It was dark already, but the moon was up, and it was easy enough to make his way towards the deserted market place of Kinigi. He thought of what his father had said. He was ready to do what was necessary though beating up Joe with his friends was hardly a challenge. Still, it rankled him that Joe had stood up to them. He was not the coward he had been as a child.

Grégoire's memory conjured up other images of Joe; racing him up the hill, playing football, they were night-watchmen together once. The tiniest flower of sympathy for Joe began to bloom deep within him, but Grégoire quickly shut such thoughts of his mind. It was not Joe's fault he was a Tutsi, but it was the Tutsi's fault that they were outcasts. They brought it on themselves. Grégoire could not allow himself to feel any sympathy for Joe. He would not let his people down and Joe was not his people.

As he walked on he dreamed of being the hero in battle, bullets flying and bombs exploding. He would protect his family against the RPF rebels. His father would see the man his son had become and be even more proud of him. He conjured up the scene in his mind, the parade ground and the military band, the applause as President Habyarimana pinned a medal to his uniform, his comrades cheering in ranks behind him while Rwandan flags fluttered in the breeze.

In the thrall of his daydream he stood to attention in the centre of the road, his chest was puffed proudly out, his arms rigid by his sides. As he paused there, he became aware of rustling footsteps on either side, as if many people were creeping alongside and past him. A shiver went down his back and his ears twitched and tensed as if seeking more information. He leaned forward, his eyes searching for a sign. Then he heard whispered voices, but it was not clear what they were saying, and he wondered why. Then he realised, it was the language that had fooled him. They were speaking English. He gasped in surprise and as he did so a hand came from behind him and covered his mouth. A voice spoke in Kinyarwandan but with an accent he could not place.

'Do not call out. It's OK young man. Do not be afraid. We are not here to hurt you.' Gently Grégoire was turned around and he found himself staring into the face of a tall soldier wearing army camouflage and black rubber wellington boots who smiled indulgently at him.

'Run along young man, run along. Stay indoors tonight, there are soldiers about.'

Grégoire ran.

12

Three hours earlier Melanie had walked with Ishimwe back to the Church. The car was not locked and Ishimwe dropped the keys from behind the sun visor down into his hand.

'Are you sure you are OK to drive Ishimwe? You've had a drink.'

'Only two beers. I'm fine. I will drive slowly'

'You have to, there are no street lights.'

It was a cloudy night without moon or stars and Ishimwe's small Citroen trundled slowly down the road to Ruhengeri, hitting most of the pot holes he would have seen in daytime. The car's headlamps created a corridor of shifting, eerie light to steer down. The wall of darkness on either side was unbroken except when they passed the occasional home where a flicker of an oil lamp, or an open fire, showed there was life in the countryside.

'Doesn't look like anyone else is going into town this evening,' said Melanie.

'I was not expecting much traffic!'

'No, but there's nothing in either direction.' Melanie said. Ishimwe did not reply. He thought it was a bit odd too, it made him feel uneasy, and he did not want to worry Melanie.

After an hour it seemed that there were more and more of the occasional lights along the roadside and the road itself became smoother; it was better maintained near the town Melanie recalled. Within five minutes they had pulled into Ruhengeri town centre and the glimpse of electric lighting gave it a feel of civilisation. There were some basic shops, cafes and restaurants. The bars looked like places you would want to go for a drink, unlike the Kinigi cabarets which were basically garden sheds that sold alcohol. There were even some white tourists walking about as the town catered for the gorilla trekking trade. Ishimwe slowed down and parked the car.

'Come. Let's see if there's any gossip' he said.

They walked into a brightly lit cafe and took two stools at the bar. There were not many customers in and they all briefly turned to assess the newcomers. Two middle aged white men quickly resumed their conversation in French; the locals looked at them suspiciously. Melanie was almost certain more than one had said 'Tutsi' to their partner.

'It's even worse than Kinigi here,' muttered Ishimwe. 'They could rename Ruhengeri 'Habyarimana Hutu town' and they'd all be happy,' he then turned to the bartender. 'Excuse sir, a coffee for myself and...'

'A beer,' said Melanie 'Primus?' The bar tender went to get their drinks. 'Do they assume you are a Tutsi because you are tall?

'Yes, and of course they are right!' laughed Ishimwe. 'Mind you both of my brothers are short. If they walked in, they'd probably nudge each other and say 'Look! Tutsi dwarves'.'

'I've thought that before today. This Tutsi tall and slim, Hutu short and broad-shouldered stuff is crap.'

'It gets worse. You'll hear some people complaining that Tutsi women have nicer skin.'

'Rosine has nice skin.'

'Rosine has a nice apartment, a professional job and a good diet.'

'And good skin.'

'Yes. Great skin. Beautiful, smooth, skin. Skin any woman would be proud of. Skin any man would long to...' he paused looking into the distance with a pretended dreamy expression on his face. 'Ah! Celibacy is not easy sometimes.' Then he turned with a wry smile and a wink. 'To Rosine's skin!' And raised his coffee cup in salutation.

'Rosine's skin,' laughed Melanie, chinking her beer bottle against Ishimwe's cup. But before she could bring the bottle to her lips, the lights went out. The silence that followed was quickly filled with conversation, some groans and some laughter. The electricity failed regularly in Ruhengeri. With a resigned sigh, the face of the bartender seemed to float away into the darkness, illumined by the flame of his cigarette lighter.

'It's not just the bar. The whole street is dark,' said Ishimwe as he got up off the floor, walked to the door and looked out. He leapt backwards at the sound of a large bang that was quickly followed by the 'snap', 'snap' of automatic gunfire down the street.

'Melanie, get down.' shouted Ishimwe as he rushed over to her, though she was already crouching on the floor. They huddled down next to their stools at the bar. The gunfire continued sporadically, there were indecipherable shouts too, but shouts of excitement rather than anger or fear.

'What's going on?' she whispered.

'I don't have a clue,' he replied. The shadow of a man appeared in the doorway. He shouted something in Kinyarwanda to the cowering customers. Ishimwe translated.

'He told us to keep quiet, stay down and not to move. We are not to go outside, or we could be shot. They don't want to hurt civilians.'

'Oh God,' gasped Melanie.

'And, I think he just told me something else. His accent. He's not from round here. That was a Ugandan accent.'

'What do you mean?'

'This must be the Rwandan Patriotic Front. The RPF, here, in Ruhengeri. Good Christ what are they up to?' said Ishimwe.

'Do you think it's an invasion?'

'I don't know. I must get you somewhere safe.

'Is this a war?'

'I don't know Melanie. I'm guessing. There has been no more gunfire. Shhh... the soldier has come back.'

Just as he returned so did the electricity supply and the lights came back on in the bar. The soldier came in and spoke in Kinyarwandan, after he had finished the Rwandans in the room stood up, collected their belongings and made ready to leave. Ishimwe went over to him and had a brief conversation, pointing over his shoulder at Melanie. Their chat was relaxed and Ishimwe's smile suggested it had a positive outcome, he soon returned.

'It's OK. They are telling people to go home and remain indoors; they don't expect to be here long. He will escort you to the Hotel Muhabura; there are some Americans and other foreign nationals there. You will be safe.'

'What about you?'

'He says it is OK for me go on to the Church. Do not be afraid, this soldier will escort you there. His name is David, he's alright. In fact, he is quite talkative.' Melanie followed Ishimwe to the doorway where David waited, leaning against the doorframe, his green army uniform unbuttoned at the collar. 'Hello David,' said Ishimwe, 'this is my friend Miss Hickman. Please look after her.'

'Do not worry Father. She will be perfectly safe with me, there is no fighting where we are going. The streets are empty except for RPF soldiers. Miss Hickman, please follow me and be assured we mean no harm to any civilians.'

David led the way out onto the street. He had a casual, loping stride and he was very calm though his eyes scanned the quiet street attentively. The distant gunfire she had heard earlier had faded to the occasional far off 'pop' of small arms. It was a quiet, warm evening and stars shone overhead. Lights peeped out from homes as people twitched their curtains to see what was going on outside. Melanie spotted other RPF soldiers patrolling the sidewalks, occasionally David waved to these men, and they acknowledged him as if he were a superior officer. He seemed confident they were in a safe area and it was not long before he attempted to engage her in conversation.

'You are American Miss Hickman?'

'Yes, you spotted my accent then, not all Rwandans do. Your English is very good.'

'Thank you. I speak four languages. English is a useful one to have. Are you here on holiday to see the gorillas?'

'No, I am teacher.'

'That is good to hear!' replied David, 'Do you teach in Ruhengeri?'

'No, but near here, in a little village called Kinigi.'

'Ah yes! The village is small but Commune Kinigi, the local area, it is quite big actually. We have been through there tonight.'

'Do you mind me asking what is going here? My friend Father Ishimwe seemed very surprised to see you here.'

'Not at all Miss Hickman, I want you to ask. When you get home please tell the truth about us, tell people what you see,' he answered. 'Firstly, we have paid a visit to Ruhengeri which will make the government very angry. Then we have, I shall say, withdrawn some money from the bank; money which had been stolen by President Habyarimana from the people. We have freed 200 political prisoners all of whom want to join us. We have also visited bases belonging to the army and captured many weapons.'

'Visited?'

'Yes.'

'You mean attacked?'

David gave a deep giggle. 'Visited is a much nicer word!'

'Were there many casualties?'

'Not many, it is hard to kill soldiers who are running very

fast in the opposite direction!' he replied with a grin. 'OK we have arrived, this is the Hotel Muhabura.'

David led her up some steps onto a paved patio area in front of a humble single storey building. There were some cheap plastic chairs and tables scattered around as if hastily abandoned. Dim lights were visible inside and she picked up a quiet hum of conversation from within. 'We say goodbye now. It has been a pleasure to meet you Miss Hickman. Tomorrow we will be gone. I wish you all the best in your teaching career.' David tilted his head slightly and, with a smile, he left. She watched him go for a second, but he turned and waved her in through the patio doors. As she reached them, a man came out to greet her.

'Hi. Come in. Are you OK?'

'Yes, I'm fine,' Melanie answered. Once inside she was introduced to the other people the RPF had brought to the hotel. There were about half a dozen; a couple of researchers from the Karisoke Gorilla Centre in the mountains and an IMAX film crew. All were Americans except for one French cameraman, they had been filming a movie for National Geographic. Introductions over they all sat down at the bar on plain wooden stools with square raffia-work seats.

'Can I get you a drink?' said the guy who had first met her at the entrance. He introduced himself as John and was dressed like the others for a day's work in the rain forest; muscular hiking boots, safari clothes stained with dried mud, and such an excessive number of zipped and button-down pockets that he looked like a khaki advent calendar.

'Yes thanks, a beer would be nice.' John turned to the bar and ordered her a Primus. The bartender had a spring in his step and served drinks with a snappy panache. John turned back to Melanie.

'Yes. This is a weird situation but the RPF guys seem OK. Gilbert, the owner here, is the happiest hotelier in town.' At this Gilbert smiled and served up Melanie a cold beer on a paper drip mat as if he were handing out Singapore slings at

Raffles. Running the bar was a humble calling, but he elevated the role to a profession with his attention to detail.

'For you Madame, may I present, one cold Primus,' he beamed.

'Thank you,' said Melanie, turning to John she continued. 'The soldier who brought me here was pretty talkative, like he was enjoying himself.'

'Was it a guy called David?' asked John scratching his chin through his beard.

'Yes.'

'He brought us in too. Maybe he does public relations for them, the RPF are well organised.'

'Well it sounds like they got a massive chunk of money, weapons and new recruits tonight according to David.'

'And a propaganda victory,' said John. 'It's so cheeky and it makes the Rwandan regular army look incompetent. The RPF are so well disciplined. They have amateur resources but a professional attitude. The regular army has it the other way around, the RPF would take this country fast if it weren't for French support.'

'French interference you mean,' chipped in Georgia from the chair behind John.

'It sounds like you've met these RPF people before Georgia,' said Melanie.

'Yes, from time to time. Their camps are in the Parc National des Volcans, and just over the border in Uganda. They don't bother us, and they don't bother the gorillas. They pass through and leave us alone. Have you been up to see the gorillas?'

*   *   *

The evening panned out from there and more rounds of beer came over the bar. As in her weekend in Kigali Melanie enjoyed hearing the accents of home. Georgia spoke with a passion for the mountain gorillas. Melanie was initially impressed but wanted to know her opinions on the local people. It was late in the evening and Georgia slurred her answer a little.

'The Rwandans? Listen if we left it to the Rwandans there would be no gorillas, there would be no Parc National des Volcans. Nothing. There would be empty bloody farmland.'

'But farmland isn't empty. It grows food.'

'Really? Amazing. Food for the Hutsi and the Tutus?'

'Comic genius,' replied Melanie.

'Oh, come on, Hutty Tutty whatever. You've seen how these people live. Don't get me wrong, the poverty is sad and all, but they bring it on themselves. They're so corrupt. We throw millions of dollars at this country and 90% of it gets stolen by Habmariyana and his cronies.

'Habyarimana.' Corrected Melanie.

'Whatever. Listen, there's only three hundred mountain gorillas left in the world. They are a species under threat of extinction. They are precious.'

'So are the people.'

'The people have a choice. Every few years they are at each other's throats, murdering and raping like savages. Because that's what they are. Savages.'

'Savages? Did you say that to Gilbert when he served your drink?' Melanie shot back, Georgia flushed, and her eyes flashed around the room in the silence that followed. Gilbert looked uncomfortable as he polished a glass behind the bar.

Georgia sat back in her seat. 'Shit. I mean, sorry folks, it's getting late and I guess I've had a few too many.' She turned to Gilbert behind the bar. 'I apologise Gilbert. I did not mean that honey, give me a hug and say goodnight. I need to go to bed.' She stood up and leaned over the bar to hug Gilbert, who accepted it with a meek smile. 'Ijoro rwiza, Gilbert, goodnight. Goodnight everyone.' Then Georgia left for her room down the corridor. The group was subdued, and Melanie felt, unjustly, that she was part of the reason for it. John was quick to play peacemaker.

'She was wrong to say that, but don't think badly of her. She would die for the mountain gorillas.'

'The local people are close to dying for them. They're malnourished because they don't have enough farmland. Hey, I care about the monkeys; I just care about the people more.'

'Ah now you see, actually, they aren't monkeys, because they have....' began John, but he stopped when he saw Melanie's raised eyebrow. 'You knew that! Ha! You got me. But I think the gorillas and the people can live side by side. The gorillas earn big money for the country. Do you know how much you have to pay to see them? Just for one hour even?'

'I've no idea,' said Melanie.

'Hundreds of dollars, they could charge more, I honestly think there's no limit. They should build a few discreet luxury hotels; have them staffed with local people. Gilbert here could make a fortune. Employ guides and park guards from this area. It is tourism that could save both Hutu and Tutsi one day.'

'Maybe. I'd like to think the kids I teach have a better future than Disney Gorilla Land.'

'But it could be a part of their future. Many countries earn big bucks from tourism. Rwanda is a country with great prospects.'

THE JEALOUSY OF CAIN

1

Rumours of trouble in Ruhengeri spread quickly to Kinigi. Angelique heard the whispers of anger around her home and interpreted them as a warning. If they ran now, they could escape the coming storm of anger, any delay and they could be caught in it. After waking Joe she quickly packed some supplies for hiding in the mountains. She knew a place and hoped any would be pursuers would be afraid that the RPF were active in the area. They hurried round to Grace and Denyse's house to warn them, snaking through shadowed orchards as silently as they could. All four yelped with fear when they met suddenly in a clearing under the moonlight.

'Grace! Denyse!' panted Joe. 'Thank God we found you.'

'We were coming for you,' whispered Denyse.

'Quickly, we must get out of the village as soon as we can. Up the slopes. Into the forest,' said Grace, her eyes glittering in the moonlight.

'I've got blankets and some food,' said Angelique.

'Same here. No water, but we can find that on the mountain,' replied Grace. 'Let's go.'

'No. Wait. We should separate. We make more noise running together,' said Angelique. 'There's more chance of getting caught. We should split up.'

'Mother, we don't have the time to talk about this,' hissed Joe in panic.

'You're right Angelique. Grace, come with me. We can meet on the mountain where it gets really steep.'

'Where the bamboo starts. Yes, it will be easy to hide there, it's so dense. Good luck both of you. We'll be OK, don't worry.'

The four exchanged quick hugs and then went on two separate paths under the dense cover of the banana leaves. They knew the many routes that led to the forest. In the dark it would be difficult to spot a still, crouching figure, even with a powerful torch; and nobody had one of those. Angelique strode forward with a tenacity that belied her slender physique. She had a knife and was ready to use it. If it was necessary, she would sacrifice herself to give Joe a chance to escape. Grace led Denyse with the same mother's resolve.

The first part of the journey was silent running, crouching in ditches at the faintest of sounds, hiding from the moonlight as best they could. Finally, both couples had reached the safe harbour of the trees; albeit a mile apart from each other. Once in the forest they relaxed a little. They had heard no angry shouts, saw no flashes of moonlight on machetes. They had left Kinigi behind and had a head start if it came to a chase.

After two hours going up steep slopes Joe and Angelique reached the start of the bamboo and walked along the path at its edge. Joe took confidence from his mother's experience and surety. She did not seem afraid, so he told himself he did not need to be. Yet every tree, every shadow, seemed to take the shape of a face or a crouching figure. Each rustle of the forest held a threat, and he was startled every few seconds.

Denyse announced her hidden presence by clamping her hand over his mouth and dragging him close to her. Joe's choke of terror quickly turned to a sigh of relief so deep he nearly fainted into her arms as he emptied his lungs of breath.

'Jesus,' he gasped.

'No, not him, not yet,' whispered Denyse with a smile.

Angelique and Grace clasped hands and stared silently at each other for a moment.

'We need to get away from here,' said Grace.

'Yes. We know of a cave under the cliff face,' said Joe. 'It's not too far, maybe another hour or so in the dark. There is bamboo all around it, we will be well hidden.'

'Take us there, Joe,' said Grace.

As they set off climbing Grace thought that if Joe and Angelique knew of the cave, then so did others. However, no one was following and when the sun rose, they would have a good view of the slopes to Kinigi a few miles to the south. The final journey up the slopes of Mount Sabyinyo was tiring, but they sensed an emptiness surrounding them. The volcano had plenty of animal life but there were no human predators, no human noses tilted into the breeze sniffing for their scent.

Their spirits rose a little as they climbed the mountain. Its sparkling crisp air held out the hope of sanctuary; as if it was too serene or sanctified to be the scene of violence. Finally, their tired thighs hauled them into the cave Joe had promised, a side altar of Sabyinyo's cathedral, where they could see out the last few hours of darkness. It was time for a brief rest and to gather their strength for whatever lay ahead.

2

At the same time Angelique and Grace were leaving their homes for the mountain Grégoire sprinted through Kinigi to tell his father what he had seen. He sped over the rough ground, leaping over the pot holes made visible by the moonlight. He knew the RPF was all around him hiding in the night, and a frisson of fear shivered down his back as he headed home.

Yet after a few minutes he slowed to a walk and took a deep breath. His fear dissipated to be replaced by feelings of excitement and anticipation. This was the turn of events Interahamwe had trained him for. Strength and energy coursed through him. He was a man, not a boy, and he was not afraid. As he walked on, he felt the thrill of being the bearer of shocking news. The RPF rebels were upon them. He had seen them, spoken to them. He doubted others had done the same, he was wrong in that.

The alleys and passages were dark and empty as he turned the corner into his own yard to find his mother Gloria leaning in the doorway. She stood on her tiptoes and strained to see him as he approached. When it was clear Grégoire was home safe she relaxed and stood back on her heels.

'Mother, I have seen the rebels. They have sneaked through Kinigi. Where is father? Quick. I must tell him.'

'He already knows, others have seen them too. He has gone back to the cabaret to meet his friends. Where did you see them?'

'On the main road to Ruhengeri. One of them grabbed me.'

'Did they hurt you?'

'No.'

'Good. Go to your father. Tell him what you have seen. I will stay here and guard the home.'

As Grégoire turned to sprint off to Evariste's cabaret he did not see his mother reach behind her into the darkness of the house, checking her freshly sharpened machete was within reach.

At the bar the earlier disagreements had been forgotten. Only Hutus were present no Tutsi were to be seen in Kinigi. They were outnumbered ten to one, and they avoided their angry neighbours as best they could. About thirty local men had gathered and Jean Damascène knew them all. Grégoire leaned against a wall in the shadows and watched his father address the meeting.

'Brothers we know what to do. Go home and come back with sharp pangas. We must defend our homes and our families. We must hunt out the spies in our village.' But his words were slurred with drink and he swayed as he fixed the men with a glassy stare. 'Come on. What are you waiting for?'

No one responded to Jean Damascène and Evariste spotted his chance to address the group and take control before it got out of hand.

'We're waiting for the army Jean.'

'We don't need soldiers to fight for us.'

'No, Jean, not FOR us, we need them to fight WITH us,' he stressed, 'the rebels are armed, we have no guns.'

'We must protect our homes,' said Jean.

'Has any home been attacked?' Evariste asked the on-lookers and a range of replies came back.

'No Evariste', I've seen nothing myself' said one, 'My wife saw soldiers at the side of the road' offered another, 'I heard shots in the distance, in Ruhengeri for sure.'

The conversation fell to a rumble of comments and side-long questions between the men.

'Nobody round here has been attacked, not a shot has been fired,' said Evariste. 'Has anyone else had sight of the rebels?' The group fell silent. 'So, we only have rumours,' said Evariste.

Grégoire leaned forward pausing at the crossroads of op-portunity that could bring him to the attention of the older men. Something in him, a wordless certainty, told him this was the not his time, and these were not his comrades in arms. He chose to say nothing. His news would be drowned by the boozy indecision ruling the cabaret gang. One option was to exaggerate and say how an RPF soldier grabbed him, but he had punched him and escaped, but he believed it was shameful to lie. He felt the truth was worse, because the soldier had smiled and promised no harm would come to anyone. The rebel's re-assuring *'we are not here to hurt you'* was an insult. The rebels did not perceive him as a threat, and he longed to prove them wrong. He decided he would save his news for a later day. The anger of these old men was futile; they would do nothing, an aggressive response would only come from a new, younger, force. Grégoire's time was at hand. Interahamwe would be his team. Meanwhile Evariste closed out the discussion.

'OK everybody, I think the best thing we can do is wait till the morning. The army will be here. We will be by their side,' said Evariste, trying to sound a note that was soothing and yet promised future action. He got the balance right because he had dealt with angry drunks many times. 'The only thing we can do till then is go home and protect our families. The army will be here soon. They will need us when they arrive.'

'We should find the Tutsi spies in Kinigi. That is how we should fight,' shouted Jean bitterly.

'Well Jean Damascène, let me guarantee you this,' replied Evariste calmly. 'If we know there is trouble at hand, then so does any Tutsi spy around here. You will find their houses empty. They will have run away. If we are patient they will return, and we will catch them. But we will not catch anyone tonight. Tomorrow we will be ready.'

'And who are you to make this decision for us?' enquired Jean.

'I am not making a decision for anybody.' Evariste calmly but he knew he had won a victory. He had taken leadership of the men this night. Jean's semi drunken state had ousted him from favour. 'I am not telling anyone here what to do. I am just saying what I think is good sense. I will act, when I am ready, I will not run around in the night chasing shadows. I don't know if other people think that is a good idea. That is up to them,' he turned to the men, 'what do you think?'

Again a hubbub ensued but the support for Evariste was clear from the louder comments; 'he's right', 'we don't know what we're looking for in the dark', 'tomorrow is better', 'Evariste is talking sense'. It was as good as a democratic ballot and Evariste had won a landslide victory over Jean, but the ex-leader had a parting shot.

'OK. Tonight we stand by our homes and tomorrow; you will lead us into action Evariste,' said Jean, but then he added more slowly. 'Make sure you lead by example.' With that he left.

Evariste knew what Jean Damascène was referring to. As soon as he heard the news, he had hidden his wife, Sonia. If there was killing, she could be spared, if they were lucky, but he had better not be caught going soft on any other Tutsi.

Tomorrow he would have to lead from the front, machete in hand.

3

Grégoire was awake before dawn the next day. He heard the familiar sounds of morning, his mother preparing some porridge for breakfast, his father breathing heavily as he lifted a large jerry can of full water. There was the same chill in the air and the same smells of home; the smoke from the fire, the pot that hung over it. But in his soul he knew everything had changed. At last there would be action and he would be part of it. The time for talking was over, now was the time for the solutions. Talk was for the old men. He got dressed quickly.

While he ate his porridge stood in the front yard, the recent turn of events announced themselves via the crackle of automatic weapons in the distance. He and his father shaded their eyes and looked towards Ruhengeri.

'The army arrived in there a few hours ago,' said Jean. 'I heard them in the night.'

'Yes, they woke me too,' replied Grégoire, which was nearly true, something had caused him to turn over, but he wasn't sure what. 'The RPF came out of the forest through here. Do you think they'll return this way?'

'They could do, but I doubt it. It's not the quickest way back to cover. The cockroaches will run for the safety of the trees as soon as they have to face a proper army.'

It was hard to tell from the gunfire where the battle truly raged. It seemed to be sporadic over quite a large area from Ruhengeri back to the mountains a few miles to the north. There was the occasional loud bang and a puff of distant smoke to suggest something bigger than bullets. Neither Jean nor Grégoire wanted ringside seats; they wanted to be in the fight.

'Come Grégoire. Let's go to Evariste's, see if our new leader has the stomach for fight,' he winked at his son but Grégoire saw through his ploy, Jean had been deposed as leader of the

Kinigi men and both of them knew it. He nodded but there was no enthusiasm in his response.

'Lead the way, father.'

At the cabaret Evariste served the ammunition while the men shouldered their arms. Alcohol would ensure the variety of clubs, knives and machetes did their work. An army marches on its belly, a mob marches on its liver. Seeing Jean enter he acted promptly to maintain his position as leader.

'Right men. In five minutes we leave for Ruhengeri. Finish your drink or bring it with you. Vincent, if you need a piss go and have one, we don't want to wait for stragglers.'

The men laughed, Vincent was more enthusiastic for beer than battle.

'Hey Evariste! I get here early, and you make a fool of me? I am ready to fight AND support your cabaret. You should be thanking me,' replied Vincent getting a few laughs.

'And Evariste.' The group fell silent as Jean Damascène's humourless tone changed the mood. 'Lead us into action Evariste. A strong leader leads from the front, with actions not words.'

'Ah Jean, you made it I see. Well if I lead from the front, promise you'll not get left behind at the back old man.' Evariste's reply drew a gasp and some more laughter from the men. Jean was forced to smile and acknowledge the put down and Evariste continued. 'At least keep up with Vincent, make sure he doesn't fall over.'

Again, the crowd laughed but Grégoire did not join in. He was sober. He was not one of the old gang. He was a little ashamed of his father's fall from grace and he made a mental note of Evariste's remarks; he would avenge them one day. He gave Evariste a blank, humourless look to make it clear he did not see the funny side. Evariste paused for a second but did not aim a barb in Grégoire's direction. He decided Grégoire was youngster and not worth his time; but one day he would be a man and it was best he was not an enemy.

The crowd amounted to about 50 men and they set off to

Ruhengeri much as they would to a football match. They chatted in groups and passed round bottles of beer. Oscar put an arm round Grégoire's shoulder.

'Here, have a drink of this,' he offered the straw that was poked into his bottle of urwagwa, Grégoire accepted. 'Are you excited Grégoire?'

'Yes, a little. I wonder what will happen when we get to Ruhengeri?'

'Ah do not be afraid. When the time comes, you will know what to do. You won't let us down.'

'I didn't say I was afraid...' Grégoire began, but Oscar continued regardless.

'There is always a first time, but you are ready. You are a strong, fine young man. Your father is proud of you.' Oscar clapped him on the back, turned away and tuned into another conversation with Daniel and Vincent. Grégoire merely shrugged his shoulders, he found Oscar irritating and patronising. However, the urwagwa had tasted good. Sweet and strong, with the texture and appearance of a muddy puddle, it warmed his throat though it smelled of over-ripe bananas. Grégoire had a look round to see if he could get some more. He spotted Vincent with a bottle and stepped alongside him.

'Hey Vincent. An exciting day.' Grégoire wondered how to encourage Vincent to hand his drink around. 'How's it going with you?'

'Grégoire, young Grégoire,' slurred Vincent. 'Good boy. Have a drink with your father's old friend.' And he passed the bottle over. 'Easy!' thought Grégoire and did his best to disguise a deep slug of the booze as a mere sip.

'Thank you, Vincent.' Grégoire replied. Vincent took the bottle back and raised an eyebrow when he saw how the level had dropped.

'Grégoire, you are your father's son!' he laughed. 'You drink like him, let's hope you can cut like him.' Vincent put his left hand on Grégoire's shoulder, the urwagwa stayed in his right hand, out of Grégoire's reach. The gang moved on at a steady pace.

Halfway to Ruhengeri the sound of heavy vehicles and the bibbing of horns caused the men to stop and step to the side. The regular army, with some units of French troops came trundling up the broken clay road, banging into pot holes and kicking up clouds of dust. The Kinigi men cheered and waved their pangas, shouting encouragement to the soldiers. Though the troops were greeted as comrades in arms they were less impressed by the rabble that hailed them and bestowed only the occasional nod of appreciation. Grégoire looked on in envy, they were not much older than him, and he felt passed over when the trucks had bounced by.

*   *   *

On the outskirts of the town troops government troops manned a road block. There was a lorry on either side of the road and a makeshift barrier with a red and white striped pole, barring their way.

Evariste strode forward to the soldiers. He did not know what to say but hoped, somehow, he and his men would be allowed through to take part. But now that he stood there he felt a fool. 'What did we think they would do when we got here?' 'We had no plan', he thought to himself. Still, he had to play his hand as best he could, he had to be the leader, his wife's life was at stake. He stood tall and tried to appear confident and in control.

'Friends, we are here from Kinigi. We are ready to fight the cockroaches alongside you.' The soldier said nothing but scratched his head, then turned to another and held a whispered conversation. Finally, he turned to back Evariste.

'Wait here.' Then he walked over to a nearby Landrover where an officer was speaking into a radio headset. Evariste waited and watched. Eventually, the officer finished his radio conversation and spoke to the soldier from the road block. He turned around and surveyed Evariste and his raggle taggle mob. With a shake of his head he got out of the vehicle and walked over to Evariste. He put his hand on Evariste's shoulder and led him back to the men so they could hear his words.

'Men. Thank you for coming here today. I salute your courage and patriotism.' The officer leaned forward and shook the hands of some men at the front of the crowd. 'You make me proud to serve my country.' Evariste knew what was coming next. His next sentence would begin with 'but...'

'But, you know, today we have things under control. The rebels have already fled. They are cowards. This battle is won, and soon the war will be. Thank you for your support but the best thing you can do is return to your village. Be vigilant. Watch out for Tutsi spies, they are everywhere. If you find anything suspicious, you must report it to the police.' The officer had said his piece, it was clear he wanted the gang out of his sight. Evariste saw that they, and definitely he, needed to retreat with dignity. He turned to speak to the soldier, gripped his arm firmly and looked him straight in the eyes.

'Thank you. Sir. We will do our best. We wish you every success. If ever you need our help you only need to ask for it.'

At this Jean Damascène thought saw his chance and pushed to the front on the group. 'We did not come here to be sent away like women. We came to fight.' Evariste wanted to reply to Jean, but the officer cut him short.

'You heard what I said. Not today. Thank you. Now it is time for you to go home. My soldiers and I have our jobs to do.'

'And what if I cross your road block?' answered Jean.

'You will be arrested.' Jean was silenced by this and wondered if he should just cross it anyway, but he waited too long.

'Jean,' cut in Evariste. 'Nobody doubts your courage, old friend, but a soldier must obey his orders. The officer has his, and he has given us ours. It is our duty to obey them.' Evariste's words struck a chord with everyone. Obedience to authority was embedded deep in every Rwandan. None of the men thought they had the right to disobey an army officer, and they were beginning to be embarrassed by Jean. Everyone wanted to go back now, the moment had passed.

They were becoming resigned to a sombre journey home when their downbeat mood was contrasted by a new sound; of drums, whistles, running feet and singing. On the other side of the road block a gang of forty or so young men came into view trotting by the side of a French army vehicle. Grégoire instantly recognised the Interahamwe anthem 'Tubatsembat-sembe' - 'Let Us Exterminate Them', ringing with the same energy and power it had at the training camp.

Those were surely his friends' voices, and he dashed forward to see them. A cavalcade of colour jigged along the clay road. It was as if an army had dressed for battle in Hawaiian shirts. Instead of marching they danced and jogged. They sang like a football crowd. Interahamwe looked like a carnival. The new had replaced the old. There was Albert, Cyprien, Placide, and Patrick. They jogged and danced along behind Fabrice who called him.

'We've been waiting for you Grégoire. Here are your colours,' he shouted, running up to the barrier and throwing him a crazy, brightly patterned shirt. 'I have a machete for you too, but I won't throw that!'

Grégoire laughed and slipped off his tee shirt. Turning around he saw Evariste, his father and the Kinigi men watching. He did not need their or his father's, approval. He was in and they were out. Waved on by the army officer, he leapt the barrier and stood face to face with Fabrice.

'Grégoire. We've been here a few hours. I looked for you this morning. Where were you?'

'In the cabaret with my father.'

'I hear he was a good leader in his day.'

'Yes. And now I will be. Do you understand?' Fabrice sensed unspoken danger as Grégoire bristled with violent energy and anger bred by generations of poverty. Grégoire's slow burning rage was like his father's. It fermented during long hard days sweating in the fields and was fed by the knowledge that, when the day was finished, the next day would bring the same unrelenting toil.

'Grégoire! I understand. Hey. Come on, it's me you are talking to, Fabrice.'

'Yes. Fabrice the man who used to be my football captain. I am the captain now rich boy.' He paused to see if Fabrice would challenge him. He didn't. 'OK. We need to hurry, we are falling behind here.' Grégoire broke the contact, and they sprinted to catch up with the rest.

The Kinigi men knew it was time to go; they turned and began the walk back home. However, they were proud that Grégoire had been able to join the fight on their behalf and cheered him as he ran off. This gave Jean some his credibility back. Evariste was still their leader, he had to pass his first test, but he had done well today.

4

A few hours earlier it had still been dark on Mount Sabyinyo when the eerie calls of the night gave way to the affirming birdsong of dawn. There was a blending of the two shifts for five minutes until the daytime sounds filled the air. Grace, Denyse, Angelique and Joe had wrapped themselves in woollen blankets as best they could, but the chill mountain air was damp, and they had slept little. As the sky lightened from black to grey it became possible to look out into the distance and try to guess what was taking place in their village a few miles below them.

They listened to the same sporadic snap and crackle of distant gunfire as did Jean and Grégoire during their breakfast. Unlike Jean and Grégoire they wished to avoid it.

'Well, I think we have three choices,' offered Angelique.

'We go back to our homes if it is safe to do so. If it's not safe, we stay here for a while. Or we go on and find a safe refuge, Uganda has the nearest camps. What do think Grace?'

'The same as you. We can wait here a few days, there is water and food. It's a long walk to Uganda through the mountains and the rainforest; maybe five days.'

'Could we go to the RPF?' suggested Joe. 'They have camps and bases in the forest to the west of here and control some villages just outside the forest.'

'It's not a bad idea. We could go there, but that is where the fighting is, or will be. The RPF has an army camp not a refugee camp,' said Angelique.

'Your mother is right Joe,' said Grace. 'I don't think they would welcome us. They are also surrounded by government troops. Maybe if we could get to Goma in Congo but, again, the army is in the way and they would treat us as spies.'

They all knew that Joe wanted to join the RPF, but this was not the time. Denyse changed the subject. 'What did we manage to bring with us from home? It would be useful to know.'

The little band of refugees pooled their resources. They had two old kitchen knives, the blades bound into the wooden handles with string. Joe had picked up an old machete, but it was not too sharp. Angelique had a plastic water jug that would hold four litres, Denyse earned everyone's respect by producing two plastic cups. They had all grabbed some food and there were a dozen or so cobs of corn, more bananas, and a loaf of bread. For clothing they only had what they wore and the blankets they had draped around their shoulders; they did not need shoes. What they had was not enough, but it was better than nothing. In silence they ate a breakfast of bread, bananas, fresh water and wild melon at the entrance of the shallow cave where they had slept.

After an hour, confident that no one was about, they walked down to the edge of the bamboo thicket and peered through the foliage at the farmer's fields above Kinigi. The only sound nearby was that of nature, constant birdsong, the occasional animal, and the whispering of a slight breeze in the trees and bamboo cane. From the direction of Ruhengeri there was some gunfire as if one army was unsuccessfully searching for its enemy and emptying its weapons in frustration when they could not find it.

'It's very quiet down there. The smoke from cooking fires is all I can see,' said Denyse. 'None of the farmers have gone to their fields. I've never seen them so empty before.'

'I can hear the cows,' said Joe. 'They want to be fed and milked. There owners are not around to see to them.'

'No. I can't think of Tutsi who would stay there right now,' replied Grace. 'I don't know where Charles and Uwase would hide with young children. Maybe they have a Hutu neighbour they trust.' They continued watching in silence for ten minutes until Angelique spoke up.

'Grace, I have made my decision. I am going to go back. There are no men in the fields because there are no men in the village. My guess is that they have gone to Ruhengeri to look for trouble. The sensible, good men will be all that remain. The women I am not afraid of, many are my friends.'

'I will come with you,' said Joe.

'No Joe. The worst that can happen to me is a few insults. You have already had trouble from these idiots, you would be a target. You would only make it riskier for me. I want to bring one of our cows up here. It will only take me four hours at most. Then we will at least have milk no matter what we decide to do, stay here or walk to Uganda.' Angelique stood face to face with Grace and placed her hands on her shoulders. 'Will you stay here with Joe and Denyse? There is no safety in numbers down in the village.'

'Yes, of course I will. But you are tired already Angelique. Maybe you should rest first.'

'No. Kinigi is quiet now. It may not be later. I might even talk to some neighbours and see what the mood of the village is.' With that Grace and Angelique hugged and, for a moment, held each other with a steady gaze.

'Take care Angelique and do not be long.'

'I won't. Joe, you look after these two, they need a strong man like you.'

'Don't you need a strong man to go with you?'

'Ha! No, to me you are always my little boy.' She ran her fingers through his short hair and smiled, shaking his head with her hand. 'Seriously. I'll be fine and I won't be long. You find us more food and water and we'll have an evening meal under the stars.' With a confident smile Angelique turned away and headed down the slope through the forest towards the farmer's fields.

Joe knew she was right, the Hutu men would pick on him, they probably just would wave and say hello to a woman. Grace put her hand round his shoulders and Denyse lightly held his hand.

'Come on Joe. Let's go and find some food,' said Denyse. Joe glanced down the hill once more at his mother, as he did so she turned and waved. Joe waved in return, then turned his back on the slopes, and threaded himself into the shadows of the forest with Denyse and Grace.

*   *   *

After two hours of the steep walk down Angelique climbed over the low stone wall that was the boundary of the national park and stepped out into the sunshine. Walking amongst the crops she kept to the narrow grassy paths, striding or jumping over the many ditches that criss-crossed the hillside. From time to time she looked around to check if she had been seen. The crops grew waist high and she could crouch and hide but other than that there was no cover, fortunately, there were no onlookers. Half an hour later she was at the banana plantations on the northern edge of the village where they had met Grace and Denyse the night before. Walking quickly but trying not to appear as if she was rushing, she went to her home. Her two cows were there, they seemed quite calm and Angelique could see they had been milked and given fresh fodder and water. There were some drops of milk on the floor and a trail to her front door.

She tried to make sense of the scene. Was a thief helping themselves to her empty home or was it a friend looking after her property? The milk droplets had yet to soak into the ground. Her faded and flimsy front door was closed. She decided a thief would have taken her cows, ransacked her home and not bothered to close the door. If someone was still around, it was a friend. She decided the best approach was to appear calm and confident. She stepped up to the door and laid her hand on it.

'Hello?' She called and paused, listening. 'Is there anyone here?'

Gently she pushed the door open, just inside, on the floor, was a plastic bucket filled with milk. As if someone had reached in and placed it there. The room was in silence, fingers of sunlight filtered into the darkness through the gaps in the broken mud wall. The thin rays of sunshine picked out tiny particles of dust that sparkled as they swirled in the air. The corners of the room rested in deep shadow.

Angelique sat down on her only chair and looked around. Though the place spoke eloquently of poverty, it was rich with memories for her; watching Joe grow up, sharing his trials and games, his tears and laughter. She had spent herself on more than ten years as a single mother, nurturing him, preparing him to be a man in the world. Her life was one of sacrifice but sacrifice gladly made. Resting on the table was a faded colour photograph of herself, Joe, and Daniel his father. She held it in a stream of light that broke into the room and stroked the surface of the picture gently with her hand as if she was caressing Daniel's face, connecting with him again. She wondered where he was right now, and whether they would ever live together again. Hopefully he was safe. The thought of safety brought her back to the present as she heard a sound outside the door.

'Angelique?' said a familiar voice.

'Gloria?' replied Angelique, rising with the picture still in her hand. 'Is that you?' Gloria's frame filled the doorway, blocking her view outside and any escape route past her. With the bright sunlight behind she could not read the expression on her face.

'Angelique, where have you been? I was worried about you? The words expressed concern, but the tone lacked warmth thought Angelique.

'I have been here Grace. Where else would I be? Let's go outside. How are you? We haven't chatted for a while.'

'I'm very well thank you. I was passing by this morning and heard your cows making a fuss, they had not been milked.' Gloria turned and stepped into the sunlight, Angelique followed.

'Ah, yes. We milked them last night because Joe and I went into the forest looking for wild melon early this morning. It is in season. Did you milk my cows again this morning?'

'No, I do not know how to do that. I would be afraid in case one kicked out at me. I told Sonia, and she did it for you.'

'Oh, thank you.'

'Looking for wild melons?' asked Gloria after a pause.

'Yes,' replied Angelique and another pause ensued.

The silence continued for a few moments till Angelique continued. 'Gloria, why are you playing this game with me?'

'What game?'

'You know where we have been, and you know why we went there.'

'Oh, Angelique, I am not playing a game with you. I know why you ran to hide, and I know why you are here now. You are a Tutsi spy. The guns of your rebel friends are firing as we speak. The real men of Kinigi have gone to fight in Ruhengeri even though the enemy is on their doorstep spying on them. Go and live in the forest like an animal or go to Uganda. If you or your son come back here...' Gloria's voice trailed away.

'What?' Demanded Angelique. 'What will you do Gloria?' But Gloria had said what she wanted to and began to walk away. As she left she half turned and looked over her shoulder.

'You have heard my advice. Go back to the forest. Do not come back to Kinigi. Ever.'

Angelique wanted to shout something at the departing Gloria but there was no point. The woman was married to the meanest drunken bully in Kinigi, she and Jean Damascène were a well-matched couple. As Angelique watched her walk away she realised that, ironically, her advice was good; the best thing Angelique could do now was to leave and never come back. Joe had been beaten up once. The threat of murder hung in the air; she had heard it in Gloria's voice. The country was bad and getting worse. The gorillas in the forest had better protection than the Tutsis, more people cared about them. It was time to leave.

Angelique looked up at the sky. It was almost noon, and she had already stayed longer than she intended. Her reason for being there came back to her, she could take one cow back with her, the milk would help and at some point they could sell it. She chose the younger of the two called Umuseengo, it was her favourite and was brown with white patches. The cow would slow her down, but it would be worth it. She unhooked the gate to the small pen and went in, slipping a rope harness over its head.

'Umuseengo, come on beauty, come with me now. There's a good girl. Come with momma.' She led the cow out and it followed obediently. The cow resisted when Angelique began to lead it through the banana plantation, this was not the usual route to the fields of fresh grass, but it trusted the soft voice and steady hand that stroked its back.

The plantation hid Angelique from the village but it also hid the village from her. She did not see that Gloria had waited out of sight to see which direction she left in. She did not see Gloria run off to meet the angry, drunken, gang return from their unsuccessful trip to Ruhengeri. She did not see Gloria telling them where they could find a Tutsi spy.

Angelique's pace slowed after they left the shade of the banana plants. As soon as they entered the farmland, the cow was attracted to the juicy green cassava leaves and it was too much of a struggle to stop her snacking. Angelique had to hope that she would quickly eat her fill and move on. While the cow ate, and trampled the crops, Angelique scanned the horizon and the edge of the village for any sign of pursuit. The cow showed no signs of finishing her meal. Finally, Angelique could wait no more and she tugged fearfully at the rope.

'Come on, please, Umuseengo, we cannot wait here. Come on!' said Angelique, her voice an angry, frustrated whisper. At last the cow seemed to get the message, and it gave into the insistent pulling on the rope biting into its neck. It stepped back from the field and began slowly, too slowly, to trudge along the narrow grassy path, up the hillside towards the forest and safety.

During the struggle to control the cow Angelique had stopped looking about her. The Kinigi men had advanced up the slopes on her right and left flanks, a dozen or so on each side. A ripple of disturbance was flowing through the crops from the direction of the village where another line of men advanced up the slope towards her, crouching low. She looked ahead to her escape route, but the trap was closing, she would not make it to a hiding place in the forest. Angelique dropped the leash attached to Umuseengo and ran a few paces in desperation but already she could see it was too late. She could not outrun them, barefoot and uphill on a ploughed field. She looked down into her hand and saw that she still held the picture. She saw Daniel, baby Joe, and herself smiling. She held the picture tightly, finally crumpling it in her fist. She would not die without a fight. Evariste signalled to the men, and they closed in the circle.

5

The Muhabura aspired to be a two-star hotel. However, despite the enthusiasm and energy of the Gilbert the owner, manager, bartender, cook and cleaner, it would be some years before this lofty ambition could be achieved. The rooms were clean but basic. Each had a plain wardrobe of pale, cheap, wood that had a distant memory of varnish on the door. There was a table with a red formica top, chipped at the edges, and a bedside lamp with no bulb in it. The bed sagged in the middle, but the sheets smelled fresh enough. As a concession to getting ready for sleep Melanie had removed her shoes before climbing in. The 'guests' had gone to bed about 3.00 am when even Gilbert's eternal smile had begun to look jaded. Throughout the night the occasional metallic click of gunfire would ordinarily have woken her, but the alcohol ensured she only turned over and mumbled.

She was not sure what woke her up, but there was sunshine coming in through a gap in the curtains, morning clatter from the kitchen, and the smell of cooking. She popped her shoes on and wandered into the corridor, following her nose to the dining room. Her fellow guests, the gorilla researchers and the film crew were already up and enjoying a breakfast of omelette, bread and coffee.

'Melanie, come and join us.' John stood up and pulled a chair out for her. 'Gilbert! Another breakfast please, and more coffee it's superb.'

'Of course, Rwandan coffee, best in the world.' Gilbert said with a smile and, as anxious to please as ever, almost skipped into the kitchen.

'Yes, the coffee is great,' said Georgia. 'I'm not sure about the powdered milk though.' She smiled at Melanie as a peace offering, embarrassed by her behaviour the previous night. Melanie conjured up a return smile. She was not in the mood for pointless arguments with people she would never meet again.

Melanie struggled to remember this was supposed to be a

war zone and that a battle of some sorts had taken place the night before. The street outside was quiet.

'You seem very relaxed,' said John pouring her coffee. 'You must have slept well!'

'I dozed, kinda in and out of sleep I guess,' said Melanie taking a deep slug on her hot coffee, it sluiced the taste of stale beer from her mouth and, she hoped, from her breath. 'I had a nice enough room actually, with a French window opening out onto a garden.'

'It's weird isn't it?' said John looking thoughtfully through to the garden which be glimpsed though an open door. 'So far from home. A third world country, so different and yet we're here having coffee, with the smell of fried eggs coming in from the kitchen. You'd think it would be so different. It is. And it isn't. It's hard to explain to family and friends when you get back.'

'I know what you mean,' replied Melanie. 'People talk to you like you've been living on this other planet, but some things aren't different at all, really. And yet other stuff...'

'Like hearing gunfire during the night. Crazy,' said John, raising his eyebrows incredulously.

'I'm from New York!' laughed Melanie. 'Just like home, but no police sirens.'

'Yes, I forgot. Hey. But maybe you are used to life on the front line now you've been living in Rwanda?'

'No. It's really quiet in Kinigi where I teach. It's a snoozy little backwater with a church, a school, a market square, and nothing much happens there. Mind you, it's very pretty with the mountains and rain forest in the background. Most of the people are nice, but they've got this big 'we hate Tutsi' thing going on.'

'Yes. It's hard to explain.' John continued, leaning over the table towards her. 'This country is so beautiful, yet there is something ugly lurking beneath the surface.'

'Yet the people can be so kind, so welcoming...'

Their conversation was disturbed by noisy diesel engines

growling down the street outside. Everyone in the Muhabura dining room left their places to investigate. The Rwandan army had arrived, a column of vehicles filed into the street. One stopped outside the hotel and dropped off ten soldiers, who quickly crouched next to the hedge at the front of the hotel. The guests, cradling cups of coffee, watched them go through the clichéd soldierly posturing, hands were waved, fingers were pointed, soldiers swapped positions, like a macho chorus in military stage show. Stationary marksmen stared warily through rifle sights at the empty street. Their play acting was such a contrast to the relaxed demeanour of David, the RPF rebel. Melanie was tempted to walk over and offer them a cup of coffee; there was clearly no enemy combatant with ten miles.

Fifteen minutes later, the sergeant decided the area was safe and walked onto the patio area to speak to them. Melanie could not resist it.

'Are you Luke Skywalker, here to rescue me?' The soldier paused and gave her a blank, humourless look.

'I do not understand what you say. Get your things and come with us. You are going to a safe area at the edge of the city. Go and get your bags.' The soldier barely looked at Melanie as he spoke, his gaze being reserved for Gilbert who stood with a breakfast tray in one hand waiting to clear the table. Gilbert's eyes shifted around the room and when they met Melanie's they seemed to appeal to her for help. Melanie did not know what help she could give nor why he felt he needed any. She smiled at him, hoping that would make him feel better. This exchange took only a few seconds, but it was enough to make the sergeant impatient.

'Go. Get your bags,' he insisted.

'Excuse me we are USA citizens...' began Georgia pompously.

'This is not America. It is Rwanda and we are at war. Get your bags or you leave without them. You have one minute.'

The Sergeant's anger changed the atmosphere. With his

military fatigues and AK47 dangling round his waist he brought an air of menace into the room. There was violence in his eyes that was just waiting an opportunity to break out. He looked at Gilbert like he had found a focus for his pent-up rage.

The group quickly made their way out of the dining room and into the corridor behind it to collect their luggage. Melanie had none but looked in the drawers and wardrobe out of habit; as she always did when checking out of a hotel. Possessing only the clothes she was stood in she retraced her steps to the dining room. Two more soldiers had arrived and stood on either side of Gilbert as the sergeant interrogated him. Gilbert's papers, his portrait stamped 'TUTSI' lay discarded on the floor.

'Why did the RPF bring the Americans here?'

'I don't know...'

'Why here? Why did they pick your hotel? Why not another hotel?'

'I don't know. They just brought them.'

'Friends of yours? I bet business was good last night.'

'No this was the nearest hotel. I think...'

'So, you do know why they picked this hotel. They told you it was the nearest. They told you because they know you, and you know them. They are your friends. You are a spy for the cockroach army.' The sergeant made as if to slap Gilbert but saw Melanie had entered the room and was watching him. He stayed his hand and glared in frustration at Gilbert, then he shouted at Melanie.

'What are you doing here? Get in the truck,' he turned to one of the men flanking Gilbert. 'You. Take her to the truck.' The soldier came over to lead Melanie outside.

Before long the party was assembled outside the hotel and soldiers were helping the film crew and the researchers load their gear onto a large truck. Georgia and Melanie sat next to each other on a wooden plank in the back and watched what was going on. Army trucks rumbled by occasionally, dropping off troops in various parts of Ruhengeri to secure the town.

There did not seem to be much of a battle taking place if the snippets of faraway gunfire were anything to go by. The aggressive tension was supplied by the attitude of the government troops, eager to face an enemy who had vanished in the night. Soldiers stalked the street, machine guns at the ready. It occurred to Melanie that any sudden movement, a child running out, could lead to the accidental shooting of a civilian. Meanwhile the only potential target, Gilbert, stood on the grey and white checked patio outside the hotel. The sergeant stood facing him, shouting, and occasionally jabbing a finger into his chest.

With the gear packed it was time to go. The hotel party and three soldiers climbed into the truck to join Melanie and Georgia. Their luggage made a big pile on the floor of the truck between them. The soldier banged his hand on the driver's cab as a signal to set off, the truck driver started and revved the vehicle, choking his passengers with diesel fumes. Slowly they backed around the corner and set off down the road at the rear of the hotel. But they found this blocked. Approaching them was a big gang of brightly dressed youths; waving machetes, blowing whistles, singing and dancing like it was Mardi gras.

'What the fuck...' began John but his sentence, even had he finished it, would have been drowned in the noise of the wild jamboree that drew up to their truck. The column was led by a jeep containing two French officers in their burgundy berets. About thirty Interahamwe militia jogged behind it. The jeep driver pressed his horn to get Melanie's transporter to move aside, fortunately there was just enough room and their driver got out of the way. The jeep drove by; its passengers anonymous and arrogant behind their cool sunglasses. The Interahamwe youths glanced up as they squeezed past but made sure they kept up with the jeep.

Just as the last of the young men passed by one looked up and briefly held Melanie's gaze. In that instant of recognition, he stopped, and the boy behind ran into his back. Grégoire stared at her unsure of what to do. A flicker of a smile began on his face, but it was quickly replaced by a snarl of anger. He shouted something inarticulate and shook his fist in the air. Then he sprinted off to bring up the rear of the raggedy column as it rounded the corner to the front of the Hotel.

'Melanie,' asked John. 'You OK?' Melanie's mouth still hung open in surprise.

'I know him. Yes. Sorry. I'm fine. I know him. I teach him.' She stammered. 'What is he doing here?'

'Looks like he's with the militia. The Interahamwe,' said John.

'But he's a schoolboy. Why is he here?' asked Melanie, to no one but herself.

She pondered the situation as the driver pressed the accelerator and revved the engine. As he engaged the clutch the roar dipped as the tyres fought to drag the truck out of a deep groove in the road. Then, suddenly the truck fell silent and rolled back into the rut as he stalled it. Straight away he turned the ignition, but he was impatient and flooded the carburettor. He would have to wait a moment. A silence fell over the truck as the driver let the engine rest. Melanie saw her chance to satisfy her curiosity. With an energy that surprised her she grabbed the side of the truck and leapt down onto the dusty road. It was higher than she thought, and her knees gave way under the impact as she hit the ground. A soldier shouted something in Kinyarwandan, she guessed it was along the lines of 'where are you going?' Melanie did not care. She wanted to see what was happening.

The garden at the rear of the hotel was just across the street and she ran from the truck and onto the dry lawn. The French windows to her room were still open, so she entered and made her way to the door of the dining room. Peeping in she could see through the front windows to where Gilbert stood on the patio with the sergeant and his guards. The jeep was parked at the front of the hotel surrounded by the Interahamwe. The two French officers strode purposefully up the steps to the patio area. Melanie watched, her view was excellent, and her face was hidden as the audience could only see their own reflection in the glass.

6

Melanie could see the Rwandan Army officers having a heated conversation. Gilbert looked on in growing terror, his head twitching this way and that, while the big guard gripped his slender upper arm with his meaty fist. Occasionally the guard would drag him a little to one side or another to show who was in control. Gilbert's hands shook with terror.

At the bottom of the steps the crowd of Interahamwe stood, waving machetes in the air, jeering and blowing whistles. One of the officers stepped toward the crowd and waved his arms to quiet them down. Machetes were lowered, and the whistles fell silent, Melanie could hear the engine of the jeep running. The officer spoke to the crowd, Melanie guessed he was asking for a volunteer as a number of hands were raised, and he selected one young man to step up onto the patio with him. As he brushed by other Interahamwe members, they clapped him on the back as if wishing him luck. It was Grégoire.

On the patio the officer put a hand on Grégoire's shoulder and led him centre stage into the sunshine. Meanwhile the guard, having tied Gilbert's hands behind his back, brought the shivering bartender forward, pushing him to his knees in front of the crowd. The officer shouted instructions in a business-like fashion to the audience, then he pushed Gilbert's head forward, so his neck was exposed. Next the officer indicated what Grégoire was to do, pointing with his finger and making a chopping motion with his hand at the side of Gilbert's neck.

By now Gilbert had almost lost all control of his body he was shaking so violently. He looked up at the watching crowd and made an effort to peer round to see what was happening behind him. A sharp blow from the officer's fist on the back of his skull turned his head to face forward and down again. He looked down at the floor in front of his knees. As if to distract him his mind coughed up an old memory, he had ordered these patio tiles a few years ago. He had always liked them. This odd thought drifted away as he noticed his trousers had a big wet stain on the crotch though he did not remember urinating.

Grégoire did not to look up at the horde that was shouting and blowing whistles in encouragement. He was concerned that any eye contact with a friend might put him off and make him miss with the machete. He wanted to do a deliver, a hard, accurate blow to impress the officer and his comrades. He made certain of his grip on the wooden handle. As he raised the blade, the roar of support and approval grew louder, the sense of sudden popularity added energy and strength to his arm. He swung down with all his might, aiming exactly where the French trainer had ordered. However, halfway through his swipe Gilbert lurched forward. Grégoire was unable to adjust his trajectory and Gilbert avoided the full force of the blade. Instead only its tip caught him, and it stuck in a few inches lower down the back his neck. His body jerked forward and shivered, but he was not dead. As Gilbert writhed in agony and shock, blood spurted from the wound onto the patio he had been so proud of.

The officer shouted and gesticulated again at Gilbert's neck, furious at Grégoire's lack of professionalism. Embarrassed, he began hacking at the ripped neck to complete the execution. It took several blows as his victim was not lying still. Gilbert spasmed unconsciously, as his nervous system responded to the assault, taking over from the mind that was fleeing into darkness. Grégoire was almost chasing the shivering body around the patio electing, at the finish, to put his foot on Gilbert's back. One final blow to the base of his skull ended both their struggles. Grégoire stood up straight, panting, his machete by his side and his foot still on the back of

Gilbert's corpse. His instructor consoled himself with the partial success of the execution; this young man, all of them, was able to kill without mercy. Their training had been a success. Finally, ignoring the officer and the corpse, Grégoire looked to Interahamwe. They cheered him like a hero, and he raised his bloodied blade to the sky, while Gilbert's wounds bubbled tears of blood onto his white waiter's shirt.

Behind him, and out of sight, Melanie stood open mouthed, rigid with shock and horror. The desire to be brave was quenched by fear. The civilised need to understand was swamped by the animal cruelty of what she had witnessed. Soundlessly mouthing a scream of horror, she fainted, sliding down the door frame and onto the floor. Her last word was a gasp of anguish; 'NO!'

Back on the truck John had been arguing with the soldiers because he wanted to go with them to fetch Melanie back. They had been uncertain what to do for a few minutes and seemed more concerned with the stalled truck. Finally, two of the soldiers left and found her after searching the garden and the rooms at the rear of the hotel. They picked her up and took her back to the road at the rear of the hotel. Their struggles to get her back onto the truck whilst unconscious woke her up. Melanie wanted to speak, to say what she had seen, to witness the violation of life, but she could not find the words.

'Oh my God. Oh my God.' Was all she could manage and mumble through her tears. 'Gilbert. Oh my God.'

'What do you mean?' Asked Georgia. 'Gilbert? Who, I mean, when, what did you see? What's the matter?'

John found a blanket, wrapped it around her shoulders and put his arm around her. Georgia embraced from the other side. They realised Melanie was in no state to talk. They did not know what she had seen but from its effect on her they figured the worst. For now, Melanie was an elective mute.

7

The rain forest remained beautiful, aloof from the fear and anguish of the humanity that scurried about in its shade. The foliage soaked up the afternoon sun, insects buzzed in the haze, birds called, and animals foraged. Hidden in its depths, safe for now, Joe, Denyse and Grace sought food for their refuge. Fruit was plentiful, so they made several trips to build up a store for their secret cave. When their supplies were squirreled away Grace led the search for dry grass to sleep on.

The morning soon passed in the warm shadows; on any other occasion it would have been pleasant work. However, despite the picturesque surroundings they were not on a picnic. Joe was aware of a tension and sickness in the pit of his stomach. He would not relax until his mother returned safe. Each time they approached the cave from a trip into the forest he listened more and more intently for some sign that Angelique was back. Each time they entered the cave to find it empty his anxiety increased. Denyse and Grace's assurances carried less weight with each repetition. When the hideout was ready, the question gnawing his gut like an ulcer had to be asked; 'how long to wait?' Grace knew why Joe was silent and edgy.

'Joe. Why don't you go to the edge of the forest and see if you can see your mother coming back? She made need some help with the cow. Denyse and I will get the beds ready for tonight. If it's really quiet, we could risk a small fire.'

'Yes. Good idea. I'll take a look.'

'Go where we were this morning, that way we know where we can find you.'

'OK. I'll go there. See you later.'

Joe headed off down the slope, gently pushing the bamboo cane aside so as not to leave an obvious path back to their hiding place. After walking for a while, he found the vantage point that gave him a good view of the farmer's fields and, further down the slope, the village beyond. It looked like a typical Sunday afternoon because nobody was working the land but then Joe realised; it wasn't Sunday. Clearly something was going on. The sick, anxious feeling churned in his stomach once more. He pondered his options; Angelique had told him to stay and wait, there was probably little he could do to help, he could even make things worse for them both, she was probably sat chatting with friends. Joe took a step forward then a step back as each argument swayed his mind. In the end it was emotion, not reason, that decided it for him. His worries would subside if he could just see his mother, so he began to creep down the slope to seek her out.

He decided to follow the stone wall skirting the edge of the forest; he kept low and peeped over it cautiously. This westward journey kept him away from the main paths leading up from Kinigi. If anyone went north towards the forest, he would be out of their route. At the western end of the slopes the crops were higher and offered more cover. There were banana plantations that would hide him. In half an hour he was where he needed to be to skip over the wall and creep towards the houses on the outside of the village.

Crouching low, crawling on his hands and knees when needed, he made his way. He had only been going ten minutes when he heard a desperate whisper.

'Joseph, Joseph.' It urged him with a note of panic. 'Joseph, stay down, come here, it's me Charles.' Charles leaned out from his hiding place and beckoned Joe over.

Joe bounded over and joined him under the cover of the thick foliage. He could see Charles's was distraught; there were lines where tears had run down his cheeks.

'Charles. My God! Are you OK? Uwase, Claude, Clement, are they OK? Are they safe?'

'Yes, they are safe. They are hiding. We live in terrible times Joe. Terrible times. Where are you going?'

'My mother has gone into the village. I am going to find her.' At this Charles' face crumpled with anguish and Joe carried on. 'Have you seen my mother?' Charles paused and then said.

'Yes. Come with me. She is hiding with Uwase and the boys. We will be safe. This way.'

'My mother is with them?'

'Come quickly Joe.' Croaked Charles as his tears fell once more. 'We have no time. They are looking for us. We must hide.'

Charles tugged on Joe's shirt and drew him deeper among the banana plants. They headed back up the slope and were soon over the wall, going back into the forest, heading west, in the opposite direction to where Grace and Denyse waited. Joe kept trying to ask where they were headed but Charles' answers were vague, he only insisted Joe follow him. After half an hour they found Uwase with the twins, hiding in the roots of an enormous tree.

Uwase leapt to her feet, she hugged and kissed Charles with desperate intensity but she soon turned to face Joe.

'Is my mother not here?' He asked with a quaking voice 'You said my mother was here,' he said desperately. Uwase turned to Charles.

'You have not told him?'

'I could not. I had to get him away from the village. It's not safe there. He would have been killed.' Charles turned to Joe, but he was barely able to speak. 'I'm sorry Joe. I'm so, so sorry,' he covered his face with his hands and leaned against the trunk of the tree.

Uwase reached out and hugged Joe tightly to her chest.

'What do you mean? Where is she? Where is my mother?'

Uwase leaned back and held Joe by the shoulders. 'Joe your mother is gone. She is dead. They killed her this morning. They killed any Tutsis left in the village. I am sorry.' Joe stood still as if not understanding what she had said.

'My mother?' he wanted to say something more but found he had no words to make sense of his feelings. He was panting and soon felt dizzy. After a minute he slid down till he knelt on the forest floor, trembling in front of Uwase. She knelt down and hugged him. Charles joined them, his arms round them both, kneeling on the leaves and grass on the floor of the forest. Joe's body shook and convulsed as he sobbed. Uwase and Charles cried with him, holding him up so he did not fall into the dirt. Joe felt that what he had heard was not news; he felt that he had known it all morning, on the deepest level of his being. His mother was gone, and he would never see her again. He was alone.

The three of them stayed that way for more than an hour. Uwase and Charles looked at each other over Joe's bowed head knowing that being with him was all they could do. Gradually Joe gained some control over his tears. He let go of Uwase and sat down on the root of the tree. He could not be consoled, but he was grateful that they had tried. As he sat on a tree root staring at the ground Claude tugged at his elbow and Clement moved to sit in his lap. Joe looked up and Claude offered him a daisy chain to go around his wrist. Joe tried a smile, but the tenderness of the little boy started his tears to flow once more. He put the bracelet on and hugged the children to him. 'Thank you,' he whispered. Charles and Uwase stood and held each other, quietly sharing ideas about what to do next.

It was another hour before Joe felt able to stand up and speak. Slowly he put the twins down and rose to his feet facing Charles and Uwase.

'I don't know what to do,' he spoke in a quiet, defeated voice. 'Is my mother buried?'

'We don't know,' replied Charles, gently laying a hand Joe's shoulder. 'But you couldn't go back into the village. It's not safe for Tutsis now. Who else is with you?'

'Grace and Denyse Keza. We ran into the forest to hide. They will be waiting for me. I have to tell them, to tell them about...'

'Yes. You should go to them. You must go soon Joe.'

'We were thinking of going to Uganda. Over the mountains,' he said in a slow and distracted manner. 'We found a cave to hide in. We have some food.'

'Could you find your way to the cave from here?' asked

Uwase.

'Yes. I will go to the edge of the forest and turn left, back along the wall to where we went in. Do you want to come with us to Uganda?'

'It's a good idea Joe,' said Charles. 'But Claude and Clement are too small to make that journey. We will have to stay here. We have some food and we know where to get more. We will be OK. But you should get back to Grace and Denyse. You must look after them.'

Charles and Joe stood face to face and looked at each other in silence. Uwase put an arm round Joe's waist and leant her head on his shoulder. Finally, Joe spoke.

'You are right. I have to go now if I am to make it back before nightfall.' After hugs and goodbyes Joe made to leave their hiding place. Charles walked with him as far as the edge of the forest. When they got to within sight of the farmland what they saw made them drop to the ground to hide. About half a mile away a line of men was working slowly through the farmer's plots, up the hillside to the forest; they were going exactly where Joe was headed.

The Kinigi men had made some guesses on where Angelique had been aiming for when they caught her. Led by Evariste, they were making straight for Joe's look out point at the edge of the bamboo. Suddenly, one of them stood up and pointed up the hill into the distance. Several of them shouted out; they had seen something suspicious. They began to labour up the slope towards their prey.

And they blocked the route for Joe.

'You cannot go back that way,' said Charles.

'But... Grace and Denyse?' He asked in despair.

'They know they are coming, they will be able to run away. They have a good start and they will lose them in the forest. In two hours the sun will be gone. They will escape.'

'Should I wait and go then?'

'No. They will have left. They have to run. They cannot wait for you. You will not find them in the dark and you risk being seen near Kinigi. Come back with me. Stay with us to-night. You should not be alone walking in the forest. We will rest and tomorrow we will have a plan.'

8

Grace and Denyse had been collecting more food as the morning ticked by. They kept wary eyes and ears open; sounds in the distance reminded them of the trouble in Ruhengeri and kept them on edge. They had plenty to eat but neither had any appetite. Finally, they went back to the cave to see if Angelique and Joe had returned. They were not surprised to find it empty.

'Mother, it's been too long. They should both be back by now. What should we do?' Denyse's arms hung loose by her side and her shoulders sagged with despair. Grace pulled the young girl to her and hugged her.

'We'll have a look for them. It's all we can do.'

They made their way to the lookout point they had sent Joe to a few hours earlier. There was no sign of Angelique or Joe but they both saw the thing they had dreaded; a group of men heading up towards the forest. Someone at the front looked directly up at them, even though he was nearly a mile distant Denyse knew they had been seen. Her stomach knotted, and she felt sick as the man, easily recognisable as Jean Damascène, started pointing and gesticulating towards his friends. They began to run up the slope in their direction. Grace wasted no time.

'Run. Follow me.'

'What if they catch us?'

'They won't. We've got a good start. They will be slow in the fields.'

Grace led the way. Denyse had never run so fast, her heart pounded as her muscles pumped with energy and adrenalin. Within seconds the two women were out of sight on the forest trails. Denyse was tempted to look back and see if her pursuers were gaining on them, but Grace sprinted relentlessly ahead spurring her daughter on. They ran for an hour before they paused to listen for danger. Trying to pant as quietly as they could they stood in perfect stillness, straining to hear the faintest sound of pursuit.

There was nothing, only the gentle rustling of trees and innocent birdsong.

'What shall we do?' whispered Denyse.

'We carry on. We cannot stop, but I think we will be safe if we are fast.'

Grace was right. The Kinigi men had given up as soon as they reached the edge of the forest. They had no chance, the women had a head start, and it would be dark soon.

Grace and Denyse however would not cease their flight.

9

Melanie was glad of the blanket John had wrapped around her, she covered herself in it to shut out the world. She hid her face from the others and pretended she could not hear their questions. Georgia and John hugged her and the weight of their arms on her shoulders gave her some comfort. Gradually her trembling grew less as her breathing became easier. Still she opted to hide from the others and looked down at the steel floor of the truck and its chipped coat of green paint. Images from the slaughter of Gilbert kept flashing into her mind. Towering above his agony was the crowing, triumphant figure of Grégoire. She shut her eyes tight to push the memory back, but the darkness made it easier to recall. Finally, she looked up and stared ahead as the outskirts of Ruhengeri trundled by.

After fifteen minutes of a bumpy ride the truck stopped at a checkpoint. Though she did not understand the language, she heard a familiar voice and recognised some of the words in the sentence it seemed to be repeating with some desperation.

'Hotel Muhabura? ... Hickman...? Melanie Hickman... Hotel

Muhabura...?' Somebody was making inquiries of the drivers. It was Ishimwe. Within moments his face appeared at the back of the truck. The soldiers let down the rear of the vehicle and helped her down into Ishimwe's supporting embrace. She had little time to speak as the metal plate was clanged shut, the engine revved ready to move off. John and Georgia leaned over to say goodbye.

'Take care. Sorry, I never got your number. Look kid, get out of this mess, get out of this country, it's fucked up.'

Melanie looked up but had no small talk to offer, her arm twitched upwards, but the wave of farewell never quite made it. With a splutter of black exhaust fumes, and a cloud of red dust, the truck launched itself off again. Soon it, and the people whose life paths she had crossed, were out of sight around a corner. Ishimwe took her hand.

'Melanie, what has happened? You look dreadful. Have you been hurt?'

'Take me home. I mean back to the school. Then I'm going home, back to America, as soon as I can. I have had enough of Rwanda.'

'My car is over here. You are safe now. Don't worry. Come with me, we'll go back.'

Ishimwe led her over to the car holding her arm in case she stumbled. He went to open the door but before he could, Melanie was sick down the side of the car. Slumping to her knees in the road she was sick again and carried on retching till there was nothing left. Ishimwe gently rubbed her back through the blanket.

'It's okay. It's okay,' he murmured. 'You are safe. You are going to be okay.'

He found a bottle of water in the door pocket, it was warm, but it soothed her throat and stopped her throwing up. Slowly Melanie managed to stand. She drained the bottle and turned to look at Ishimwe.

'Thank you,' she said.

'What has happened to you?'

'To me? Nothing.'

'Something has. What is wrong?'

'I... can't, I can't...'

'Please. It might help you to tell me.'

Melanie took a deep breath and found an inner, hidden source of emotional strength. 'Ishimwe, an hour ago... I saw a man butchered like a piece of meat,' she said, her voice quiet and drained of emotion. Ishimwe stood silent for a minute.

'I'm sorry. I don't know what to say. The anger is so great, it runs deep,' he replied, his arms listless by his side. 'Come on. Let's go. I'll take you back to the school.'

'I want to go home,' said Melanie when they were back in the car, Ishimwe was driving quickly as if escaping from Ruhengeri.

'When we get back, you can pack your things,' he shouted over the whine and clatter of the engine. 'I'll make some phone calls; the American embassy and the Peace Corps offices.'

'They butchered this man. He was innocent, just because he was a Tutsi. There were French soldiers watching.'

'The French have trained the presidential guard and the army.' Ishimwe nodded. 'They have supplied weapons, ammunition, everything, for years.'

'They have been training Interahamwe too. They helped them do it. I saw them. Ishimwe, my God! What about you?'

'What do you mean?'

'You are a Tutsi. You were in danger back there. What happened at the Church?'

'It was OK. The Church was full of people visiting Ruhengeri, or those who could not make it to their homes safely. Many slept on the benches, but I was lucky, the priest knows me, and he let me use a guest room. The RPF were gone in the morning. When the government troops came, they just wanted to get everyone out. They were setting up roadblocks, but they were not ready. They just sent us on our way and, thank God, did not check our papers.'

'What would they have done if they had seen your papers? They say you are a Tutsi.'

'They did not check them. It was very early this morning, and they had more urgent things to do.'

'You could have been killed.'

'Well, I was lucky,' he replied with some irritation. 'Like I said. They did not check them.'

Ishimwe did not to want to talk about it and they said little more on the way home. The journey passed in a shocked trance for Melanie as she looked at the lush landscape with a new understanding. Its grandeur and beauty told a lie and if you fell for it, you would be blind to the suffering that stalked the land. The rough roads connecting the cutesy villages, with their mud and grass roofs, looked great in a travel brochure. They held out a promise of a simpler life, shorn of the complexities of the modern world. But the mirage only worked if you stayed in the hotels and game parks and avoided the real people. The porters, and waiters, and receptionists, and cleaners smiled for you; not for themselves. As they drove along, they passed two children playing at the side of the road. To prove her wrong, they looked up and smiled when they saw Melanie's face.

'Mzungu, mzungu.' They shouted, running after the car.

'Yes, that's me. Mzungu,' thought Melanie. 'It's like I'm an alien.'

10

While Grace and Denyse ran into the safety of the forest Charles and Joe returned to their hiding place. They had made a primitive camp in the roots of a large tree, with dry grass for a bed they settled down and sought elusive sleep. Charles and Uwase took turns to listen in case any pursuers had ventured out in the night. In truth one watched while the other lay awake, but with their eyes closed.

Joe looked up at the stars he could see through the branches above him. He wondered if his mother was somewhere up there, watching over him. His tears fell as he cried silently for her. Grief created an emptiness within him; it was a hunger that no food could satisfy. He ached for his mother's face, her voice, her smell, her touch; but these could never be had again.

For a tiny moment he was terrified he could not remember her clearly enough, then a memory flooded in, he saw her only too well and a wave of sorrow swept through him. In the end, exhausted by grief, he slipped into a light doze. He dreamt he was looking for his mother in their old home. He could hear her voice, singing quietly around a corner, but when he got there, she was gone. Just out of sight he heard her sing a lullaby;

'Kabuye Kanjye
Kabuye Kaniye ni keza pe
Kabuye Kaniye ni keza pe...'

It was her surely! He opened his eyes only to see Uwase singing to her two boys. He watched how they listened to her, knowing how they took her singing for granted as he had done his mother's. With a deep sigh the tears returned but also, deep within him, the smallest spark of determination. He would not give up on life; that was not why his mother bore him, he would carry on. Joe looked up at the at the sky turning from grey to orange with the coming of dawn. He did not know what 'carrying on' meant yet, but he was determined to do something. His life, won by his mother's struggles, would not add up to nothing. He had a debt to repay.

Noticing he was awake Charles walked over and gave him half of a wild melon. He scraped the seeds out with his thumb flicking them onto the ground, looking into Charles concerned face he bit into the flesh. It was juicy and sweet. Refreshed, he wiped his chin with the back of his hand and looked nodded gratefully at his older friend.

'Thanks,' he could not bring himself to smile in appreciation, but Charles understood why.

'So, what are you going to do?' asked Joe.

'Wait. Stay out of sight. Maybe go to the Church for protection. They will not harm the priests and they would be witnesses to any more crimes. Things will change, this has happened to Tutsis before.'

'Yes. Too often. So much for peace.'

'You are right Joe. Look, I have something for you,' he reached into his pocket. Joe frowned and looked at the crumpled card offered to him.

'What is this?'

'I found it. In the fields yesterday. It belongs to you.'

Joe took the crumpled photograph from him and smoothed it out on the palm of his hand. The faded colours were broken by a patina of creases where his mother had gripped it in her fist and hugged it to her chest. Joe could not bear to look at the picture. He knew what it was, a sacred thing that spoke of the happiness that should have been his childhood. In the last 24 hours he had suffered too much to feel any more. He put the photo in his pocket for later veneration and tears.

'I'm sorry, but I had to give you that now,' said Charles.

'I know. Thank you, Charles.'

'That was your father wasn't it? Daniel? I never met him. Is he still alive? I heard he was a good man?'

'As far as I know he still is a good man. I think he is alive. And now I know what to do.'

'What?'

'I'm going to go and find him.'

'How will you know where to look?' asked Uwase.

'The last I heard he was with the Rwandan Patriotic Front in Uganda. He is a soldier.'

'The RPF is often in the national park they may still be here,' he replied. 'They have camped in the forest on Mount

Karisimbi. It is the most westerly volcano.'

'Yes, I could make my way there under the cover of the forest.'

'It would take two or three days,' suggested Charles thoughtfully. 'If you could get there you would be as safe with the RPF as you would be anywhere else.'

For the second time Joe made his farewells with Charles, Uwase and the children. While he said goodbye, he gave brief thought to the journey that lay ahead and noted that it held no fear for him. He stood on an abyss of anguish and felt an urge to fall but, if he gave into that, he knew it would destroy him. He took a deep breath and the tiny spark of determination deep within him grew brighter. The young man who was easily scared was fading away to be replaced someone new, someone who had been re-forged by grief.

As their paths separated, they wished each other luck and safety. Joe still could not smile but he was able to offer a wink as he shook hands with Charles. He thought it was what men did in these situations.

'Take good care of your wife and children Charles. I will be fine. And we will meet again, I am sure.'

With that Joe strode off through the forest making a path to the west and an unknown future.

11

It was late afternoon when Ishimwe pulled up at the school grounds. The gates were closed but unlocked and the caretaker that usually looked after 'security' was not to be seen. Melanie got out of the car to let them into the compound. She was tired and drained; the part of her brain that dealt with grief had shut down to rest. She appeared diffident but this was a defence mechanism to protect her from her sadness. The familiarity of the school grounds held some comfort for her; the paths worn through the grass, the single storey school buildings and staff houses. It was quiet and peaceful but then, just as she was starting to savour the tranquillity, a thought struck her.

'Ishimwe?' she asked.

'Yes, what?' he replied and stepped out of the car to stand by her side.

'What day of the week is it?'

'Monday.'

'So why is it so quiet?'

'Yes. I see what you mean. Well it's past four o'clock. The school children will have gone home.'

'But there are usually some people around.' Melanie walked over to the front of her house. 'Everything is just as we left it. Empty beer bottles and stuff.'

'So?'

'Angelique always comes on Monday mornings, so she has not been today.' Melanie stepped inside her front door and quickly emerged back into the late afternoon sunlight. 'No water has been delivered so Joe hasn't been here either.'

'I'll check on Rosine.'

Ishimwe turned and walked quickly over to Rosine's rooms calling her name as he went. Melanie walked back inside looking at her room as if it were a crime scene. Yet nothing had been touched, nothing was missing. The only evidence was the eerie silence; the school compound was a like ghost town. As she looked round, she heard Ishimwe's footsteps approach the door.

'Rosine is not there. Is she usually in on a Monday evening?'

'Well, it varies. She could be at Pascale's house in the village, he is back from Kigali,' replied Melanie. Ishimwe looked thoughtful.

'Are you OK here for a while? I'll go to the Church. Father Patrice will be able to explain what's going on.'

'Yes. I want to pack my things.'

'OK. I won't be long.'

When Ishimwe had left Melanie reached up and pulled her

suitcase down off the top of the wardrobe, cast it on the bed and flipped the lid open. She made an attempt at folding a few things then stopped as she felt her eyes filling up with tears again. Scattered, disparate images of Gilbert's slaughter flooded back into her mind and she felt faint. She had to pack but now was not the time. In the sink she saw four bottles of beer sat in a bucket of water and pulled one out with a clink of glass, the label slid off slickly into the cold water. 'This will help' she thought.

She opened the bottle and went outside to drink it in the late afternoon sunshine. The beer gave her no satisfaction, it was a means to an end, an anaesthetic. Yet it was a relief to taste it, an innocent pleasure at the end of a day where she had peeped through the open gates of hell. Melanie sat down heavily in the chair outside the front door and swigged a big mouthful from the bottle. The beer fizzed inside her cheeks. The sensation was normal, familiar and reassuring. Her mind compartmentalised her experiences that day to protect her from the horror. Watching the murder of Gilbert was this morning, in a horrible place. Drinking beer in the sunshine was now, in a different place. She felt dizzy and sick as she placed the two experiences side by side. There was only a faint whisper of a breeze in the sparse foliage on the trees and again the campus felt too quiet. Melanie closed her eyes, leant back in her chair, and longed for a familiar voice from home.

*   *   *

Meanwhile Ishimwe walked over to the Church in search of Father Patrice. He entered the vast nave via the big, wooden, back doors. It was empty and silent. His eyes were drawn upwards by the searchlight beams of sunshine that streamed through the high windows. The soft breeze drifted through the light and blended with the creamy, smoky aroma of extinguished candles. His footsteps echoed as he walked slowly down the central aisle towards the front. As he approached, the large crucifix hanging behind the altar seemed to rise up, as if Christ were ascending to heaven before his very eyes.

Ishimwe stooped to his knees on the steps of the altar, on the boundary of the sacred space, bowing his head in reverence to what lay beyond. Out of habit he clasped his hands to pray. He spoke so quietly it was almost to himself, but his lips moved as his mind framed the words.

'Lord, I am not worthy to receive you, but only say the word... Our Father who art in heaven...' But his tongue stilled, and his prayer died heavy in his chest, the old formulas would not work. He decided to try to just put his feelings into words. 'Heavenly Father... Lord, help me, help us all... God, oh God help us... Lord, it's me Ishimwe, here in Rwanda. I'm sorry. I am afraid. Give me courage, give me strength. Give me the words to say to bring peace. Oh God, speak through me, and bring your healing in this place.'

He ran out of words, but his emotions flowed without conscious expression as he knelt alone in the Church. With his eyes tightly closed he was yet aware of the emptiness around him and his own position as its focal point. It was as if the building was aware of him. In the quiet he realised the walls were not silent, there were tiny, comforting ticks and clicks as the building responded to the sunlight bathing it outside. The sacred space held an invisible presence.

Ishimwe thought of the hundreds of hours he had spent saying mass in this place. The thousands of hymns and voices he had joined in praise. The prayers that had been offered up to the heavens. He felt as if all those moments, the joyous and the reverent, were still present, suspended in the atmosphere of the Church. The walls themselves recorded and remembered it all.

The sum of these memories welled up in him as a new feeling of peace and confidence. All that he had done was still known here and always would be. In that moment he understood that his calling to be a priest, to heal and uplift the human spirit, came from outside of himself. He was merely a conduit to a power beyond his body and this world. It was a force which desired to reach into the human race with love. Ishimwe felt that love as it surged into him and radiated out from him. His vocation was to give that love to others as it was needed. It was not for him to judge those who God placed in his life, but to love them. He felt affirmed. Tears of appreciation rolled down his cheeks as he opened eyes and looked up into the face of the crucified Christ above him. At last a prayer came, and he said it out loud.

'Thank you.'

Ishimwe knelt in front of the altar for another ten minutes suffused with tranquil reassurance. He did not hear Father Patrice enter the Church from the vestry at the side. His brother priest stood and watched him for some minutes before he spoke. He stayed by the door, he did not step too close in case Ishimwe smelled the beer on his breath.

'Father Ishimwe where have you been?' He said, steadily. 'I have been looking for you. You were missing all last night.'

'Father. I came to find you,' said Ishimwe with a slight, calm smile, as he stood and turned to face Patrice. 'I went to Ruhengeri yesterday evening, and we got stuck there.'

'We?'

'Yes. I went with Miss Hickman. The American teacher from the school.'

'I know who she is,' replied Patrice with a blank expression. 'Do you think that is what you should be doing as a priest? Spending a night away with a woman?'

'I did not spend the night with her,' said Ishimwe. 'We went to see what was going on. The rebels attacked while we were there, she was taken to a hotel, I went to the Church and they gave me a room for the night. I found her this morning and brought her back.'

'Do you think that is what people will think?'

'Well...,' he began, but stopped himself. 'And what do you think Father Patrice? Please. Me and a young American woman? It's a little unlikely isn't it?'

'What I think is not the issue here. We have to be above suspicion to maintain our dignity. We are representatives of the Church. We must set an example. We are representatives of...,' he paused realising he was repeating himself. 'You chose a bad time to go to Ruhengeri; the very night the Tutsi RPF brings its violence to the town.'

'It was a coincidence Father, that is all. What is this? Do you think I am a spy for the RPF? Is that it?' Ishimwe laughed incredulously as he asked the question. Patrice did not answer but maintained his fixed expression. 'Come Patrice, we are friends, fellow priests,' said Ishimwe with his arms held apart and taking a step towards the older man.

'I am not accusing you of anything Father Ishimwe. I am just warning you what many people think.'

'You think people in this parish think I am a spy for the rebels?'

'Not you. I didn't say that. Don't put words in my mouth. Hutus are afraid. They are worried their neighbours may be spies. The radio has warned them to be vigilant.'

'That's insane, it's paranoia.'

'It is not insane or paranoid to want to protect your family.'

'I am a priest and I...'

'And you are a Tutsi. Your friends in the RPF attacked a nearby town last night.'

'They are not my friends. You do not believe that. I do not discriminate between Hutu and Tutsi parishioners. We are all equal in the sight of God.'

'The Hutus in this parish do not need your condescension Father Ishimwe. And the Kinigi Tutsis... well... where are they?'

'What do you mean 'where are they'?'

'They are not to be found. So many empty houses.'

'You mean they have gone into hiding? Why would they do that?' asked Ishimwe narrowing his eyes in suspicion as he tried to read Patrice's expression. What has happened here? If anybody has run away, it would be because they were afraid of being attacked.'

'Seriously Ishimwe? You come in here wondering where the Tutsis might be? You have just come back from Ruhengeri where their rebel army is terrorising innocent Hutu civilians and you ask that question? It is not who they were running from that is the problem, it is who they were running to! Their friends, the RPF!' he shouted. 'The cockroach army. That is where they have gone. That is who they have been in regular contact with. Deny that if you can!' Patrice's fists were clenched so tight the knuckles in his old hands ached. He shook with rage, fuelled by alcohol, as he stared at Ishimwe's relaxed face.

'Father, this is a house of God, and your accusations...'

'Don't you dare lecture me,' spat Patrice. 'House of God? I've served in God's house longer than you. I know the sacrifice and the service of the priesthood. And I know the rules of mother Church and my duty to obey them. I shall be writing to the Bishop to inform him that you do not.' Father Patrice swivelled on the ball of his foot and made for the door, swaying slightly as he did so. Ishimwe noticed the slight lurch as Patrice reached for the doorframe to support himself, it was early in the day to be drinking.

Ishimwe had guessed his superior's anger was fuelled by a few drinks but he had learned what he came to find out. He knew where all the Tutsis were; they were in hiding. Most of them would be in the forest he was sure of that. He did not blame them, but he would not follow them. He looked up at the cross and knew he had the courage to stay and reason with the parishioners that remained. His flock. The truth would set them free. The words of Saint Paul came back to him; 'there is neither Jew nor Gentile, slave nor free, but all are equal in the sight of God'. Hutu and Tutsi were equal in the sight of God too; it was a message he was ready to preach. He strode to his rooms to write his sermon.

Father Patrice walked heavily into the presbytery still angry and planning the letter to the Bishop in his clouded mind. In his room his drinking partner sat waiting for him. Jean Damascène clicked the top of another bottle and offered it to Patrice.

'Where has he been then, your fellow priest?' he asked.

'He is no priest.' Patrice replied. 'He is just another Tutsi.'

12

Joe headed west thorough the forest keeping the low stone wall that marked the park's border to his left and the line of volcanoes far away on his right. It was a simple enough plan, but hard to stick to. The way was easier near the wall and the villages on the other side, but that was where the danger was greatest. He followed what felt like a reasonably safe route for thirty minutes only to freeze in fear when he heard voices. Only a few yards away two farmers were talking in agitated, excited tones amongst their crops near the wall. Joe listened long enough to catch the thread of their conversation.

'Have you seen any?'

'Not one. All their houses are empty...'

He did not need to hear anymore, he knew who 'they' were. Nervously he allowed himself a shallow, quiet breath, and mastered his fear. It was not safe here. The path worn by generations of passing feet naturally swerved down the slope towards the villages all the time. He realised instantly it was safer higher up the mountainside although there the vegetation was denser, the slopes steeper, and his pace would be slower. He wanted to make his journey as short possible, but it also had to be away from people. It was his only option, so he crept away from the voices as silently and as speedily as he could. From there he found a way up towards the mountains and deeper into the tangled wilderness.

Though he had lived in its shadow all his life Joe had never felt at home in the forest. He was afraid of the shadows and the unknown creatures that dwelt, veiled behind the barricade of foliage, dripping with spiders and insects. He had played in it as a child, foraged for food many times, but only in daylight and never alone. However, as he cautiously sprinted into it now, pausing like a wary deer snuffling the breeze for predators, he felt as if the trees were welcoming him into their outstretched arms. For all the dangers it was safer here with so many places to find cover. The voices were soon way behind him and his nervous, pounding heartbeat subsided to be replaced again by his determination to get to find the RPF.

It was hot and humid and every time he passed a stream, he drank gratefully from it. If he recognised a fruit, he ate some and kept what he could in his pockets for later. The steady drone of buzzing insects punctuated by the calls of exotic birds drowned all other sounds. It made it difficult to hear any pursuing gangs, but it also masked his own progress. After a while he noticed he was not charging madly through the undergrowth, but following, as if by instinct, a myriad of routes made by animals. Some routes were mere narrow side streets through bamboo thickets, only wide enough for a small antelope; others broadened out between the trunks of vast African redwood trees, wide enough for the elephants and buffalo that carved them. Joe had headed north, away from the village for about two hours up the slopes, then he headed west as best he could, making use of the forest highways.

From time to time he found himself in a clearing and could see over the trees as they stretched into the distance. Joe felt the eternal power of the forest. In its many guises and shades of green it conquered the mountains. It hummed with life making human attempts to shape the world look puny. The farmers fought the wilderness at its edge where they marshalled the power of nature and soil into rows of fragile crops. If they paused in their vigil for even a single season, the army of trees would march in and reclaim its territory from the human usurper.

Joe journeyed on; using the paths instead of struggling

against the vegetation. His progress was steady until he reckoned it was about thirty minutes from sunset. The fear of being followed had subsided, but there were dangers in the forest at night. He decided that the safest place to sleep, if he could sleep at all, would be up a tree. After a quick search he chose one with a hollow between a group of branches about eight feet above the ground. This seemed high enough to climb, but not too far to fall from. From a nearby clearing he gathered some dry-ish grass, pulled out the nettles, gave it a good shake to knock the insects out, and went up the tree to make his nest. It took several trips to finish the task but before the sky quite darkened, he had built a bed for the night.

Joe watched the sun plunge below the horizon as he peeped through a screen leaves. The brief twilight was soon overtaken by a wave of darkness from the east and the first stars began to emerge and twinkle in the cold blackness. The volume of noise from insects and birds grew as the night deepened. Once the warmth of the day had been buried under the horizon Joe began to feel the cold. The physical exertions of his journey were overtaken by the anguish that had led him to travel so far from home.

As the word 'home' came into his mind his spirits sank and tears flooded his eyes, dripping from his cheeks onto his chest. With a heart-breaking ache he understood that 'home' was gone forever. It had never really been the village of Kinigi or their tiny house. Home had been his mother, the two of them looking after each other; it was a state of love, not just four mud walls and a leaky roof. Home was something inside him that had been burnt out, he was left with only the shell of it. Grief for his mother lurched and ached within him. He longed to watch her combing her long, straight hair by the firelight. He longed to hear her voice. He touched the pocket where the picture was, it was still there, but he was glad it was too dark to see; it would have brought him more pain than comfort.

Minutes that had sprinted past in the day trudged by like hours in the night but, eventually, exhaustion brought with it the fleeting gift of fitful sleep.

After some hours he awoke in terror to feel the tree shaking and hear the crash of undergrowth being destroyed. Just as he was about to scream in terror a word came into his mind; elephant! He held on to a branch and peered over the edge of his nest as it lumbered past, barrelling through the forest, oblivious to all in its path. He could make out its shape and saw its mighty back lit up in the silver-grey moonlight. He smiled as he enjoyed the spectacle from his perch; the elephant was alone, just like he was. Their shared solitude gave him a strange sense of safety. When the elephant had gone, he took a deep breath, climbed a little higher up the tree, and looked for dawn in the east.

He guessed sunrise was less than an hour away but there was more news. Clouds had gathered in the darkness and it would be a wet day in the mountains. He was used to the cold but not immune to it. This did not depress him however, there was always a silver lining; he would be harder to see or follow in the rain. This weather would put any trackers off the chase. He reckoned the journey would be tougher, but safer, for the downpour.

He climbed down and set off westwards once more, chewing on a piece of the wild melon that he was now heartily bored of. It was not raining yet, but the atmosphere was close, warm and sweaty. Within an hour the first drops fell, spattering off the leaves above him and forming rivulets on the muddy soil. Before long all his attention was devoted to keeping his footing as he kept up a stooped, loping run. Occasionally he had to stop under a great tree as the downpour thickened.

He panted in the shelter and steam rose off his upper body as he stole a drink of the fresh water running off the leaves. It was a struggle to motivate himself to keep going; he knew what he was running from, but not what he was running to. As doubts crept in and challenged his resolve, he felt the temptation to just sit down, give up, and wait for whoever to catch him. Still his determination won through and he drove himself ever onwards although, at times, the journey seemed as pointless as it was arduous.

Later in the afternoon the sun came out and within forty minutes it had dried away the rain leaving a warm mist shrouding the mountains. Joe looked to the north east and saw clouds covering Mount Sabyinyo. His thoughts went out to Grace and Denyse with a pang of loss and he wondered if they had been caught in the same storm. Crouched on his haunches he held his head as if feeling the weight of his thoughts. Looking down, he noticed mud caked his feet and legs, so he found a nearby stream to wash. It would make his steps surer, but it was also nice to be clean. He massaged his feet and calves as he rinsed them.

In the late afternoon he walked at an easier pace, ever westwards. He let the sunshine warm and dry him, as it did the rest of the mountainside. The blue sky lifted his mood and, though memories caused a pang of sadness in his gut, his spirits were high enough to keep him going. Finally, with half an hour till sunset, he found a tree and, as he had the day before, he made himself a nest. This time he slept reasonably well, the needs of his tired and aching limbs kept cold and grief at bay.

When he awoke the sun had been up for two hours, the air was warm and filled with the racket of forest life. It had been too dark the night before so he climbed his tree a little higher to take in the view to see if he could work out where he was. The volcanoes rose behind him and below him the silver blade of Lake Kivu glittered and pointed south in the daylight. A hundred miles long it ran the length of Rwanda's western border; on the other side lay the dense jungle of the Congo. Joe had never seen the lake before, but he knew enough of the geography to know that, if he was near the top end of Kivu he was in the right part of the forest.

Joe began to climb down the tree, grasping branches and creepers with his hands as his feet searched for a foothold that would take him lower. Once a foot was secure, he shifted his weight and found the next move for his hand to take him safely downwards. If he fell and injured himself in this wilderness, it could be his last mistake. In a minute he had climbed down past last night's nest, hanging from a branch and reaching out beneath him. He was aware of his foot wafting in the air, searching for safety, as his hands grew tired.

But his foot found no ledge and instead his ankle was gripped by a powerful hand. In that second of shock he forgot to hold on and fell down heavily from the tree, seven feet onto the ground. The bang of the impact momentarily shut his eyes. When he opened them, he was looking at a pair of black rubber wellington boots into which were tucked a pair of olive army fatigue trousers, the uniform was topped by jacket of the same dirty green colour. A battered and worn AK47 hung loosely in the soldier's grip but it pointed away from Joe. The face of the man was hidden by the bright blue sky that shone above him but the voice that questioned Joe was curious not intimidating.

'Young man. What is your name?'

'Me? Joseph. Sir.'

'So, Joseph, what were you doing up in that tree?'

'I slept there last night.'

'OK.'

'I felt it was safe.'

'OK.' The soldier replied then, with a chuckle. 'There's not much meat on you for a gorilla. Where are you from gorilla boy?'

'I am from Kinigi...' Joe stopped as he heard other voices stifling laughter. At that moment his hands involuntarily came up to cover his face, the movement was beyond his control. His lungs emptied of air with a great gasp of a sigh. His body shook, and he was wracked with sobs as the stress of the last few days caught up with him once more. 'She's gone.' Was all he could say.

The soldier knelt beside him on the tussocky grass and put a powerful arm round his shoulders. 'Who's gone son?' He asked and, through his tears, Joe managed to stutter...

'My mother.' The soldier said nothing but stayed where he was, nodding to show he understood. Another soldier leaned over and ruffled Joe's hair.

'It's all right young man,' said one voice. 'You're going to be OK,' came another. 'You'll be OK with us.' Joe looked up.

'You're the RPF aren't you?'

ABEL UNLEASHED

2

Melanie carried her bag out of her room and placed it on the ground next to Ishimwe's Citroen. Her suitcase was light as she had left most of her clothes on the bed. Angelique and Rosine needed them more than she did. Ishimwe lifted her bags into the boot and, chivalrous as usual, opened her door for her. Melanie paused, leaned against the car, looking into the distance. She felt she was deserting them all; the school, the children, and Ishimwe but she could not wait to leave the country. Ishimwe understood her dilemma.

'You are doing the right thing Melanie. You signed up to be a teacher, no one expects you to stay and be a part of this... this horror.'

'I'm sorry. I know I'm running away.'

'You don't need to apologise. This is not your problem it is ours.'

'It's because I'm afraid. I'm running because I'm a coward.'

'Being afraid is not cowardice, it is sensible after what you have seen here.' Ishimwe put a hand on her shoulder. 'Come on, we need to get going.'

'Yes, we do. Thanks for being so understanding.'

'It's OK,' said Ishimwe with a smile. 'Let's get you to Kigali.'

'Which hotel will we try?'

'The Kifalme Park is good, and you've been there before. It shouldn't take long to get a flight. The telephone system works in Kigali; unlike here!'

'I wish I could just pick up a phone. I haven't even said

goodbye to Angelique, or Joe, or Rosine.'

'I will pass on your goodbyes when I see them, I'm sure it will not be too long.'

'How can you be sure?'

'We have seen this before. They are hiding till it is safe. Trust me. Look. I have your address in New York. We will all write to you. I'll put all the letters in the same envelope to save on postage. We can send pictures too.'

'You don't know where they are.'

'If I knew where they were hiding it would not be a very good hiding place would it?' Ishimwe smiled. 'Come on, we'd better get going, it will take us five hours to get to Kigali.'

Melanie was silent for most of the journey as the countryside rolled by. From time to time children ran down to the side of the road alerted by the trail of dust they had seen approaching in the distance. They shouted, 'good morning' and waved when they saw Melanie, holding their hands out for gifts of sweets or chewing gum.

After a couple of hours, they pulled in at a roadside cabaret; Melanie recognised the shabby bar and white plastic chairs from her first visit months earlier.

'It's not changed.' She said as Ishimwe brought two soft drinks over to their table.

'No, it hasn't, but we have. Is cola okay?'

'Yes. Mm, it's cold too,' said Melanie as she rubbed the cool bottle against her forehead and then wiped the moisture off with her sleeve. 'It sounds pathetic to say this but, how does he get it cold? Does he have a fridge? He can't have electricity.'

'He does have a fridge!' smiled Ishimwe. 'But it is not plugged in to anything, he has a large block of ice in it.'

'Then how...' Melanie stopped.

'I think ice is delivered to all the bars along this road, it's the main route to Kigali.'

'God, that says a lot about me. How can I not know a detail as tiny as cold Coke? I'm pathetic. I know nothing.'

'Don't be so hard on yourself. You've only been here a few

months, you can't know everything. You know more than many, many people about this country.'

He fell silent and looked thoughtful for a moment. 'When you get home, tell people about us. Don't you forget us.'

'Ishimwe, I will never forget the people I have met here. I will never forget you. You've been so kind to me. Thank you.' She reached out and put her hand over the back of Ishimwe's where it rested on the plastic table.

'Thank you, the children will always remember you Melanie. You made them feel special. Do you know that?'

Melanie felt tears prickling the back of her eyes as she answered, quietly. 'Yes.' They were both silent for a moment.

'Well,' said Ishimwe. 'We've got a way to go yet. But it's not long after we've driven through Butare, two hours I'd say.'

He was right, after Butare the road switched from the rough gravel on clay to a tarmac road, they were able to drive faster and before long they were in Kigali.

In the city centre the traffic was chaotic and often stood still; 'just like Rwanda', thought Melanie. Eventually, Ishimwe pulled the car up under the concrete canopy at the front of the Hotel Kifalme Park. Melanie walked into the cool shade of the entrance and up to the reception desk. Ishimwe followed with her bags.

The receptionist confirmed that they had a room for two nights and a porter took her cases. The relaxed and professional atmosphere of the hotel was a contrast to the noise of the city. Melanie turned to face Ishimwe, she wanted to speak but her eyes welled with tears. They embraced briefly but Ishimwe quickly put her at arm's length and smiled saying,

'Come on now. Take a deep breath. Thanks for everything you have done. It has been a pleasure to now you.'

'Oh God I wish... I hate goodbyes,' said Melanie struggling to maintain her composure.

'Ah, do not worry. You will be back here again, I am sure of that. And I will write to you, so will Angelique and Rosine.'

'Do you think this will pass?'

'Yes. It is bad of course, terrible, but life goes on, crops have to be planted and harvested, and the cows have to be milked. There's too much work to be done to waste time fighting. This will blow over. You'll see.'

'OK. I hope so.'

'It will. I have to go now, I need to do as much of the journey in daylight as possible, these roads are dangerous in the dark.'

They embraced one last time. Melanie watched him as he left. As he opened the car door he looked up, smiled, and waved. Within seconds he had pulled away. Melanie followed the porter up to her room. Melanie kicked her shoes off and lay back on the bed. She felt emotionally and physically drained. The linen was clean and the room sleepily fragranced by a vase of lavender on the writing table. It was late afternoon as she drifted into a doze.

She awoke with a start a few hours later. It took a second to remember where she was. The daylight was almost gone, so she went to her balcony to watch the sunset, taking a small bottle of wine out of the mini bar for company. Lights were being switched on in the city centre as the sun began to sink behind the rippling slopes that stretched into the distance. Beyond where the buildings petered out firelights flickered in countless front yards where people cooked their evening meals on the hillsides that surrounded the city. The scene was beautiful, the air was warm, and the wine soothed her anxiety. Already Gilbert's murder seemed unreal, yet it was real, and she decided she had to stop herself dwelling on it. It was an experience that could unhinge her mind. Soon she would be home and then she would deal with it. She headed down to the restaurant.

She dined alone and headed out to the bar by the bright blue swimming pool, that was lit up for the night. Nondescript, ambient jazz drifted lazily above the scene.

With a large Martini in her hand she scanned the seating area for an empty table. She did not really want company as she knew she would end up talking about events in Ruhengeri. It was not a story she was ready to tell, but as she looked about, she spotted a familiar face pointed in her direction.

Michel.

He was at with another man; he grinned and waved her over. The man had greying hair and looked in his mid-fifties. He had no middle-aged spread however but a stocky and powerful build that suggested a lifetime of keeping fit in a hard life. Melanie guessed he was ex-military. She could not think of a good enough reason to decline and so she joined them as Michel stood up and got her a chair.

'Please...'

'It's Melanie.'

'Yes! I know! I had not forgotten. It is just such a surprise to see you here. A lovely surprise. How are you?'

'I'm OK.' She decided on pleasantries. 'How are you?'

'I'm good. Very busy in fact. What brings you here? Are you alone?'

'I'm going home. There's a flight in a couple of days that I can catch.'

'Well, you must keep Francois and I company this evening,' he turned to his friend who stood up to shake Melanie's hand. 'This is an old friend of mine, Melanie, she came here to teach. She is a noble and courageous person I would say.'

'Ha. I'm neither noble nor courageous Michel. Just a teacher.' As she spoke a rocket shot high into the air. Everyone at the bar looked up to see its flight. 'Michel, I'm impressed! Did you order a firework display just for me?'

2

As Melanie drank her Martini in the Kifalme Park an unhappy President Juvenal Habyarimana sat in his personal jet as it circled above Kigali airport returning from negotiations in Dar Es Salaam. The United Nations had twisted his arm a few years ago, and he had signed the Peace Treaty in Arusha, Tanzania, with the RPF. It had not achieved much peace, but he had agreed to sharing power, to democracy, and to having RPF soldiers integrated into the Rwandan army. He allowed himself a snort of derisive laughter when he thought about the farce of the negotiations. He had no intention of honouring the agreement; the plans were already in place for a 'final solution' to the 'Tutsi Problem'.

'What amuses you Juvenal?' asked Cyprien Ntaryamira, President of neighbouring Burundi, whom Habyarimana was giving a lift home. A selection of their senior government ministers chatted in the background.

'Not enough these days.'

'What do you have to worry about? This time next year the RPF will be history.'

'Yes. Of course. But a powerful man must look over his shoulder. The people must know I am strong, when I signed that peace agreement it looked like I had made a weak compromise. I must act soon.'

'You will be fine with your French friends to help you. They won't have the English-speaking Tutsi telling them what to do!'

'No, they are good allies. They even gave me this jet.'

'Complete with French pilots. I must make friends with the French government too!'

Both men laughed as Habyarimana looked out of the window at city below him. Somewhere in the darkness were his palace, his wife Agathe, and their six children. In an hour he would be sat in the palace grounds enjoying a glass of wine. Peace at last.

With clearance to land granted, the pilots began to lose altitude in preparation. From the cockpit the runway of Kigali airport shone the welcome road home. Next the pilot saw the glaring tail of the rocket streaking into the sky and wondered what it was. Then they noticed it was headed for them. Incredulity was quickly followed by indignation, anger, and finally fear.

There was no time to warn the passengers. There was no point in doing so.

It was significant where the wreckage fell. President Juvenal Habyarimana was at peace in his palace grounds sooner than he planned.

3

At the Kifalme Park a large bang and a flash high in the night sky interrupted the mellow poolside atmosphere. Conversation stopped and people looked up in mild surprise. Dozens of guests simultaneously asked one another variations on the theme of; 'what was that?' There were further streaks of light and bangs as the wreckage plunged into the city. The stone had been dropped into the pool and, though the waters closed in over it, the ripples quickly began to spread wide and far.

When conversation recommenced, the discussions fell into two camps; those civilians who had no idea what the spectacle was, and those from a military background who knew precisely. Michel and Francois were in the latter camp. They stared briefly at each other. Melanie spoke first.

'That was no firework.'

'No,' replied Francois with a slight frown.

'It was one of ours, a surface-to-air missile,' said Michel.

'A 'Mistral'?' offered Francois.

'Sounded like it, but firing at what?'

'That was not a big plane. A small jet I'd say, a personal jet. Mused Francois, then he looked directly at Michel. 'And I know of only one person in Kigali with one at his disposal.'

'Habyarimana!' whispered Michel. 'Shit.'

'Keep it quiet. We might not be right, and he might not have been on it. We must not cause a panic. There must be a radio in the hotel bar. There may be some news.'

'What's going on here guys?' asked Melanie.

'Err, I don't know,' replied Michel. 'I'm well, we are, only guessing. But that sounded like a plane being shot down. And over a crowded city, the wreckage could fall anywhere,' he turned to Francois who, with a furrowed brow and shake of the head, indicated he had said enough. 'I'm going to see what I can find out. I'm going to the bar. Do you want another drink?'

'No thanks.' She replied with an indifferent shrug of her shoulders.

He and Francois got up and made their way inside. At the bar a waiter had already got a radio out and was searching for a station. After a lot of high frequency whistles, he finally found RTLM radio. It was playing classical music.

'That's strange' Said the barman.

'What?' asked Michel.

'Classical music. They never play classical music on RTLM. Never.'

'Something's going on,' said Francois. 'Michel, do you have a friend, a contact, you can telephone?'

'Maybe,' he replied, and went down to the end of the bar. He hadn't finished dialling when the music abruptly ended and a quiet but harsh, angry, voice came on the radio, oozing menace.

4

Radio Télévision Libre des Mille Collines

The announcer spoke in a low, threatening voice.

It is 8.45 here in Kigali. They will be struck by misfortune, they will indeed be struck by misfortune. And you have clearly heard that those who desired it, those who desired and provoked it, are themselves being struck by misfortune, Kanyarengwe, the traitor, has just died, Pastor Bizimungu, the traitor, has just died. Whatever made them go and sign a blood pact with the cockroaches who will exterminate us? Whatever prompted them to do that? Aren't they the ones who have just killed them? Aren't they responsible for killing them?

However, they themselves are being struck by misfortune at this moment, at this very minute, at this hour, at this moment I am talking to you! You the people living in Rugunga, those living over there in Kanogo. YES! Those living in Mburabuturo, look in the woods of Mburabuturo, look carefully, see whether there are no cockroaches inside. Look carefully, check, see whether there are no cockroaches inside. Fill up the empty graves. Cut down the tall trees.

The announcer carried on in the same vein until the hotel manager, Justin, switched it off and turned to Francois.

'This will only alarm the guests. Please. Can I get you a drink?' he said with a smile.

Taken aback by his cool demeanour Francois ordered two beers and they returned to their table.

'What was that about?' Melanie directed her questions at Michel. 'What were they saying on the radio?'

'I don't think it is good though I only speak a little Kinyarwanda, but, at a guess, I'd say that ten minutes ago the president got assassinated.'

'Michel...' murmured Francois cautiously.

'Who by?' asked Melanie.

'Again, I can only guess,' continued Michel, 'but that sounded like one of our missiles, but we're only arming one side in this war, so I'd say...'

'That's enough speculation Michel.' Francois cut in. 'We don't know yet, there will be official news tomorrow and it may be that your guesses would be dangerous to say out loud. Even if they are correct.'

'Yes, you're right,' he clinked glasses with Francois. 'The king is dead.'

'Long live the king,' replied Francois, they turned to Melanie and held out their glasses.

'Someone just died,' she said, 'mind if I don't join in?'

'Sorry. You are right. Look there's nothing for you to worry about. You're an American citizen, the UN is in town and they'll look after you. Major General Romeo Dallaire is in charge. I know him. He's a good guy, I saw him here earlier.'

'I already checked for Romeo, he left here as soon as he heard the explosion,' said Francois.

'See?' said Michel to Melanie. 'The UN general's a regular here.'

'Great,' said Melanie. 'What else was the radio saying?'

'Well, it was just a wide-ranging message for calm and to stay indoors. That's good advice, if there are rumours there's trouble in a place like this.'

At that moment the bar was plunged into darkness as the power was cut. A gasp went up from the guests around the pool. The manager was the voice of calm.

'Don't worry; the generators will come in a moment. This happens,' he announced, walking through the bar and to the pool area. Please, normal service will be resumed...as soon as possible,' he looked up at the hotel. 'Let there be light.' The electricity came back on. '...And there was light,' he beamed a smile at the guests who responded with a smattering of applause and laughter. The wallpaper jazz returned.

Melanie turned to Michel and Francois. 'Well it's late and I'm tired. I think I'll turn in.'

'Would you like me to walk you to your room?' offered Michel with a raised eyebrow.

'Ah, chivalry lives on! But no thanks, I know the way. Goodnight.'

She left the men conversing in low whispers at the bar. Up in her room she got herself a drink and looked over the city from her balcony. There was a tense atmosphere created by random shouts of anger, screeching car tyres, and the distant metallic tick of gunfire. Her tiredness was a blessing, and she slept well.

When Melanie awoke on the morning of the 7th of April 1994, she went down to breakfast and wondered what was coming next. She was not alone in this. Joe was in the RPF camp. Grégoire was the leader of the Interahamwe gang in Ruhengeri following his first successful execution. Charles and Uwase hid in the forest and speculated when it would be safe to return to Kinigi. Rosine and Pascale were in hiding. Grace and Denyse were running towards Uganda. Ishimwe woke to bad news. RTLM had repeated its advice that everyone should stay at home till calm was restored, but at the same time the announcer mobilised Hutu men to join the police, the army and Interahamwe in their work.

She did not know yet what the 'work' was.

5

When Melanie looked out in the morning, it seemed that the tranquil clime of the Hotel Kifalme Park struggled to hold out against the storm of fury that had begun to rage beyond its pristine lawns. The command to stay indoors did not apply to everyone. The police, the army and the Interahamwe militia were joined on the streets by hundreds of men. They drank beer and waved knives, machetes, and homemade clubs. Hundreds of roadblocks had been set up across the city to paralyse the movement of its population. At every junction everyone who defied the call to stay indoors had to produce identification papers. They waved them frantically at the barricades as if trying to prove their innocence of some crime.

The atmosphere of violence robbed Melanie of her appetite and she settled for a coffee. Through the lobby windows she could see the blue helmeted UN soldiers on the hotel drive. They reassured her that there was someone to protect them. Rwandan army officers swaggered arrogantly down the corridors but left their murderous intent at the door. For now, they seemed wary of confrontation with the UN.

She watched Michel and Francois working the room, shaking hands conspiratorially with the Rwandan military, whispering in ears and clapping friendly hands onto their client's shoulders, wishing them luck. They were more cautious talking to the UN troops, more concerned to say the right thing. Michel's smile, merely professional at the best of times, now appeared greasy and obsequious.

Melanie took her coffee and walked casually, she hoped, onto the sunlit patio at the side of the hotel. There were other guests walking around too, supposedly 'taking the air'. Their pretence of nonchalance was laid bare by the fact that everyone was glancing fearfully beyond the grounds. It was as if the perimeter of the hotel was an invisible castle rampart beyond which a besieging army clamoured to break in. Rwandan military jeeps sped by and thuggish looking militia strolled past and peered over the walls on tip toe. Melanie glanced up at a cruel face that looked her way; for a second the man's eyes held her own, they were filled with contempt and malice. She quickly turned to go back inside as he bared his teeth in a mockery of a smile and drew his finger across his throat.

As she walked in Michel walked over to her and gently took her arm.

'Melanie, did you arrange a flight yet?'

'No. I was going to ask the hotel to help me with that.' She replied, gently but firmly removing Michel's hand.

'You won't need to, I have good news. The UN are ferrying foreigners to the airport soon. You will be safe. It might be a good idea to pack your things and be ready.'

'Thanks. I'll do that.' She turned to leave but stopped as her anger rose to the surface and a question occurred to her. She turned to face him. 'Michel!'

'Yes.'

'What are you doing here?'

'In this hotel? In Rwanda? What do you mean? You know what I do, I work for the...' She cut him short.

'No. What the fuck are you doing here? Why are you here at all?'

'Well, I thought I explained, my business is...'

'You didn't explain that you're helping a bunch of murderers. You didn't say you were on their side.'

'What do you mean? Of course, there is a war but...'

'I saw a man killed yesterday morning. Butchered, for an audience. French soldiers were there, they organised it.' She pointed a steady, tense finger at him. 'We visited that training camp. You're with these people. They're your friends.'

'No! I'm shocked and sorry to hear this. I'm sure there is another explanation.' Michel held his arms open with his palms facing outward.' Perhaps he committed a crime... could it have been it an execution, perhaps?'

'A crime? You mean like he was guilty of being a Tutsi?'

'Come on, I am not racist. Many people are very frightened and very angry. I'll look into this. If anyone is responsible for a murder, I'll see to it that...'

'You'll see to what?' Melanie stepped up closer to him. 'You'll see to what? If you're just a 'businessman'... you can't 'see to' anything.'

Michel paused, choosing his words carefully. 'Yes, but I have friends... and I know people...'

'Yes, and your friends murder people and you help them to do it,' said Melanie, and finally Michel was silent, his face expressionless. 'I guess I don't know what's really going on here Michel. But one day I'll find out. I'll do something about it. God knows what. But I'll do something.'

*   *   *

The airport was closed to civilian traffic for two days, but the UN made arrangements for all foreign nationals to be flown home at the weekend. Everyone was relieved to be getting out. The hotel was an island in a sea of anarchy. Noisy gangs roamed the streets, while the police and army did nothing to calm the situation. Melanie's last hours at the hotel were disturbed by the sounds of fighting; gunshots, mortars and screams of terror. That the nightmare did not break into the hotel seemed like a miracle. A veil of secrecy surrounded the hotel. Nobody would say what was happening in the city, but rumours of slaughter began to be whispered if not believed.

Finally, on Saturday morning she and dozens of other guests boarded the coach for the journey to the airport. No African citizens were leaving the hotel; in fact, quite a few Rwandans seemed to be moving into it. They arrived at the gates waving Tutsi identity cards shrieking with relief, like shipwrecked sailors who had washed up on the beach of paradise. Melanie sat at the rear of the vehicle of the bus and Michel, to whom she had not spoken since their argument, sat at the front talking to the driver. He had not packed any suitcases and only seemed to be there as an observer.

With UN troops in vehicles at the front and rear the vehicle made its way out of the hotel grounds.

Many of the passengers gazed out of the windows wanting to see an image to explain the chaos that they had so far only heard. Their curiosity was soon brutally rewarded. There were many roadblocks, and although their coach passed through unhindered, the function of the barriers was evident. At every one of them butchered corpses were dumped by the side of the road. The slaughter was no respecter of age or gender. Blood stained the tarmac and congealed in the gutters. Interahamwe whooped and staggered around as they blew whistles and chanted football songs. They waved bloody machetes and bottles of beer and laughed at the departing white faces.

Some on the coach shrieked in horror, others wept silently, and others sat still in numbed silence and fear. As the coach rumbled and bounced along the rough roads Michel walked down the aisle and stopped near where Melanie sat. His face was almost expressionless as he searched for a comment that could match what they had seen.

'My God. It's chaos, out there. Anarchy.' It was only when he had had uttered the opposite of the truth that Melanie finally saw it.

'No. It's not chaos. It's organised.'

'What do you mean?'

'There are no coincidences here. It's all been planned. Everything. Interahamwe did not set all these roadblocks up spontaneously. They're not killing people at random; they're selecting them. The army is not stopping them because they're helping them, they trained them. And the radio station. It's organising them. Why do you pretend you do not know?'

Michel looked at her intently; he gently massaged his forehead with his fingers as if physically searching in his head for a reply. He said nothing and walked back to his seat. Thankfully the coach picked up speed on the main road to the airport outside the city centre and they sped through the few remaining roadblocks. Melanie stared at the back of the seat in front of her, shutting out the world outside. She had seen enough and there was nothing she could do.

The coach swung into the airport car park which was defended like a military base. UN soldiers formed an extra armed perimeter around the coach as the passengers got off. There was fighting taking place to the north west of the airport and they could hear mortar and machine gun fire in the direction of the football stadium. The UN troops were keen to shepherd them off the concrete and into the airport building. Melanie watched as the coaches waited for another convoy to join them and return to the Kifalme Park and collect more passengers. She could see Michel perched on his seat next to the driver.

Once they were safely in the departure lounge Melanie and the other Kifalme Park guests sat and waited. Soldiers handed bottles of water around and a captain apologised for the lack of food. They were assured they would get something to eat on the flight which was due to take off within the hour. The tiny, single counter cafe looked like it had been looted and no Rwandan staff were to be seen. There was no electricity; sunlight stole through the dirty windows and failed to lift the gloom. Slumped in their seats the evacuees were quiet as if what they had witnessed had robbed them of trivial conversation, and yet not given them anything meaningful to say.

A young man with a ruck sack at his feet sat next to Melanie and looked to her as if he was going to speak. In the event he changed his mind, nodded and pursed his lips thoughtfully. They all wanted to be far away and free, but survivors' guilt robbed them of the joy of escape. It was not their war yet still they felt like deserters. Their grim expressions were replicated on the faces of the UN troops. It was as if they knew that this day would haunt them for years to come; when the soldierly virtue of following orders without question would be revealed as a vice. Brave men turned into seeming cowards by their leaders in New York.

The plane taxied up to the departure building as the second group of coaches arrived. The evacuees and some soldiers climbed the steps up to the body of the jet that gleamed white in the sunshine. It held the promise of safety and civilisation. At last a sense of relief stole over some people's faces.

At the top of the stairs everyone paused briefly and took one last look around before they stepped inside the door. The looks they gave to the city differed, some offered an unspoken prayer, others asked forgiveness, but all turned away with regret. Melanie looked as far as she could into the distant hills as if she could see Angelique, Rosine, Joe or Ishimwe, as if by looking she could help them. She had paused too long and the irritation in the queue behind her became audible.

'Please, can we get on the plane lady?' said an agitated and sweating passenger before he pushed past her. Behind him was a nun who paused before she too walked by. She turned and laid a sympathetic hand on Melanie's arm as she spoke sadly and quietly.

'I know. We're running away aren't we?' She looked into Melanie's eyes. 'I wish I could stay. But what else can we do? We can't change the world?' With that she patted Melanie's arm and stepped into the aircraft.

At that moment the faces she had searched for on the distant horizon came into sharp focus in her mind. Suddenly Melanie realised the nun was wrong and the little message her mother written down for her rang clear in her mind: 'you can only change the world one person at a time'.

She did not know what she would achieve by staying, but she knew that if she left, she would never forgive herself. Not bothering to apologise she barged down the crowded stairs and onto the tarmac apron and sprinted back to the terminal building. The departure lounge was filling up again as

another coachload of guests from other Kigali hotels, sluiced
their terrified refugees into the airport terminal. The makeshift customs arrangements were nothing more than a couple
of tables manned by UN staff and Melanie stomped past them,
ignoring their half-hearted requests for her to stop. She was
soon through the front doors of the Kigali airport and into
the parking lot in the bright sunshine. The Kifalme Park coach
was revving its engine and readying to go back to the hotel. As
it set off she ran alongside it, banging on the door.

'Stop! Stop!' She shouted. 'Let me on. I'm coming back
with you.' With a slight squeal of brakes, the coach halted, and
the door opened with a hydraulic hiss. Melanie pounced up
the steps with an angry energy. 'Thank you.'

Michel was again sat on the foremost seat and as Melanie
bounded on his mouth dropped open in dumb surprise. Eventually he managed to lamely exclaim; 'Melanie!'

'Michel.' she replied with eyebrows raised.

'Why are you...'

'I couldn't bear to leave you Michel.'

'Well... but I...'

'I'm joking! I don't even like you! But right now, I need you.
Don't cross me Michel. You won't like me when I'm sarcastic.'
With that she leaned over and held her face close to his. She
paused. 'You'll like me even less when I'm angry.' She gazed
into his eyes. 'Don't make me angry. Michel.'

Michel leaned back in his seat. He was a man of influence
and some power. He didn't like the threatening tone in Melanie's voice. He didn't like her attempt to turn the tables on
him.

'What do you think you are doing?' he asked.

'I'm coming back with you.'

'But Melanie, it is dangerous here.'

'Michel. I'm wearing a suit of armour. It's my skin. I'm
white. And I carry an American passport. I've got a bodyguard;
you! And you're going to make sure I'm safe.' She reached out
and patted his cheek. 'I had a good chat with the UN guys in the

airport and I told them you're going to look after me Michel. Or you're going to have to explain to them why you didn't. Do you understand?'

Her lie worked and Michel took a deep breath. He understood.

6

It was late in the evening when a weary Father Ishimwe made it back to Holy Family Church. Father Patrice was sat in the presbytery lounge waiting for him.

'Ishimwe, you've been driving all day, you must be tired. Freshen up then come and have a beer with me.'

'Yes. Good idea.' Patrice's friendly manner took Ishimwe by surprise. 'It was a long journey and I'm glad to be back. I'll have a quick wash; I could do with that beer!'

Rinsing the dust and sweat off his face with cold water revitalised him. Briefly he pondered his colleague's change of attitude, came to a conclusion, and whispered it to the mirror; 'Well, I guess he's as stressed as I am after all,' he said as he patted his face dry. Feeling much better he switched off the light in the bathroom and strode down the dark corridor to the lounge. Patrice had a beer ready for him on the table. He picked it up and slumped backwards onto the old sofa.

'Cheers,' he offered with a slight smile and Patrice clinked bottles with him. 'Are you OK? You look concerned Father.'

'I'm fine. I had a good sleep this afternoon. I apologise if I was harsh on you earlier today, I was not feeling well.'

'That's OK father, we all have our moments!'

'Yes, me more than many I suppose. Anyway. You haven't heard the news on the car radio, have you? I can tell.'

'No, it's broken. What news.'

'Have a good taste of that beer first.' Patrice advised, Ishimwe obliged with a shrug.

'OK. It's bad. This evening the president's plane was shot

down as it came in to land in Kigali. Everyone on board was killed. Habyarimana is dead.'

Ishimwe froze. He quickly tried to foresee the consequences of this disaster. 'Do they know who did it?'

'No, I don't think so. The radio has blamed the Tutsi rebel forces.'

'Who is in charge? What has the government said?'

'They are advising people to stay indoors until the situation calms down. It looks like the army are taking control.'

'Oh no! Melanie is in Kigali.'

'She is probably in the safest place Ishimwe. The UN are there and will look after her.' For a few minutes the two men sat and drank in silence.

'What do you think we should we do Patrice?'

'We must play our part for the Church, for our parishioners in Kinigi Ishimwe. Many people will be worried. They should do as the government suggests but I think it would good for us to visit those we can and reassure them.'

'Many local Tutsi went into hiding since the trouble in Ruhengeri. Have any come back home?'

'I think so, yes, so our friend Jean Damascène tells me. Others will surely come home soon. They must; that is what the authorities want. We will be here to look after them.'

For the next hour, before they went to bed, the two priests talked about who they would visit over the next couple of days. Ishimwe was glad that Patrice had got over his bad mood, he had been drinking then anyway, surely that explained his anger. He was fine now, back to his old self, and showing what a good shepherd of his flock he truly was. Ishimwe pushed his doubts about Patrice to the back of his mind, with his experience the old priest would be a rock in a crisis.

*   *   *

The next day Patrice and Ishimwe went out and about in

Kinigi. They travelled about their large parish separately and on foot. They checked on as many people as they could. About half of the Tutsi families that had gone missing had returned. They were careful about staying indoors and locking themselves in. For some people that meant jamming a chair behind the door, for others a padlock and chain on the metal gates to their yards. Once they got the message off the radio the people, obedient as ever, complied with it.

The responses Ishimwe got from people depended upon who he was visiting. Tutsi families were edgy, peeping through cracks in doors from inside their darkened houses. Often, they pretended not to be in when he knocked or called through an empty window frame. They waited in silence, hiding where they could. When it was obvious the visitor was Ishimwe they relaxed a little and he was able to reassure them they would be safe. At Hutu homes he was greeted quite coolly or met with a sullen silence. They did not want to talk when they found it was the Tutsi priest. Worse was the false bonhomie he got from Jean Damascène and some of his friends. Jean invited him for a drink at Evariste's bar. He went along to be diplomatic, but he felt the conversation from the men there; Evariste, Thierry, Daniel, Oscar and Vincent was forced as though they were hiding something.

He only stayed for one beer. The older men would only talk about the weather, or their crops, which in fact they were ignoring. Nobody was working in the fields. When he tried to bring up the current situation, they were evasive and offered platitudes; 'Ah, yes, these are difficult times', 'The president, such a shame. 'He was still young'. 'He's left a wife and children behind him.' Their words were empty, but their coded glances to one another were full of meaning.

In the shadows sat a group of younger men he had not expected to see there; Albert, Cyprien, Placide, Patrick and Fabrice all sat round Grégoire who acted as if he were their leader; though leader of what Ishimwe could not say. He said hello to them, but group just stared at him and did not return his greeting. Grégoire's stare in particular was filled with contempt and just before he left, he felt he had to challenge it, to see if he could disarm him with his avuncular charm.

'Young Grégoire. How are you? Are you well?' he said, but he drew only silence in response. 'You'll be wanting to get back your studies, won't you? Back to school.' The others looked between the two of them but Grégoire did not look away only stared at the priest more intently. The silence became an embarrassment to Ishimwe, so he decided to break it off. 'Well. I'll be going now. See you soon. At Church I hope.' As he turned to leave Grégoire spat loudly onto the floor. The other boys roared with laughter at the priest's departing back. Ishimwe pretended he had not heard it and left.

*   *   *

By the weekend the tension in Kinigi had increased still further. Rumours of massacres began to spread. At night one could hear occasional gunfire and, by day, disparate columns of smoke to the south of the village suggested a number of mysterious fires. People connected these signs up; tales of families being murdered, and homes being destroyed were passed around amongst the scared Tutsi. On the Saturday morning Ishimwe had his update meeting with Pascale. As he arrived Jean Damascène was just leaving Patrice's office, he looked up and twisted his mouth into a smile for Ishimwe as they passed one another.

'Good afternoon Jean.'

'Good afternoon Father, it's always a pleasure to see you.' Ishimwe paused for a moment and then entered Patrice's study, knocking gently on the door as he did so.

'Ah good, you are back. How was it today?' asked Patrice brightly.

'Same as yesterday. A bit worse, people are panicking a little. Frightened by rumours, I don't know. It's not good but...'

'Yes, I understand,' replied Patrice, nodding and blinking slowly. 'Things will get easier. You are doing the right thing. In fact, I have an idea. Why don't you celebrate the mass tomorrow? Prepare your sermon, spend a day on it. I will go around the village now and visit what people I can. I think our Tutsi parishioners in particular should come to Church, they need our support most.'

'Which mass? We have two scheduled.'

'I've put a notice on the Church door. We'll just have one at 11.00 o'clock. You take it and bring our community together. You can give them the gospel message of comfort and reconciliation. Let the words of Christ himself heal our people. What do you say?'

'Yes! That's a great idea. But you could do it so much better than I Patrice. You are so experienced, they respect you as the parish priest, you are the senior.'

'Oh Ishimwe! You do me an honour. Thank you, but, come on now, I am getting a bit out of date with my 'burn in hell sinners' nonsense. It belongs in the past. You have the gift to reconcile. You are a healer.'

'Well, I...' Ishimwe was taken aback, it was a privilege to say the main Sunday mass, and he sensed an opportunity. 'Thank you, Father. What is the gospel?'

'Change the gospel of the day; choose one that fits, one that meets the people's need. Nobody will know you did it.'

'Yes. There's only one gospel message; 'love your neighbour'. All the rest flows from that.'

'Love your neighbour, yes, Hutu or Tutsi. That is the central teaching of the Church.'

'Thank you, Patrice. Look if you don't mind, I'll get started on this. I'll check out the other readings. What are they?'

'Ha! Ishimwe. I'm good but not that good! Check the Lectionary.'

'You are that good, come on, 2nd Sunday of the Church's year,' said Ishimwe, narrowing his eyes and smiling at Patrice as he threw down the challenge the older man could not resist.

'Hmm... 2nd Sunday. The Old Testament one is from Genesis. There's going to be something from the Book of the Acts of the Apostles because it's just after Easter. Gospel would have been... from Saint John on the resurrection?'

He was pretty close. Half an hour later Ishimwe stood alone on the altar looking at the texts he was to preach on. When he looked at the Old Testament reading, he could not believe his luck. This was a message that needed to be heard. He knew the passages well enough and went to his room to write his sermon.

*   *   *

He was in the church two hours before the mass on Sunday morning. He wanted the building to himself, to pray alone in the empty space and listen to the Holy Spirit for guidance. He knelt down before the altar and took out his rosary beads. He did not say the lengthy prayer often, he found the meditative themes too dry and his attention tended to wander till he was daydreaming. On this day however he knew it was just the thing he needed. The act of participating in the ancient tradition with its cycle of Our Fathers and Hail Marys would soothe his worries. At first the prayer went well as each prayer split neatly in half, his breathing fell into the correct rhythm, turning the words into a chant. The empty Church was a good place to pray as the silence in the large space gave it a more intense spiritual focus. For a while Ishimwe was at peace.

However, as he prayed, he became aware of noises beyond the closed doors. It sounded like people were arriving early, waiting for the Church to open. Finally, a loud knock meant Ishimwe could pray in solitude no more. He had to open up and see what was going on. He walked down the aisle with a slight frown on his face. 'Why are they so early?' He wondered.

He pulled back the wooden beam that locked the big doors and swung them open. Around three hundred people were gathered in front of the Church clutching bags of clothes, cooking equipment and small children. They were not dressed for mass but carrying belongings like refugees seeking sanctuary. The people were different shapes, sizes, ages, and wore a kaleidoscope of different colours, but the look on all their faces was identical:

Fear.

At the front of the crowd was a familiar face. Charles stood clutching a broken cardboard suitcase with Uwase and the twins. The unwashed faces of the children were streaked with tears. Charles spoke.

'Father Ishimwe, thank God it is you. What time is mass today?' His voice aimed for dignity, but he was unable to hide the fact that it was a plea.

'You are a bit early,' replied Ishimwe, noting that there was a clear sign on the door as Patrice had promised. He spoke a little louder over Charles' shoulder to those nearby. 'You are all early. Did you not know the first mass was cancelled?'

'Please, you must let us in.' Charles replied. 'We will be safe here.' A part of Ishimwe wanted to say no. This was a Church not a refugee camp, the bags, pots and pans would be out of place, they would detract from the holiness of the setting. But he knew he could not deny them. His job, the Church's job was to meet their needs. If they wanted shelter, he had to give it, even if he felt they didn't need it. He pushed the doors back.

'Of course, Charles, of course.' Ishimwe then addressed the crowd opening his arms out wide. 'Please, everybody. You are welcome here, after all this is not my Church but yours. As Jesus himself said 'there are many rooms in my Father's house',' he smiled at them in the sunshine. 'Well, of course, there's only one room here, but it's a big one. Big enough for all of us. And safe.' With that he stood back, and the throng slowly trudged wearily and warily in, looking over their shoulders as if to spot an invisible pursuer. Within half an hour the crowd that had been three hundred was being added to by people walking in from the hills and fields around; it would soon be more than doubled.

Ishimwe busied himself helping those who were clearly tired after the long journey from the far corners of the parish. The elderly and the young had struggled, and many were thirsty. He got some volunteers to fill jugs with water in the kitchen and encouraged them to go around giving people a drink from whatever receptacle would hold liquid. Finally, he managed to hunt down Charles, who was slumped against the cool brick wall with Clement in his lap.

'I went to your house Charles. You've not been there for days. I was worried about you and your family.'

'We have been hiding in the forest. We'd still be there, but the children are too young.'

'Are you really so scared?'

'People have been murdered Ishimwe. Whole families.'

'How do you know this?'

'I have heard.'

'It's just rumours Charles... panic and hearsay, come on. I know you well. You aren't taken in by this nonsense. Can you even name a single person?'

Charles looked at Ishimwe, narrowing eyes now drained of tears. 'Ishimwe. Do you not know?'

Ishimwe looked back. His only answer was 'I do not know' but he knew it was the wrong time to advertise his ignorance. 'Who?' was all he could say. Charles reached and placed a heavy hand on Ishimwe's shoulder, drawing him near so he would not have to speak out loud.

'Who, Charles, who?'

'Angelique,' said Charles in a low voice. 'Angelique. She is gone.'

'Oh my God. Who did this? No, I do not want to know. What about Joe? Was Joe killed too?'

'Joe was not with her, but he knows. I met him in the forest and told him. He is safe, or at least as safe as anyone can be. He has gone to find his father and join the RPF.'

'Oh my God. Angelique. Joseph.' Ishimwe rocked back dizzily onto his heels and held his head in his hands. For a moment he did not know what to do. Images of Angelique and Joe flashed through his mind. He felt shock, not grief; he knew that would come later. There would be a time for tears. At the back of his mind a voice told him that time was not now, though he could not reason why. Then, with the Church bell chiming he remembered; he had to say mass. Patrice was ringing the bell calling the faithful. He had something he could do. A comfort he could offer the hundreds that had filled his Church. He could offer the sacrament of the mass. He was relieved to find a worthwhile course of action that avoided confronting and slumping against the brick wall of grief. He stood erect and looked down at Charles.

'Charles. Thank you.'

'For what?'

'For helping Joe. For being a good man, a good husband, a good father, a good friend and a good… well, thank you.' Ishimwe ran out of categories, but he was readying himself for his priestly preaching role. 'Charles I am glad you here. This is the right place to be. The right place to be safe, and to hear the word of God, that we may find comfort.'

He looked about him at the Church that was already full, and even more were arriving at the door, called by Patrice's bell. It was a congregation of refugees perhaps, but a congregation all the same. 'I had better get ready for mass Charles, I'll see you later,' he looked down at the father cradling his son, knowing that his sudden grasping of the priestly role was just that, an act. But it was the part he had to play.

Charles smiled faintly. 'Yes, Father Ishimwe. We need God now. We need you too. Good luck up there! I couldn't do your job.'

Ishimwe smiled in return and turned to walk to the vestry and robe himself for the celebration. As he passed through the crowd desperate upturned faces looked to him for help and reassurance. He felt their fear and, though he knew he had little protection to offer, he acted as if he was a rock they could cling to. He smiled, shook an outstretched hand, and caressed a proffered babe in arms. There was nothing he could say, but he hoped his calm and confident manner would comfort them. And though he did not realise it, it did.

In the vestry he noticed that Father Patrice was not yet here, but he brushed away the split second of concern. He could say mass on his own. Patrice needed to be out amongst the congregation. That was his strength; he was a good pastoral man by instinct. Ishimwe figured that was why he was not here yet, he would be with congregation already.

Ishimwe passed the vestments over his head and tied the white rope cord around his waist. He kissed the embroidered red cross on his stole before putting it over his shoulders. As he dressed, he remembered his conversation with Charles. Angelique! The horror! Who could... but he stopped the train of thought. There was nothing to be gained by giving in to sadness. There would be time for that. And a time for justice too, he would be reporting this to the police and demanding they investigate this. 'Yes', he told himself, 'there is a great deal of work I can do'.

He checked his appearance in a full-length mirror in the vestry. He wore a green stole over a white chasuble. He nodded approvingly at his reflection. He looked the part, and he knew that was important. A good liturgy, a good service, was theatre. Religious costume was part of the spectacle. Some men were waiting by the door and were ready to be his altar boys. He sent one ahead with a box of matches to light the two candles on the altar. The mass would be as normal as possible, and that would reassure them in this abnormal time. Indeed, as the candles were lit, the crowd hushed and formed itself into a congregation awaiting their priest.

As Ishimwe stepped out from the vestry, all eyes turned toward him. Knowing he had their attention he made his way in a solemn and dignified manner down the central aisle of the Church; his makeshift group of four altar boys made a brief procession behind him. There was no hymn sung, but the silence was respectful.

On reaching the sanctuary Ishimwe genuflected and climbed up the three steps before turning to face the people. He began with the sign of the cross.

'In the name of the Father, and of the Son, and of the Holy Spirit.' To his relief the congregation joined in, quietly, but they were with him. He began the introductory rite. 'The grace of our Lord Jesus Christ, the love of God and the fellowship of the Holy Spirit be with you all.'

'And also with you.' Came the response, like an echo.

'My dear people we are gathered here today to celebrate the Holy Sacrifice of the mass. We have come with many worries, with many fears,' he paused to offer a slight and gentle, knowing, smile. 'But we come together, before our creator, who so loved us that he sent his Son to free us from the slavery of sin. That Son who died to prepare a place for us in heaven. With this faith let us ask our Heavenly Father for forgiveness. Let us call to mind our sins.' After a suitable pause he began... 'I confess...'

'...to Almighty God, and to you my brothers and sisters...' It was working, the shared responses were growing in resonance, next he began the penitential rite...

'Lord have mercy...'

The congregation chimed back with the responses and, it seemed to Ishimwe, that they relaxed a little more with each one. The Catholic mass had a rhythm and a consoling familiarity; it was working its magic on these trembling souls thought Ishimwe. It was soon time for the readings and, with no lay reader organised, Ishimwe walked calmly to the pulpit.

'The first reading is from the book of Genesis.' Ishimwe cleared his throat and spoke in a voice that, whilst it was clear and authoritative, was also warm. His tone reflected what he felt deep inside; this was the truth, it was a message of liberation and hope. It was the good news. He hoped the Old Testament reading would speak for itself.

'Now Abel kept flocks, and Cain worked the soil. In the

course of time Cain brought some of the fruits of the soil as an offering to the Lord. And Abel also brought an offering - fat portions from some of the firstborn of his flock. The Lord looked with favour on Abel and his offering, but on Cain and his offering he did not look with favour. So, Cain was very angry, and his face was downcast...'

At first, he did not notice it but there was some noise or disturbance going on outside and it was beginning to distract his listeners. He was aware that people were increasingly turning around and looking at the doors at the back of the Church. He looked up and paused momentarily but decided his only option was to carry on.

'...Then the Lord said to Cain, "Why are you angry? Why is your face downcast? If you do what is right, will you not be accepted? But if you do not do what is right, sin is crouching at your door; it desires to have you, but you must rule over it."

He stopped once more. The noise outside was now unmistakeable, singing voices, whistles blowing, there was a crowd gathering. From the benches came soft moans of fear. Mothers clutched children tightly to them. Fathers tried to stand tall and see what danger was coming their way. Very few people were listening to Ishimwe's reading, yet he took up the story again, there was nothing else he could do.

'Now Cain said to his brother Abel, "Let's go out to the field." While they were out in the field Cain attacked his brother Abel and killed him. Then the Lord said to Cain, "Where is your brother Abel?" "I don't know," he replied. "Am I my brother's keeper?"

As he finished the reading, he tried to remember what he had planned to say. His memory faltered, it was something about how Christ had come to save both Cain and Abel, but the words would not come out. He gripped the pulpit to cover the fact that his hands were shaking, anxiety swirled in the pit of his stomach and he felt sick. A loud bang on the back doors made his head jerk upright, and he stared down the aisle of the Church.

Cain had arrived.

7

The cabaret opened earlier than usual that Sunday morning. Four government soldiers bought cases of beer and urwagwa off a smiling Evariste. He did a week's trade in ten minutes. The soldiers took the booze down to the square in Kinigi and put it on a trestle table there. As leader of the local Interahamwe Grégoire had sent his comrades out around the houses making sure local men were ready to help in the work of the day. Any male over the age of fifteen and fit enough to wield a machete was expected to take part.

Fabrice, Albert, Cyprien and Patrick jogged into the square where Grégoire waited with the soldiers. Hutu men from all around streamed behind them carrying clubs and machetes. The air was filled with excited chatter as bottles of free beer were handed round. Evariste stood talking and drinking with Jean Damascène, and their crew.

'See Jean Damascène, I am better equipped than any of you.'

'How so Evariste?' Jean asked.

'I have a bottle opener and a machete! Here give me your bottles.' The men managed a laugh despite the tension. Evariste was keen to be at the forefront, his only chance of saving his wife from slaughter was if he could prove himself to his friends and Interahamwe. Grégoire ended a conversation with the commanding soldier by clinking bottles with him, and then he turned to his friends.

'Fabrice, Albert, stand by me while I speak to the men. Keep an eye on them, report to me the name of any man who looks unwilling or tries to walk away. Patrick, Cyprien, stand at the back of the crowd, let them know you are there watching them. We are all in this together, everyone must take part,' he looked about him. 'Has anyone seen Placide? He's got to be with us.'

'He was here. He said he forgot his machete, so he went home for it,' said Cyprien.

'If he turns up without one, then give him one from our store. In fact, fetch the little coward if he's not here in ten minutes,' replied Grégoire. 'Placide is not getting away with standing by. Today he will kill or be killed. It's his choice. Let's get this started.'

Grégoire surveyed the crowd. There were about 200 men present all were armed with a weapon of some kind. The soldiers had grenades and rifles. He blew hard on his whistle.

'OK everybody. Now listen to me. Today we have the chance to rid Kinigi of the Tutsi forever, the chance to be safe. All across Ruhengeri province good Hutu men are gathering to defend their communities. It is time to destroy your enemy.' The crowd cheered. 'And I have good news that will make our work easier.' Grégoire indicated to his left, Father Patrice stepped forward and stood by Grégoire's side and spoke.

'Our plan has paid off. All the local cockroaches have been advised to gather at the Church. They are all inside with Father Ishimwe, the traitor and spy, who is their leader. They think they are safe in there.' Patrice triumphantly shook his fist in the air. 'They are like rats in a trap. Waiting to be exterminated,' his announcement was met with cheers and applause. Grégoire took over.

'We need four groups for the work. There needs to be a roadblock at both ends of Kinigi. Check the papers of anybody trying to get in or out. If they are Tutsi kill them. If they do not have papers and say they are Hutu, take them prisoner and try to find someone who knows them personally to make sure.' Grégoire strutted around like a general while Jean Damascène looked on with pride. He outlined his plans to the members of Interahamwe in their brightly coloured shirts.

'I want at least twenty men for each one roadblock, and I want the same number to sweep round the town to catch any who may be hiding. That should leave over a hundred of us for the work at the Church. Interahamwe will lead you to victory. Today is not a day for farmers to tend crops; it is a day for heroes to protect their wives and children. We must kill or be killed. We will be finished before the sun has set. There will be meat and beer for all at a celebration here in the square tonight.'

Half an hour later the roadblock groups had gone off to begin their work, each armed with machetes and crates of beer. The group tasked with searching the village was left to some younger men as they might need to be quick in the chase. The main body of Interahamwe made their way to the Church. Grégoire and his friends, Kinigi United, led the way singing 'Tubatsembatsembe' once more; 'let us exterminate them'.

After ten minutes walking, they rounded a bend past the school and the red brick Church came into view. Above its door a large statue of Christ was attached to the wall. Its arms were stretched wide in an open gesture of welcome.

On their arrival the crowd fell silent, hushed by Fabrice, Albert and himself. They hoped not to alert those inside just yet. Patrick and Cyprien brought up the rear of the gang making sure no one slipped away. With them was Placide, clutching a brand-new machete. Grégoire called him over, they stood face to face and Grégoire gripped the smaller teenager by his skinny shoulder.

'So, here you are soldier. And with a new machete, these come all the way from China I understand. I will be checking it later, make sure it is red with blood. Do you understand?'

'I won't let you down.'

'Of course, you won't, you're one of the boys, you played for Colline Kinigi United. Tonight we'll have a beer together.' Grégoire released his grip and patted Placide on the head. With that he walked over to the soldiers who stood outside the Church.

'Let's let them know we are here. Have you got a grenade for me?' Grégoire asked.

'Yes, here, have you used one in training?' asked the army

captain.

'Yes, of course,' Grégoire shot back, keen to demonstrate his confidence and leadership. 'I'll throw it in through one of the windows. That will create chaos inside, then we'll open the doors and you can fire off some shots.'

'Not too many, we don't want to waste bullets.'

'No problem, anyway, I want plenty of cockroaches alive for these men to do their work.

'OK, we'll fire a dozen or so rounds then back off to let your men in. We'll stay outside in case any climb out of a window or sneak out of a side door. Ready to throw the grenade?'

'Yes.' Sensing action the crowd had begun singing again and whistles were blowing. Grégoire walked to the front and faced the big Church doors. He stood silent, as if in contemplation.

'What are you waiting for?' shouted one of the soldiers, Grégoire turned and smiled with a curl of his lip.

'It is good manners to knock.' Suddenly he sprang forward and, with a bang, planted his foot on the door to announce his presence. He ended Ishimwe's reading of Genesis. Looking up, he saw a big window open six feet above him to his right. Taking the pin out of the grenade he tossed it in, and it dropped on the other side of the door. Then he stood back, folded his arms, and waited for the explosion.

8

The bang on the door had broken the spell cast by Ishimwe, the knotted snake of fear that coiled in everyone's stomach churned and writhed. Some women shepherded their children towards the altar and away from the threat at the back of the Church. All the men stood up; some in front of their families in a vain gesture of protection, some moved towards the door to confront the violence that waited to charge in. These saw the grenade fall in through the window and quickly turned to run back, some made it down the aisle, some tripped and fell over each other. One or two had the idea of throwing it back out and stepped towards the metal object spinning on the floor but they were not quick enough; Grégoire had timed his throw too well.

When the grenade exploded the noise deafened those nearby just as the metal shattered into thousands of pieces of shrapnel to tear into their flesh. The Church filled with screams of panic, dread, and the agony of the injured. A cloud of dust spread from the back of the Church towards the altar. Ishimwe pushed through those at the front and walked down the central aisle with his arms wide open. He wanted to appeal for calm but was too shocked to speak. Near the door the dead and dying lay in a quickly spreading pool of blood. Ishimwe pushed through the fleeing people with a few men, hoping to assist the injured. They did not know what to do, but they wanted to be by their sides.

As they got to the bloody mess at the back, the doors flew open and the soldiers started firing into the crowd. They did not need to aim, they could not miss. There were so many targets that none of their bullets did not make it to the back wall, and all found its mark in somebody's flesh.

By this time the 'lucky' ones were already dead.

Despite being stood near to the door Ishimwe was unhurt. Still walking forward, he was blinded by the blaze of light that came through the open doors. He saw the shapes of men come sprinting in whirling machetes above their heads, shouting and blowing whistles, whilst behind him the crowd screamed in terror. He recognised the first face running towards him.

Grégoire's first concern was to set an example to those following him in. He would teach them that indiscriminate slaughter demanded merciless violence. Anyone who showed mercy to a Tutsi was a traitor. He recognised the face of the priest; it did not concern Grégoire to remember his name. Ishimwe gasped in recognition and formed the first syllable of Grégoire's name.

With all his strength Grégoire swung his machete at Ishimwe's face. Ishimwe saw the movement as if in slow motion and raised his arms to protect himself. He watched the blade in disbelief, knowing that he would be in pain soon, but he was not yet. Not till it made contact with his arm. Then he would feel it, he was aware that these were his last moments of not suffering. Deep inside him was the hope that even now this monstrous intrusion could be avoided.

Grégoire harboured no such complexity of thought. The priest was meat to be butchered, and then he would turn to his next victim. He felt some resistance as the blade sliced through the flesh, followed by a knock as the keen edge bit into the bone cutting his arm almost right through. Ishimwe shuddered in agony and shock, as he staggered back feeling dizzy and sick. His right arm spasmed and flailed aimlessly at his side with blood spurting from the gaping slash in his flesh. Ishimwe looked down in horror. He did not feel Grégoire's next blow as the machete caught him in the throat cutting right through to the cervical vertebrae, just above the collar bone. Ishimwe's head flopped backwards under its own weight. The last thought he had, other than a desire that this be over, was a recognition that he could see the ceiling of the Church. There was no more. The person Ishimwe had been fled. He was now solely represented by his corpse that lay flat on its back in the aisle of the Church.

Exhilaration and victorious energy flushed through Grégoire's body as gloried in his achievement; a swift kill to inspire his followers. He turned to see that they had indeed watched his work and his example had empowered them to join in. With a roar of anger and a lust for death Interahamwe hammered their machetes into the fleeing crowd. They did not care who or what they struck, as long as the rigid blade met yielding flesh, they were happy. Quickly, screams of terror, and useless pleas for mercy, were replaced by screams of pain. The killers did their work hacking, slashing and stabbing.

As the orgy of violence surged and howled around him Grégoire remembered to keep a cool head. He had a responsibility to make sure everyone was involved. He could not afford to leave a witness who did not have blood on his hands, someone who could point an accusing finger at a later date. They were all in this together. He went to find Placide.

Grégoire soon spotted him and strode up to him. Inevitably Placide stood at the rear of the church and away from the violence.

'Placide. My favourite Hutu warrior. Show me the blood on your machete.'

Looking nervous he held up his blade for inspection. It was red with blood but Grégoire suspected he had wiped it on from a corpse.

'Who did you kill?' Placide pointed to a body lay under one of the benches.

'I killed him and another over there.'

'Did anyone see you?'

'I don't know. How would I know?' Cyprien stood nearby.

'Cyprien. Did you see Placide kill this man, or anyone else?'

'I was not looking, he may have. I'm not sure.'

'OK, let's make sure. Let's find him someone.'

There were not many people alive at the rear of the Church by now but Grégoire spotted a man moving, perhaps twitching, sat against the wall. He gripped Placide's arm and led him over, Cyprien followed. The man was maybe in his thirties he had shrapnel wounds to his leg and what looked like a bullet hole in his shoulder. He clutched a dead child which flopped in his arms like a rag doll.

'Here Placide. Finish this one off. I want to see you kill,' he pushed Placide forward. 'Kill him.' Placide raised his machete, but the blow did not fall. 'Kill him you coward!' The man looked up. It was Charles. His child, Clement, lay dead in his arms. Uwase and Claude were stretched out to his right, blood still oozing from their flesh. He looked into Placide's face.

'It's Charles!' Placide pleaded.

'It's a Tutsi. Kill it.' Grégoire poked his machete in Placide's back, cutting him and drawing blood under his shirt. Placide looked into Charles' eyes and in that split second, he realised that Charles wanted to die. All he had ever loved had been taken from him and slaughtered by his side. He had not been able to save them, and he did not wish to save himself. Placide swung his machete down with all strength he could muster onto Charles' shoulder near the neck. Placide prayed he had ended his agony.

Grégoire looked on, satisfied that Placide was no longer innocent. 'What do you think Cyprien? Is Placide one of us? Or is he a coward and a traitor?'

'I think his arms are too thin for the task,' he swung a powerful blow where Placide had struck and Charles' head fell onto the floor. Blood bubbled from the remaining stump of his neck.

'Tomorrow Placide, you are on the roadblocks. You can check the papers.' Grégoire clapped Placide on the back and moved away as Cyprien tugged at his arm.

'Grégoire, one thing.'

'What is it Cyprien?'

'There are still some Tutsi left. At the front, they are mostly women.'

'Yes.'

'Maybe we should save some of the women. Not kill them yet. If you know what I mean.'

'Good idea Cyprien. Let's go and choose some of them. They don't all need to die today.'

They left Placide looking down at the bodies of Charles and his family. Blood dripped from his blade to the ground and formed a little puddle at his feet. He dropped the machete and walked slowly out of the Church into the sunshine. At the rear of the Church one of the soldiers called to him.

'You there. Come here.'

Placide walked over to the uniformed man and stood gazing into his face.

'It's not over yet.'

Placide said nothing, but slightly titled his head and continued to stare at the man.'

'You can't go till you've been dismissed.'

Placide looked the soldier up and down, turned and walked away.

'You will get in big trouble for this.' The man shouted at Placide's retreating back.

Placide had nowhere particular to go but, led by his deeply troubled conscience, his feet took him to Joe's house. He looked around, but it was obvious they had fled. Placide hoped Joe at least had found safety.

Within an hour the frenzied feast of slaughter had subsided. The only sound was the sobbing of a group of forty young women who were sat with their feet and hands tied at the foot of the altar. They trembled with horror at what they had seen and fear at what would come next.

9

Around five o'clock the killers finished at the Church and headed back to the village square. The soldiers led the way in the jeep, Interahamwe and the men from Kinigi followed on foot. All were tired and, although the younger men in Interahamwe chatted about what they had seen and done, there was not much conversation from the older ones as they thought back over the day.

Several fires had been lit and the women of the village were cooking big chunks of fresh meat; the Tutsi cattle had been slaughtered like their owners. A table was set up with plenty of free beer and the potent urwagwa. Groups of friends gathered together to discuss the events of the day. Gloria handed Jean a beer.

'Here, take this. You look tired. How did it go today?'

'We did our duty.'

'There must have been a lot of people in the Church, they came from miles men, women...'

'Away with your questions. This isn't the time.'

'What happened to the women?' Asked Gloria after a pause. 'Did you kill them all?'

'Enough questions I said.' Jean took a long drink of his beer. 'What did you do?'

'Laurette and I found an empty Tutsi house. We took some things, I have some pans for the kitchen and some bedding.'

'Did you find any money?'

'None, we looked.'

'They probably took it with them. Trying to bribe their way out of trouble. It didn't work, the cockroaches got what they deserved.'

'If you get some time tomorrow, there's some good tin on one of the roofs. It looked like new, no rust on it. I couldn't get it off without ladders.'

'We may get some spare time soon. We have been told to come back here in the morning. There may be more work to do. Grégoire thinks there may be still Tutsi hiding in the forest. They plan to send out search parties.'

'It's a young man's work. Let the Interahamwe boys do it.'

'I will offer to help. That's what the beer and meat is for. And if I am doing the work, you can visit more houses.'

Gloria drank some beer and looked at Jean over the top of her bottle, then she turned away and went in search of her friends leaving Jean alone with his thoughts. Her mention of the 'women' would not go away, he was sure of that. He was not concerned; Tutsi women were part of his pay. It was not illegal to rape a Tutsi before they murdered the president, so it certainly wasn't now. Jean grabbed another beer off the table then sought the company of his friends. He could hear Evariste laughing nearby. He picked up a strip of freshly cooked meat off the barbeque and joined the circle of men by a fire.

'Here he is. Still strong for all his years,' said Daniel in greeting, clinking Jean's bottle. Jean tugged the brim of his battered cap.

'Yes! Still strong and ready for beer and meat at the end of a hard day's work.'

'Meat?' said Oscar. 'Beef Jean. This is the good stuff, real beef. The stuff Tutsi keep for themselves, today we eat like rich men.'

'You deserve it too.' Jean turned aside and moved to let the speaker into their circle.

'Father Patrice. Good to see you here.'

'Yes Father,' added Evariste. 'You did well today.'

'Now now, careful what you say. I am a priest. I did nothing much, but I am a good citizen. Today was about politics not religion. We have all done our duty for our country. Especially you I hear Evariste.'

'Evariste was excellent. His arms must get their strength from carrying beer around,' said Jean Damascène. 'We should never have doubted, you have done us all proud.'

Evariste chose not to mention the fact that the doubts had been Jean's and no one else's, but it was best to say nothing. He had killed with a frenzy to prove his loyalty to the Hutu cause. Jean had given his blessing, and it was a reassurance that his wife Sonia would be safe as a result. He knew Jean would pass the message onto his son and Interahamwe would, hopefully, leave his family alone. Hopefully. All he could do was be the most willing volunteer and keep the beer flowing. It had been chaos in the church that day but amidst the mayhem one memory was indelible. In the flurry of knives and slashing one face was vivid in its horror and her voice begging for mercy still rang clear. He had killed Sonia's sister. His only consolation was that, given the fate of the other women, her death had at least been swift.

Grégoire stood drinking with his friends. They were in good spirits, their weekends of training with the army and Interahamwe had borne fruit. They had proved themselves. Grégoire believed this day had been coming for years and felt he had fulfilled a prophecy. He had been brainwashed with anti-Tutsi propaganda since childhood. His mother and father blamed Tutsis for their poverty. They made sure he had no

Tutsi friends. At school Clement had reinforced the message by teaching them his warped view of history and making them recite the Ten Hutu Commandments by heart. The government had used the radio stations to spread its message that ensured the Tutsis became the scapegoat for their corruption and failure. Grégoire believed that what he had done was necessary retribution and justice.

'Grégoire. What about Placide?' asked Fabrice. 'Did he do his duty today?'

'Just about. Not very well, but he did enough. He cannot plead innocence.' Grégoire thought a little on the 'Placide problem'. 'He is weak, but we need people on the roadblocks. He can read and he can be useful there.' Albert nodded his agreement.

'I always liked Placide. If you are happy with that then so am I.'

Cyprien looked around. 'Is he here tonight? I haven't seen him.'

'He'll be around. Somewhere,' said Grégoire. 'I'll speak to him tomorrow. In fact, just send him to the road block at the north of the village if you see him before me. Who wants another beer?'

Grégoire wandered off into the darkening evening lit by the flickers of firelight. He bumped into Yves and Charles, both drunk, and invited them to join the others. They stumbled back together.

'Yves, is that Charles? Hey, drink with us,' said Cyprien. 'How did it go today? Did you find any cockroaches in the village?'

'Oh man it was crazy.' slurred Yves. 'We went to the school and had a look around there. We saw nothing, heard nothing.'

'We did hear something,' said Charles.

'I'm getting to that. We heard nothing, but just as we were about to give up, we heard a noise coming from one of those big water tanks that collect rain from the roofs? Someone coughed inside one.'

'Who was it?' asked Albert.

'This is the best part,' continued Charles. 'It was teachers! Tutsi cockroach teachers. Do you remember Miss Isaro?'

'Rosine Isaro?' asked Albert.

'That's the one; she was quite young for a teacher.' said Charles.

'I remember her,' said Grégoire. 'Her boyfriend used to play football for us.'

'Yes, Pascale was his name. He went off to be a student in Kigali, a real big head, thought was clever because he went to university.'

'Anyway, we got them out of the tank. Miss Isaro she was screaming for mercy and this Pascale guy, arrogant as you please just stood there like he was daring us to do something.' Charles started giggling at the memory.

'Anyway, we did something!' Yves continued the story as Charles could not speak for laughing.

'I said to him. You think you are so clever with your education. You think you are better than me because you have been to university? Then Charles pushed him down onto his knees. Let's see how clever you are Pascale.'

By this time Charles was speechless and crying with laughter.

'That's what I said. Then I whacked him with my machete and split his Tutsi skull wide open, and you could actually see his big, educated, teacher brains. It was crazy, they spilled out down the side of his face and into his ear like porridge.'

'Isaro was screaming and going mad.'

'What did you do to her?' asked Albert.

'We killed her next,' said Charles, getting his breath back.

'Straight away?' asked Albert.

'Eventually,' said Yves.

'What do you mean "eventually"?' asked Albert.

'After we fucked her!' roared Yves.

At this most of the gang laughed and clinked bottles round the group; only Albert did not join in and looked on, stony faced.

'You did the right thing boys,' said Grégoire. 'Don't forget the Ten Commandments; 'we must show no mercy to the Tutsi'. Mercy is weakness, and they would only exploit it. But it's getting late and we have a busy day tomorrow. Some of these Kinigi men will be hungover in the morning and we will have to rouse them from their beds. There is still work to be done all around this area. Goodnight.' Grégoire nodded at them, drained his bottle then made his way back home.

By ten o'clock most of Kinigi's inhabitants were at home getting ready for bed if not asleep in it. But many did not sleep well. Albert had brought three beers back from the evening celebration and sat outside his house drinking on his own in the darkness. His mind ran over the memories of the day. The killing he did not mind too much, that was his duty. He did not like the raping of the women though. He watched but did not join in. He wondered why. He liked women enough but this, he decided, was cowardly. It was not right, women should be showed respect, even Tutsi women, they deserved a quick death.

He grimaced when he thought of Rosine and Pascale. Rosine was his favourite teacher. They had to die because they were Tutsis, but they did not deserve to be laughed at. Albert remembered Pascale playing football when they were kids. He had always liked him. Come to think of it, he frowned; he liked him more than he had ever liked either Yves or Charles. The soldier should kill his enemy, that is war, but the enemy should be allowed to die with dignity. Albert made himself a promise; they had better watch what they said, or they might give him a reason to lose his temper. He finished his bottle and threw it into a nearby bush before opening another. Killing today had been a job, and he had to get it over with as quickly as possible. These were times of political problems. He wanted to get back to normal, be a farmer like his father, but safer, with the Tutsi threat gone.

He tasted the fresh Primus and his mind flicked back to the day he first drank from a bottle like this. It was at a game of football, that game against... who was it now? He could not remember. Pascale had played that day and they kicked him when he was down. The cowards. The memory made Albert leap to his feet with anger and walk around. It had been a day of fury and now he directed some at himself. He felt sorrow for Rosine and Pascale and shame at their fate. A tear spilled from his eye and ran down his cheek. He wiped it away and told himself to stop. It was too late for regrets. It had started, and it had to be finished. But Yves and Charles needed to be careful, he might make them pay when this was all over.

10

For three days Grace and Denyse walked deeper and deeper into the mountains. They found food and water enough to keep them alive, but it was a diet with little variation. Grace wanted to put as much distance between herself and Kinigi as possible. She did not know what was happening back home but would not risk returning to the village to find out what she needed. They journeyed when the sun shone and slept fitfully, hugged together for warmth, at night. It was hard to know for certain, but she guessed they had probably left Rwanda. The density of the trees hid the topography, and they were now probably somewhere on the Ugandan side of the border; it was hard to tell.

She was worried about Denyse who said little and was clearly depressed. Grace tried to cheer her up but there was not much she could say. Their only hope was to find some haven, hopefully a refugee camp in Uganda. She had heard that the Ugandans did not particularly want the Rwandan Tutsis in the country, but they did not persecute them.

In the middle of the day they stopped walking and looked up at the sun at its highest in the sky. Nearby a mountain stream tinkled and sparkled so they took the opportunity to have a drink and swill the sweat and dirt from their faces.

Afterwards Grace felt refreshed, but Denyse dropped down on the grass, her head slumped in her hands, as though it was too heavy for her neck to keep it upright.

'Are you OK?' asked Grace.

'I'm tired. This heat makes me thirsty, it so heavy.'

'It's better than walking in the rain, at least we are warm. The air is heavy though. A large storm just missed us a few days ago. There were big clouds in the west.' Grace sat down next to Denyse and put her arm around her shoulders. 'You are doing very well. You are a very brave girl. I'm very proud of you.'

'Mother, I'm so worried about Angelique and Joe.' It was a conversation that had taken place many times.

'I know. I am too. One day we'll see them again. But not soon, we cannot go back yet.'

'When can we go back?'

'Well. I don't know Denyse. One day, but not one day soon. I need to know if it's safe.'

'But we don't know if anything really bad has happened mother.'

'No. We don't. But I won't take any risks, not with something as precious to me as you are. We are in Uganda now, I think. We will be safe here for a while.'

Shading her eyes with her hand she stood up and scanned the terrain. She was stunned by what she saw.

There, only a hundred yards away under the trees up the slope, stood a cabin. It was made of corrugated tin and painted green to camouflage it against the background of the trees.

She quickly dismissed the stab of fear that came with the thought of detection. If there was any enemy or threat in the cabin, they had been in full sight of it for a good twenty minutes.

'Look!'

'Where?' asked Denyse barely lifting her head.

'There is a little cabin over there. Under the trees. Do you see it?' Denyse stood and followed her mother's gaze. 'I wonder what that is doing here?'

Denyse's mouth opened as a memory returned. 'I know what it is. I've seen these before.'

'Really? What is it?'

'It's a park ranger's hut. For the gorilla tourists.'

'Perhaps there's someone in there?'

The two looked at each other. They had little choice. They walked over to the hut to explore whatever secrets it held.

11

At that moment, a hundred miles away in an army camp on the western slopes of Mount Karisimbi Joe stood in rank formation with his Kalashnikov AK47 by his side. The sun was hot and high overhead, his shadow hid under his standard issue rubber wellington boots. It was the only part of the uniform that was really 'uniform' in that every soldier, man or woman, wore them. The rest of the soldiers' clothes were variations on a theme; mainly dark greens and browns, ideally in a camouflage pattern. A passer-by would conclude they were soldiers, but maybe from several different armies.

It was the headgear which would have taken a Western observer by surprise. Any soldier needed a hat on a hot day but there were no rules and no standard issue; anything was acceptable. Most of the men chose green or brown headgear with camouflage in mind but some had clearly opted for a more dashing look that made a statement. Dark peaked caps were popular, as were French berets, some sported bandanas, others flat caps. Joe had a tatty peaked cap with flaps that buttoned over the top of his head but could be pulled down to protect the ears in the unlikely event of snow.

He was being sworn in as a soldier. Training had lasted

three days during which he had been given his wellingtons and shown how to fire an automatic rifle. He had been rather scared of the gun initially and he trembled as pulled the trigger the first time he fired it. He didn't want to fire too many shots and was worried that the recoil punch against his shoulder would cause him to lose control and spray bullets everywhere. His instructor smiled, he had seen this before, he laid a calming hand on Joe's shoulder and it went well. The rifle had been made in Romania and sold to the RPF, in a display of equanimity they also sold them to their opponents. The global arms market, sensing a bloody conflict in the offing, was falling over itself to get weapons to both sides in the coming Rwandan civil war. Like high street stores in the January sales they had plenty of offers and discounts to tempt the would-be buyer.

Unlike the French backed Rwandan Army, the RPF was not rich and therefore poorly armed; Joe's parade day Kalashnikov was just for show. After the ceremony it was handed back to an experienced fighter. When his unit was given orders to advance his role was to follow in the rear of the group to watch and learn. He carried no weapon at first and would only get one if a comrade died or the enemy abandoned a firearm.

Despite the lack of equipment there was no fear or dread amongst the young rebels. Some were as young as 16 while others were in their late thirties, but they stood tall and proud as their commander, Major Gatanzi, stood at the front flanked by two other officers. The leading figure in the RPF military was General Paul Kagame and there was a rumour that he would attend this humble passing out parade, but Joe couldn't see from the back row. The men and women of the RPF stared directly ahead, squinting in the sunlight, hoping that standing rigidly still was the same as standing to attention.

After some brief words congratulating the soldiers their commander and his colleagues strolled down the ranks appraising individuals and offering encouragement. When they reached the end of his rank Joe peered as much he dared down the line without moving his head; it was Kagame! Joe stiffened even more and every soldier in the line seemed to grow another two inches. As the party approached him, he heard Major Gatanzi addressing individuals and introducing them to General Kagame and the other officer. Finally, his turn came, he stared directly proudly ahead, with his back straight, and his shoulders square. He tilted his head a little in that hope that his jawline looked more rugged.

Major Gatanzi did not smile; he swallowed a pang of worry that such a young man, only a boy, should be going to fight.

'General, this young man has newly joined us. His name is Joseph, he is a fine soldier and very brave.'

'Excellent. I am glad to hear it.' General Kagame answered and fixed Joe with a piercing gaze. The strength of the rebels flowed from this man; he was tall and slender with angular features. His facial expression showed the intensity of passion that burned within him and inspired everyone in the RPF. He made great demands on his troops and they knew he made the same demands of himself; Kagame led by example.

'How long have you been with us Joseph?'

'I came to the camp earlier this week General.'

'But already Major Gatanzi knows you are a fine young soldier!' Kagame smiled and turned to his colleague. 'The Major is a good judge of character is he not?'

'I hope so sir,' replied Joe a little concerned that he was being gently mocked. General Kagame dropped his smile, reached out and placed a slender yet firm hand on Joe's soldier.

'Look at me young soldier,' he stood directly in front of Joe, paused, and looked into his eyes. 'I believe you. Listen to the Major and your comrades. Take their advice. When the time comes, you will be ready. You will do well and be a liberator of your country.' Kagame turned to the other officer behind him and beckoned him forward. 'Colonel Shema, Daniel, what do you think? This young man will make Rwanda proud will he not?'

'Oh yes, he will General. I have no doubt about that.' With

that the Colonel stepped out from behind the others. 'He is my son.'

THE LIBERATION
OF ABEL

1

The coach journey back to the Kifalme Park was as horrifying as the journey to the airport. Worse than the sight of the dead was the plight of those waiting at the roadblocks. They knelt in terror awaiting execution and it was a 'when' not an 'if' situation. Interahamwe were checking names against lists, but if your pass was stamped 'Tutsi' that was a death sentence. Melanie noticed two men leading a young girl down a side alley. Her execution would be delayed.

Tears rolled down Melanie's cheeks, but they were tears of anger not fear. Michel spoke to her with an edge of genuine concern.

'Why have you come back? You knew what you would see. It is not good for you to be here.'

'Oh, I may not save a single person but at least I can be a witness. One day I might get to tell people what happened here.' She looked across the aisle of the coach at him. 'And you will protect me Michel.'

'Being white is no guarantee of safety anymore. They killed ten UN Belgian soldiers this morning, butchered them.'

'You're still here. You could have flown away just as easily as I could have done. You must feel safe.'

'The Kifalme Park is safe because the UN protects it. The militia know this coach belongs to the hotel, so it too is safe from the anarchy out there.' Michel looked over his shoulder out of the window, Melanie crossed the aisle and sat next to him. She made him face her as she spoke.

'It's not anarchy Michel. We have been waved through every roadblock, there are no UN troops on this coach. There is some kind of agreement in place. Some organisation is behind this. What do you know about it?' Michel rose to the challenge and held her in a steady gaze.

'Melanie, I work here that is all. You are in the education business, I am in the arms business and that's all it is; business. I'm no saint, I'm just doing my job. OK?'

'Don't tell me. If you didn't sell them weapons someone else would.'

'Yes.'

'But you do have influence here, don't you?'

'Look.' I am a kind of salesman. I have a catalogue of my products. When people buy from my company, I am here to see the shipment gets to the right people. I advise them on its correct use. I try to get them to buy other goods from us. I keep my customers happy with bottles of brandy, whisky or champagne. I take them out to dinner at hotels like the Kifalme Park or the Mille Collines or the Diplomat. I know some people high up in the army. The army knows the militia, and the militia knows the army. They know not to interfere with me. Is that influence? Maybe it is, maybe it isn't.'

Melanie listened with a blank expression, then sat back looking silently ahead for the rest of the journey as a plan formed in her mind. Finally, they pulled into the front drive of the hotel, passing through the final Interahamwe road block. The door hissed open and as Michel stepped down, she followed him and asked him a question.

'Can I travel safely about the country with you?'

'Rwanda is not a tourist country right now. I would advise against travelling anywhere.' He spoke to her without looking back to her, then he turned to face her with his hand on his hip. 'In fact, I would advise you to leave the next chance you get.'

'I'm not a tourist. I work here, I've got friends here.' Melanie jumped down behind him. 'I'm serious Michel. I've got friends and I want to help them.'

'Where are your friends Melanie? Think about this. Where are they?'

'In Kinigi at the school, near Ruhengeri.'

'And where is the rebel army, the Rwandan Patriotic Front?'

'What do you mean?'

'Well the problem is that they are in the forest to the north of there and they are heading south into Rwanda. One of their first objectives will be, where? Where do you think?' Melanie had no answer, so Michel supplied it. 'Ruhengeri. They are bound to attack there.'

'So...'

'So, you cannot go to your friends, they are in a war zone, on the front line to be precise,' he lifted his arms then dropped them loosely by his sides. 'All you can do is pray for them.' The realisation hit Melanie like a physical blow. She felt a rush of fear chill down her back. 'Do you hear me Melanie? There's nothing you can do. There's nothing I can do either. Not until the situation changes.'

Melanie knew Michel was telling the truth, and she stared listlessly at the ground in despair. 'But, surely...' She did not finish the sentence and fell silent.

'Come on, let's get a drink.' Then he added quickly before Melanie snapped at him. 'As friends. Come on. I'll tell you what I know.'

'OK... friend.' She replied with a little sarcasm.

The two of them headed into the hotel bar, they chose not to sit outside as the noise of men shouting, car horns blaring and whistles blowing menaced the patio area.

'OK.' Michel began. 'This is the way I see it. Don't be fooled by the Interahamwe militia, they behave like drunken thugs, but the government is pulling their strings. The murder of President Habyarimana, probably by the RPF, has made people angry so they are taking revenge. It's horrible I know, because people, innocent people, will be murdered. The army will take control, they are well trained, well-armed and they are moving against the rebels who are poorly armed and poorly trained...'

Melanie cut in. 'They took Ruhengeri two days ago, what's to stop them doing it again?'

'The regular Rwandan army was not there then, but they will be next time. I'll be surprised if the rebel attack lasts two weeks before they are wiped out. When the dust settles, I'll take you to see your friends. With a bit of luck they will have avoided the fighting and these crazy revenge killings.

'So, we are safe here?'

'Yes. From what I understand there are a couple of hotels in the city, a technical college and two stadiums that have Tutsi refugees. They are safe as long as the UN keep soldiers posted there.'

'There are only a couple of guards here,' said Melanie while Michel took a mouthful of beer and paused for thought.

'This place is safe, look over there'. He indicated a small group of men laughing and drinking together at a table. 'Do you know who they are?'

'That's the manager isn't it? Justin Shimana? Who are the other three?'

'The two real soldiers are General Augustin Bizimungu and Colonel Bagosora, you've seen Bizimungu before.' Michel smiled and raised his glass in their direction. Bagosora returned his greeting quite cheerfully, while Bizimungu nodded his head slightly. 'The other man is Georges Rutaganda, he's an Interahamwe leader.

'Yes, I recognise the General and Shimana. So?' She took a pull on her beer while Michel continued his theme.

'They are regular customers of the Kifalme Park, here and at all the top Kigali hotels. There's an army communications post on the top floor of the Milles Collines. With all this killing going on the Rwandan government needs to be careful of bad publicity. Some of the refugees are high profile 'guests' and questions would be asked if they were killed. The UN is watching and there are too many witnesses. General Roméo Dallaire faxes reports to New York every day. The army are wary of him and he's not afraid of them. People will be killed, but not at places like this where the spotlight of the media could fall, or worse.'

'Worse?'

'Murdering civilians is classed as a crime against humanity. Those who did the murders at the roadblocks, Rutaganda and his gang, they may well face a trial when this blows over. But nobody will be murdered in the Kifalme Park, there would be too much evidence and the UN are on guard. The violence on the streets will not last long. It will calm down when the army starts getting results against the rebels. People will be less angry and less afraid.'

'From what you are saying it sounds like I should wait.'

'That is up to you. There will be other chances to leave the country if you wish to, but if you wait, I am sure you can get back to the school to see how your friends are.'

Melanie thought for a moment. 'You think this will all be over in a couple of weeks?'

'Sure. The RPF will be wiped out. They are outnumbered and have few weapons.'

'Then I guess I have no choice but to wait,' replied Melanie.

2

When he heard his father speak Joe did not know what to say or do. Fortunately, all that was expected of him, once the officers moved on and continued their inspection, was to stand to attention and stare straight ahead. In the absence of any other ideas that is what he did, but he was no longer thinking about how exciting it was to meet General Kagame. He had hoped to find his father, but now that they had met, he realised he had not planned what to say to him. As the parade inspection continued, he gathered his thoughts.

Eventually, the officers were stood at the front of the men once more and the orders came to 'stand easy', and then 'dismissed'. The other soldiers drifted away but Joe remained stood where he was. His father walked across the dusty makeshift parade ground towards him. He stopped in front of Joe who let the older man speak first.

'Joseph. It is good to see you, I have not seen you in a long time,' he paused, and his eyes scanned the distant mountains as he tried to find the right words. 'I do not know what to say Joe. I wanted to sit down one day and explain everything to you, but life has not given me, us, that opportunity. I am sorry. I wish it had. I hope your mother has explained our situation to you,' he stopped there, he knew he had not said nearly enough, but he had made a start.

'It's OK. Mother... she did explain. I understand.'

'Good. How is Angelique? Is she back at home in Kinigi? I hope she is safe, she...' It gutted Joe to speak the words, but this was the time to say them. The responsibility to deliver the blow of bad news could not be ducked. He looked steadily at his father's face as he spoke. 'No. She is dead. They killed her.'

Daniel rocked back on his heels; his body tensed as the news him like a punch in the solar plexus. He felt light headed, and he struggled to breathe. Questions fought with the shock and anguish that flooded his mind; 'how', 'when', 'who'? He knew they were pointless inquiries, and he did not raise them. The answers would not change the brick wall of death's finality. That wall cut across the road of Angelique's life. She was gone. Death was impervious to reason and negotiation. As a soldier he was familiar with the reality of loss and he regained his composure. Today, now, was not the time to grieve.

Grief, he knew, was not a companion you chose, it was a predator that stalked you and took you unawares. It could capture you with an accidental memory, a familiar phrase, or a snatch of an old tune. Your guard dropped and grief took you in its jaws. Daniel could not drop his guard here. Today, after the shock, grief would wait in the dark shadows of night, under the eaves of the forest, watching for its chance to strike. Daniel fought for mastery over his emotions.

'Joe,' he said, taking a deep breath. 'I am sorry, I... I have no words.'

Father and son instinctively reached to the other, but they were too unfamiliar to embrace. Instead they shook hands only to be embarrassed by the superficiality of the gesture. They released the handshake and held each other by the forearms, a short distance apart. Close enough to share the moment but not so close as to offend the minimal conventions of personal space.

'We will talk later. Look, if you agree I will have you moved to my company. Major Gatanzi will understand. Is that alright with you?' Daniel paused, he realised Joe did not owe him affection or loyalty, despite his good reasons he had still been an absent father for too long.

'I don't know. I am friendly with the guys in my company; I've got to know them.'

'Come on Joe. How long have you been here? Two, three days? I'd like to have you in my company. Will you think about it?'

'I'm sorry. I don't wish to seem... why? It has been a long time.'

'Yes. Too long. You don't owe me anything.' Daniel pause and eyes looked left and right as he searched for the right words. 'I owe you. I want the chance to, be a father somehow, to explain why our family has been what it has. Whatever you decide, I will understand.'

Joe looked down at the ground, finally he found something that might help him make a decision. 'We are going south to Kigali tomorrow. Where is your company headed?'

'Ruhengeri then, hopefully, south to Kigali.'

'You'll be near Kinigi,' said Joe, he turned and looked away thoughtfully.

'Yes,' said Daniel to his son's back. Joe turned to face his father with a faint smile of resignation and acceptance; he nodded slowly.

'Transfer me. We'll go home together.'

3

Joe's parade was on the afternoon of Thursday the 7th of April, Juvenal Habyarimana's plane had been shot down the evening before and events were moving quickly. The genocide began. On the Friday morning the RPF force of 25 thousand marched out of its hiding places in the mountain forests and began its advance into Rwanda. The attack split into three, the overall aim being to surround Kigali in the centre of the country. In doing so they hoped to defeat the Rwandan Army and force the government to surrender.

The vanguard of troops set off eight hours before Joe's unit moved to join them. The company walked for several hours along the edge of forest before heading south to join the battle that had just begun to take Ruhengeri. Joe struck up a conversation with an older and more seasoned comrade called David who, Joe suspected, had been assigned by his father to keep an eye on the inexperienced recruit.

'So, Joe, I hear you lived near Ruhengeri before you joined us.'

'Yes, in a village called Kinigi, near the forest. Do you know this area well?'

'I have been here before, I spent an enjoyable evening in Ruhengeri quite recently actually!' replied David with a laugh.

'Really?'

'Yes. We'd paid the place a visit a few days ago. We freed some prisoners who all joined up with us. It will be different this time.'

'They will be waiting for us.'

'Definitely. They know we are coming. The army will fight hard for Ruhengeri, they have to, our beloved ex-president was from there. It is the capital of Hutu Power. But, do not be afraid. Right is on our side, we are the liberators, we are the good guys.' Joe knew he was meant to feel encouraged by that, but he could not hide the tension he felt.

'Does that make any difference? I mean, I believe in our cause, we are the good guys, but this is not like a story in a book is it?' David raised his eyes in surprise.

'No of course. But I think it does make a difference. We want to fight and win; we are determined. I have fought against the Army before and they are not so good without the French paratroopers by their sides,' he waved a finger in front of Joe's face and grinned. 'The only time they ever really pushed us back was with French help. The French military have trained the government's troops, and armed them, but they will not fight with them anymore. We lived in the mountains and the forest for years. We are disciplined like proper soldiers. The Rwandan Army is not as efficient as we are. Do you know what I think? They are not happy fighting because nobody wants to die for a bad cause. We fight to free our country. We are fighting for a better future. There will be no more Hutu or Tutsi, we will all be Rwandans. That's why so many Hutus fight alongside us.'

'No more Hutu or Tutsi?'

'That's right.' David looked intensely at Joe, determined to make his point. 'If you cannot forgive and forget you cannot move forward. We cannot stay locked in this cycle of revenge. You were born in a refugee camp in Uganda, weren't you?'

'Yes.'

'So was I. We long to return home, of course we do, but it is not just our home, it is the Hutu homeland too. It is called Rwanda; so we must be Rwandans! We have to live together in peace.'

Joe wanted to keep his thoughts to himself, but his expression gave him away.

'Joe, your silence says it all, I understand. You are angry. You want revenge.'

'They killed my mother.'

'They have killed many mothers. I am sorry for you Joe. We

will win, those who have committed crimes will be arrested and they will face justice. But we must not sink to their level.'

The company carried on walking and, although Joe and David were at the front, they did not fear the enemy as they knew their comrades had cleared the way before them. The countryside was practically empty; most people had fled the oncoming RPF. Occasionally they would come across some elderly individuals sat outside their homes. They showed little fear, as if they were resigned to whatever fate threw their way, when Joe called out 'miriwe' (good afternoon) to one elderly grandmother she nodded in response.

A hundred yards down the road was another house like all the others, set back twenty feet from the road, lifeless and abandoned except this one seemed different. Joe simply knew it was different, a deep, animal sense told him so. His vision sharpened and his hearing tuned into every sound. He became more alert though he did not yet know why.

Slowly he walked across the scrubby grass to the front door of the humble shack which was open. It was quiet inside but as Joe listened, he carefully he picked up the humming drone of flies. David was close by his side as they approached the front door to look in. The smell ambushed them as they stepped into the shadows, sweet and nauseating in the heat; rotting meat and faeces. The odour penetrated and violated their nostrils; both men gagged and staggered backwards. They fought the desire to retreat but could not yet look properly into the room.

'Joe, wait here. I'll have a look first,' said David covering his mouth with a handkerchief and gripping Joe by the arm.

'No. We cannot hide from these things.' Joe looked squarely into David's face. 'This the truth. We know what is in there. It is obvious. Whatever we see we must not turn away. We must remember that it was a person. They still deserve our respect whatever state they are in.'

On the mud floor of the house lay a middle-aged couple. Joe guessed they had been dead for two days; their eyes stared sightlessly into the banana leaf roof over their heads. Both had been hacked to death by machetes. The woman was naked from the waist down, there were broad ravines, thick and encrusted with congealed blood, where her genitals had been. The man was a few feet from her, it may have been an accident of their placing, but it seemed the man's arm stretched out to try and reach her. It was probably the last thing he tried to do in his life.

Joe's eyes filmed tears, but he did not weep. He looked at David, nodded his head, and walked out into the sunshine. Fists clenched, he took a deep breath and searched his soul for the right feelings. Anger, disgust, grief and reason fought for supremacy in his mind. Eventually the emotions cancelled themselves out and reason won. David walked out of the doorway and over to him.

'You okay?' He asked.

'Yes. This is the truth of this war.' Joe replied surprised at the calmness and clarity of his thought, surprised at his emotional control. 'It's an ugly disgusting truth. You are right about revenge David.'

'How so?'

'Those people in there. They have lost their lives, but they did not need to lose their dignity,' he paused and looked into the distance. His experience of suffering, grief and lifetime of being bullied coalesced into courage. 'We must give them their dignity back by fighting their killers with honour.'

'Good Joe. Well said. Brave words,' replied David, taken aback by the younger man's wisdom.

'I am not afraid of Interahamwe or the Army. I am afraid anger might make me become like them. I won't let that happen.' As Joe spoke the rest of the men and women in their group had caught up with them. Some had been in the house and seen the horror within. More than a few were in tears and several vomited by the side of the building.

Daniel arrived and David went over to him. After Daniel had looked inside, he called the soldiers together. They sat on the grass on the other side of the road from the house, out of reach of the sickly scent of the tragedy. His face did not give away his feelings, but his body was tense as he fought to control powerful emotions and address them.

'We have new orders. We are not going to join the fight in Ruhengeri, we have the town surrounded. The Army are making a defence of it and we don't need to waste time there. They are going nowhere. We will go south to join the forces heading to Kigali. The sooner we take the capital the sooner we will win. Factions of the Army have already started to retreat; it is if they have other things on their mind.'

Daniel paused and scanned the company making eye contact with every soldier he could. 'OK. I hope you all looked in that house there. It is the reason we must get to Kigali as quickly as possible. As we feared the Army and Interahamwe have begun a full-scale extermination of Tutsis.' Again, he stopped and looked towards Ruhengeri. From a nearby tree birdsong mingled innocently with the crack of gunfire and the crump of mortar shells ten miles away. A cloud of smoke hung over Ruhengeri. Daniel took a deep breath, he knew what the soldiers would want to do, the scene in the hut had enraged them, but they had other instructions.

'Our orders are clear, we are professionals. There will be no looting. There will be no revenge killings. Any soldier disobeying this order will face instant court martial and the death penalty. I will carry it out personally. Any prisoners we take will be handcuffed and taken to the rear of the line to prison camps. Are there any questions?'

One soldier raised a hand. 'Are the French helping the Army?'

'Not as far as we know.' Daniel replied.

'And the UN. Are they doing anything?' asked another.

'I do not know. They are in Kigali but not in great numbers.'

4

Grace pushed the door of the park ranger's hut open and the sunlight followed her into the room. It was simply furnished; there was a wooden table, three chairs, some cupboards, a gas stove, a food preparation area, a metal draining board and sink with holes where the taps had never been fitted. There was a faded canvas camp bed with metal legs and several more folded up next to it on the concrete floor. Denyse opened one of the cupboards and found plates, bowls, cups and tins of food to last weeks. She turned to her mother, her mouth open in awe.

'It's... it's like a palace.' Denyse turned back to gaze at the labels on the tinned food.

Grace sat on one of the chairs, propped an elbow on the table and rested her weary head on the heel of her hand. She raised her eyebrows and managed a smile, her first real on in three days. 'Yes, it is a palace, our palace for now.' There were scraps of paper on the table one of them was headed notepaper which told her where they were, she read the heading out loud.

'Mgahinga Gorilla National Park'.

'That's not our park' replied Denyse.

'No. We've crossed the border. We're in Uganda. The writing is in English.'

'We are safe?'

'Yes. They will not follow us here.'

The realisation that she was no longer stalked by a brutal death suddenly swept through Denyse and she dropped to her knees. Leaning forward with her hands splayed out on the rough concrete floor she sobbed and panted for breath. Her mother knelt by her, wrapped arms around her and hugged her tightly to her chest.

'It's OK. We are safe my lovely girl, safe from harm.' She kissed Denyse's hair and rocked her gently for a few moments. Eventually the ache in Grace's stomach reminded her of a pressing need.

'Come on. We've not eaten decent food for days.' She stood up and helped Denyse to stand up in front of her. She stroked the young girl's short hair, pushing it behind her ears, trying to impose an order and a shape on it. 'Look at you, your hair needs washing, and your dress, oh dear.'

'It's got bigger!' At that Grace laughed gently.

'I think you have got thinner!' She smiled and gently brushed the back of her fingers over Denyse's face. 'Let's eat.'

'The food is not ours. What if someone comes? We might get in trouble.'

'We'll be in worse trouble if we don't.' Grace walked over to the cupboards and pulled a tin off the shelf. 'Mandarins in syrup.'

'What is a mandarin?' said Denyse as she and Grace eyed the picture on the label.

'They look like little oranges. There's only one way to find out.'

The foray into mandarins was such a success that they found another tin and ate those too. Denyse tilted the almost empty tin to her mouth and drained the sweet juice from it.

'How do you feel?' asked Grace.

'OK. Tired.'

'How's your stomach?'

'Fine. I feel very full.'

'I don't think you should eat too much straight away. It will make you sick.' She laid her hand on Denyse's neck, caressing her skin. 'Why don't you lie down? Try to sleep.'

'I am very sleepy. Eating has made me tired.'

'That and running through a forest for four days!' said Grace as she led her over to the camp bed and wrapped three blankets round her as she settled onto the canvas. 'Sleep.' She whispered and kissed her on the forehead.

She lay next to her for a few minutes, but it did not take long before Denyse was in a deep, exhausted slumber. Grace was tired herself, but she wanted to check out the safety of their little 'palace'.

As it was a ranger's hut it had enough food for a stay of several weeks. She was certain there would be a water supply of some kind and a quick search revealed a tap at the back of the hut. Not before time good fortune had finally smiled on them; a roof over their heads, food and water, a bed to sleep in. If park rangers came along, they might not be happy with the uninvited guests but they would not harm them, Grace was certain of that.

The front step of the cabin made for a nice place to watch the sun set and catch its warmth before it faded in the west. Now that she was no longer concerned with her and Denyse's immediate safety her mind wandered to those who they had left behind. Were Angelique and Joe safe? What was happening in Kinigi? They were not questions she could answer, she feared the worst, but she pushed those thoughts out of her mind. Although she stared in the direction of home, she did not hear its voice; it did not call her name with love or tenderness. Her last memory of Kinigi was of the men running up the slopes towards them; she had sensed their violent intent. All she hoped was that the same sun that set on her that evening also set on Angelique and Joe. Perhaps it warmed them too.

As these hopes and thoughts focused in her mind, she realised she wanted to pray, after all, she had always believed in God. However, the words would not come; only questions. 'Where was God?' She asked herself. 'Did he not hear the pleas of her people?' 'Was He deaf to their cries?' 'Was He blind?' 'How could God stand by and do nothing?' 'He cannot be there.' With nothing else to say she offered her doubts up to the heavens. It still helped to pray, if only to the empty sky. With one last look in the direction of Rwanda she went inside the cabin and quietly closed the door.

5

As the weeks passed in the Kifalme Park Melanie observed a tense stand-off between four forces: The United Nations troops had guns, but were not allowed to shoot. The Tutsi refugees wanted to shoot, but did not have guns. The Rwandan Army had guns, and wanted to shoot, but dared not with the UN watching. Interahamwe sat outside the hotel frustrated; they threatened, they sang, they blew whistles, and they drank, while they waited to swing their machetes.

Each day dragged by and the threat of violence remained just that; a threat. The days were packed with rumours. Melanie did what she could to help, especially for families with children and she got to know a few people. Generally, she was not trusted however because she spoke to Michel and everybody was suspicious of him. It was difficult to commit to friendships in a situation where everyone wanted to escape and consequently, she had a lot of time on her hands. If you had money, you could buy a drink at the bar, she had money.

'Interahamwe are quiet tonight,' commented Michel as they sat on the terrace with a warm beer. It broke the silence and Melanie was grateful for that as it stopped her thinking about her friends in Kinigi. Worrying about them was fruitless as she was powerless to help them.

'Yes, like they're waiting for something.' Melanie looked over to the roadblock on the top of the drive at the hotel entrance. 'Maybe Georges Rutaganda ran out of beer and they've gone to find him.'

'Rutaganda still has beer, if he didn't, we'd have none. He supplies this place, and he's well paid I'm sure.' Michel sipped his beer thoughtfully.

They were silent for a while listening to the sounds of the city. After the first week or so the random gunfire which engulfed the city had faded to a specific, if occasional, battle around the football stadium where an RPF battalion had been camped prior to the war in the hope of a peaceful hand over of power. Michel had explained the weird situation to her. It was yet another stalemate in a country waiting for one dam or another to burst and change the status quo.

'It's so strange isn't it,' said Melanie. 'We're all waiting and hoping. We're just waiting for different things.'

'What are you waiting for Melanie?' asked Michel.

'Well, I guess you know that. I want some word that Kinigi is safe so I can go there.' She looked at him in a focused way. 'Don't tell me again; I'm wasting my time.'

'OK. I will say nothing except that I hope your waiting has a happy ending.'

'What about you?'

'I have to stay in case there are questions about the goods I have sold.'

'Guns.'

'Guns, yes, I know you don't approve of that. An American concerned about too many guns in the world, there had to be one,' he winked at Melanie who raised a solitary eyebrow in return. 'But I too am waiting to leave. To go home. See my parents.'

'And then?'

'Go somewhere else.'

'And ruin some other...' Melanie began but Michel cut in.

'I'm not the world's only arms dealer. But I will be out of this game soon. Trust me. I do not enjoy this work. When I have made enough money, I will be gone.' Michel took a breath, closed his eyes, and pictured his ideal future. 'I will buy a farm. Plant a vineyard and make beautiful wine. Or keep pigs and make great sausages,' he gazed over the rim of his beer glass to a different future. I don't know which yet. But every evening I will sit and watch the sunset and enjoy my wine.'

'Or your sausages.'

'Yes. I might have to buy the wine from a supermarket. I need to work on my dream!'

'Well, who knows, maybe it will come true for you. What about the people here? What are they waiting on do you think? What are their dreams?'

'To be honest. I hope they don't dream, it would be better for them.' Michel nodded sadly. 'I don't think their dreams can come true.'

'Really?' said Melanie. 'None of them?'

'Well, the guys in the army. They should be OK. They will win. Interahamwe? No chance. When this is over the United Nations will come running in full of apologies and they will want to punish the guilty. The army will hand over the peasant militia.'

'And the Tutsis?'

'Life will go on as it always has. They would be better to leave this country than live here dreading the next massacre. It's not good, it's not nice, but it's the truth.'

'You said the Hutu extremists will win in two weeks.'

'OK, it's going slower than I thought, but they can't lose. They are too powerful.' As Michel finished his predictions General Augustin Bizimungu walked by their table talking heatedly with Justin Shimana who looked very concerned. The general left through the front entrance, leaping into his jeep which tore off at a pace. Shimana strolled back in slowly and thoughtfully and Michel saw his chance to get an update on the situation.

'Justin! How's it going? What's the latest? Are we winning?' Shimana stopped by the bar and leant onto it, he paused, as if in search of a sentence, then gave up, and stated baldly.

'The army is retreating before the RPF. The government is abandoning Kigali and moving to Gitarama today.'

6

In Kinigi Grégoire and his Interahamwe comrades were the new troop leaders at Evariste's cabaret. The old silverbacks led by Jean Damascène had been usurped and the old boys listened from the shadows. The last couple of days had pulsed a strange new rhythm into the life of the community: The Kinigi Hutus met in the village square in the morning. Grégoire sent search parties out to various areas to hunt surviving Tutsis out of their hiding places and kill them. No mercy was shown, they were an infestation to be cleansed. As the slaughter was carried out the Hutu women were pillaging the houses of the dead for valuables. Usually these did not amount to much; cheap plastic kitchenware, serviceable blankets and clothes, anything that could be carried home as booty. Both killers and scavengers celebrated the end of every day with a boozy barbecue.

Yet the mood at the evening parties had the forced jollity of a party that could not last. For the men it was a welcome change from the drudgery of farming and the rewards were tangible as the free beer washed away the coagulating, beefy fat from their mouths. The women enjoyed the easy access to material goods, but they had misgivings about the rumours of rape that the men failed to conceal. Sure, the men were killing cockroaches not people, but they were raping women not insects. It was betrayal no matter how one justified it. Conversations between husbands and wives were uncertain and smeared with the silage of mistrust. Sonia made Evariste sleep on a makeshift bed in the cabaret. He had only killed so enthusiastically to ensure her safety, but she knew his zeal had not been confined to killing. Several other killers complained that their wives now preferred to sleep alone. The tongue savoured the sweet fruits of victory but, once swallowed, they congealed and rotted in the gut. Deep down everyone knew these days were a passing phase and a return to normality would be followed by recriminations.

The men sat in Evariste's cabaret and listened to the fighting in Ruhengeri. They wanted news of the battle, even to join it, but they had new instructions. It was Grégoire's duty to deliver them and silence fell as he stood up to speak.

'OK. Tomorrow will be a busy day. We have worked hard, we have done well, but we have new orders.' Many nodded their heads and murmured in agreement. Grégoire paused, he knew what he had to say, but could not find an appealing way to dress it up.

'Our work here is finished. Tomorrow we must leave Kinigi; women, children, old people. Anyone who can walk must come with us,' as he spoke, he scanned the group with the expressionless face he used for the business of command. 'There is no choice. We will take as much as we can carry. If you have a handcart or a bicycle, then use that for your goods. We will travel south west to Gishwati Forest, when we are there, we will await further instructions. We may go on to the shore of Lake Kivu.'

The announcement was met with a stunned silence that lasted a while until it was broken by Patrick.

'But we are winning! Why are we running away?' He asked.

'We must have killed most of the Tutsis in the area,' said Fabrice.

'Several hundred just in the Church,' added Cyprien.

'Yes, yes. We have done well, but the fight is moving south this way,' explained Grégoire. 'That is a battle for the army not us. We must protect our women and children so they can enjoy the safe future we have worked for.'

'And we have all worked for that future. Everyone has played his part,' said Evariste, keen to remind them of his role.

'Yes,' agreed Grégoire. He had made sure that every man fit enough to kill took part. A man without blood on his hands could have a loose tongue if questions were ever asked, consequently Interahamwe murdered anyone who did not join in. Few resisted the command to kill. Some were more enthusiastic than others but there was no shortage of volunteers. Tutsis young and old were butchered by neighbours they had known for years, even those who had been their childhood friends. "Fill the half empty graves" broadcast RTLM radio, but in Kinigi they hadn't dug many. Bodies lay where they fell.

'Everyone has played his part,' Grégoire continued, 'and now our part is to do as the army asks. That is to secure our families away from the RPF murderers. Give our soldiers the space to fight and win for us. Then we can return to our homes and rebuild our lives free from fear.' Grégoire reached down for his bottle of beer. He raised it in the air and invited the others into the toast. 'We have done our work well. We will have our reward. Tomorrow we march.' All those present stood and took a draught of beer, clapping each other on the backs and shoulders after they had finished.

'OK. Back to your homes. Tell your families to prepare for a journey.'

Grégoire and his lieutenants; Patrick and Cyprien, Fabrice and Albert stayed back for a few minutes at Grégoire's request.

'Tomorrow we must go round the village and make sure everyone able to make the journey comes with us. We do not need to take the very elderly. Use your judgement.'

As they left the cabaret, they were distracted by the noise of a crowd that had gathered outside one of the nearby homes. They walked over and pushed to the front of the drunken gathering.

Yves and Charles had found two small boys hiding near the forest and they had brought them home. The taller was about ten years old and the other, probably his younger brother, looked about seven. Yves and Charles had brought half a dozen boys out from a hut and staggered around them laughing and waving their machetes.

'Come on!' shouted Charles, at the children slurring his words. 'This is how to do it.' With that he pretended to strike the older child with his blade. He then handed the weapon to one of the children, urging him to take a swing. The blade was a too heavy for the kid and his blow landed at the feet of his trembling and seemingly paralysed victim.

'No, no. That is not the way.' laughed Charles. 'Show them Yves.' Yves stepped forward and, decapitated the older boy with one blow of his machete, leaving the younger one shivering and confused, staring at the headless body of his brother.

He soon shared the same fate at the hands of the young apprentices, though it took them several attempts.

Yves and Charles clapped and cheered the juvenile killers.

They did not understand the congratulations but accepted them as better than a telling off. There was little response from the crowd. No applause, but no condemnation. Grégoire decided to move them along. 'Come everybody. You will need your sleep. Wives ask your husbands, they have news for you.' The onlookers dispersed to their homes.

The next morning the population of Kinigi trickled out onto the main road. Some elders remained; Grégoire spared his own mother and father the hardship of the journey. For the rest, the so-called victors were transformed into refugees. Grégoire led the way and Interahamwe brought up the rear, herding their friends, neighbours and families as a human shield. Hundreds of people took to the road with everything they could carry; on their heads, on their backs, or in tottering piles on handcarts. They were joined by many more, ss the countryside emptied and joined the procession. However, many were weak or ill and, before long, it became a death march.

7

Daniel, Joe and rest of their company skirted Ruhengeri walking through the farmland and villages to the east of the town. It took them over a week to sweep the countryside checking abandoned homes for booby traps moving cautiously forward looking out for snipers. They grew used to the sight of corpses. Everywhere it seemed their enemy ran before them, avoiding confrontation. The houses had been abandoned, stripped of all their minimal valuables such as battered pans, plastic jugs and corrugated tin roofs. The fields they advanced through were deserted and an army of weeds awaited their opportunity to invade. One of the soldiers, Odette, walked alongside Joe.

'You are Daniel's son, aren't you?'

'Yes. Who told you?'

'David.'

'Ah. David. He's a nice guy. He's been teaching a few of us hand to hand fighting in the evenings.'

'Ah, he's good, very experienced, you will learn a lot from him. Are you from round here?'

'Yes. Not far. Kinigi. How can you tell?'

'The way you look about you. You seem to know what you are seeing, like it's familiar.'

'Yes, I'm from Kinigi. It's not far from here.'

'Do you have family there?'

'Not anymore.' Joe's replied in a 'matter of fact' way, but Odette guessed that, like so many others, he was masking a personal grief. She didn't press him any further, and they walked along in silence. Joe appreciated her tact and was comforted by it.

Two hours later Kinigi came into view, nestling below the slopes covered by the farmer's small plots. They were ordered to approach silently using the cover of the long grass at the side of the road. It was not long before Joe was stood at the edge of the village. The only sound was the whisper of leaves and occasional birdsong above the kiss of the summer breeze. In other circumstances it would have been a beautiful day. They made slow progress, checking each house in pairs for fear of ambush. Joe worked with Odette, sneaking up to a doorway then bursting in, weapons at the ready. The houses had been ransacked, anything portable had been taken. Some had even had their corrugated roofs removed. Joe turned to Odette and spoke quietly.

'Everyone has fled.' She nodded back at him.

'It looks that way.'

'There are no hens, no goats, nothing.'

'There's got to be somebody left.'

David emerged from a nearby doorway and motioned them to keep silent; he pointed them along the path to the next house. Joe and Odette nodded, he was right. They could not relax until the village had been declared clear. As they made their way towards the centre of Kinigi, they began to meet up with other RPF soldiers who had worked their way in from different parts of the perimeter. It seemed ninety percent of the population had left a day or two earlier. Some old folk remained, sat outside their homes cooking on tiny fires. Occasionally partially dismembered bodies were found, they still lay where they had been murdered. To Joe's relief he heard no rumour of Grace or Denyse.

The RPF continued their sweep of Kinigi until, finally, the company crouched on the various routes into small the central square facing each other. Using pre-arranged hand signals each reported back to Daniel that their sector was safe. When all had reported back, Daniel stood up and walked into the middle of the space. As he did so group leaders stood up and walked over to him and began to talk normally. Kinigi was clear.

No grass grew in the square, the very possibility of roots had been grouted out by the passing of so many feet. There was a blackened patch littered with crumbs of burnt charcoal and shards of animal bone. Broken glass was trampled everywhere; no beer bottles remained intact, as if smashing them had been a game. Daniel allowed the company half an hour for lunch then they would move on. He walked over to Joe and stood next to him, avoiding direct eye contact.

'Well. Are you OK?' Daniel asked.

'Are you?'

'No. I am not. Do you want to look for your mother?'

'Do you mean look for her...' Joe could not add the word 'grave'. Daniel paused, his voice faltering.

'Yes... that is what I mean of course. We have a little time.' Joe did not answer and stood motionless, deep in thought. 'We could go to the old house if you like?' Daniel continued.

'I don't think she will be there.' Joe looked in the direction of the forest. Somewhere in those fields his mother lay, in a shallow grave at best. 'I don't want to go home just now. It's not that long since I was there.'

'It's OK. I understand.'

'Maybe you do, father.' Joe looked into Daniel's face. 'Can I call you father?'

'Yes. Of course. If you'd like to.'

'I just don't think today is the day.' Joe turned once more to the distant forest slopes. 'We cannot give her the... respect... time... burial... I don't know. I, we, must come back. Give her the time she deserves,' he turned to Daniel. 'Am I making sense?'

'Yes. I feel the same... when I let myself feel at all.'

'This is what it is.'

'What do you mean Joe?'

'This. Now. It's all there is. On another day, a tomorrow, then we can be sad.'

'OK.' Daniel let out a sigh of relief. 'Another day. Come Joe, liberator of Kinigi, we must eat.'

'Shame there was no one to liberate!'

'Actually, I was coming to that. Don't you think there's something odd here?'

'Yes. There are not enough bodies.'

'Go on.'

'Well Odette and I must have looked in twenty houses as we came in. I know three or four of them belonged to Tutsi families, but there are no bodies and no graves. And that is just the village centre. There are many more houses in the sur-rounding area. Hundreds of Tutsis live round here.'

Their conversation was cut short for, at that moment, Jean Damascène wandered into view. He looked scruffier than usual and held his tatty leather cap in his hand. He addressed the RPF soldiers like a weary victim grateful for rescue.

'Please, good men and women take me to your com-mander. We have been through terrible times here.' David led him by the arm to Daniel. Jean did not recognise him, but his mask of confidence slipped when he saw Joe.

'Are you in charge of these soldiers?' Jean asked Daniel, his eyes flicking from father to son and suspecting a link. 'Ah, young Joseph isn't it? It's good to see you back. I was worried about you.'

'I am the commander, Jean Damascène. I remember you, even if you don't remember me.' Daniel moved closer to Jean. 'What have you got to say?

'Really? I... terrible things have happened here. Law and order and peace have all been broken by madness.' Jean began the speech he had prepared, but he was rattled by the situation. He was not expecting to deliver it to people who knew him. 'So much anger. So much killing.'

Daniel and Joe said nothing but waited for Jean to continue.

'People were angry. Afraid... Our president dead... the army gave orders... it was kill or be killed. We had no choice.'

'Did you kill people Jean?' asked Daniel.

'No, not me, I'm too old for that. It was the young men, angry and afraid...'

'Where is everyone?' said Daniel, cutting Jean short.

'They ran away. They knew you were coming and thought you would kill them.'

'Everybody?' inquired Daniel. 'The Tutsi villagers too?'

'No, of course...'

'Well, where are they?'

Jean Damascène was silent for some time then added in a low, quiet voice. 'You will find them in the Church,' his eyes shifted left and right. 'I had nothing to do with it. It was the young men. The Interahamwe.'

'Dead?' Again, Jean was silent for a moment then he turned to Joe with his empty palms held open.

'Joe, you know me.'

'Joe? You call me Joe?'

'Yes. Young Joe. My son's friend.'

'Please, Jean. Call me cockroach.'

'What do you mean? You looked after my fields with Grégoire. You, we, our families are old friends.'

'Jean!' said Joe in mock horror. 'You just broke the 8th commandment.'

Jean looked confused. 'The Hutu must stop taking...'

'...pity on the Tutsi? No. Not that one,' said Daniel. 'The real 8th commandment; you shall not bear false witness against your neighbour.'

'What do you mean?' asked Jean, wide eyed and confused.

'I mean I think you are a liar.' Daniel spoke firmly and dispassionately.'

'How do you...? What do you mean?' Jean trembled following his Hutu Commandment gaffe. 'Am I under arrest?'

'Not yet. But we will investigate what has happened here and if you are suspected of any wrongdoing, you will face a trial. If you are innocent, you will be freed, and if you are guilty, you will go to prison or face the death penalty. It all depends on what you have done. Tell your judge, not me.' Jean stood still not knowing what to say as Daniel continued. 'You will stay here in Kinigi and we will leave some of our soldiers to patrol the area. If you don't report to them every day, they will find you and you will be arrested on suspicion of murder. Now you can go.'

Jean Damascène slunk away. As he left two soldiers ran into the square, out of breath and shaking.

'Captain.' they panted. 'Captain you must come. The Church...' Daniel left with the two men taking another, older soldier called Eric with him.

*   *   *

It was twenty minutes before Daniel returned alone. His face and voice seemed drained of energy when he called the company together with a weary voice. 'We leave in ten minutes. I am leaving three behind to patrol the area. They will stay up at the Church.' The group was silent for a moment.

'What did you see up at the Church Captain?' asked Odette.

Daniel paused, scrunched up his eyes and looked into the sky. He rubbed his jaw with his left hand while he searched for the right words. He did not find them.

'We will not be looking for any survivors from Kinigi. They are all dead. Massacred. We came too late to save them, but we must go forward, so that we can save others.'

8

Grace and Denyse spent several weeks in the park ranger's hut in the Mgahinga National Park in Uganda. Their fatigue drifted away as sleeping on comfortable beds eased their tired limbs. With food and water their spirits lifted a little. They never forgot the fear of violence that lay beyond the horizon, but they did not believe it could touch them here. Many question marks lay over their future and they were feeling ready to explore the possibility of returning to Rwanda. They wanted to return to their secret cave and see if Kinigi was safe once more, however, they were no longer alone.

As the days and weeks passed other refugees came by their hut in groups of twos and threes. The two women shared their treasure trove of food with them. Some of the visitors stayed a night, slept on the wooden floor, and then moved on the next day looking for official refugee camps. Many of the people toiled under the weight of grief for loved ones who were either killed or lost. The chaos and confusion added to their suffering as the only life they knew, for all its faults, had been ripped apart. They did not know what the future held. Their only consolation was that the storm of war had tossed them like fallen leaves out of its path. Survival was a possibility.

Amongst the flow of people there were small groups of orphaned brothers and sisters, often led by the eldest. Some did not want to journey further. More than a dozen latched onto Grace and Denyse who had little choice but to become foster mothers for a while. The youngest of their newly found family was only about three years old. She could just about walk but could not, or would not, speak. She stayed as close as she could to Grace; either sat in her lap or holding her hand. Grace had given up asking her name when a little boy broke his vow of silence.

'Her name is Carene,' he said, patting Grace's arm as they sat outside the hut in the afternoon sunshine. 'She is my sister, I am Raymond.'

'Thank you, Raymond. Can she not talk?'

'She does not talk anymore.'

'Why? What happened to her?'

'She saw bad things.'

'What bad things Raymond?'

'The bad things.' Grace made several attempts to find out more but 'bad things' was all Raymond would say. She decided to give him more time.

*   *   *

One night, when the children were asleep, Grace and Denyse sat under the stars by the small fire they had lit. The twigs crackled and spat tiny sparks, its warmth and light gave them comfort. Denyse wrapped her woollen blanket closely around herself and she stared into the fire, watching its shifting images. Embers glowed red, orange, or bright yellow as the gentle night breeze fed the flames. Spent particles of dust would glow and fall from the wood; the branches would shift, crack, and tumble as they were consumed. It was like watching a play where you had to invent the storyline, the fall of an empire in flames. She held out her hand to be fed by the heat, curling her fingers in its golden glow.

Grace watched her, relieved that Denyse was recovering from the desperate flight from Rwanda where death had snapped at their heels. For her daughter's sake she was glad of the children that had joined them. They were a burden and a responsibility, but they enabled both of them to exercise their womanhood. Caring for them was rewarding and gave them purpose; a challenge they could rise to. Denyse was aware of Grace's gaze, she looked up, and smiled as she spoke.

'Isn't this strange?'

'What?'

'This moment of silence.'

'What do you mean?'

'I don't know. Silence, when there's all this noise of war.'

'Yes.' Grace replied as she leaned back her head and looked up at the stars. She stretched her hands out to the fire and took a deep breath. 'It is peaceful here and yet, over there...' She looked in the direction of Rwanda.

'How long shall we stay here?'

'Well. I don't know. For now, let's enjoy this peace. We could go on, maybe find a refugee camp, they are only two or three days walk away. Maybe we should do that.' She shrugged her shoulders. 'But these children need rest. They have been running like we have.'

'What if the park rangers come? We are eating their food. Will we get in trouble?'

'Probably, but whatever trouble there could be here, it is nothing like the trouble back home.' She smiled at her daughter. 'No. I don't think there would be much of a problem. The Ugandans are OK.'

Grace was silent for a moment, but the realisation of their comparative safety made both women think about Angelique and Joe. They looked at each other, knowing that their fears did not need to be spoken. Grace acknowledged their shared intuition.

'We can only pray and hope for others.' She reached out and clasped Denyse's hands in her own. 'Pray and hope.' Denyse nodded and entwined her fingers with her mother's, slightly surprised that the tears she expected did not fall.

'I will pray, and I will hope.'

'Good girl. Let's go to bed.'

'You go mother. I'll be just a minute. I want to watch the

fire a little while longer.'

Grace kissed her on the forehead and headed into the wooden hut. Denyse looked up as the world spun on its way through the nothingness of space. She looked at the fire, she looked at the stars. She wondered if life meant anything to a God in the clouds, tugging His beard about the lives and deaths of people in Rwanda. It made sense when Father Ishimwe talked about God's love in Church but here, under the stars, by the whispering fire, with the night calls of the forest all around, she could not give life an easy meaning. As she looked south a memory of Joe tugged at her heart. The warmth she felt inside was quickly doused by the grip of icy fear. The hope that she would ever see him again was a fruitless one. Hope was a mirage that could rob you of the strength to survive; should would not blow hope's slender, fragile flame; but nor would she encourage it to burn more fiercely.

9

After nearly three months of weathering the storm, the peace of the Kifalme Park remained fragile. Sometimes the fate of more than 1200 inmates seemed to reast on the presence of only two UN guards at the gates. The lucky refugees had managed to escape the blades of Interahamwe so far but, for weeks across the city, the slaughter had continued mercilessly. Radio RTLM continued to encourage the drunken militias to 'fill up the empty graves'. When the carnage finally began to decrease, it was only because they were running out of victims.

Melanie's attempts to travel north and help her friends were fruitless. No matter where she asked it was made clear that travel was not an option until the violence ceased. She was forced to admit the advice was sound, and she felt helpless. The more she thought about it her reasons for getting off the plane and staying were flimsy, ill-considered and futile. She was embarrassed that Michel had been right that day at the airport, she should have left.

The hotel, and other refugee centres like it, evolved a micro environment of their own. It seemed amazing that the presence of the UN guards was enough to hold back the tide of racist hatred that foamed at the hotel gates, but it was. Threats and screams of anger splashed up against the walls but they did not flood the grounds. Melanie helped look after the many orphaned children who had arrived seeking sanctuary under the UN troop's watchful eyes. Most of them had to sleep rough outside the hotel. Her efforts had won people round; but she still longed to get to Kinigi.

Michel fared worse than her. His influence waned as his contacts lost interest in him. They had no money to buy weapons and did not need his advice to fire the ones they had. Michel marked the decline of Rwanda's civilisation via the availability of food and drink at the hotel. The menus shrank and meat finally disappeared off the table. First to go was steak, finally rabbit and goat disappeared from the stews; he became a vegetarian by default. Likewise champagnes and brandies put in less frequent appearances, then wine was unavailable, finally even the beer was in short supply though Melanie kept a secret stash for emergencies. They were all refugees by the end, and they were reduced to boiling water from the swimming pool to drink. They made fires from broken furniture on the carpeted floors of the rooms.

The quiet courage and resolution of General Dallaire and his troops held the besieging army on a leash. He was a source of hope. He toured the remaining safe sites in the city, making sure the Army and militia saw him. He could not offer salvation, but his presence stayed the hand of damnation by Interahamwe. One night Michel sat with Melanie enjoying the last days of beer and he tried to engage a senior UN officer as he walked through the bar.

'Monsieur,' he enquired politely. 'How are things going?'

Though he was clearly in a hurry to leave and visit other refuges across the city, the Captain paused to speak to Michel. 'I know you. Yes. You are Michel Jaubert, the arms dealer.'

'That's right. We have not been introduced,' replied Michel. 'I have always wanted to speak to you.'

'Is that so? You've had plenty of opportunities. Why Now?' Michel was silent. 'Well Jaubert, I guess I wanted to ask you some questions.' The Captain pursed his lips, as he nodded his head gently and thoughtfully. Michel sensed he was getting somewhere and replied chirpily.

'Well, that's great, please, how can I help you?'

'OK... OK, let's start with this. Why did the French arm and train the army of a government that planned to kill its own people?' The Captain held his head sideways at a slight angle, but Michel could not tell if he was waiting for an answer or considering his next remark.

'Well, err... policy, that is for, I mean it is not for me to say, to tell my superiors...' the officer stopped him with a raised finger.

'Oh shut up Jaubert! Your government, and you personally, have made money from this.' The Captain's anger and disgust were palpable. Michel shifted and turned as if he wanted to hide somewhere. Sentences formed in his mind only to be discarded. In the end it was all he could do to stand and say nothing in the face of the accusation. He looked like a schoolboy caught doing wrong. The Captain slowly looked him up and down. 'Your government, and you...' he raised his eyebrows and leaned forward as if he might spit an insult or slam a fist into Michel's face. In the end his sense of dignity won through, he nodded his head almost imperceptibly, turned on his heel, and walked briskly out of the bar. Michel was below his contempt.

A day later the Captain returned to the hotel and from his animated conversation with the manager it seemed he had good news at last. Within 20 minutes the 1200 plus refugees that sheltered in the Kifalme Park were gathered on the wrecked bar area by the swimming pool cum reservoir. Not a splinter of patio furniture remained, and the pool was half empty as it had become their supply of chlorinated drinking water. The Captain addressed the crowd.

'Ladies and Gentlemen.' The mood in the silent crowd shifted almost imperceptibly on the faintest inward breath of optimism. 'Tomorrow a convoy will take you from here to a safe place. The army and the militia have agreed your safe passage to an RPF camp. Please be ready at eight o'clock in the morning.'

Melanie and Michel stood side by side to listen. A question formed in Melanie's mind and she whispered it to the Frenchman.

'Why?'

'The RPF is getting close to the capital. You can tell by the increase in shelling.'

'So why don't the Interahamwe just come in and kill everyone?'

'They cannot. We are the bargaining chips that get the killers out of Rwanda. It's trade off.'

'We were safe all along?'

'Yes, because the Kifalme Park was protected by the UN. Also, the survivors here have been used as evidence to soften the impact of the genocide; a token to show that they haven't killed everyone.' Michel replied with a snort of resigned sarcasm.

After the General's speech the various groups of listeners drifted off to wherever they had made a temporary home for the last ten weeks. For some that was a proper room, for others a stretch of carpet on a corridor, for many a space with a blanket on a once pristine lawn. All gathered their minimal possessions for the exodus from the hotel. For many that 'minimal' meant the clothes they stood in and that included Melanie who had given away the non-essential clothing she had, in that she surprised herself. She had never been overly vain or materialistic, but she had never thought the day would come when her appearance didn't matter at all. Every evening she washed her clothes in the bathroom sink using three cups of chlorinated water, and then she let them dry over the cold radiator. The baggy tee shirt she slept in got the same treatment every morning; a quick rinse in water then she left it somewhere to dry.

When the UN convoy left the hotel the next morning, Melanie joined the rivers of humanity streaming across Rwanda. The RPF advanced on Kigali from several directions. The government troops resisted them but lost every battle on the way to losing the war. In the end there was only one open road, to the north west of the city, and finally the army fled up it. Interahamwe left with them and they continued to butcher in every suburb till there were no Tutsi's left. They dragged the remaining Hutu civilian population along with them, using them as a human shield.

Melanie looked out from the back of a UN truck onto a packed road that was a boiling tsunami of misery and fear. The first consequence of the murder of a million innocents was this rushing turmoil of their killers and the bystanders who did not raise a finger to help. Rwanda oozed refugees like pus from an infected sore. The few people who managed to remain to greet their liberators did so in fear lest the RPF find them guilty. It was a land of troubled souls.

Only part of Melanie's mind could take in the information fed to it by her eyes. She was tired, and beneath her veneer of courage she was also depressed. She gazed out over the rear tailgate at the weary people that trudged by, exhausted, on the dusty, red road. As she looked, she remembered how she had got to this place a lifetime ago. A vision of Positano Ristorante in New York leapt into her mind. Her family. What did she eat? Pizza? A boyfriend. What was his name? Tom! Ha, fuck him. Jesus. A plane flying across the ocean in the dark of night. Driving to Kinigi with Fr Ishimwe. Her heart sank as this memory flicked into focus. 'God, I hope he's OK'. Children smiling, children angry. Joe... Angelique... Grace...

The faces of people intruded into her thoughts. She had not forgotten them, and she never would. She leant against the metal rim of the truck, insulating herself with her forearm against the thumps of the hopeless road and wept. The tears were a release. Each one drained a little of the tension that had built up over the days and weeks. Maybe at last an end was in sight but there was one more journey she must take.

10

After they had made the terrible discovery at the Holy Family Church, Joe and his company remained in the centre of Kinigi for thirty minutes to rest. Following this Daniel called the company together. Three soldiers were to remain in Kinigi to guard the Church, the rest were to march on with him. The plan was to head south west, via the Ruhondo region, joining other RPF companies and engaging the enemy on the way. Their objective was Kigali in the middle of the country; Ruhengeri was to be left behind in a besieged stalemate.

*   *   *

The journey took several weeks of fighting and as they approached the capital, they began to encounter ever fiercer opposition. The population had fled the countryside, but government troops fought for every road, every village and every hilltop that led to what had been the seat of power, the heart of the nation. Joe felt as if he spent five weeks of his life either asleep in a ditch or running in a crouching position. The experience of war had hardened him, and David was impressed with his progress in combat training. Despite his fatigue he had never felt fitter in his life; his muscles were wiry and hard.

The men and women of the RPF were tired, but optimistic. They advanced inexorably and took few casualties, as if being on the side of right were a coat of armour. Their enemy's disillusion dissipated their strength and undid their courage. Despite greater numbers and better weapons, the regular army did not believe it could win; so it lost. The RPF advanced southwards and were joined by more troops from the east of the country where they had quickly dominated. The army dug in to defend the capital, but it was disheartened by the knowledge that their leaders had abandoned it. The Tutsi rebels flowed like an incoming tide around a sand bank, slowly cutting off the escape routes.

On the 5th of May Joe looked down on Kigali airport while the artillery shelled the buildings and runway. He gazed at the vast expanse of tarmacked runway and, country boy that he was, wondered how such an enormous plain of asphalt could be built. Munitions thumped into the runway and airport buildings. With each advance the RPF were becoming better armed as they took ownership of weapons abandoned by the retreating forces. Every day the balance of power shifted in favour of the advancing rebels. The battle for the city took three weeks of fighting, with mortars discharging ahead and infantry closing behind the fire. House by house, and street by street, Kigali changed hands. Early in July, almost out of ammunition, the government troops withdrew from the city and followed their leaders. They headed west for the new seat of government at Gitarama on the way to the Congo. Three months after the assassination of President Juvenal Habyarimana had started the war the RPF moved into the city centre and claimed the capital. It was a milestone victory, though half the country remained to be liberated.

Daniel's company walked along 106th street towards the former President's Palace.

Joe edged cautiously along the side of the rubble strewn tarmac. He tried to stay as low as he could but still presented too much of a profile.

'Joe! Keep your head down,' urged David from behind him. Joe flapped a hand in response.

'I am doing. Sorry. I know, you're right,' he replied.

'He's too tall!' giggled Odette, from further down the line. 'Joe. You'll have to get down on your hands and knees.'

'OK. Quiet back there...' The command came from the

front of the line, led by Daniel.

They were at the top of the drive that led to the presidential residence. The shattered remains of the guard posts were empty sentinels, reminders of a battle that had been lost. As they crouched and listened other RPF troops appeared at sections along the perimeter wall. Soldiers peeped over and nodded tentatively at one another as they gazed at the debris spattered on the remains of the lawn. Daniel was joined by two other company leaders and they held a brief discussion. Finally, Daniel stood up in the centre of the road. No sniper's bullet came and after a nervous few minutes he stopped waiting for it.

'OK. We are declaring this area safe. There are no enemy troops. Do not go into the palace grounds, they are probably mined and there are likely to be booby traps in the buildings, so we have to stay out of there.'

The company relaxed, everyone stood up, and stretched. Joe arched his spine and pushed his shoulders back to relieve the cramp. He stood with Odette and David as they stared at the pock marked and burnt out palace.

'We made a mess of that place!' he said.

'I wonder if it is true that Habyarimana had gold taps in his bathroom?' said Odette.

'If he did, they won't be there now,' said David with a smile. 'They'll be tucked away in the back pack of one of his loyal guards.'

'Habyarimana has no need of them anyway,' said Joe. 'Is that the wreckage of his plane there?' They both looked over to where he was pointing. Shattered and torn shards of metal had ripped wounds out of the lawn.

'Shot down by his own Presidential Guard,' said Odette.

'Didn't we do that?' asked Joe.

'No. We'd have been boasting about it if we had!' replied Odette.

'I heard they were ordered to assassinate him by his wife!' added David and went off to talk to Daniel. The soldiers sat down on the grass or leant with their backs against the palace garden wall to rest.

'War is strange,' said Joe.

'What do you mean?' asked Odette.

'Yesterday we were ducking, hiding, running around, dodging bullets, and today; relaxing in the sunshine.'

Odette smiled. 'Yes, I have been with the RPF for five years. It's been like that all the time.'

'What will you do peace comes? What are your plans?'

'I want to open a little cafe here in Kigali with my husband, we will have children and they will be the finest waiters and cooks in the city.'

'That's a good dream. I didn't know you had a husband.'

'I don't. I did have.'

'I'm sorry, I didn't mean to...'

'There's no need to apologise. It was a few years ago.' Joe remained silent, not knowing what to say. 'I still have a life to live. Maybe I will find a new husband, a young strong man!' She added, slapping Joe hard on the thigh.

'Ow! You're 25, you are too old for me,' laughed Joe.

'But Joe, think how much experience I have.' She replied and gave him a hefty nudge.

'Yes, well, I hear experience is a great teacher,' said Joe.

'You can call me 'experience' from now on then,' grinned Odette, 'unless, of course, there is someone else?'

Their conversation was cut short by David's return from his meeting.

'Well, we shall be staying in luxury tonight. Our company has four-star luxury at the Kifalme Park.' Let's get moving, we can rest there,' he led the company towards the hotel.

As Joe walked, he pondered Odette's words. She was clearly interested in him. He found the thought both frightening and exciting. As he turned the idea over in his mind however the image of Denyse surfaced in his internal monologue. Was it worth being faithful to a dream? He had not promised anything. It was not just the question of what the future might hold, he was a soldier in a war and his future could be a bullet the next day. Death had taught him life was fragile, he would be a fool not to live in the present and take what pleasures it offered him.

He looked up at Odette's sensuous, swaying hips as she walked in front of him. Odette was reality, she was the present. If he got the chance, it was a present he would be pleased to unwrap.

*   *   *

It was clear from the outside that, as an ex-refugee camp, the Kifalme Park was not much more than a concrete shell. Most of the windows on the first two floors were smashed, and the grounds were littered with broken glass. The sharp edge of stale smoke caught at the back of Joe's throat as they approached the concrete canopy in front of the main entrance.

'I'm no expert but I think the hotel is in danger of losing some of its stars,' he confided to Odette as they walked into the ruins of the hotel reception.

'I heard many people survived here. Is that right David?'

'Yes. Mostly Tutsi and some Hutus who refused to get involved,' he replied. 'The UN stood guard, the army kept Interahamwe out and finally they used the people in here to guarantee their safe passage.'

'The plan worked,' said Odette.

'Yes, and over a thousand people were saved here,' said David. 'Credit to Dallaire and the UN troops that remained. The place has been messed up though. You won't find anything of value that's for sure.'

'I don't think you'll find anything you could even burn,' said Joe looking into the offices behind the reception desk.

'We should have a look around. Don't touch anything that looks interesting, that's a call sign for a booby trap. Do not open closed doors or draws, just look into rooms. If you find anything suspicious come and tell me, we'll check it out properly.'

David organised the company into pairs to carry out the search. Joe and Odette made their way up the stairs to survey the top floor. Blackened holes were burnt into the carpets and fire smoke had stained the walls. Odette quickly realised what they were.

'Joe these were cooking fires!' she exclaimed with surprise. 'They didn't just live in the rooms, they camped in the corridors.'

'No wonder there isn't any furniture left, they used it as fuel. They were lucky they didn't set the whole place alight.' With that he entered an open door to the last room on the corridor. There was a metal bed frame propped against the wall, the glass doors to the balcony were intact and opened out onto the city. He stepped through to take in the view and look down he noticed something wedged between the metal rails of the balcony. The shade of navy-blue cotton was strangely familiar. He tugged the item out and examined it. It was a blue peaked cap with the letters N and Y superimposed over one another in white cotton. His heart skipped, and he forgot to breathe as the memory flooded back. Odette stepped up behind him.

'Are you OK? You look like you've seen a ghost?' She said fixing him with an inquisitive, wide eyed look.

'I've seen this cap. I'm sure I...' Unable to finish he turned the cap over in his hands and looked inside it. There was the label "Melanie Hickman", he gripped it tightly in his hand. 'It's her New York Yankees baseball cap.'

'Whose?'

'Melanie's.'

'Who's Melanie?'

'This American teacher I used to know. I worked for her, fetched water and she helped me with my English.'

'Are you sure?'

'It can't be a coincidence. A hat like this is rare round here.

This is the real thing, not a cheap copy, you can tell by the weight. I've seen this cap before. She said she'd give it to me before she went home.'

'You think she was here? This teacher?'

'Look it's got her name in it. She would have to leave Kinigi and come to Kigali. All the foreign nationals flew out of Kigali. I remember her telling me she had stayed here before. What a weird coincidence.'

'Well, you did need a hat.'

'Yes, I lost mine weeks ago, and now I have a new one!' chirped Joe with a smile and popped it on his head. 'It's fate. She wanted me to have it. Thank you, Melanie,' he said, flicking the peak of the cap with his forefinger and beamed a grin at Odette.

'It suits you,' said Odette with a smile. Joe popped the cap on his head, and they carried on their search.

*   *   *

Half an hour later the soldiers were gathered in the hotel entrance with nothing to report. David gave orders.

'Find yourselves somewhere to sleep for tonight, anywhere in the hotel or grounds, it's up to you. Be here tomorrow at 6.00 am. We are heading west in the morning.'

'Where to?' asked Joe.

'We are heading for Kibuye near Lake Kivu, but we think the way may be blocked by French legionnaires.'

'Where have the government's troops gone?' Odette asked.

'They headed north west to Ruhengeri and Gisenyi. The French will try to protect them on their retreat, but we are going to pursue them,' he paused to invite more questions.

'What about Interahamwe?' asked Joe.

'Scattered in every direction we think. Many will have gone with the troops and they have taken millions of refugees with them as you may have guessed.' As no more questions were forthcoming David dismissed the company. 'Get something to eat. Get as much rest as you can. We are safe here tonight, I'll see you tomorrow. Goodnight.'

The soldiers separated into small groups to find places to sleep. Joe went upstairs to Melanie's old room as the top floor suites were more intact than the lower floors. He looked into rooms wondering what the place would have been like full of guests and laughter and life. He noted brighter patches on the walls where pictures had been taken down to be burned, all the light fittings were broken, and many carpets had been ripped up. It was eerily quiet. Reaching Melanie's old room, he pulled the metal bedframe away from the wall, set it on its legs and tested the springs with his foot. As it squeaked and bounced, he heard a noise behind him. With a sharp intake of breath, he spun round, ready to fight. Odette stood in the frame of the door.

'Damn, you beat me to it,' she said with a smile and a raised eyebrow.

'Ha! You scared me. This is my room, telephone the manager if you want to complain.' laughed Joe.

'I'd rather call room service.'

'Good idea. I could use a beer or two.'

'Well, there's no chance of that...' Odette stopped as she noticed a question pose itself on Joe's face. 'Joe?' She asked but no reply came. 'Joe what is it?'

'Well, if I know Melanie, and if this was her room... Where would you keep beer cool?'

'I don't know.'

'I do. Cold water.'

'But there's no water at the hotel.'

'Not now, but there was.' Joe mused. 'Where's the bathroom?' He added in a flash of inspiration and sprinted out of the door.

'Are that you desperate?' chuckled Odette at his fleeing back.

In the next room Joe found the toilet, lifted the lid off

the cistern and peered inside. 'Melanie. I think I am in love with you,' he said, and, with a deep breath of satisfaction, he reached into the tank and pulled out four bottles of Primus. The labels had floated off and stuck to the dry sides of the porcelain, but the treasure remained.

Clutching the bottles, he walked back into the bedroom. 'Room service madam?' he asked with a little bow.

'Joe! That's enough beer for two,' said Odette as Joe handed one over and sat on the edge of the bed frame. 'That's big enough for two as well.' remarked Odette.

'What is?' asked Joe, puzzled.

'The bed.'

'Ah...' Began Joe, but it was not a sentence he was to finish. Odette took the bottles out of his hand, placed them on the floor.

It was half an hour before they had a drink.

11

Grégoire's plan was to lead the Kinigi Hutus south before heading west to Lake Kivu. Within hours they were joined by others leaving the countryside and in days they joined the rippling roads of refugees that washed through the country in growing numbers. He was a shepherd leading his sheep, his Interahamwe lieutenants were the faithful border collies tasked with keeping the flock together. However, it was a task that soon became impossible in the chaos caused by three million people trying to escape. The men who killed were murderers, their wives were accomplices, and their children necessary baggage.

Most refugees headed for the nearest safe border be it Congo, Tanzania or Burundi. Grégoire and his friends had to go south because they knew the RPF had cut off the route to the north. Grégoire knew the paths through Gishwati Forest National Park to the west because his Interahamwe training camp had been there. He had not reckoned on sharing the country roads with so many others. Within a few days his group had become hopelessly fragmented along the way.

A march that should have taken days turned into a confused scramble, this way and that, and it dragged on for weeks going backwards and forwards. At first, they walked proudly, their heads held up by their hopes for a Hutu victory; but the optimism leaked away as bad news and rumours chipped away at their confidence. The government was losing every battle. The march to victory became a rout into exile as Interahamwe, cowering behind their hostages, flushed civilians before them away from the rebel forces. With little food and no medical supplies those too young, too old or too sick, literally fell by the side of the road and died. The 'lucky' ones were comforted by the tears of their loved ones.

Still the killing continued; when a hiding place was uncovered, when a Tutsi hiding in the crowd was denounced, or when a tall Hutu lost their identity papers. After the first kill it became easy, after several it became habitual, after many it was addictive and finally it was an indiscriminate leisure activity.

Grégoire and some friends sat around a feeble fire of damp twigs late one afternoon. It gave out little heat and the grey clouds overhead drizzled a light rain.

'Patrick, Cyprien. How many of our people are still with us?' asked Grégoire wearily.

'I keep seeing people I know from time to time,' replied Cyprien.

'Yes.' offered Patrick. 'They are hereabouts. I saw Yves and Charles earlier and told them to find us later tonight. They have been working with Hutu refugees from Burundi.'

'Those Burundi guys certainly hate the cockroaches!' said Fabrice.

'Yes, they had to run from them because...' Grégoire cut his sentence short as he spotted a familiar figure walking by them down the road. 'Placide! Is that you?'

The man turned and stepped toward the group.

'Grégoire, Patrick and Cyprien... Is that you with a beard Fabrice?' said Placide. '... It's good to see you guys.'

'Yes, good to see you too.' 'Sit down.' 'Join us.' Came the varying responses, Grégoire laughed quietly then added quietly; 'Yes, I bet you are really pleased to see us Placide.'

'What do you mean Grégoire?' asked Placide in an innocent yet guarded tone as he crouched down on his haunches. Grégoire looked at Placide and weighed him up. He was still no fighter, but he could see the weeks of trudging through the country had sharpened him.

'Nothing Placide, my old friend. So, you have survived this march to nowhere. That shows courage and strength. Well done. I am sorry we have no food or beer to offer you tonight, but stay with us, it's good to have you around. Do you have any news?' Grégoire asked.

'Yes. Actually, I'm on my way to some good news right now. Is this the furthest west you have been? You've not been to Lake Kivu yet?' The silence and shrugged shoulders answered his question. 'This part of the country is to be taken over by the French.'

At this news everyone lurched forward excitedly to Placide. 'What?' asked Cyprien.

'The French. The Legionnaires are coming.' Placide explained. 'They call it Operation Turquoise. You must come with me and see them. They are not far from away. The road is only a few miles from here. Come. I'll show you.'

The news shook the weariness from their aching limbs and the men jumped to their feet as a pencil flame of hope was rekindled.

They walked for an hour until they could hear the rumble of military diesel engines in the near distance.

'Those are armoured cars,' said Patrick.

'Lots of them too,' added Grégoire. Within minutes the

group crested a hill and joined a crowd of a hundred or so people watching the scene being played out before them.

A mile in the distance a forest road was just visible, threading its way along the floor of the valley. A column of army vehicles rumbled along, kicking up dust and shaking the dense foliage.

'Liberation!' Said Cyprien through a gritted smile, his fists clenched with joy.

'Vive la France!' Went up the shout from several of the onlookers. With cheers, whoops of delight, the crowd took up the mantra in full voice; 'Vive la France', they clapped and chanted, blowing whistles and dancing.

'Let's go down and greet our allies,' said Grégoire, his arms round the shoulders of Patrick and Cyprien. As he said this, he saw Yves and Charles in the crowd. 'Brothers come with us. Let's say hello to our French comrades.'

Before they could set off however the situation changed. The column in the valley seemed to falter and then pause, the noise of their engines faded as they sat quietly idling, awaiting unseen events. The armoured division had not merely stopped. Something had stopped it.

12

A hundred miles north of Gishwati Forest, Grace and Denyse took stock of their situation and decided to leave the hut in Mgahinga. Grace reckoned they had enough food for the journey back to Kinigi. They had no guarantee of safety in Rwanda but no certain future in the Ugandan park once the food ran out and that day fast approached. They knew it was time to fly their borrowed nest.

For five days they trekked through the rain forest until they reached what they believed were the wooded slopes of Mount Sabyinyo. The going was slow as they now had 14 children following them closely on the narrow paths. The older ones could carry food and bedding which was helpful, as the younger ones wanted to hold hands or even be carried. The maximum load was an infant dangling from each arm, and one sat on their shoulders.

They women advanced with as much caution as they could, wary of unnamed dangers. Not that they really knew what there was to fear but nor did they know if the journey was safe. That the forest sang with the calls of animals and birds that could also mask a human threat. Finally, the constant downward direction, the thinning of the trees, and the brushes of bamboo made Grace feel certain they were not far from their old cave. She turned to Denyse.

'We should try to keep the children quiet now,' she said, Denyse nodded, and both of them turned to their charges with fingers on their lips saying 'Shh...'

'We need to hush.' Denyse whispered, and consequently the children made even more noise shushing each other holding fingers over their lips. She turned to her mother. 'It's almost too quiet round here. I have not heard the birds for a few minutes.'

'Nor I. Keep still for a moment. Let's listen.' They tried to reach out and penetrate the forest with their hearing, but the children found it impossible to stand still. Little movements and whispered voices of the youngsters distracted the attention. Denyse turned to face her mother.

'What would make the birds...' immediately she froze looking over Grace's shoulder; across the grassy clearing, under the low branches of a tree behind her, a man stood perfectly still, watching them silently. In his hand he carried a machete. Sensing Denyse's fear Grace spun round. She knew him in an instant; Jean Damascène.

His face brought a sick feeling to her stomach as she remembered the last time, she had seen him as her pursuer and would be killer. Jean leaned his head back and scratched his head under his old cap as he considered what to say. He remembered the chase into the forest maybe three months earlier, but he did not know if he had been seen by them.

'Grace Keza... and young Denyse... Hello. It is good to see you both... and with so many children.' Jean attempted a smile, but it seemed to Grace that he merely bared his teeth and she noticed how the machete twitched in his hands.

'Jean Damascène. You are pleased to see me? Really?' Grace took a step forward to confront the threat. She had no weapon, if he attacked the only thing she could do would be to encourage the others to run while she died first; hopefully slowing him down. Her hope lay in her relative youth and speed; Jean was an old man, cunning and mean, but not strong, and not fast. Maybe she had a chance.

'Yes, of course Grace,' said Jean taking a step towards her.

'But I remember the last time I saw you... Not so pleased then eh?' She took a step forward and stood with her hand on her hip, facing him down.

'Ah... I see.' Jean knew she guessed his intentions; he gripped his machete more firmly. He did not know what they had seen and therefore they were potential witnesses. 'But that was then Grace. This is now. Those times were... political times, problems. That's all over now.'

'Is it?' replied Grace.

'Yes,' said Jean as he edged a little further forward, there was now only twenty yards between them. 'You can trust me... the war is over. Your friends in the RPF have as good as won. Times have changed. So much anger and mistrust back then.'

'Ah yes, Jean. So long ago now.'

'Hutu and Tutsi, we can be friends. You and I... we can be friends.'

While Jean spoke, Grace whispered to Denyse. 'When I say 'run', then run as fast as you can, take the children. He cannot catch us all. He wants kill us because he thinks we are witnesses to his crimes.'

'Mother!'

'Just do it. I can handle him.'

'Let me show you the way out of the forest.' Jean took another step closer. 'You must be lost.'

'NOW! RUN!' shouted Grace, pushing Denyse away from her. Denyse turned, ran and, mercifully, the terrified children followed her lead.

'Stupid cockroach!' shouted Jean as he stumped forward quickly with his machete raised. 'I'll cut you like I did Angelique.' As he ranted Denyse appeared from the trees ten yards to his right. Jean stopped; he could not run in two directions at once. No matter who he attacked the other would be bound to escape. They would outrun him.

'One of us will escape Jean. One of us will tell the truth about you.' shouted Grace, bracing herself for his charge.

'Not you.' Bellowed Jean in fury as he ran forward a few steps ducking under a tree, which seemed peculiarly bent, like an archway. 'Not you Grace Keza.'

Jean didn't make it very far. His right foot stepped directly into a wire trap and jerked him upside down into the air. The tree sprang upright as his weight pressed on the trigger. The impact knocked the machete from his grasp, and it lay on the soft grass, tantalisingly just out of his reach. He tried to swing over and reach the blade, but it was no use. Grace walked over to him.

'Do you want this Jean?' she asked, picking up his machete.

'Grace... I..,' he began.

'Oh, shut up. Your lies won't save you now.' Grace turned to her daughter. 'What do you think Denyse? What should we do with him?'

Denyse stepped forward, careful to stay out of reach. 'That wire looks strong, it's a well-made trap. One of yours Jean?' She looked over to Grace. 'He's going nowhere.'

Jean tried to reach up to where the steel wire cut into his ankle. Already the pain was vicious and sharp. As he flopped back down the wire cut in further, tightening more with every struggle. He groaned and snarled in fury, but the trap was strong enough to suspend an antelope, it coped easily with him.

'Come Denyse. Let's gather the children. We're going home.' Both women turned away from the inverted and slowly pirouetting, Jean Damascène.

'Hey!' he bellowed. 'You can't leave me here. I will starve. There are wild animals!'

'Then you'll be in good company Jean,' replied Grace.

As the two women disappeared into the forest Jean made another attempt to reach the noose but it was no use. He tried grasping onto his trousers to pull himself up but there was not enough strength in his bony old hands. A young man would have struggled. As he fell down once more the wire dug further into his flesh, he could feel a trickle of blood running up towards his right knee. His left leg hung painfully down hurting his hip. Tilting his head back he looked at the dried grass six inches from his grasping fingers. If he could reach it, he could take the strain off the trap; but he could not.

His heartbeat was sounding heavier and louder in his ears as his head filled with blood, causing his eyes to bulge. He took a deep breath and tried to think of a way to escape. There was none. Jean peered at the grass beneath his head and looked up into the sky. His only hope was that someone would find and free him. He knew there was little chance of that. He always hid his traps in this part of the forest precisely because it was less frequented. His breathing became harder, he felt sick and giddy. Like so many of his prey he decided to preserve his strength and not fight the wire noose. In the silence that followed he listened to the sounds of the forest; the breeze in the leaves, the birdsong and, somewhere hidden in the nearby undergrowth, a deep, throaty growl.

Jean was not the only one searching for food.

THE MARK OF CAIN

1

In Gishwati Forest Joe sat leaning against the stump of a tree listening to the approaching vehicles. His AK47 rested casually in his lap as his father stood in the middle of the road awaiting the column of French troops.

'What are the French doing here? What is this 'Operation Turquoise?' asked Joe. 'The United Nations have their people in Rwanda.'

'I'm not sure how much use the UN was,' replied Daniel. 'I heard their General Dallaire speak last week. He seemed a decent man, they saved many lives in Kigali, but the UN never fired a shot; except at some stray dogs.'

'Yes. If the UN takes a shot, it's with a camera!'

'The UN has stood by with its hands in its pockets while our people have been slaughtered.'

'Yes, you are right. Anyway, to get back to my question, what are the French going to do? Anything different?'

'Dallaire was furious about it all. We think the French troops will just protect the fleeing Interahamwe and government troops.' Daniel bent over, picked up a pebble, and rubbed it clean in his hands as he spoke. 'Operation Turquoise is meant to be a protection zone to get humanitarian aid in.'

'Do you believe that?'

'No. They are liars. France has always been on the side of Hutu Power, they know what has been going on. They see Rwanda as part of the French African Empire. They don't like the RPF because we have come from Uganda and we speak English.' Daniel cocked his head to one side. 'Hey, listen up, they are close, they will be here in a few minutes.'

'We are ready for them. Do you think they will fight?'

'Maybe, we shall see. I think they'll just be too shocked when they meet us!' As Daniel finished speaking the front vehicle of the column came into view. It was a jeep mounted with a large machine gun. When the soldiers saw the two RPF soldiers in the road they began to slow down and signalled down the line that the road was barred, however feebly.

'They don't look like they are stopping,' said Joe, gauging the progress of the lead vehicle.

'Do nothing. Let them get closer,' said Daniel as he stood casually and arrogantly in the centre of the road with his arms folded. He gazed immovably at the soldiers in the lead jeep. 'We'll call their bluff,' he turned to Joe and winked. 'You sit there. Don't get up yet and don't threaten them with that gun. Hide it in the ditch. If they look at you; smile.'

Twenty feet from Daniel the jeep stopped and pulled to the side to let the vehicle behind it pass. It stopped a foot from Daniel. In the passenger seat sat General Menteur, who stood up to speak.

'D'accord. Vous êtes dans le chemin. Respectueusement, je vous demande de déplacer de côté', said the general.

'OK, yes, respectfully, I am stood in your way, I am stood on the road because it is under my jurisdiction.'

'Qui etes-vous?' the General asked.

'I am a Captain in the Rwandan Patriotic Front and this is our territory. The boundaries of Operation Turquoise do not extend this far north or east,' replied Daniel calmly. 'I am ordered to insist that you and your soldiers turn around.'

'Vraiment?'

'Yes, really.'

General Menteur raised an eyebrow and looked silently at Daniel. The three other soldiers in the jeep turned and smirked at each other. Silently the General raised a hand. It was a signal that altered the mood of the stand-off. Joe heard the metallic click of ammunition loading into the breach of weapons that were being turned and trained on his father.

'Eh bien, capitaine. J'ai mes ordres pour continuer. Il n'est pas nécessaire pour nous d'avoir une dispute. Mais je ne vais pas répéter cette instruction une seconde fois. Ecartez-vous ou je vais commander a mes troupes d'ouvrir le feu. Est-ce que vous comprendez? Je vais compter jusqu'à cinq.'

'Oh yes general. I understand.' Daniel leaned forward till he was almost touching the jeep. 'Turn around,' he tapped a finger on the bonnet and gave his final command. 'Now.'

The General knew his bluff was being called. In the seconds it took for him to assess the threat Daniel tossed the small pebble to Joe who caught it as he stood up and waved down the road. At that signal the RPF troops lining both sides of the road stepped out from their hiding places under the trees. There was a second chorus of metallic clicking as the RPF troops aimed their weapons. The general turned and scanned down his line of armoured cars: as far as his eyes could see it was completely surrounded on both sides by the RPF. His men were lined up like they were in a shooting gallery at a funfair. It was the perfect ambush. He could do nothing. Realising this he turned and fixed Daniel with a piercing glare.

'Congratulations on your ambush, Captain.'

'Congratulations on your English, General,' replied Daniel with a smile. 'Now if you would turn your troops around. We are not at war with France, we are merely establishing our borders.'

'We are here to establish a humanitarian mission and...'

'So I understand,' said Daniel cutting him short. 'But you cannot do that in territory we have liberated. Good morning to you sir.' Daniel nodded his head politely and stood with his hands behind his back. The debate was over.

General Menteur sat down heavily in his seat and, after a thoughtful pause, muttered to the officer next to him. The man stood up and shouted orders in French. Under the watchful eye of the RPF each vehicle did a three-point turn on the gravel track and headed back west in the direction of Lake Kivu.

The French column retreated with a rumble of dust and fumes. After the French left most of the RPF dissipated like morning mist back into the forest. Daniel's company stepped down into the road and walked up to their captain. Daniel quickly issued new orders.

'We need to search this area and we are looking to for two things. First, if you find any Tutsi in hiding from the killers send them east away from here, not towards the French. The FAR army is retreating north and through here, but it's still dangerous.

'Will the French kill them?' asked Odette.

'No, but they won't stop Interahamwe from carrying on the killing, out of sight of the French troops. According to our reports the French soldiers do not really know what has been going on here.'

'What do you mean?' continued Odette. 'Have they not seen the bodies? Thousands of corpses floating in the rivers, piled up on the streets. What is it they don't see?'

'The world thinks of this as a civil war,' he paused. 'Anyway, our second problem is refugees, there are many on the roads on the other side over the hills close by here. Interahamwe is herding the people out of the country and gangs are still active in the area. If you see one or two, then engage them as the enemy. But be careful. If it is a large group, you must come back to our rendezvous here at four this afternoon. There is no point in getting killed when we are so near victory. We can attack them together, as a team. OK? Right, choose a partner, you have about five hours and I repeat; be careful. If you can't win... don't pick the fight.

At that the company split up into pairs to search the area. Daniel looked to see if Joe would approach him but smiled to see him heading off into the forest with Odette. David walked over to his side.

'Looking for a partner sir?' He asked.

'Yes. So it seems.'

'Young Joe works well with Odette,' said David with a chuckle.

'Yes. It is good to see them... forming strong bonds!' Daniel smiled for a moment but then he stopped. 'He's my son and I don't know him, David. I have let him down.'

David put a friendly arm round his commanding officer's shoulder. 'No, don't be so hard on yourself. What you have done you did for him, and many more like him.'

'Yes... I know. Oh God, I'm so sick of this war.'

'You are tired Daniel, we all are. Hopefully there is not long to go now.'

'Yes, hopefully.'

As they walked off to begin their search Daniel hoped David would not see the tears that had formed in his eyes. Out of respect for his friend David chose to ignore them.

2

After five hours of bumping along dirt roads the UN trucks carrying Melanie, Michel, and the other Kifalme Park refugees reached the RPF camp to the north of Kigali. It was in the grounds of a school. The UNHCR had supplied the tents and the Red Cross the medical support. Thousands of people were living there under the protection of the RPF guards who patrolled the perimeter.

Melanie and Michel walked into the main building which housed the administrative staff who were busily writing names onto lists. It had originally been the school dining room. When she got to the front of the queue, she said her name and put her passport on the desk. The clerk looked up in surprise.

'American?' I did not know there were any left here.'

'I was in the Kifalme Park Hotel.'

'Wow! Well, good news is you are now safe here. We have arriving daily transport to take people to Entebbe in Uganda and from there you get airplane home.' The woman finished off her paperwork and looked at up at her. 'You will not be here more than one night...'

'I don't want to go Uganda, I'm not ready to leave the country yet,' replied Melanie. 'There's somewhere I have to go. Where I used to work.'

'I'm sorry, I don't know if that will be poss...'

'Well, when will it be?' The clerk clearly didn't have an answer, so Melanie continued. 'I want to go to a village in the north, a few miles out of Ruhengeri. It's called Kinigi.'

'Ah! Colline Kinigi. I know that. It's near the gorilla tracking places. Very popular with tourists.'

'I was a teacher. I've got friends there.' Melanie stood hands on hips. 'Look. I'm sorry if I seem unreasonable. I know this is a difficult time, but I have to go. Will it be possible for me to get there?'

'It may take time. Ruhengeri is still a Hutu town, but the army is trapped in there. You will have to wait I think, most transport is allocated to refugees or the military. The coaches going to Uganda don't go at Ruhengeri.'

'I'm happy to wait. I've been waiting for three months already.' The clerk was thoughtful for a moment.

'OK. If you go to the desk over there,' she indicated another queue, 'they will find you somewhere to sleep and give you with blankets. I will see what I can do.'

'How will...'

'Do not worry, I will come and find you as soon as I have news.' She smiled and held out her hand, Melanie shook it gratefully.

'Thanks. I know I'm being a pain in the ass.'

'It's OK.' Melanie walked off to join the next line with a glance at Michel who took his turn to register.

'Good afternoon. My name is Michel Jaubert.'

'Are you a French citizen?' asked the clerk.

'Yes.'

'Do you have a passport?' Michel handed it over and the

clerk read the details as she copied his name onto her list. After she finished writing she called a male colleague over and they held a quiet conversation away from the desk. The man walked away with Michel's passport as if to show it someone else.

'Excuse me. That is my property.'

'It will be returned to you in a moment sir,' said the clerk. 'Could you stand aside for a moment please?' Michael stood back, irritated by the wait and wondering why his process had been different from Melanie's. He turned to watch her as she made her way steadily up the next line to be allocated a bed. He did not see the two uniformed men walk up behind him. One of them tapped him on the shoulder.

'Mr Jaubert?' Michel spun round to face them.

'Yes. Is there a problem?' asked the older of the two men.

'Would you come with us please? We have a few questions to ask you.'

'What is the meaning of this? By what right...'

'If you would just step this way sir,' said the officer, indicating an office at the back of the room.

'This is outrageous. I demand to speak to the authorities.'

'You are doing, sir,' the man replied.

'Am I under arrest?'

'Should you be?'

Gently, but firmly, Michel was led into the office and the door was closed behind him. When Melanie turned around clutching a couple of blankets, he was gone. She scanned the room but could not see him. Wondering where he was she approached the clerk at the desk again.

'Excuse me. Did you see where the man went? The one stood next to me in the queue a moment ago.'

'Mr Jaubert?'

'Yes.'

'Were you with him? Is he your partner or a friend?'

'I know him. I travelled with him.'

'He is being questioned. He will not be long,' she said

with a non-committal shrug of her shoulders and hands. Ten minutes later Michel came out of the back room with the two soldiers. He was wearing handcuffs. He looked over at Melanie.

'So, this is goodbye.'

'What is going to happen to you?' Melanie asked.

'I am wanted for questioning apparently, they're taking me to an army barracks back in Kigali.'

'What do they think you have done?'

'I cannot imagine. I have told them I am just a business-man. I have not broken any laws and I have nothing to be afraid of. I'm sure I will be released soon enough. Don't worry about me.'

'Michael, I won't.'

'What do you mean?'

'Goodbye Michel. Good luck. Not that you'll need it. Your type always wriggles free.'

Michel did not reply as the guards led him away. Later, when Melanie walked outside to find her tent, she had her last sight of him; he was sat under guard in the back of a jeep.

3

Leaving Jean behind Grace and Denyse called the children to them as they ran through the forest. They had not gone far, but it took an hour to gather all fourteen in. The mute Carene grasped Denyse's leg and looked up into her face with wide, beseeching eyes. They gave no more thought to Jean and walked on for another three hours before they climbed the old stone wall that marked the boundary of the Parc National des Volcans and stepped into the bright sunshine beyond the trees.

Kinigi lay silent before them. There was no fire smoke from the houses. The fields had run wild with weeds, the neat rows the farmers had taken so much pride in were barely vis-ible as thistles and thorns choked the drainage troughs. Na-ture corrupted man-made order with its wild profusion. Only the main paths remained, and they led them down into the village. As they walked through the dusty passageways of Kinigi, it was clear that the abandonment was not complete. Some people remained, quietly getting on with their lives, hoping to bend with the storm of war rather than break in it. Grace and Denyse felt hidden eyes follow their journey, but nobody called out to them. Guilt and fear lay on the village like a silent carpet of thick snow. Gutted and derelict, Kinigi awaited a reckoning.

They spotted three soldiers sat by the path leading up to Holy Family Church. Something about the men told Grace they were not a threat, but she did not know where that confidence came from. She just knew it was the RPF, and that they had nothing to fear. As they approached the behaviour of the children changed; the nearer they got to the Church the more panicky and tearful they became. Eventually Denyse was unable to walk with so many little hands anchoring her still. Carene shook and trembled, Raymond tugged at her dress with silent tears falling down his face.

She looked down into the children's faces. She felt needed and somehow chosen; at that moment, Denyse knew it was her fate to be their mother.

The oldest of the three soldiers came over while the other two stood up and barred the path.

'Good afternoon. My name is Eric, I am with the RPF. Please, you are quite safe madam. What is your name?'

'Grace. Graze Keza. I am from here. We have been hiding in the forest.

'And the others with you?'

'My daughter Denyse and some children. I can't remember all their names. They found us in the forest, a long way from here. We are looking after them till we find their parents. There are too many for our small house. I was going to visit the Church.'

'Please, come over here.' Eric gently took her arm and took her out of earshot of the others. 'You cannot take the children to the Church. I advise you not to go there. The children's parents are probably in there but...'

'Then surely... I need to speak to them. To find them.'

'Listen Grace I cannot and will not stop you, but my advice is not to go to the Church. I will not let you take those children there.'

'Why?' was all Grace could muster.

Eric looked thoughtful for a moment then he turned and spoke in a low voice to his two comrades. The two men stood up and motioned for Denyse and the children to come with them.

'Who would like a drink of water?' One of them asked. The nervous children did not respond but Denyse realised Grace wanted the children to be distracted and out of the way. The group shuffled off with the two soldiers. As they left Eric turned to Grace.

'Come with me.' With that he led her up the path.

The front door of Holy Family Church was a hundred yards away but even from that distance Grace could see the damage, the burn marks on the walls, the shattered wood, and the broken windows. As they got closer, the smell grew stronger, a smell of meat decaying in the cloying warmth of the shadowed building. The hum and buzz of flies stopped Grace as the stench grew overwhelming. She dropped to her knees in horror and retched into dust, clawing it with her fingers.

'Oh God. Oh God. How...'

'Grace do not go in there. You do not need to. You know what you will see. This is not the day to look after the dead. The living, the children, need your care. Come back here another time.' Eric helped her to her feet, put an arm round her shoulder and led her down the path. 'Come, I will walk with you.'

'But, where do we go?

'Back to the village. Rebuild your lives.

'But our home is too small, how do we feed so many?'

'There are many empty houses now. We will help you

move into a bigger one. We can get you some food, not much, but you will not starve. The farmers abandoned their crops and there are some things to eat. Is that your daughter with you? She needs you to be strong. These children are orphans and they are going to need you.'

Grace looked at Denyse standing tall in the midst of their new family. She knew Eric was right. 'You'll help us find a house?'

'Yes. I think I know just the place.'

'I don't want the home of someone who has been murdered.'

'Don't worry there are plenty to choose from.' Eric was a great help and by late afternoon they had taken over two houses that were close by each other. Their tin roofs had been removed but the RPF soldiers had put big thick banana leaves up which was good enough. There were many empty houses and with some scavenging they managed to get enough straw and some sheets to make beds for the children. As the sun went down Eric joined Grace to share the soup she had made on a fire between the houses. Denyse had gone to bed.

'So. Kinigi is your home?' said Eric.

'Yes.'

'How does it feel to be back?'

'I don't know. It's hard to have feelings. Or it's hard to understand them and put a name to them.'

'Yes, that is natural. You have survived. That is the main thing.'

'Is the danger passed?'

'For Kinigi I think so. The fighting is in the south and west now. There is a stand-off in Ruhengeri.'

'Did the RPF win?'

'Not yet. But we will. We have taken Kigali. The government and the army have gone as far west as possible and many are hiding in Gisenyi, right next to the Congo. Ruhengeri will fall soon. The French are in the west of the country, but they won't be for long.'

'What are the French doing?'

'They've called it Operation Turquoise. They are supposed to be stopping the massacres of Tutsis, maybe they are, but they are also making sure their friends in Hutu Power get away.'

'How many people have been killed?'

'I don't know. A lot, but some will have escaped like you did and they may return.' Grace fell silent, she wanted to ask about Angelique and Joe but choked on the question. She feared what the answer would be. Eric realised what the unasked question was about.

'You must be concerned about old friends?'

'Yes.'

'I'm sorry... at the Church... Well, you must not give up hope. Not everyone was killed.'

'But many were.'

'Sadly... It would be wise to prepare yourself for the worst. I am sorry.' The two were silent for a while.

'There are so many people I want to know about. I wonder if I'll ever have the answers.'

'Nobody knows, Grace.' Tears rolled down her cheeks as they quietly stared at the flames. Eric wished there was some good news he could give her, suddenly a thought struck him.

'Hey. One of our guys came from here. Maybe you knew him.'

'Really,' said Grace. 'Who'.

'A young man called Joseph. Joseph Shema. His father is our captain...'

'JOE!' Screamed Grace. 'You know Joe?' She leapt to her feet, flung her arms round Eric and shook him vigorously. 'You've seen him? Where is he? Is he safe?'

Eric tottered to his feet supporting Grace as she trembled with excitement and gripped his shoulders with her hands. 'Yes. He joined us just before we left camp in the mountains.'

'Where is he?'

'He has gone south with the others. He was in Kigali, I don't know where our unit went after that.'

'Is he safe? Please. I have to know.'

'As far as I know. He was OK up to Kigali, we had very few casualties and he wasn't one of them.' Grace wept again but this time it was tears of joy. As he looked at her another thought occurred to Eric. He knew that Joe's mother, Daniel's wife had been killed. It was news Grace would not be able to take in her current state, he feared that telling her would break her.

'Did you meet his mother? Her name was Angelique.'

'No. It was a while before we got to Kinigi. By the time we arrived most of the population had left. Some people remained, mostly those who were too old to make the journey.'

'Why? Where did they go?'

'Why? To avoid us. Where? I'm not sure. We think they started off going south, but they headed west later. It has been chaos.'

'And somewhere, out in that chaos, Joe is still alive.' Eric hugged Grace close to him as she rested her forehead against his shirt.

'Let's hope so.'

4

A mile away up the hill from where the French column was performing a clumsy U-turn the euphoria of Grégoire and his friends had subsided. They had seen their French allies turn around. They did not understand why but it was clearly a retreat and the reversal dashed their hopes. Heads and shoulders drooped as they remembered their exhaustion and growing despair. Grégoire's arms dangled by his sides, his hands were twitching and clenching in rage.

'What are they doing?' asked Fabrice rhetorically. 'Why aren't they coming up to us Grégoire, why don't they fight with us?'

'Don't ask me your stupid questions!' roared Grégoire, he

stepped over to Fabrice and pushed him so hard in the chest that he stumbled backwards. 'How would I know?'

Grégoire turned and glared at the gang. In the silence that followed whatever remained of his authority slipped away. His leadership had been unravelling steadily as the march descended into chaos. It started with little things, surly looks and questions. Then followers began to back off and lose themselves in the horde. His orders began to produce more excuses than results as power leaked from his grasp. Grégoire was loth to relinquish it and he tried once more to show he still had control.

'We need to head over to the French and speak to them,' he pronounced, but the suggestion was met with sullen silence.

Rubbing his chest Fabrice looked at him, turned, and silently walked away.

'Fabrice! Come back! I order you. Come back!' Fabrice kept on walking. Grégoire, animated, turned to the others.

'Patrick, Albert, Cyprien! You are like my brothers. I can rely on you. Come with me and we'll meet the French.' Patrick answered for them.

'The RPF are everywhere. If we don't walk with the refugees, they'll know we aren't refugees. Grégoire... they'll know what we are.'

'We are not refugees, we are Interahamwe.' snapped Grégoire. 'The ones who work together.'

'And they'll know what we have done,' added Cyprien. 'Walking with the refugees, getting to the Congo, that is our best chance.'

'Our best chance is running?' asked Grégoire. 'What about winning?'

'Our best chance now is surviving.'

'You're running from the cockroaches when our allies have arrived?' Grégoire fired the questions but their minds were clearly made up. 'Think of what we have done together.'

'That's what I am worried about,' said Patrick. 'Come Cyprien, Albert; let's go back to the road.' As they turned to leave, they paused. They took off their once brightly coloured Interahamwe shirts, now muddied and torn, and slung them into the bushes by the path. During the conversation Yves and Charles had already disappeared up the track. Grégoire shouted at their departing backs. 'Why leave now? With the French by our side victory is certain.' They did not turn around.

'The French are here because we have already lost,' said a voice behind him. Grégoire whirled on Placide. 'Traitor!' He screamed and slapped Placide across the face. 'Coward!' He bellowed, punching Placide in the chest, and knocking him to the ground. He stood over the cowering Placide his fists clenched. 'You... you ...no... wait. You are one of us Placide. Never forget that. 'He leaned over and stared manically into his eyes. 'Do you remember? I do. I saw you kill Charles in the Church. Oh yes, there is blood on your hands. Not enough, but it is there.'

Placide said nothing but looked up at Grégoire figuring a way to distract his anger and escape another blow. 'Yes Grégoire, you are right. I have killed, you were right to make me do it.'

'Yes. I was right!' Grégoire stepped back and looked up into the evening sky. 'I was right. And you are one of us.'

Grégoire leaned over and picked Placide up with one hand under his bicep. 'That is why you must come with me to speak to the French. Yes?'

Placide wanted to say 'no' but knew that would trigger more violence and he was worried about the revolver that was tucked into Grégoire's waistband. 'Yes Grégoire. You are right again. They can help us, we have not lost yet.'

'Come. We can reach them before they are out of sight if we are quick.' Grégoire let go off his grip of his upper arm and set off jogging down the slope, Placide followed. 'Don't lag behind, and if you try to run...' he stopped and jabbed a finger in his chest, 'I'll catch you.' There was enough of a threat in his last, growled, remark to stop Placide running off.

The two ran through the undergrowth, Grégoire out in front. Placide struggled to keep up but, though he dare not risk escape just yet, he knew his chance would come. The gap between them slowly grew. The French troops had been a mile off and the column was already headed in the opposite direction. The terrain and undergrowth made running difficult. They sprinted a few paces, walked a few more, and jumped over gullies that crossed their path. In his heart Grégoire knew the truth was that French were pulling further away, but he was in no mood to face the truth. He was going forward because going back was not an option. He ran because running was his only hope.

He almost fell over Odette, bumping into her as she came from behind some dense foliage. Grégoire quickly recognised the uniform and landed a massive blow to her jaw which knocked her unconscious and sent her flying to the ground. She lay there utterly still. Grégoire stood astride her and looked down at her prone body. Placide was nowhere to be seen. He shouted as he began to undo his leather belt. 'Look! Placide, look! She's just lay down waiting for me.'

He did not see Joe's leap into the air behind him, but he felt the blow from the edge of his fist as it smashed into the side of his neck. Grégoire screamed in pain and anger; there was no way she would have been alone, he should have been more cautious.

Next a vicious stamp on his lower back sent him sprawling and rolling ten feet across the grass. But Grégoire was a powerful man, and despite the long march across country he was fit and strong still. He leapt to his feet ready to fight, though before he could focus on his opponent, a sharp punch on the jaw sent him staggering backwards. This time he did not fall though he spat blood from his mouth and looked up. Joe and Grégoire looked into each other's eyes.

Joe spoke first. 'Grégoire!' he smiled ironically as Grégoire adopted a muscular fighting stance in contrast to Joe's louche sway and dropped guard.

'You! I thought you were dead, like all the other cockroaches.'

'Do I look dead old friend?'

'You soon will. You are still a skinny weed Joe. Why do you call me friend? Is that your way of begging for mercy?'

'Ah, Grégoire, Grégoire! No, I am not begging for mercy just yet. But, you know, actually, I do have a question.'

'What question?'

'I know this will sound strange, but my question is, why? I want to know why. Really, the big WHY?'

'Why what?'

'Come on Grégoire, as children we were friends. We played on the same football team. How did you turn into one of these killers?'

'I grew up. I learned what the Tutsis did to the Hutu. We have to protect ourselves from liars and murderers. I am only guilty of self-defence. The Tutsi are responsible for their own deaths. They have caused this. We had no choice; kill or be killed.'

'No. I don't believe that. You're not stupid, Grégoire, you don't believe that shit either.'

'How do you know what I believe? Get ready to join your mother. We killed her you know,' he sneered.

'Yes. I do know. So, I'll get to the point. You are under arrest for the crime of murder. Surrender. If you resist, I will use force.'

'Joe. You dirty cockroach. How will you arrest me? You are not even armed.' Joe had already realised that his AK47 was still in the ditch where he had left it. However, nor did Grégoire have a weapon, his revolver had fallen out when he undid his belt. It was several feet behind Joe next to Odette's unconscious body.

'I don't need a gun Grégoire. The only time you ever beat me you needed your friends to help you,' he held his arms wide with the palms open. 'Where are they now? Did they run Grégoire? Interahamwe running away? You should change your name to 'those who run together'!'

Grégoire roared in anger and charged at Joe his arms whirling and hurling his clenched fists. Joe had not wasted time in training, just before Grégoire got near he spun round on his left leg and his right heel smashed into Grégoire's nose, knocking him backwards spurting blood. Joe laughed with derision.

'Grégoire! Are you resisting arrest? You're not resisting it very well.' Joe stepped forward, his fists clenched but held low, his upper body leaning forward to offer Grégoire a target. Behind him Placide stepped forward and picked the gun up off the grass.

'Placide! Good man.' Grégoire called. Joe heard the footfall behind him and whirled round to face Placide. As he did so Grégoire lurched forward and kicked him in the back, knocking him face forward onto the ground. Grégoire knelt on him gripping the back of his neck. He punched him, heavily, several times in the back of his skull. With Grégoire's weight Joe could not move and after seven or eight blows his vision clouded as consciousness began to seep from his brain. He had not long left. Grégoire knew it and so he stopped.

'Joe I am going to kill you, rape this whore and then kill her. Or I could do it the other way round, so you get to watch. Which do you prefer?' Joe could barely speak through his pain and anger, but he felt no fear.

'Ah, you attack from behind like a coward as usual.' Grégoire punched him several more times for that remark, his knuckles banged into Joe's skull, then he stopped again.

'Your choice. I'll kill you first, I'll still enjoy the bitch knowing you are dead beside us. Placide give me the gun.' Then Grégoire paused. 'No! Another kill for you my friend!' He leaned back and pulled Joe's head upwards, arching Joe's back so that he grimaced in more pain. 'Placide, shoot the bastard.'

Placide did not respond. He was thinking. To their right, a dozen yards away, among the ferns under the trees, he saw a bird pecking at the ground. Here, in all this violent ugliness, the bird was beautiful. Its tentative steps were innocent and purposeful as it looked for food on the ground. Its sharp eye flicked this way and that and its crown of spiky feathers twitched and swished with every move of its long neck. The bird was free, Placide was not.

'Placide!' roared Grégoire.

Joe's eyes were closed, and he heard the bang as the gun fired. He waited to die and, for a split second, was surprised that death was not more painful. He was confused when his head dropped forward, released from Grégoire's grip. His head and back were slick with warm liquid, and he opened his eyes to see blood everywhere. But it was not his. Grégoire rolled off him and onto his back by his side. That must be Grégoire, he thought, but his face was missing. A mush of blasted flesh and shards of bone were all that remained.

He was in too much pain to get up and for a few moments he lay face down on the grass. He felt a hand gently pat him on the shoulder. Joe managed to look up at the man who had just killed for the second time in his life.

'Placide,' Joe whispered.

'Hi Joe. Are you okay?' Joe turned onto his side, wiped bits of clay off his face, and looked up at Placide. After a bewildered pause he managed to speak.

'Placide. Thank you. You saved my life.'

'Yes. I'm glad I had the chance to.'

'Why did you kill Grégoire? Why didn't you kill me? You're with them, aren't you?'

'Ah, good questions Joe.' Placide turned away in thought and was silent for a moment. 'But there are no good answers, that's the stupid thing. So many people have died, people will ask why, but the answer never seems enough to explain the deaths. It's just… hate. There's no really good reason. Is hate a good enough reason? I don't know. But here we are, and I didn't want to kill you.'

'Thank God,' said Joe, and managed and a lop-sided smile as he sat up. 'Did you want to kill Grégoire?'

'Not really, but I never liked him, he was always a bully,' he said as he looked down at Grégoire's ripped face and broken, blood-spattered skull. 'Fuck him.'

Placide helped Joe up and meekly handed the gun over. Joe put it in his pocket.

'Placide,' he said, 'I know thank you is not enough but... thank you.' Joe noticed that Placide looked down at Grégoire's body with a certain amount of satisfaction. He had no regrets. This was not the same young boy who had been tormented all those years ago.

As he gazed at Grégoire, Placide realised he had killed one of only two witnesses to his murder of Charles in the Kinigi Church. Only Cyprien remained. He looked at Joe with eyebrows raised.

'Are you going to arrest me or take me prisoner?' said Placide with a slight smile.

'Err... I don't know. No, of course not. What do you want to...?' But before Joe could finish a groan from Odette alerted both of them that she was coming round.

It was twenty minutes before Odette felt able to walk but Joe was confident that they would make it to the company rendezvous point before a search party was sent out. She was dazed but otherwise OK. The three of them set off down the slope supporting Odette carefully.

Before long before they could hear the voices of Joe's company gathered at the meeting point. Placide paused, unwilling to go on.

'Joe. I think I'd like it if we said goodbye here.'

'Yes, sure, I understand,' he let go of Odette and stood face to face with Placide. 'Where will you go?'

'I had better go with the refugees for now. We'll make our way to the Congo I suppose.'

'You don't have to you know.'

'I do Joe. Your RPF guys are angry and they're going to want revenge.'

'We are under strict orders not to take revenge.'

'Well, that's nice to hear but if I was on your side, I'd be disobeying those orders, especially if I saw my family had been killed.'

'Have you killed many Placide?'

'No. You know me! I was never the type. But I am not innocent of blood. Interahamwe killed those who wanted to be innocent.' Placide took Joe's hands and held them as if in prayer. 'I have to go, but I hope we will see each other again. Wars can't last forever, friendships can.'

Joe could find no reply. He gripped Placide's hands tightly in a gesture of affection and goodbye. Finally, Placide let go, turned, and disappeared among the trees.

'He was an old friend?' asked Odette.

'Yes. I had forgotten. But he is a friend. He always was.' Joe took Odette by the hand. 'Come on, let's join the others. Our job is not done yet.'

5

Joe's unit remained encamped on the edge of the French zone created by Operation Turquoise. They watched the refugees walking for a few days on the lookout for members of Interahamwe, but it was impossible to filter them from the crowds. Three million people, exhausted and hungry, were trudging out of the country. Many thousands were guilty of murder, hundreds of thousands were accomplices and witnesses; all were afraid to tell the truth. The wandering hordes shared a code of silence created by guilt and fear. The bodies of one million Tutsis and moderate Hutus rotted in fields and floated down rivers behind them but, when questioned, nobody had seen anything. Interahamwe threatened reprisals on anyone who spoke.

*   *   *

On the morning of the 10th of July 1994 Daniel called

them together. He had been contacted by radio and had new orders.

'Our commanders are confident that hostilities are over here and in the south. The Hutu government and army occupy a tiny area in the north west; Ruhengeri and Gisenyi on the Congo border. We're going back there to clear them out. You have an hour to get your gear together, then we set off. This war isn't over, there is a battle or two left, but do not doubt that we will win. Any questions?'

'What about the French?' came a voice from the back.

'They are not interfering and do not want a conflict with us.'

'They are not helping the Hutu government then?'

'No. Not anymore. Once we win, they will leave.' Daniel looked among the men and women of his command. 'Any more questions?' Silence followed. 'OK, let's get ready, we march in an hour, we can be there in two days.'

As the group dispersed Joe spoke quietly to Odette. 'Two days? I know we are fast but, fifty miles a day?'

'Yes,' Odette chuckled, 'your father can be a bit of an optimist sometimes.'

* * *

On her second morning in the refugee camp the registration clerk, Carene, came to look for Melanie. She found her stood in a muddy puddle, cleaning her teeth at a water standpipe with a small towel draped around her neck.

'Carene! Hi! Excuse me a moment.' Melanie flushed her mouth with cold water and spat out into the puddle at her feet. She wiped her face vigorously on the towel, looked up and smiled at the clerk who she had got to know a little. 'Did I get it all off?'

'Yes. You look great. Big clean smile for you.'

'Thank God I got a tooth brush and paste. I can't remember

the last time I gave them a thorough clean. My mouth feels civilised at least! Any luck getting me a lift up north?'

'Yes. I spoke to the couple of doctors of this earlier and they are going at one o'clock this afternoon.' Melanie had got used Carene's unique take on English.

'Is that one o'clock Africa time or one o'clock real time?'

'Real time. Hey, I think you are used to Africa time. It will be a shock when you go home.'

'I bet. Is the news I've heard true?

'Yes, Ruhengeri surrendered yesterday. The RPF had sent troops north, and it was quickly won.'

'Does that mean the fighting is over?'

'The government only has troops in Gisenyi next to the Congo border. All they do is watch refugees walk out of the country. The war will soon be finished.'

'So, it's safe to go back. It seems like a long time since I was there, about three months I guess,' said Melanie and then she fell silent.

'Are you sure you want to go?' asked Carene.

'I have to. It's the only reason I stayed. I can't explain why very clearly, it's not because I made a promise to anyone. It's like I made a promise to myself. It would be wrong to abandon them even if I achieved nothing by staying.'

'I think you are a brave person.'

'Carene, what do you think I'll find?' Carene read the worry on Melanie's face and rested a hand on her arm.

'I can't know that Melanie. You have to have your hope. You must be prepared for hope to be wrong. Not many survived.'

'Yes. Well, I will hope, and I'll pray.'

'Come to main office at one o'clock. I see you later. The doctors are from Bangladesh, very nice men.'

'See you later.' As Carene walked back to her desk in the main office Melanie returned to her tent to pack her belongings into a plastic carrier bag.

*   *   *

Daniel's company were twenty miles from Ruhengeri on the 12th of July when news came back from the front that the RPF had taken the town and the remaining government forces had fled to Gisenyi on the Congo border. They sat by the side of the road and rested on the grass.

'One hundred miles.' mumbled Odette.

'In two days,' replied Joe wearily.

'Yes, we are fast!' chuckled David who stood over them looking into the distance, shielding his eyes from the afternoon sun. 'But there is no more marching today for you weak youngsters.'

'You are made of different stuff than me David,' answered Joe, sitting up.

'Practice, that's all it is.'

'What do we do next?' asked Odette.

'Our troops are following the retreat to Gisenyi, but they will only make a show of defending the town. They want to get into the Congo and the UN camps that are waiting for them. Daniel doesn't think we will need to go. But here he comes now, maybe he has news.' Daniel approached them with sheets of paper in his hands.

'Our orders,' he said, waving the paper at them.

'Is it good news?' asked David.

'I have been asked to take a handful of our soldiers to Gisenyi. I'm setting off in an hour. The rest of our company can take a rest for a while. We will call upon them soon.'

'Who are you going to take?' asked Joe.

'Those who have been with us the longest. We are not going to fight. If there is any kind of formal surrender, we think they should be there to witness it. Some of us, like David here, have been in the RPF for seven years now. How long have you been with us Odette?'

'About five years.'

'I was going to take David with me obviously, would you like to come too?'

'Yes. I would like to see them running.'

'Joe,' Daniel said, turning to his son, I'm sure you understand.'

'Yes, of course. It's OK.'

'We are not far from Kinigi. I want to go back there and, see what I can find.'

'Wait there for me. I will meet you there before too long.'

Joe rose to his feet and stood face to face with his father. For a moment neither spoke but looked into the other's eyes. Daniel broke the silence.

'I will see you soon. In Kinigi. We have unfinished business. Peace will give us the chance to make up for the time we have lost.'

'I hope so, and I can wait a while longer.' Joe replied. The two hugged and, as they separated, Joe gave his father a salute followed by a smile.

'And you are fine soldier too Joe. The RPF will not let you go easily. When we have won this war, we will need people like you. Our enemy has not been destroyed, it has only been evicted.' As Daniel turned to leave David made to follow him. He clapped Joe on the back and smiled.

'I'll see you soon Joe, and don't worry, I'll look after the old man for you!' David walked away but Odette paused for a moment.

'Well Joe. I will see you when we get back from Gisenyi, if you want.' Joe paused, only for a second, but it was a second too long.

'Yes. I would like that.'

'Are you sure there's not someone else Joe?'

'Well, there isn't, really. I mean... of course I would l love to see you again. I...' Odette smiled, laid a hand on his chest and did one of his buttons up.

'Joe let's neither of us make promises we can't keep.' This is a war; war is a strange time for lovers.'

'But what I mean is...' began Joe, but Odette cut him short.

'What you mean is you don't know. That's OK. I understand. Take some time to think. You will know your own heart better when we have been apart for a while.' She kissed him lightly on the cheek and held his hand. 'Right, this is goodbye for now. Our company will be called together again I'll see you then. Joe watched her walk away, Odette waved over her shoulder as if she could feel his eyes on her back. They were certainly on her rear.

Joe looked up at the familiar profile of the Virunga mountain range. Ever since it had come into view on the march Kinigi had called him home, a tug of emotion deep in his gut. It was a view he had known all his life, and he realised that he loved it. He would be in Kinigi the next day.

6

Joe was almost the sole traveller on the route to Kinigi. Fields and plantations by the roadside were abandoned. Perfectly fine houses stood empty, their fireplaces cold, their Hutu owners vanished. Some houses were ransacked, the possessions not worth stealing were strewn in front of damaged doors that creaked on broken hinges; the Tutsis that had once lived there were missing or dead.

Eventually Joe walked through the silent main square, it was market day but there were no stalls set up and no produce to sell. The few permanent shops there had been were burnt out wrecks. Kinigi was not empty but nobody came out to greet the returning son with a Kalashnikov over his shoulder and a New York Yankees cap on his head.

Now that he was here, he realised he did not really have a plan of action but, inevitably, his footsteps led him in the direction of his old house. The terrain sloped gently and steadily upwards from the village centre. He could see the banana plantation where he and his mother had bumped into Grace and Denyse on the night of their flight. The memory stopped him where he stood as emotion welled up. He had thought and prayed for them many times. With a deep breath he mastered himself and the tears did not come; not yet. He knew this return held pain for him but, then, so did being away. It was a pilgrimage he had to make.

Their house was set back from the road and his footsteps became heavy as he walked the path that would bring it into view. There was the door, the cracked mud walls, the banana leaf roof that was intact because the leaves weren't worth stealing. His expectation was that it would be derelict but, with a pang of sadness, he realised why he saw so little change. At its best his home was not many steps above derelict anyway. Then came the shock. Barely visible, but surely real, a faint wisp of smoke rose from the fireplace in the front yard. Their fire was lit! Joe ran to the door and looked in. The house was clean, tidy, and the crazy idea that it had been prepared for a guest leapt into his mind. Joe ran out of the front door in confusion.

'HEY!' He shouted, uncertain both of what he should shout and who he thought he was shouting to. Realising it was dumb but having little option he repeated the call. 'HEY!'

'Hey to you to,' came a quiet voice behind him. Joe spun round recognising it in an instant.

'Denyse?' He gasped in a stunned, broken tenor. 'Denyse!' She stood before him smiling, her arms full of corn cobs ready for the pot that was heating up on the fire. Joe leapt over to her and hugged her close. He wanted to be happy, and he was, but the intensity of the joy broke down the defences that had kept his boiling emotions at bay. They burst through in a fury of sobs, tears, and laughter.

'Oh my God, you are alive,' he stammered. As the storm of emotions poured from him he rested his head on her shoulder and soaked her dress with his tears. Denyse held him close and gently massaged the back of his head with her hand. It was five minutes before he could pull himself together enough to speak. Finally, he took a deep breath, leant back and held her at arm's length by her shoulders.

'Thank God. There's so much I want to say. So much I want to ask. So much I... I don't know. There's...'

'Too much?'

'Yes. Too much.'

'Me too. It's OK.'

'How come, why the fire, and how come you are here?'

'Ah! Well that much is easy to answer, our mutual friend in the RPF, Eric.'

'Ah yes, Eric, we left him here.'

'And he's become a very, very good friend of my mother!'

'Grace is here too?' cried Joe. 'I don't believe it.'

'Yes. And Eric told us you were nearby. We guessed you would come back to the house. So, we made it ready for you. I was boiling this corn as a welcome present. If you didn't show I would just take it to our house, like I did yesterday.'

'Wow. I don't know what to say.'

'Then say nothing. Pick up that pan of water. We'll go and see my mother.'

'You don't live near here. I'll spill most of it on the way I'm sure.'

'Well, we live near here now, in two houses, and there are plenty of people to feed, so don't spill it.'

'Really?' said Joe, picking up the cauldron off the fire by its handle.

'Yes, really.'

As they walked along the pan clanked against the machine gun that swung round his back. It did not take long to get to Denyse and Grace's new home. From a distance Joe could hear the shouts of children playing and chasing each other around. When the place came into view there was a fire set between two nice, small houses. Children darted about and Grace stood side by side with Eric arranging cooking pots on an open fire. She screamed with delight when she looked up and spotted him. Dropping the ladle she was stirring with she ran over to him.

'Joe.' Was all she could say. She hugged him with all her strength and wept into his shirt as Joe tried, with limited success, to put the pot of warm water down without spilling too much.

'Grace, Grace...' he murmured. 'How wonderful.' Eventually she pulled back and said what she had to.

'Angelique... I'm so sorry,' she said. Joe's answer surprised her.

'Yes, so am I. But let's not be sorry now when we have so much to be thankful for. There will be sadness, tears and memories for sure. All of that. But let's be glad we are alive to remember, yes and to feel the pain, but to remember those we loved. And still love.' Joe took a deep breath. 'I'm sick of sadness and tears.'

Grace looked up into the boy's eyes and saw the man he had become in the space of one hundred days.

'Ah! My hat. Could I possibly have that back please?' said a voice behind him.

'What?' Joe turned around to see Melanie.

'My cap. Always was my favourite. No way was I gonna leave Rwanda without it.'

'You stayed?'

'Of course. I'm not going home without this. It's a very good cap.'

'Shut up about the cap. It's mine now,' said Joe bending over, weak from laughing. 'And you promised it to me!' Melanie walked over to Joe and, for the third time in fifteen minutes, he found himself hugging a weeping female and for the third time he wept with them. Eric came over to the huddle, gave Joe a mug of freshly brewed urwagwa and shook Joe's hand.

The sun began to set as the group settled down for an evening meal of corn stew and banana wine, with children running around them, darting in and out of the shadows and firelight. They had much to say to one another, this night would not be enough. But many more lay ahead.

AFTERWORD

You may wonder how I came to write this book. It starts here...

My wife Anne, Preston, 1979

She is watching David Attenborough's 'Life on Earth' series on television. Like millions of others the little girl is stunned by the scene with the mountain gorillas in Rwanda. He reclines on the mountain side and an adolescent male, young black-back, lies on him, using him as a pillow. It was a moving, beautiful scene and one she wanted to experience for herself.

Of course, it was nigh on impossible at the time except for the rare lucky few. However, David Attenborough, backstage if you will, was making the case to Dianne Fossey for gorilla tourism. It would provide the money she needed to protect the great apes. Many years later my wife found out it could be done but it still seemed a dream out of reach for a little girl from Preston.

Leigh, Lancashire, England, 1994

I was eating cheesy baked beans on toast, with plenty of black pepper, and watching the news. God knows why I can remember what I was eating. A story came on about some country in Africa that I'd never heard of. I wasn't listening too clearly at first, but the images were so shocking, so I tuned my ears in. The news reader's script delivered the horror and confusion we were meant to feel. Indiscriminate slaughter, people hacked to death with machetes in the streets. At first it was clear that Hutu were murdering Tutsi but there were also reports of Tutsi murdering Hutu. Who knew what was going on in the madness? 'They were all at it', so the BBC told us.

The images and information sickened me. At heart I'm an optimist and believe in humanity. I believed (I still do actually) that global civilisation is on an upward trajectory. Civilisation was surely part of God's plan? I was brought up a good Catholic boy. The events didn't just offend my morality, they challenged my beliefs about humanity, about all existence. How could humans do this? I wondered. I was disgusted, and I exclaimed out loud between mouthfuls.

"Fucking savages. Fucking animals."

And then I turned the television off and finished my tea. I did have the occasional conversation about the news at work, and we all agreed that they were savages, animals, etc. How could we have known any different? We believed what we were told. Slowly, a more accurate account would emerge, but who cared? I didn't. The Balkan civil war was closer to home.

It would be a long time before I learned the truth about Rwanda.

HMRC

By 2011 Anne had been married to me for over a decade and we had grown steadily more courageous in our holiday travelling. Her dream to see the gorillas was still there, alongside another to go on safari in Kenya. But they would be expensive trips, way beyond our budget. Then, one morning an envelope from the local office of Her Majesty's Revenue and Customs popped through the letter box. We regarded the letter apprehensively, HMRC aren't famous for good news. We read the contents; my wife had been paying too much tax for five years! A hefty cheque was on its way. So, we had a choice. We could put the money away for the future or squander it. Life is short. A 'once in a lifetime' holiday was booked, Rwanda and its mountain gorillas were to be the grand finale.

Rwanda

I did some research about the country before we went and what I learned amazed me. I gave some lessons on the subject in school. Via the charity CAFOD I heard genocide survivor (and Guardian International development Achievement Award winner 2010) Odette Kayirere give a talk. I presented her with a CD the children at school had made to raise money for the charity she worked for, AVEGA. I arranged to meet her in Kigali on the last day of our holiday.

Inevitably the gorillas were amazing, but it was the people we met that moved me, specifically Feza Mediatrice who had been denied a visa to the UK when Odette visited. With Odette we visited Feza at her home in Musha. Their stories were stunning and moving, and the women themselves truly heroic. Equally, the Rwandans I met at the hotels and on the gorilla tracking trip made a profound impression on me.

On my return I wanted to do something practical to help the people I had met. I came across the Rwanda Group Trust (RGT) in my home town, Preston, and became a member. Eventually I became the chair of the board of trustees and helped run the charity shop they have in Preston. As chair of the RGT I went to Rwanda in 2014 and toured the country meeting our partner groups there. Again, I met many genocide survivors and heard their compelling stories. I resigned from the RGT in 2016.

Parallel to this activity I started writing 'The Luck of the Crane' (LOTC). There are very few *novels* available on Rwanda and the genocide. I felt it was a story that needed to be told but much of what is available, though some of it is brilliant, does not offer a narrative as such. I wanted to frame the events

THE LUCK OF THE CRANE

of 1994 to make it available to more people. I think we should know about Rwanda, its tragedy and the astonishing progress it has made since.

Historical accuracy?

The events in the book are real enough but I have 'telescoped' them, so they fit into my storyline. For example, the RPF attack on Ruhengeri actually took place a couple of years before the genocide of 1994. My characters are fictional apart from the obvious well-known figures. I mention the Hotel Milles Collines and it was, of course, the setting for the movie 'Hotel Rwanda'. However, Odette Kayirere, UN General Romeo Dallaire, and many other Rwandans, dismiss much of the movie's plot as a fabrication. Edouward Kayihura's book listed below is very informative, I hadn't read it before I wrote LOTC, but I had spoken to enough people to guess the truth.

LOTC is not a history book, it's a novel. I don't think a complete history has been written about the genocide or, indeed, Rwanda. I read pretty much everything I could find as part of my research and I can recommend the following books to anyone interested.

'We Wish to Inform You That Tomorrow We Will Be Killed with Our Families' by Philip Gourevitch.
'Machete Season: The Killers in Rwanda Speak' and 'The Antelope's Strategy: Living in Rwanda After the Genocide' by Jean Hatzfeld.
'Shake Hands with the Devil: The Failure of Humanity in Rwanda' by Roméo Dallaire.
'Season of Blood: A Rwandan Journey' by Fergal Keane
'Inside Hotel Rwanda: What Really Happened at Hotel des Mille Collines', by Edouward Kayihura

About the author.

John Poulton is a writer, teacher and was until 2016 chairman of the Rwanda Group Trust which is a charity dedicated to helping education, health and small businesses in Rwanda.

'The Luck of the Crane' is his first novel he has also written an autobiography 'Missing the Bus'. A follow up to 'The Luck of the Crane' is planned.

I am very grateful for the cover artwork which was done by Janet Riley, please visit her Facebook page 'Art by Janet Riley' if you wish to see more of her superb work. She has items for sale there and on eBay.

Printed in Great Britain
by Amazon